# THE
# DIVIDE

## A JADE HARRINGTON NOVEL

# J. L. BROWN

# ALSO BY J. L. BROWN

## *Books*

*Rule of Law*

*Don't Speak*


## *Short Story*

*Few Are Chosen*

The Divide © 2019 by Julie L. Brown

Printed in the United States of America.

For information address JAB Press, P.O. Box 9462, Seattle, WA 98109.

Cover Design by Damonza
Library of Congress Control Number: 2018915314

ISBN 978-0-9969772-6-5 (paperback)
ISBN 978-0-9969772-7-2 (Kindle)
ISBN 978-1-7354750-1-1 (EPUB)

First Edition: May 2019

*To my mother, Julia, who raised me to be the best that I can be. And I shall be forever grateful.*

*Divide and rule, the politician cries; unite and lead,*
*is watchword of the wise.*

—Johann Wolfgang von Goethe

# PROLOGUE

---

# One Week Ago

*Philadelphia, Pennsylvania*

THE FIRST ONE to leave the meeting, he jogged down the stone steps of the historic building, cinching the lapels of his coat to ward off the late-autumn chill.

Thanks to "Franklin," his sponsor, he had been inducted into the Paine Society, or the Society, as his fellow members called it. Membership lasted for life, either a member's natural-born life or otherwise. Standing before the ninety-nine other members, he pledged to preserve and protect the democracy of the United States.

How had he ended up in this predicament? Parliamentary government worked just fine, thank you very much. Was assigning him the name "Madison" someone's idea of a joke? The real James Madison, a founding father and the fourth US president, known primarily for his part in drafting the Constitution and the Bill of Rights, was less remembered for leading the fledgling country into war against the newly elected Society member's homeland in 1812.

The present-day "Madison" stopped and stared at his reflection in the window of a closed clothing store. His gray eyes stared back at him.

Under Franklin's direction, Madison had been covertly working for the Society, deterring his boss from pursuing the Robin Hood case and discovering the Society's role in it. His job was to ensure that the case remained closed. Permanently. The warning he issued to Jade Harrington a couple of months ago had not given him pleasure. Over the past year, working alongside her, he discovered that she was one of the good ones. Always trying to do the right thing. An agent he could learn from and aspire to be like someday.

But he had a higher calling, and as his dad used to say, one's calling wasn't a choice.

A SEPTA bus swooshed past. Glancing at his watch, he hurried toward the 30th Street Station to catch the 10:18 p.m. Amtrak to Washington, DC.

He had to report to work at the Federal Bureau of Investigation headquarters first thing tomorrow. And he couldn't be late.

# PART I

@TheGodOfVeritas: While thousands of NYC citizens won't be eating dinner tonight, Sebastian Scofield is attending a $1000-a-plate dinner at the NYPL. #shame

# CHAPTER ONE

# Washington, DC

"WHAT DO YOU want to show me?"

Jade Harrington leaned forward, forearms on her thighs. Next to her, Pat Turner sat perched on a seat cushion, a sweater draped over the back of her chair. Photographs of TV characters from *Star Trek*, *The Twilight Zone*, and *The Big Bang Theory* covered the three walls of Pat's cubicle. A space heater under the desk blew hot air against Jade's legs.

The rest of the agents on the fourth floor had left for the night, their cubicles dark.

Pat, gray-haired and in her early fifties, had been with the bureau long enough to understand how to get things done within the bureaucracy. She knew where all the bodies were buried— Jimmy Hoffa's included, it was rumored.

She pointed at the monitor. "Read it for yourself."

After selecting a blue peanut M&M, Jade slipped the small bag back into her pants pocket while she read the text on the screen. It was a report from CART, the bureau's Computer Analysis Response Team.

"What the… ?" She looked at Pat. "This means…"

The other woman nodded. "He didn't do it."

Jade leaned back in the chair and briefly closed her eyes. Not in prayer, but in shame. "How could I make a mistake like this?"

Pat's shoulders sagged. "It wasn't just you. It was all of us."

"But the buck stops with me. Damn!"

She jumped out of the chair and paced back and forth a couple of times before returning to her seat.

"Explain," Jade said.

"We messed up. As I told you months ago, something about fingering Noah Blakeley always nagged at me. All the evidence pointed to him, but his technical skills lacked the proficiency to create a hack as sophisticated as Astrea."

"The Goddess of Justice."

"The perp used Tor to anonymously send malware via email asking for donations from prospective donors of Noah's nonprofit. The program stole the victims' passwords to their online banking sites and then drained their bank accounts. The hacking of Blakeley's computer made it seem like all the transactions originated from there."

"If it wasn't Noah, then who was behind the hack?"

Pat sighed. "*That* we're still working on."

Jade glanced down at her watch. "It's 6:00 p.m. there. I need to make a call." She looked the older woman in the eye. "Good work, Pat."

Popping out of the chair, Jade sprinted down the corridor between cubicles to her office.

# CHAPTER TWO

# Camp David, near Thurmont, Maryland

"WHY ARE WE here?"

Her younger son stood in a wide stance in the middle of the living room of the main house. Once his bangs had flopped on his forehead, but now his hair was cut close on the sides and in back, the hair on top a little longer. His hands were in the front pockets of his dark blue slacks, and his white shirt was open at the collar, the uniform of a young staffer on the Hill. His red tie was draped over the armrest of a chair.

"Mom," Chandler said, "I'm needed back in Washington. I have work to do."

"I can only imagine," she said. Chandler Fairchild was a legislative aide for Nebraska senator Paul Sampson.

"What's that supposed to mean?"

"Nothing. Although you might want to think about switching to a winning team."

Emma laughed from her chair adjacent to the fireplace.

"Shut up," he said, whirling on her.

"Don't talk to your sister that way," Whitney said.

"Yeah," Emma said. "Don't talk to me that way."

Whitney flashed her daughter a warning look. "Emma."

"He's so stupid, Mom," Emma said.

Grayson, Whitney's husband, sat next to her on the sofa.

"Don't call your brother stupid," he said.

"Well, he is. He doesn't believe half the things he says." She turned to face her brother. "They're using you to provoke Mom. That's the only reason Sampson hired you."

"You think?" Chandler asked.

Leaning toward him as if in confidence, she said, "It wasn't for your political mind."

"That's enough, Emma," said Grayson.

Chandler turned to Whitney. "Are you on the winning team, Mom?"

"History will reflect favorably on my legacy."

"Doesn't seem like you're winning. The New New will die die."

The New New Deal Coalition Act, a modern incarnation of the New Deal implemented by Franklin D. Roosevelt in the 1930s, rendered relief for the unemployed and underemployed poor and middle class, recovery of the American Dream through the provision of universal preschool and a cap on college tuition, and reform of the financial system and the national infrastructure, which would build and repair highways and bridges and provide low-income housing.

"What makes you say that?" Whitney said.

"No reason," he mumbled.

"Take a seat, son," Grayson told him, "and watch your mouth."

"Yeah!" Emma said. "When you hold a real political position, then you can talk. She's your mom and the president. You should respect both."

"Emma, I'm not going to tell you again," Grayson said.

Despite the chastisement, Emma appeared pleased with herself. Chandler, on the other hand, shot each of them a look before sitting in the chair on the other side of the fireplace.

Whitney clasped her hands in her lap. "We have something to tell you."

"You're getting a divorce," Chandler blurted.

This caught Whitney off guard. "What?"

Chandler's leg bobbed up and down with nervous energy. "What else could be important enough to drag us out here to the country? You told us about that psycho, Landon. There's not another sibling we don't know about, is there?" He barked out a laugh.

"Being a victim of rape isn't funny," she said. "You make it seem as if it was my fault."

Under her breath, Emma said, "I told you he was stupid."

Chandler's face softened. "Sorry, Mom."

She looked at her son. He had become a stranger to her. Though Emma, too, had changed. For both of them, Whitney suspected, it was more than the usual pangs of growing up. The pressure of being the president's children—not to mention the children of the first female US president—didn't help. The two siblings had been close until a couple of years ago. They rarely spoke to each other now. When they did, their words weren't kind.

Whitney glanced at her husband. "Landon Phillips," she said carefully, "believed he was my son."

"We know," Chandler said.

"It's not true," Whitney said.

Emma sat up. "What?"

"What's not true?" Chandler said.

Soldiering on, Whitney said, "For some reason, perhaps because of our mutual circumstances—coincidences—he conjured up this entire scenario that I gave him up at birth."

"Why would he do that?" Chandler asked.

"I don't know," Whitney said.

"Who's his biological mother?" Emma asked.

"I don't know that either."

"You don't have another son?" Chandler asked, hopeful.

She pondered, not for the first time, if this was the root cause of her son's drastic personality shift over the last year.

"That's not why you asked us here," Emma said. "There's something else."

"Yes." Another glance at her husband, who winked at her, bestowing a smile that nestled her in a warm blanket. He patted her hand.

"After the terrorist attack on Rockefeller Center," she said, "my press secretary needed a blood transfusion."

"Blake Haynes," Chandler said.

Whitney nodded.

"Wait a minute," he said, standing. "Haynes is your son? Is that what you're saying?"

"Yes."

"Are you sure this time?"

"Watch your tone. I've had enough of your attitude."

Chandler brushed back bangs no longer there. Was he analyzing the political implications as she had when she'd received the test results? Or were his calculations more personal?

"Yes, we're sure," Whitney continued. "DNA testing proved beyond a doubt that Blake is my son, and your half-brother."

"He's not my brother," Chandler said.

"Since his politics are more aligned with Mom's than yours are," Emma said, "maybe you're the one who's adopted."

"Emma!" Whitney said.

"Just kidding, Mom." Emma rose, crossed the room, and sat on the other side of her. Hugging Whitney tightly, she whispered in her ear, "I love you, Mom," before resting her head on Whitney's shoulder.

"I love you too." Whitney laid her cheek on her daughter's head and looked up at her son.

"Are you going public with this?" he asked.

"Not yet. This is between us for now. And Dr. Sangha." Dr. Sati Sangha was the physician to the president.

"Who's the father?" Chandler asked.

She and Grayson had agreed, for now, not to share the identity of the rapist with anyone. Another secret they wouldn't be able to keep for long.

"He wasn't a father," Emma said. "He was a rapist. You should be supporting *her*. Your mom is president of the United States!"

Chandler glared at her, grabbed his tie, and stomped out of the room. Grayson rose to go after him.

"Let him go," Whitney said. "It's a lot to absorb."

Since Chandler had discovered politics during his last year in college, a chasm had opened between Whitney and her son.

She needed to get him back.

# CHAPTER THREE

---

## Seattle, Washington

"WILL THE DEFENDANT please rise?"

From the back of the crowded courtroom of the US District Court on Stewart Street, Jade watched as a man at the defense table stood. In a mismatched tan jacket and brown slacks, he appeared bigger than the last time she had seen him, thanks to a prison weight room.

The Asian-American judge said in a soft voice simmering with anger, "Noah Blakeley, you have endured a gross miscarriage of justice." Through enormous owl-like glasses, she scanned the spectators from the dais, the polished wood gleaming. The United States and Washington State flags stood sentry. Jade could've sworn the judge's eyes paused when they landed on her.

Did she recognize Jade as the arresting agent?

The judge's gaze returned to the man before her. "On behalf of the federal government, I am ashamed and apologize for its actions. You are hereby exonerated from the ninety-nine counts of wire, bank, and computer fraud, computer intrusion, aggravated identity theft, and all other charges brought against you." She paused. "I am pleased to tell you, Mr. Blakeley, that you are free to go."

Slamming her gavel once, she gathered her black judicial robes and made a brisk exit through the door behind her.

Noah's legs buckled slightly. With a pained keen, he began to sob.

One of his hands flew to his mouth, while the other found purchase on the table, gripping the edge as if to prevent him from falling. His attorney belatedly moved in closer to hold him up. She handed him his cup of water, and he gulped it gratefully.

There was no one else to catch him. After his conviction, his wife, Diane, had left him. The couple had been childless. His brother, August, and his father, Augustus, weren't present.

Jade slipped out the door and stood across the hall from the courtroom door, waiting. Ten minutes later, Noah and his attorney came out. Up close, Jade saw stubble dotting his cheeks and chin.

This wasn't one of her better ideas. As Noah and his attorney started to walk past her and out the front door of the courthouse, she stepped forward.

"Noah."

He stopped. "Agent Harrington."

"I—"

Noah grabbed both of her hands, his eyes still moist. "I'm glad you're here. I wanted to thank you in person, and here you are."

"For what?" she said, incredulous.

"For never giving up on me. Without you, I would've rotted in that cell forever. I wouldn't have survived."

*You were in that cell in the first place because of me.*

Letting go of her hands, he hugged her. A desperate hug, like he was clinging to a life raft. Maybe he was.

She extricated herself gently. "What are your plans?"

Shrugging, he said, "Equality One is dead. The concept is still a great idea, but it'd be hard to raise money after what happened. I'm not sure my father will take me back." He hesitated. "Not sure I want him to anyway."

Just before his arrest, Noah had resigned as the chief operating officer of his family's international shipping firm to head up Equality One, a nonprofit that provided jobs and homes to people who needed them.

"You can start something else," she said.

A glance downward. "The stigma from this will follow me wherever I go. For the rest of my life. No matter what I do. But you may be right." He extended his hand. "Thanks again, Agent Harrington."

Jade hesitated and then shook it.

Noah's attorney led him out the front door, where a crowd of reporters and camera crews anxiously awaited his statement on the courthouse steps, and probably his plans to sue the Seattle Police, the City of Seattle, the Federal Bureau of Investigation, and Jade Harrington.

To avoid the crowd, Jade headed for a side door she'd spotted on her way in.

"Agent Harrington."

She turned. A woman she didn't recognize held out a smartphone, the red button indicating that it was recording.

Guarded, Jade said, "Yes?"

"My name is Iyanna Adey. I'm with KIRO7. We've spoken before, on the phone."

Jade remembered. The reporter had asked for a comment on

the Robin Hood case. When Jade refused, the woman divulged that Jade's supervisor, Ethan Lawson, had been the source for details regarding that case. Soon thereafter, Ethan took a leave of absence from the bureau.

The black reporter wore expensive three-inch heels and a tight-fitting blue dress, despite the forty-degree weather outside.

Jade had never understood women who wore sleeveless dresses in the winter. Was it to show off their arms? It did appear that Adey worked out. Or was it more comparable to those football players who sported short sleeves in below-freezing temperatures? To prove… something.

Eyeing the phone, Jade said nothing.

Adey gazed through the glass doors at Noah, who spoke into a microphone on a makeshift podium. "Care to comment about Noah Blakeley's release?"

"No."

"You arrested an innocent man and were instrumental in his conviction. I'm giving you a chance to explain your side of the story. To set the record straight. The people have a right to know."

"No comment."

"Are you sure? I can portray you in a positive light."

*Sure.* Jade started to push past the reporter.

"Come on," Adey said. "We need to stick together. Won't you help a sistah out?"

"Excuse me?"

"It's hard for us to be assigned real stories."

"I can't help you."

"Can't or won't? I'm sure you feel guilty about what happened—"

Jade strode away down the long corridor, what she should have done when the reporter had first called her name.

From behind her, Adey said, "Lovely to finally meet you in person, Agent Harrington. I'm rooting for you."

*What did Adey mean by that?*

Jade kept walking. Before reaching the door, she glanced back.

Iyanna Adey had joined two people: Detective Kurt McClaine of the Seattle PD, whom Jade had worked with on the Robin Hood and TSK investigations, and Kyle Madison, the managing director of a venture capital firm, a victim in the former case, and someone Jade had become close to during the investigation.

Too close.

Out of the three of them, Kyle was doing most of the talking.

Jade watched them for a moment longer before turning, pressing the release bar to open the door, and stepping out into the misty morning.

## CHAPTER FOUR

# Washington, DC

THE WALLS OF the private room were painted gray—not an institutional shade but a modern one. Except for the medical equipment, it could have been mistaken for a hotel room.

A man was sitting up in the bed. Most of his face was covered in bandages, except for his eyes, which never left her face.

"Not bad for a hospital room," Whitney said.

"Most people would kill for this room," Blake said, "but I miss the office."

"Not home?"

"My office was my home."

They both pretended to watch the muted television on the wall near the foot of the bed.

The clear liquid in Blake's IV flowed to the needle inserted in the thin skin on the back of his hand.

"Sorry I haven't visited before now," she said.

"You're busy."

"Still."

She'd squeezed in this midday visit between meetings with the CEO of Goldman Sachs and the president of the Service Employees International Union.

"It's only been a couple of weeks," he said. "Any leads?"

Blake Haynes had been at New York City's Rockefeller Center, promoting the New New Deal and the Federal Anti-Bullying Act on MSNBC's morning show, when a suicide bomber blew himself up, killing twenty-seven people and injuring forty-five others. Five more subsequently died from their injuries.

Blake had needed multiple blood transfusions, leading Sasha, Whitney's chief of staff, to discover that he and Whitney shared the same rare blood type. DNA testing proved her maternity.

"No." She hesitated. "I guess we should talk about—"

"Not sure I'm ready," he said.

"I owe you an explanation."

"You don't."

"You deserve to know."

She described the circumstances of his birth. "Seventeen and still in school," she concluded, "I wasn't in a position to raise a child. I did what I thought was best for you."

She didn't mention that she'd wanted an abortion.

Blake listened without interrupting. "My parents were good to me. I never felt adopted." He hesitated. "Who was it? The rapist."

"I don't know," Whitney lied.

His bandaged left hand reached for hers. She slipped her left hand through the side rail, meeting him halfway, their hands resting on the thin bedspread. Their eyes met. For a few moments, they didn't speak. A bond had always connected them, even before she'd learned that he was her son. Now she understood why.

"Thank you," he said, "for donating the blood."

"Better than my liver."

His brow furrowed.

"I'm joking," she said. No need to mention the amount of wine she had consumed since the attack.

He released her hand. "It's going to take some time. To get used to."

"For me too."

"Does the First Gentleman know?"

She nodded.

"What about Chandler and Emma?" he asked.

"Yes."

"How did they take it?"

She made a face.

"That well?"

"They'll need time to adjust." *Especially Chandler.*

"How are things at the office?"

Whitney laughed. "That question is different for my job, isn't it?"

"Guess so," he said, chuckling. "How's Lena doing?"

Lena had been White House press secretary before Whitney poached Blake from his commentator job on a cable news channel. Lena left the administration to form her own public relations firm. When Whitney called after the tragedy to offer her the acting press secretary position, Lena accepted without hesitation.

Whitney wasn't sure she could be so forgiving. She looked at Blake. As either of them.

On the television screen, a reporter spoke outside the hospital. Judy Porter, middle-aged with auburn hair, had been in the press pool accompanying Whitney during the presidential campaign. In uncovering an explosive story about Grayson, her reporting led to the revelation that Whitney had given up a baby for adoption.

Whitney didn't bother turning up the sound on the TV. Judy wasn't finished digging into Whitney's past. And she never would be.

She turned back to Blake. "What's the prognosis?"

"I won't be running marathons anytime soon."

"Seriously."

"Healing."

"Well, that's great news."

"But not fast enough. My recovery will take months."

"Any friends been by?"

"A few."

"Jade?"

The bandages prevented her from seeing his face, but his eyes betrayed him. He shook his head.

Whitney frowned. "That's surprising."

"It's okay." He exhaled. "I can't face her."

"Why not?"

His eyes flashed. "I don't want her to see me like this!"

A knock at the door. Josh McPherson, Whitney's lead secret service special agent, poked his head in. The florescent light from the hallway shone on his bald ebony dome. "Is everything all right, Madam President?"

"I'm fine, Josh. Thank you."

He looked from her to Blake, then shut the door.

"I think you underestimate her." She paused. "I thought there was something between you two."

Shifting his gaze, he said, "So did I."

"She's a hard one to read, that one," Whitney said gently, "but I'm sure she's worth every word. I wouldn't give up just yet."

He didn't respond. He was still looking out the window when she left the room.

## CHAPTER FIVE

# Washington, DC

A T THE FEDERAL Bureau of Investigation, Acting Special Agent in Charge Jade Harrington was no longer in her old cramped office down the hall. She was now ensconced in Ethan Lawson's office, reviewing a report.

Jade couldn't stop thinking about Noah Blakeley and the part she played in his arrest and conviction. She hadn't forgiven herself. The details of the case replayed on an endless loop in her mind. What had she missed? She wasn't one to make mistakes. Jade was the type of person who could ignore everything she'd done right and focus on the one thing she'd done wrong. Since learning of Noah's innocence, she was figuratively sore from kicking herself.

Leaning back, she slowly spun around once in the high-backed chair. The old FBI emblem on the wall behind her, depicting the scales of justice and the motto Fidelity, Bravery, Integrity remained, as did the mahogany coatrack in the corner. Her former boss's diplomas, of which he was proud—especially the one from *the* George Washington University—were stored with his other personal effects in a cabinet in the credenza.

To an outsider, it appeared to be the temporary office that it was. No diplomas. No family pictures. Jade's only personal items were a basketball paperweight sitting on one of the stacks of files on the desk, a family-size yellow bag of peanut M&M's that she kept in the center drawer, and an old basketball she spun on her finger when she needed to think.

Jade was waiting for Ethan to return from a leave of absence that she didn't believe was voluntary. He couldn't be the source of the leaks on her last two major cases, as she'd been led to believe.

She missed him. His guidance and his unwavering support. Ethan had put her name forward to fill in for him. Jade had no idea when he'd be coming back. He hadn't called, and she suspected he didn't want her to call him.

Around the same time that Ethan left, President Whitney Fairchild had asked Jade to be a special assistant on her staff. Serving in the White House and for the person whose decisions impacted three hundred fifty million lives, even more when you counted the rest of the world, was an honor that Jade hadn't taken lightly. But it was also a temporary position lasting the remainder of Fairchild's presidency, whether that was three more years or seven.

Regardless, the FBI was in her blood now. It was her life. One day Director would be on the nameplate next to her door. Leaving the bureau, even temporarily, would put that aspiration in jeopardy. The decision had been a no-brainer; her eyes were on the prize.

"I don't pay you to daydream."

Jade started at the sound of his voice. "I was thinking," she said. "There's a difference."

Assistant Director, Criminal Investigative Division, Warren Barringer strolled into Ethan's office and heaved one of his haunches onto the desk. She cringed. He was white-haired and overweight, and Jade found it hard not to stare at his white bushy eyebrows.

"We need to talk," he said.

"Okay."

"About your cases…"

"What about them?"

"Solving them. Since you took over, the department's solve rate has decreased."

Jade offered no excuses. He was right.

Although she'd replaced Ethan, she hadn't found someone to replace her, because she'd been too busy doing both jobs. She didn't want to hire someone from the outside in case Ethan returned. Promoting someone on her team was an option, but Pat Turner didn't want to supervise people, Micah Alexander was too green, and neither Christian Merritt nor Dante Carlucci was ready.

Or she wasn't ready to let go. Jade wasn't much of a delegator.

"I hear you," she said.

"You'd better," Barringer said. "I'm not happy about the outcome of the cybertheft case."

Sitting up, she inclined her head, frowning. "But we sent an innocent man to prison."

"It was closed," Barringer said.

"You'd rather keep the wrong—"

"I can always bring Ethan back."

Jade shrugged. "Do it. That's what I want. Why is he on leave anyway?"

"Or install someone more… suitable."

Something within her ignited. Before counting to ten, she said, "What does that mean?"

"You know what I mean."

"I don't."

"This diversity stuff has gone too far."

*What was he saying?*

He slid off the desk and left, not bothering to shut the door.

Before this interim appointment, she hadn't worked much with Barringer. Clearly unenthused about her promotion, he'd been unnecessarily hard on her. Opening the desk's bottom drawer, she removed the furniture polish and a towel. As she rubbed out the moist spot he'd left, she concluded that the Robin Hood case was the real reason he'd come to her office. Even though truth had won, he wasn't happy with the outcome.

Why?

# CHAPTER SIX

# New York City, New York

SEBASTIAN SCOFIELD LAUGHED at Hasad Nasir's joke, although the city's mayor wasn't that funny. Earlier that evening, Sebastian had announced—to loud applause from the crowd of wealthy businesspeople, athletes, and entertainers—that he would make a significant donation to the sponsor of the fundraiser, a children's literacy foundation, and match all donations up to $25,000 per gift.

Laughing with Nasir now would make the ask easier later.

Sebastian loved the city. The lights. The people. The restaurants. The museums. Broadway. Times Square. The city that never slept, like him. Working almost one hundred hours a week at his day job as the founder and managing director of a hedge fund, Sebastian lived for the nights. For these dinners. He'd better, since he attended one almost every night. He loved the schmoozing, the clinking of glasses, turning on the charm, meeting new people, asking them for their money. His Rolodex, or, rather, the extensive contact list on his smartphone, contained the names of every influential person in the city, the cause or causes important to them, and what story would yield their maximum donation. Sebastian believed in the causes he supported, especially when they benefited him, his company, or his political beliefs.

But that was his secret.

Most of all, he enjoyed being seen. A picture of him sitting next to and laughing with the mayor would be on the front page of the *New York Times* style section tomorrow. Possibly the front page of the entire paper.

They would definitely make Page Six.

After a main course of filet mignon, curried potatoes, and asparagus, a chocolate hazelnut tart was served for dessert. He admired the building's architecture, including the thirty-foot-high glass and cast-iron dome above him. The men—and some women—were in tuxes. Other women wore gowns and expensive jewelry. A chamber quartet played quietly in the corner. A server exchanged his empty champagne flute for a full one.

Over the floral centerpiece, he grinned at his wife, sitting across from him at the oblong white linen–covered table. Her black dress matched her hair. The sizable diamonds around her neck, in her earlobes, and on several of her fingers—including the rock on the ring finger of her left hand—sparkled in the light of the multitude of fixtures overhead. She gave him a crisp nod. She understood why he was laughing.

The program was wrapping up. After the host's closing remarks, Sebastian stood and clapped along with everyone else in the ballroom.

Outside, at the top of the steps near the entrance of the New York Public Library, he and his wife, who was bundled in a white fur coat, shook hands, air-kissed both cheeks, and said goodbye to the who's who of the city.

"Scofield!" someone called out to him. "You did well tonight!"

"Thank you!" he said. Someone had told him the event raised over four million dollars.

Touching his wife's back, he bent to whisper in her ear that it was time to go. As he did, a stab of pain spread through his lower back. Odd. In his midfifties and in excellent health, he had never suffered from back pains before.

"Excuse me," said a gentleman wearing a formal hat pulled down low over his forehead. He picked up an event program and handed it to Sebastian.

"You dropped this."

"No, I…"

Sebastian's fingers clutched a strange object protruding from his back. His coat was wet. When he brought his fingers in front of his face, they were covered with a dark liquid. If he wasn't mistaken, it looked like blood.

*Mine?*

Lightheaded, he started to fall. He reached out for his wife to steady himself, his hand leaving red prints on the sleeve of her white fur coat. When he hit the pavement, his wife's scream sounded far away. Footsteps rushed toward him. Images of people towering over him began to converge, then grew hazy. Fingers pressed against his throat, checking for a pulse.

Sebastian Scofield fell into a deep sleep from which he would never wake.

# CHAPTER SEVEN

## New York City, New York

ACTING LIKE ANY other successful businessman late for another appointment, Devon hurried down the steps, bumping into and apologizing to people. Some of them were on their cell phones and barely noticed. The first scream curdled as Dev ran down 42nd Street. Other screams joined in, as well as loud voices shouting commands. Her deed had been discovered.

She didn't stop running, and she didn't look back.

In the middle of the block, she cut through Bryant Park, her men's dress shoes tapping on the walkway that surrounded the lawn. She passed the fountain and emerged on 40th Street. Slowing her gait, she blended in with the other pedestrians on the crowded sidewalk: businesspeople headed home, theatergoers, shoppers carrying bags, people going out for food and drinks, residents walking their dogs, dog walkers walking other people's dogs.

Androgynous, Dev had always been able to blend in, passing

for a man or a woman, white, Hispanic, Asian—even a light-skinned black person. An asset in her career.

Previous and current.

A homeless man covered with a blanket sat against a building, his legs spread in a *V*. Next to him, a trash bag was stuffed with clothes. He was reading a book in the light of a streetlamp. A John Grisham novel. *A Time to Kill.*

*How appropriate.*

The man met her eyes. Watchful. Wary. Knowing.

Dev stopped and took off the black coat she'd worn to the fundraiser. The victim's blood was most likely on it. Destroying the coat would be the smart thing to do. Instead she handed it down to the man, who gripped the coat in both hands in front of his chest. Jaws clenched, he nodded his head.

A careless act, but she didn't have the heart to burn it or throw it away. Not when he needed it.

While he struggled to his feet to try it on, she continued walking. After a couple more blocks, she hailed a yellow cab. Ten minutes later, she entered the revolving doors of a hotel in Chelsea.

Just inside, a uniformed doorman greeted her. "Welcome back, sir."

"Thank you."

He eyed her tuxedo jacket. "Bit nippy out."

Shrugging her shoulders almost apologetically and praying there wasn't blood on her pants, she said, "Thought I'd risk it." She pointed a thumb vaguely to the south. "Formal dinner in the financial district."

"Well, you're here now," he said. "Good night."

"It already has been."

"Oh… killer deal?"

Dev smiled. "Something like that."

# CHAPTER EIGHT

## Washington, DC

"YOU WANTED TO see me, boss?"

Jade looked up from the case file she was reading. A major difference in her new role was that she had to be aware of the facts of all the cases in the department, not just her own.

Special Agent Dante Carlucci poked his head into her office. His brown hair was cut short, all the curls gone. He looked handsome. And happy.

She didn't care for the new nickname, but it was better than chiefette or chief.

"Have a seat," she said.

In the guest chair across from her, he leaned back, spreading his long legs. "What's up?"

"Comfortable?"

"Yeah."

He'd missed the rebuke.

"Barringer came to see me," Jade said.

Dante raised an eyebrow but remained silent.

"He's not happy about our close rates. Since Ethan left."

"We're working as hard as we can."

"But not as smart as we can."

Frowning, he said, "What are you saying? You think it's my fault?"

Jade straightened the five pens in front of her into perfect formation. "I've been trying to run this office like Ethan did, but it's not working. There's someone missing."

"Who?"

"Me."

"You?" He shook his head. "I don't get it."

She stopped messing with the pens. "I need someone to replace me."

Dante scowled. "I get it. You're promoting Merritt." He started to rise. "Whatever."

"Sit down," she said, reaching into her center drawer and pulling out a small unopened bag of peanut M&M's. Jade threw it at him.

He caught it and looked at her questioningly. "I don't like M&M's. Or peanuts."

"It's a metaphor. Go put them in my desk."

His expression remained blank.

"Congratulations," she said. "While I'm acting as Ethan's replacement, you're acting as mine."

"Me?"

She nodded.

A grin, wide with wonder, crossed his face, then dissipated. "Is this a joke?"

"No," Jade said. "I think you're ready to take on more

responsibility." She waved him away. "Now, go claim my office before I change my mind and give it to Merritt."

He hustled to the door.

"Hey!" she said.

He turned, his expression communicating that he was prepared for the punchline.

"This doesn't mean I like you now or anything."

Dante laughed. "I got it. Boss."

❊

Later that morning, during her team's weekly meeting, Jade listened as each of her staff presented updates on their current caseloads. Sitting around the oval table in the conference room were Christian, Pat, Micah, and Dante. Absent was Max Stover, a behavioral analyst out of Quantico, Virginia, who wasn't technically on the team but worked with them on high-profile serial killer cases.

Interrupting them occasionally to ask for more detail or suggest they pursue a different angle, Jade waited until the updates were finished before saying, "I have an announcement."

"A new case?" Micah asked, his slight British accent a feather against her skin.

"No," she said. "I've been trying to do my job and Ethan's job since he left. It's too much."

"Even for you?" Christian asked.

"I thought you could do everything," Micah said.

"Someone needs to take over my responsibilities," she said.

"Be in with a chance?" Micah asked.

From a chair leaned back at its customary forty-five-degree

angle, Dante said, "What the hell does that mean? Can't you speak English?"

The second question was asked without irony.

Shaking his head, Micah stared at Dante. "Hopeless."

"Someday," she said to Micah. Glancing at the rest of the expectant faces, she steeled herself. Inclining her head toward Dante, she said, "Effectively immediately, Dante is your acting supervisor."

Pat stopped typing. She peered over her glasses at Jade and mouthed, "What the fuck?"

With a look of horror, Micah said, "Shite!"

Christian's face transformed from a look of horror to one of amusement. He laughed. "You got me."

Jade said to him, her tone soft, "There wasn't time to tell you."

Christian's laughter died as his eyes narrowed. "You're serious."

She gave a slight nod.

Dante smiled sweetly at Christian. "You may call me 'Daddy' if you'd like."

"Shut up, Dante," Jade said, glaring at him.

Pushing back his chair, Christian shot a look at Jade and walked out of the room without another word.

Micah watched him leave and turned back to Jade. "I feel as if I've seen this movie before."

He was referring to a time during the bullying case, when Christian had words with Dante and walked out of a team meeting.

"Me too," Dante said. "It's my favorite movie."

# CHAPTER NINE

---

# The White House, Washington, DC

FROM BEHIND THE nineteenth-century *Resolute* desk in the Oval Office, President Whitney Fairchild watched her chief of staff's mouth move, an actor in a silent movie. She was thinking about Blake.

Across from her, Sasha, a former Texas congresswoman, stopped talking, her lips pursed. Whitney prepared to hear it.

"Have you listened to a word I said?" asked Sasha, a look of annoyance on her dark-complexioned face.

"Pardon me?"

"I knew you weren't listening," Sasha said. "I told you that you're too thin, we might have a lead on the attack, and I'm concerned about the New New Deal."

"I missed all that?"

"Apparently. Do I need to tell my momma to bring you some

real food? Put some meat on those bones?" Sasha slid her arms down the side of her body and shimmied. "These curves didn't come from eating kale."

Whitney held up her hand. "Stop shimmying."

Her appetite had suffered in the wake of the terrorist attack as she continued to have nothing substantive to report to the press. The guilt wasn't helping either. She still didn't know who was responsible, much less brought anyone to justice as she had promised the American people she would.

None of the usual suspects—ISIS, Al-Qaeda, the Taliban, Hamas, Hezbollah—had claimed responsibility.

Because she'd avoided the press's questions about Blake's condition, citing HIPAA concerns, reporters started calling her aloof. Unapproachable. Cold. Some nicknamed her the Steel Lady in an unflattering mimicry of the Iron Lady, the former prime minister of the United Kingdom, Margaret Thatcher.

Last week's State of the Union address—her first—hadn't gone well. Although the Democrats clapped at everything she said and stood at the scripted moments, the response was subdued. The Republicans hadn't bought what she was selling, and neither had her own party.

"Do you have something to tell me?" Sasha asked.

"As far as?"

"About Blake."

"He's in better spirits."

"That's not what I meant."

*I know what you meant.*

Not ready to confide in Sasha about Blake's parentage, she said, "'Not knowing when the dawn will come, I open every door.'"

"Who said that?"

"Emily Dickinson."

Hands on her hips, Sasha said, "Are you trying to tell me to not be so curious? To mind my own business? Because you are my business."

"That's the great thing about quotes," Whitney said, smiling. "You can interpret them however you wish. Now, tell me about this lead and why you're worried about the New New Deal."

# CHAPTER TEN

# Washington, DC

S HE'D PUT OFF this visit long enough.

Shifting the Audi to park, Jade exhaled and stared at herself in the rearview mirror, smoothing the top of her light-brown hair. She hadn't seen Blake Haynes since the terrorist attack over six weeks ago. They'd planned to meet up when he returned from New York.

She'd called to check on his condition a few times, but the hospital wouldn't release any information. She could have gained access through the president but didn't want to be obligated to her.

Jade didn't want to owe anyone anything.

The administration, through its acting deputy press secretary, Lena Smith, would not comment on Blake's condition.

Jade and Blake had seen each other before the attack. They weren't dating. Or friends. She wasn't sure what they were, but she enjoyed being with him. He was intelligent. And he made her laugh.

With her promotion, she hadn't had time to visit him until now. At least, that's what she told herself. In truth, she was reluctant to face him, and not because of the changes to his face and body. What was she afraid of? Although she'd been a psych major in college, she didn't spend much time analyzing herself.

She got out of the car and locked it, the beep loud in the silence of the underground parking garage. Her eyes lingered on each gray concrete pillar as she imagined the possibility of someone hiding behind it.

Professional habit.

Jade entered George Washington University Hospital and wended her way to the information desk. Clearing her throat, she waited for the nurse manning the station to look up.

"I'm looking for Blake Haynes."

"Your name?"

"Jade Harrington."

"Relationship to the patient?"

"Uh… friend."

"One moment please."

The young man tapped several computer keys and then spoke into his headset. Personnel were being paged over the intercom system and directed to various areas of the hospital. After a moment, he looked at her.

"What room is he in?" Jade asked.

The nurse searched her eyes. "I'm sorry. You're not on the approved visitor list."

"Can you double-check? I'm sure he wants to see me."

He sighed. "Mr. Haynes left specific instructions. He doesn't want to see you."

"There must be some mistake."

"Maybe so, but you're not seeing him today."

@TheGodOfVeritas: It's no secret that the Carr brothers and their Super PAC are behind the push to repeal the #NewNewDeal They should feel #shame

# CHAPTER ELEVEN

# The White House, Washington, DC

WHITNEY PICKED AT her Cobb salad.

"You're quiet," Grayson said.

Putting her fork down without eating, she took a sip of wine. "I'm sorry, darling. A lot on my mind. How was your day?"

Grayson sat across from her at the dining room table in the Residence, his light-brown hair grazing his forehead. A fire blazed in the fireplace, warding off the chill. One of her favorite paintings, a woman with a child sitting on her lap, hung over the mantel.

"We're finally making progress," he said. "I met with business leaders from across the Metro area again today, and we're close to finalizing the plan. I'll have something on your desk by the end of the month."

Grayson's cause as First Gentleman—or the First First Man, as the mainstream media called him, or the First Dude, as the alternative media called him—was to oversee a major initiative to provide job and business training to the long-term unemployed. Although initially averse to taking on his First Gentleman duties, he had since embraced them with the same fervor as his former position: CEO of Fairchild Industries, a family-owned global biotechnology company. He'd relinquished the job to one of his brothers so he could join Whitney in the White House.

Refilling her wine glass, she said, "You seem excited about it."

"I am." He reached across the table and touched her hand. His tone was gentle as he said, "Don't you think you should slow down?"

She glanced at the grandfather clock. "A president doesn't have the luxury of slowing down."

"I was talking about the wine."

There was a knock at the front door of the Residence.

Moments later, Sasha entered the dining room, her face strained.

"Madam President, I'm sorry to interrupt."

Whitney set her glass down. "It's fine, Sasha. What is it? The terrorist attack?"

"A false lead."

"Then what?"

"My source on the Hill says Hampton and Sampson secured enough votes to overturn the New New Deal."

Whitney's first thought was not of the time and energy and political capital they'd expended to pass the legislation, but rather of her son and his comment at Camp David.

*The New New will die die.*

Chandler had known.

# CHAPTER TWELVE

## Chicago, Illinois

IN A PRIVATE upstairs dining room of the Oak Club, Jared F. Carr Jr. looked across the table at his younger brother.

"Superb steak," Jared said, wiping his mouth with a white linen napkin.

"That stuff will kill you eventually."

"At least I'll die happy. Unlike you. Your dying wish will be for a juicy double cheeseburger. With cheese fries."

"I doubt that," Jason Carr said.

The Oak Club was founded over a century ago by Yale alumni living in Chicago. It provided a place for members and their guests to meet, dine, and socialize in a refined and exclusive atmosphere in the city's North End.

The server entered and cleared their dinner plates. The two men were silent as he returned carrying a tray containing two glasses of port and clipped cigars. After lighting the cigars, the server retreated. Technically it was a nonsmoking room, but the federal, state, city, and club regulations didn't apply to them.

Rules were for those without money.

Except for their expensive dress, the brothers were nothing alike. Jared was blond, portly, and a Yale alumnus, like their father and his father before him. Jason had dark hair and a runner's physique, and had graduated from the University of Illinois business school, to their parents' eternal regret. Jared, married with three children, lived in the Chicago suburb of Glencoe, while Jason, a lifelong bachelor, owned a penthouse condo overlooking Lake Michigan in Chicago's Lakeshore neighborhood. Often photographed with wealthy women—businesswomen, socialites, models, celebrities, athletes—Jason never managed to keep a relationship going more than a few months. The press constantly speculated on when he would settle down and who the lucky woman would be.

Whenever he read such speculation, Jared laughed. His brother would never settle down with any woman. Jason was gay. Although he wasn't out, he wasn't so deep in the closet that he would enter into a sham marriage. Jason's sexual orientation was ironic—their nonprofit organization, Freedom of America (FOA), financially backed the Defense of Marriage Act in the nineties.

At the time, Jason was too busy working for their father's real estate investment firm to date anyone. In correlation with the nation's grudging recognition of gay relationships and, finally, gay marriage, Jason began seeing men discreetly, but he still hadn't come out to his family, including his brother. Jared knew only because of reports submitted by private investigators. It wasn't personal. Jared investigated everyone. He could never possess too much information about someone, even his flesh and blood.

After battling the issue of gay marriage for decades, Jared

realized that Jason's sexuality didn't matter to him. When Cole Brennan had tried to resurrect the Defense of Marriage Act II a couple of years ago, Jared quietly ordered that the topic be removed from FOA's website and all its promotional materials. It was a lost cause. He only spent his time and money on issues he could win. If Jason noticed the change, he never said anything.

Not even a thank you.

Admiring the cigar, Jared said, "A wonderful day."

"Yes, it was," Jason said.

"The free market reigns," said Jared, taking a slow, sensuous puff.

"Did you talk to Hampton?"

Jared exhaled. "I did. The Senate majority leader was a good solider on this one."

"The house we bought him on Hilton Head didn't hurt."

"True."

Jason eyed his brother. "What's next?"

"Not sure yet. I'm going to enjoy tonight and think about that tomorrow." After a while, he placed the cigar in the ashtray's stirrup. "I need to go." Jared didn't like to keep his wife, Lisa, waiting. He stood. "Are you coming?"

"No," Jason said. "I think I'll stay here and enjoy this." He held up his cigar. "Then go down to the bar."

From the door, Jared turned and gave his younger brother a pointed look. "Be careful."

Jason gave him a sad smile and saluted. "I always am."

Returning the salute, Jared thanked God again that he was straight. Living with an affliction like Jason's couldn't be easy.

Downstairs, he retrieved his coat, bracing himself before going out into the sub-zero temperature. As he waited for the valet to bring his car around, he thought about what his sources on the Hill had told him earlier about the overturning of the over-reaching New New Deal Coalition Act.

They had the votes.

Although Jared was the brains behind the brothers, he and Jason had never received the credit they deserved for their influence on US conservative politics. But that was fine. They didn't do it for the glory but for love of their country.

He disdained both major US political parties. In truth, Jared was a Libertarian, believing government had no role in the lives of the American people—period. But to make his dreams a reality, he had to choose a side. Today's victory, one of many since his ideology supplanted that of his father's Republican Party, was only the beginning. Jared wouldn't stop until he'd amassed his fair share of the economic pie, which, to him, meant the whole pie.

A homeless man shuffled toward him, the bottom of his tattered pants dragging behind him on the sidewalk. He carried a cardboard sign painted in red letters: This is what invisible looks like. The doorman of the club started toward the man. Jared waved him off. "It's okay."

The doorman returned to his place by the front door.

The homeless man's eyes shone clear in his dirty face. He held his hand out.

"I need to eat too."

"Get a job," Jared said, not unkindly. "Then you could buy food, and it will make you feel better about yourself. Give you confidence and self-esteem."

This surprised the homeless man. Perhaps no one had ever given him this advice.

The man tilted his head. "Why do you think I don't have a job?"

This brought Jared up short. While formulating a response

to this improbable question, the man whipped out a knife from under his thin sweatshirt—unsuitable for the weather, Jared noted belatedly—and stabbed Jared in the chest three times in rapid succession.

Clutching the knife in both hands, Jared hit the pavement face-first, the blood flooding through his fingers as the knife burrowed further into his body.

"Hey!" the doorman yelled.

The homeless man flipped up the bottom of Jared's coat, ripped the wallet out of his back pocket, and took off at a run, the sound of his footsteps receding into the night.

Kneeling next to Jared, the doorman said into his cell phone, "A man's been stabbed. In front of the Oak Club. Hurry." He recited the address and hung up. "Mr. Carr, you're going to be all right. An ambulance is on its way."

It wasn't true.

Jared Carr had known he didn't have much time left. As the darkness descended for the final time, he mourned for himself. He would never seize the entire pie.

# CHAPTER THIRTEEN

# Chicago, Illinois

DEV RAN AWAY, knowing the doorman would choose to try to save the life of a coveted member of the club—and reap all the rewards that that would entail—rather than apprehend her. He wouldn't have caught her anyway. She kept herself in peak condition, not only for her work, but for herself, taking pride in her long, sinewy muscles. The absence of body fat.

Before crossing the street, she risked a brief glance over her shoulder. She'd been right. The doorman was bent over, attending to Carr.

Ignoring stoplights, she sprinted another four blocks before slowing down to a homeless-man shuffle. She passed a delivery van, then ducked into an alley that bisected the block between skyscraper office buildings. Littered with takeout cartons, crumpled candy wrappers, rotting garbage, and empty liquor bottles, the alley was shrouded in darkness, most of the lights extinguished on the lower floors.

The number of wailing sirens in the distance multiplied. Reaching behind a dumpster, Dev retrieved the bag she'd stashed there earlier. A car drove by the alley's entrance. She shed the homeless persona, donned a T-shirt over her chest-compression wrap, and slipped on an Under Armour tracksuit. As she changed, she ignored the pitter-patter of rats scurrying nearby. They were looking for food like everyone else.

Balling up the rags and tucking them under her arm like a football, she ran out of the alley and back into the icy wind.

Security gates protected the storefronts at this time of night. Every few blocks, she deposited an article of clothing into a trash can. Midblock, some homeless guys and one woman gathered around a blazing barrel drum.

Serendipity.

They stared but said nothing as she approached. Eying each of them, she threw the remainder of the clothes, including the sweatshirt, in the drum.

One man said, "Thanks."

A police car rushed past on its way to the crime scene. She followed it with her eyes before resuming her run in the opposite direction.

While she ran the remaining six blocks, she daydreamed about a woman.

How she would punish her when she saw her again.

The doorman of the hotel stood under the awning and opened the front door for Dev. "Evening, sir. How was your run?"

"Exhilarating," she said.

# PART II

PLATE III

## CHAPTER FOURTEEN

---

# Washington, DC

"COME ON!" MICAH shouted down to her.

The Potomac River below her, Jade looked up at his backside, which was snug in running tights, five steps ahead of her on the Watergate Steps. This was their hundredth set.

He jogged in place at the top, waiting for her. "Slow poke."

"We're not done," she said.

Taking off at a sprint, she passed him, calling over her shoulder, "Last one to the memorial is a chump!"

"I presume that's not a good thing," he shouted back.

They ran along Lincoln Memorial Circle, avoiding the midday traffic, and ended up at the plaza at the bottom of the monument. It was nearly empty. Few tourists had braved the bitter January cold.

Micah and Jade shared a quick glance and, without a word, sprinted up the fifty-eight steps.

Jade arrived at the top first and shot both arms up like Rocky Balboa in the first *Rocky* movie, one of her father's favorites. She shuffled her feet and delivered some air punches at Micah as she hummed the movie's theme song.

He shook his head. "Gracious. You look like the female Creed."

At the reference to the main character and the name of one of the sequels, she stopped shuffling and bowed. "When you got it—"

"You did okay," Micah said, pausing, "for a girl."

He took off running—the man wasn't stupid—to the other side and hid behind one of the thirty-six Doric columns, each of which represented a state in the Union at the time of President Abraham Lincoln's death.

Jade laughed and jogged over to sit beside him on the top step. "Smart man."

He smiled, his white teeth bright against his mocha skin. "I inherited my brains from my mum."

Staring out at the reflecting pool, the World War II Memorial, and the Washington Monument, she said, "You don't talk much about your parents."

"Neither do you."

"Touché."

Her cell phone vibrated in her pocket, saving them both from a topic neither of them wished to discuss.

"What's up?" she said.

"A detective from Chicago PD called," Dante said, "asking for you. Lieutenant Tom Blanchard."

"What did he want?"

"He has a case that might interest you."

Jade had solved three high-profile cases over the last two

years—well, two, if you didn't count the Robin Hood case. Consequently, members of law enforcement from all over the country called her office requesting her counsel. She removed her hair tie and shook out her shoulder-length hair.

"What is it?"

"He caught the Jared Carr case."

"And?"

"Blanchard just got off the phone with a detective in New York City."

This caught her attention. "New York?"

"The investment guy? Knifed outside the library? Sebastian—"

"Scofield."

"There are some similarities to their cases."

Rising, she stepped back up to the monument level and started pacing. "How so?"

"Both victims were stabbed. Knives left in the body. He said that his crime looked like a robbery."

Jade stopped pacing. "Looked like?"

"Yeah," Dante said. "He didn't think robbery had anything to do with it."

❄

Forty-five minutes after hanging up the phone with Dante, Jade stared at a photograph on her computer screen of the late Jared Carr. While she and Micah had sprinted from the memorial to the FBI gym to take (separate) showers, Lieutenant Tom Blanchard had emailed Dante part of the case file, which he'd forwarded to her.

Carr's body was pitched forward, face-first, on the sidewalk, a pool of blood in a semicircle beneath him. She clicked the arrow key for the next photograph. This angle was from behind him.

The back of his coat was lifted, his pants pocket ripped, apparently empty. His clothes looked expensive, the bottom of his dress shoes barely worn. The autopsy photos revealed that he was obese. Wealth afforded him suits that masked his girth.

Carr had been stabbed three times in the chest. The medical examiner found evidence of prostate cancer, which had metastasized to other organs.

Had Carr known? Was that what had driven him? Impending death?

She called Dante and told him to come to her office.

"What did you think?" she asked after he was seated.

"He was stabbed in the aorta. The other two strikes were overkill. I called the Chicago ME, who said Carr would've bled out in two to thirty minutes from the first wound."

"Where did it happen?"

"The Oak Club. A membership club downtown."

"Any witnesses?"

"Only the doorman."

"Did he check out?"

"Said Carr was talking to a homeless guy, then said something that seemed to agitate the other man. The guy then took out a knife and stabbed Carr."

"Camera?"

"Yeah. Aimed at the front of the club. Corroborated everything he said."

She sat up. "And the perp?"

"Blanchard said you can see him shuffle into view, exchange words with Carr, and then stab the hell out of him."

"We need that recording."

Dante didn't move. "I'll get it, but Blanchard said you can't see anything. The perp's back is to the camera, and he's wearing a hoodie."

She sat back, momentarily deflated. "Any prints on the knife?"

Dante shook his head.

"We need the number of the detective in New York," Jade said.

Fishing something out of his pocket, he held up a slip of paper.

❋

Later, Jade poked her head into his office. "Busy?"

Dante looked up from his computer. "Nope."

She frowned. "You should be."

"I should've said, 'Not too busy for you.' What's up?"

"That's better," she said.

She settled into the only other chair in her old cramped office, which Dante had made his own. Photographs of him and his live-in girlfriend, Laurie, sat on top of his desk and the one filing cabinet. She was the reason he was so damn happy. Until he'd met her, Dante had hit on every woman under fifty. Including Jade. He hadn't appreciated her rebuff at the time, but he eventually got over it.

A photograph of his favorite chef, Eric Ripert, hung on the wall behind him—French cooking was Dante's hobby—as well as a poster of his father, Marco Carlucci, soaring for a jump shot in his Italian professional basketball league uniform. He'd played his twilight years in the NBA.

"Awesome," Jade said, admiring the poster. Turning to him, "Seen Christian?"

Dante averted his eyes. "He took the week off."

She waited for him to look at her. "We need to keep him. He's a key member of this team. I expect you to make that a priority."

"I got it."

She said, "Talk to me about Scofield."

"Talked to a Detective Katz, NYPD. Unlike with Carr, there were lots of witnesses, including Scofield's wife. She claimed a gentleman bumped into her husband seemingly by accident. Only after he fell and she saw the knife did she realize her husband had been stabbed in the back."

"Any visual on the perp?"

"No one got a decent look at his face. He was wearing a dark coat, slacks, and a hat. Might've attended the event."

"Katz doesn't know?"

"Not confirmed yet."

"Anyone see anything else?"

"No," he said.

They had watched the recording of Carr's murder earlier. As Blanchard had warned, it hadn't yielded much. The perp's back was turned the entire time. He appeared to be about five ten, medium build. The dark-gray hoodie didn't have any recognizable markings or logos. It was impossible to see in which direction he had run.

"So… one vic stabbed three times in the chest by a homeless guy. The other once in the back by a possible fundraiser attendee. I presume Scofield was also white and wealthy." Jade waited for him to nod. "Both of them probably attracted a lot of haters. Why does Blanchard think these cases are connected?"

"The knives were left in both victims," Dante said.

She shrugged. "Still."

"They were the same brand."

CHAPTER FIFTEEN

# The White House, Washington, DC

THE FOLLOWING MORNING, Whitney and Sasha stood close together in front of the television on the credenza in Whitney's private study off the Oval Office. She did the majority of her work in this room, the Oval being reserved for meetings and photo ops.

On the TV, men and women of the US House of Representatives walked to and from the podium to cast their votes in a synchronized process. At the bottom of the screen, in a large archaic font reminiscent of the halftime score of a seventies college basketball game, were the words H-5861, Repeal of the New New Deal Coalition Act. Underneath, the count: Yeas 86, Nays 63, the numbers ticking up by the second.

The two women didn't speak, knowing what was at stake: Whitney's signature legislation that would define her presidency and preserve her legacy. Everything that Whitney, Sasha, and her entire team had worked for during the last year would be for naught. As would Blake's personal sacrifice.

"How's it going?"

An African-American woman wearing a black dress and a gold brooch stood at the door, her expression grim. Her straightened hair, high cheekbones, broad forehead, and strong physical features, coupled with her inner strength, gave her a presence. She was the kind of person who, when she walked into a room, everyone stopped talking. A woman not to be messed with.

Whitney waved her in.

After forcing Vice President Xavier Fernandez to resign, Whitney had nominated Josephine "Jo" Bates to replace him. In accordance with the 25th Amendment, a majority in both houses of Congress—despite Republican control—quickly confirmed Jo. Everyone involved realized the urgency of filling the role to ensure a smooth presidential succession.

A popular senator from California, Jo chaired the Congressional Black Caucus. She was a former lawyer and fierce advocate for gender equity. She and Whitney had cosponsored the Equal Rights Amendment, the watershed legislation that finally gave women equal rights in the United States. They had become close while working together on the ERA, and because of them, federal and state laws were changing to eliminate bias toward men.

Equal pay was now the law of the land.

Whitney chose Jo because of her qualifications, not her Northern California constituents. Their party had a lock on those. Jo was intelligent, a savvy negotiator, fearless, a smart political operative and insider, and she didn't hesitate to speak her mind. She also possessed a rare trait for a politician these days: integrity.

Now the first woman, the first *black* woman to hold the

second-highest office in the federal government, Jo—like Whitney—understood that a lot rode on her performance. The same opportunity for all the women and women of color that came after her would depend on her success.

Crossing the room, Jo stood next to them. "This Congress didn't waste any time."

The Yeas maintained, then grew their lead.

The final vote count: 389 Yeas, 146 Nays.

"That's it then," Sasha said.

Whitney remained silent, afraid her voice would betray her roiling emotions.

"It still needs to pass the Senate," Jo said, always the fighter.

The camera cut to a man standing in a hallway of the Capitol, a Corinthian column behind him. Senator Eric Hampton, his slicked black hair parted on the side, wore a dark suit and his ever-present red tie.

Jo said, "He's smiling as if he won the lottery."

"He probably did," Sasha said.

"Turn up the sound," said Whitney.

Sasha grabbed the remote off a nearby table. "I can't stand his whiny voice."

"You and me both," said Jo.

In answer to the commentator's question, Hampton said, "This is a wonderful day for democracy, individual independence, and capitalism. Supply and demand should determine winners and losers in the marketplace—not the government."

"There shouldn't be winners and losers among the American people," Sasha said, her eyes not leaving the screen.

"Senator," the commentator said, "when will the bill be voted on by the Senate?"

Hampton smoothed his tie. "We've promised a swift vote all along. This will be on the docket tomorrow."

Whitney gasped. "Tomorrow!"

"He's not wasting any time either," Sasha said. "The little twit."

"Mute it, please, Sasha," Whitney said.

Sasha retracted her shoulders, preparing to strike.

"Not you," Whitney said, "the television." She moved to the chair behind her desk and sat heavily.

"I'm sorry, Madam President," said Sasha. "I know how much this legislation means to you."

Whitney picked up a letter opener made of wood and pewter and gently tapped it against her hand. "It's not about *me*. It's about all the people who would have been positively affected by this legislation."

Income inequality started increasing in the 1970s and had widened ever since. The disparity had grown to the point that her economic advisors reported to her on the performance of the economy for the wealthiest one percent of the population separately from everyone else. During the presidential campaign, Whitney had called the gap the "Great Divide."

Now there was nothing to stop the economic divide from continuing to grow unabated.

And becoming permanent.

Jo came to stand in front of Whitney's desk. "The New New Deal is a worthy piece of legislation."

"So I keep hearing," Whitney said.

"It's a good law," Jo said. "We need to fight for it. Even if the Senate repeals it. A lot of people supported this bill. Inside and outside the Beltway. We might not be able to resurrect it again in its entirety, but we can implement the parts that matter. I'm willing to do whatever I can to make that happen."

Sasha stood next to Jo. "Me too."

Whitney's pulse quickened as she observed the quiet confidence on the faces of her vice president and chief of staff. "Let's get to work."

# CHAPTER SIXTEEN

# Washington, DC

"HERE'S THE INFORMATION on Carr," Pat said.

"Have a seat," Jade said. "Should I bring Dante in?"

Pat settled in Jade's guest chair and said, "Updated him earlier."

"Go on then."

Pat opened her laptop. "Jared and Jason Carr own a real estate firm, estimated to be the fifth-largest private company worldwide. Their holdings span across the United States, with properties in Chicago, New York, DC, LA, San Francisco, and almost every major international city, including London, Berlin, Madrid, Rio de Janeiro, Johannesburg, and Singapore."

"Sounds like beaucoup bucks."

"Individually, they are the eleventh and twelfth wealthiest people in the world, worth roughly about forty-five *billion* dollars. Each. They're not in the one percent. We're talking about the point-oh-oh-one percent.

"They started a foundation called Freedom of America, a major GOP donor, that supports senatorial, house, gubernatorial, and a lot of down-ballot races: state, local, even school boards."

Jade considered this. "They don't leave anything to chance."

"I think that's the plan. The organization's operations are shrouded in secrecy, but I found out that they fund other foundations that support limited government, lower taxes, elimination of regulation, and eradication of services for the poor and needy. For all intents and purposes, Freedom of America *is* the Republican National Committee."

"Anything else?"

"They secretly fund grassroots protesters at events. Cyber believes they use Russian hackers to influence Americans on social media to support their causes."

"And they call themselves patriots," Jade said.

Pat clicked a few keys on her keyboard. "Jared Junior was an outspoken climate-change denier and a vocal opponent of the Department of Housing and Urban Development. During the sixties, HUD cited their father, Jared Senior, for housing discrimination against minorities who tried to rent apartments in buildings he owned in New York City. Senior fought the violations for years. The case wound up in the Supreme Court."

"What happened?"

"He lost. His firm shelled out millions of dollars in fines and reparations. The stress eventually killed him. Heart attack."

"And this initiated Junior's beliefs in limited government?"

"More than that," Pat said. "Junior never forgot what happened to his father, and he never forgave the US government."

## CHAPTER SEVENTEEN

---

# Chicago, Illinois

D ANTE WHISTLED UNDER his breath. "Worth killing for?"

"People have killed for less," Jade said.

She hadn't comprehended real wealth until that moment. Standing in the foyer of the home of Jared Carr Jr., she gazed at the marble flooring, the two sitting areas, and the side table, over which hung an oval mirror in a gilded frame. A massive chandelier dangled overhead. Dual half-circle staircases with shiny banisters led to the second floor. The foyer alone was almost the same size as the first floor of Jade's townhouse.

The gray-haired African-American butler nodded at her before leading them to a spacious living room. Jade paused at the threshold.

An older woman with coiffed white hair and a plain but expensive red dress sat on a couch between a middle-aged man in a sweater, collared shirt, and slacks, and a middle-aged woman in black tights with a long, pale-blue sweater shirt. Her medium-length dyed-blonde hair was cut at a severe angle to her shoulders.

Beyond them, an expansive fireplace displayed family photos on the mantel. A grand piano occupied one corner. Heavy draperies covered the tall windows. There were two sets of French doors: one leading outside, the other to a sun room.

Jade felt as if she were on the set of *Downton Abbey*.

The man rose to greet them.

"Thank you, Charles," he said to the butler. To Jade and Dante, he said, "I'm Jason Carr."

His eyes met hers but didn't linger. Jade shook his hand and introduced them.

"Thanks for seeing us," she said.

"This is Jared's wife, Lisa, and my mother, Judith. Please," he said, gesturing to the chairs on either side of the glass coffee table, which had a ceramic vase in the middle. He returned to his seat. One glass, halfway full of amber liquid, rested on a coaster on the table. "We'll do whatever we can to help find Jared's killer. What would you like to know?"

"Tell us about what happened that night."

"He and I met at the club after work."

"Club?"

An indulgent smile. "Sorry. The Oak Club. Near our office. When we were both in town, we stopped by there a couple of times a week."

"To do what?" Dante asked.

Jason arched an eyebrow, as if he'd never been asked that question.

*Many women would kill for those eyebrows.*

"Our weekly dinner," Jason replied. "Sometimes lunch. Our

lives are hectic; it was our time to catch up. Or unwind. To discuss business outside of the office and away from prying ears."

Jade frowned. "Your staff eavesdropped on your conversations?"

He crossed his legs. "Or competitors. You can never be too careful these days."

"Did you discuss business that night?"

"Yes."

"What did you talk about?" Dante asked.

"It has no bearing on what happened to Jared."

"Let us be the judge of that," Jade said.

Jason reached for his drink, took a sip, and replaced the glass. "We were celebrating."

"What?" Dante asked.

"The overturning of Whitney's Folly."

"The New New Deal?" Jade asked.

"There was nothing new about it."

"Why were you celebrating its repeal?"

"Because it righted a wrong."

"How so?"

"It was another example of government overreach being crammed down the throats of the American people. Never should've passed."

"And the overturning of it benefited your business."

"That too."

"So you celebrated," Dante said, waving his small notebook. "What happened after that?"

"Jared left to come home."

"What did you do?" Jade asked.

"Stayed for a drink at the bar."

"Were you meeting someone there?" Jade asked.

"My assistant stopped by to deliver some papers."

"How did you find out about your brother?"

"The doorman came running into the lobby screaming, 'He's dead!' I heard him all the way in the bar. I didn't think much of it at first. We have so many old members who, frankly, are dying off all the time."

"Did he come find you?"

Jason leaned forward, picked up his glass, and drained its contents. "He stood in front of me, covered in my brother's blood, and said, 'I tried.'" In a hushed voice, Jason said, "That's when I realized he was talking about Jared."

Lisa glanced down at the table.

Jade directed the next question at her. "Mrs. Carr, did your husband ever mention any enemies, competitors? Anything like that?"

"Why would you ask that?" she responded. "He was murdered by a homeless person."

"Please answer the question."

"Of course he did," Judith Carr interjected. "Every liberal in the country hated my son. Many in the GOP too. If it turns out to be premeditated, there would be a long list of suspects."

The older woman sat up straight, her hands clasped casually in her lap, her purse leaning against her hip.

"'Premeditated' isn't a word we often hear from civilians," Jade said.

"I watch all those shows on TV," Judith said, nodding with satisfaction. "Even the documentary about you, Ms. Harrington. What was it called?" She thought for a moment. "*Don't Speak*. Don't worry, I can speak your language."

Under different circumstances, Jade would have enjoyed this conversation with Judith Carr. "Do you think it was premeditated?"

"Who's to say? It could have been exactly as it appeared. A homeless man robbed my son for money. But it wasn't a secret that my boys frequented the club, as their father did before them. Jared took the same route to work every day."

"How do you know?"

"I'm a mother." She nodded at Jason. "I told them to vary their routes. Their routines. My sons say I'm paranoid from watching too many crime shows."

Jason sighed. "You were right, Mother."

Jade turned back to Jared's widow. "Mrs. Carr, do you know of anyone who wanted to hurt your husband?"

"He rubbed some people the wrong way," Lisa said. "You should speak with the head of security at the firm. Jared and I sent any threats we received to him."

Jason gave Dante the security head's name.

"What was Jared like, Mrs. Carr?" Jade asked.

The question was for Lisa, but Judith Carr answered.

"Disciplined," she said. "Methodical. Competitive. Jared hated to lose. Sore loser, that one."

"Mother…," said Jason.

"When he was ten, he lost his first race ever at a championship meet. Never swam again for the rest of his life." She touched her purse, as if to check that it was still there. "He was such an excellent swimmer."

"Did he ever get angry?" Dante asked. "As an adult? Lose his temper?"

"Sure. He had tantrums, but if you ignored him, he'd get over it. At least, that's what I did. You couldn't win an argument with him. No matter what. Not like Jason here, who you can reason with."

She patted her son's knee.

"Jason was the opposite," Judith continued. "Always sneaking off to be alone with his books. Jared always did what was expected of him. Jason was a little rebellious."

"Mother, that's enough. This isn't about me." Grabbing his glass, he walked over to the small bar between the French doors.

"You're right," Judith said. "This is about Jared." To Jade, "Will you find the man who killed my son?"

*Did they know Jared had cancer and would have died soon anyway?*

"We'll do our best. Is there anything else you can tell us?" Jade asked.

The two women seated on the sofa shook their heads.

"The answer appears to be no," Jason said. He drained his fresh drink and set the glass down too hard on the bar. "Charles will show you out."

※

"What do you think?" Jade said, glancing at Dante as she fastened her seatbelt.

Although the plane was accelerating for takeoff, his seatbelt remained unfastened. "Seemed nervous."

"Like he was anxious to get rid of us."

Dante raised an eyebrow. "How would he tie in to the other murder, though?"

"Not sure. We need to check him out."

"Will do."

"His mom might be right."

"About what?"

"If they ate dinner there once a week, someone could've studied their patterns. Knew they were going to be there."

He closed his eyes. "If we're not careful, she might put us out of work."

She tapped him on the shoulder and waited for him to open his eyes before she glanced down at his seatbelt. "Are you going to buckle that?"

"Didn't know you cared."

"I don't," she said. "I'm asking for Christian."

@TheGodOfVeritas: Word on the street is that Finn Hurley is in secret meetings with Senator Hampton. I wonder what Congress will do next to boost her business. #shame

## CHAPTER EIGHTEEN

---

# Arlington, Virginia

EW CYCLISTS BRAVED the cold. The odometer showed ten miles. Five to go before she arrived at her home in Old Town Alexandria. She picked up the pace as she headed south on the gravel path that paralleled GW Parkway, the mud-brown Potomac River on her left. Ordinarily, she rode ten miles every morning, but today she strove for fifteen. Because of her ever-rising stress level? Was she procrastinating going to work?

She pedaled harder.

The board of directors was unhappy with last quarter's financial performance: flat sales, escalating payroll costs, and a decline in earnings.

*They're shortsighted.*

She'd never understood why American markets focused only on a public company's last quarter. She had negotiated several new client contracts, increasing the backlog, which meant future revenues. One was a lucrative contract with the federal government.

She ran her company for the long term, a perspective that was hard to keep in this market environment.

She wanted her "baby" to be around long after she was gone.

Six months ago, she increased her employees' pay. Not out of kindness, but to retain her top performers before they left to seek higher wages elsewhere. Was she rewarded for her efforts? No. Some of her best talent still left, and profits fell. To compensate, she'd need to increase her fees, which would alienate most of her clients. She couldn't win.

The one bright side: she was still running the company.

Her front tire hit a rock. In an attempt to control the bicycle, she overcorrected. As she fell, she clicked out of the pedals and landed on the grass adjacent to the path, the cycle still between her legs.

As dew seeped into her cycling clothes, she assessed the damage. She wasn't too worried. She wore a helmet. Nothing was broken or even scratched, the grass landing having softened the blow. Sitting up, she examined the bicycle. The front tire was whacked out of alignment, but otherwise things looked okay. Easy to fix.

She heard the clicking of an approaching bicycle.

It was one of those red bike-share bikes you saw everywhere these days. The rider stopped near her and disembarked. He was dressed in all black—cycling glasses, helmet, tights, and jacket—and toted a backpack.

"Are you all right?" he asked, concern etched on the visible lower half of his clean-shaven face. He had a strong jaw.

She liked that. "Yeah. It's no biggie. My ego is hurt more than anything else." She laughed. "I fall about once a week."

He joined in the laughter. "Here." He laid his bicycle next to hers and held out his hand. "Let me help you."

"How kind," she said.

Placing her gloved hand in his, she thought how refreshing it was to meet a friendly person. A friendly man. Men in DC were pretentious, unable to be involved in a real relationship with anyone but themselves. Her husband divorced her after becoming fed up with the hours she spent at work and client dinners. She hadn't met a considerate man in a long time. She laughed inwardly. There she went again. A glance at the gentleman's gloved left hand. He might not be single.

After he helped her up, she righted her bike, preparing to adjust the tire. She turned to thank him... and a burning sensation spread up her thigh. She saw the hilt before her brain registered that it was a knife.

Eyes wide, she looked at him. "What are you—?"

He stared at her, his face neutral, as she fell again. He didn't say a word while she lay there, her blood soaking the grass. She closed her eyes for the final time. Her last thought wasn't of her company. Or her accumulated wealth. Or her ex. Or the children she would never bear.

Instead, it was, *I guess he wasn't such a nice guy after all.*

# CHAPTER NINETEEN

## Arlington, Virginia

DEV PEDALED AWAY.

She understood why the target chose to ride at this time of morning. It was quiet. Peaceful. Only a few other riders and runners were out.

The lack of nearby witnesses was advantageous.

But that's not why she had killed the cyclist here. She'd been given specific instructions, and Dev was a stickler about following orders.

But she had messed up once. Just once.

And here she was.

Following the path to Crystal City, Virginia, she reached Jefferson Davis Highway. She located an available bike-share dock on her phone and locked the bicycle, then walked back to her room at the Holiday Inn.

Showering hastily, she changed into a business suit. She hailed a taxi in front of the hotel, climbing into the well-worn back seat.

Entering the automatic sliding glass doors of Ronald Reagan National Airport, she averted her face from the surveillance camera, bypassed the check-in counters, and went straight to security. Patiently waiting in line, she smiled as she allowed a black woman with two young children to cut in front of her.

Retrieving her small carry-on and briefcase from the conveyor belt, Dev blended in with the rest of the early-morning business commuters as she headed to the gate, in time for the announcement of the 8:00 a.m. American Airlines flight to New York City.

## CHAPTER TWENTY

# Arlington, Virginia

BUSTING THROUGH THE circle of cops huddled around the victim, Jade was oblivious to their shouts of protest and dirty looks. Kneeling close to the body, she stared at the victim's face, placing her palm on his cheek, his freckles a galaxy of stars across his nose and upper cheeks.

"Wake up!" she said. Then, more urgently, "Austin, wake up!"

He didn't stir.

She shook him, but to no avail.

Special Agent Austin Miller was dead.

Jade sat up in bed, sweaty, her cotton T-shirt clinging to her back. Light filtered in under her bedroom blinds. The alarm clock on her nightstand displayed 7:00 a.m. in bright red numerals. The vibrating cell phone next to it had awakened her.

Lately, her fallen agent appeared recurrently in her dreams.

She allowed her head to clear for a moment before she picked up the phone.

"Harrington," she said.

"Agent Harrington. Lieutenant John Briggs. Remember me?"

"Of course."

Briggs had worked with Jade on the bullying case a year ago.

"I've got something for you," he said. "Again."

"Talk to me."

"A stabbing victim. A cyclist. I think there are some similarities to other cases I've been reading about. Want to check it out?"

"Where are you?" she asked.

"Not too far from Gravelly Point Park."

This stopped Jade short. "Really?"

"I know, right? What a coincidence."

Nicholas Campbell, one of the bullying victims, had been murdered and dumped in the same park. Jade didn't believe in coincidences.

She hopped out of bed. "I'm on my way."

❊

"Where's Christian?" Jade asked.

Dante shook his head.

She'd arrived to find him and Micah waiting for her. She'd called Dante earlier and asked him to meet her here. Both of them wore suits, although Micah looked like a *GQ* magazine model, while Dante looked like a character from *Miami Vice*. They stood apart from the other police personnel. Jade scanned the crowd for Briggs.

Briggs, medium-complexioned with the build of a middleweight mixed martial arts fighter, spotted her first and strode over to greet her.

"Good to see you again," he said. They shook hands. She introduced him to Micah and Dante.

The detective eyed Dante's suit. "I remember you."

Micah threw his head back and laughed.

Jade bit back a smile. To Briggs, she said, "What do we got?"

After checking in with the officer maintaining the sign-in sheet, they followed Briggs across the swath of grass to the bike path. Response techs in white space suits collected evidence. A photographer snapped pictures of the victim and the crime scene from every angle.

Looking down at the body, Jade said, "Who is she?"

Briggs shook his head. "No ID."

Jade took in the pocketless black bicycle tights and bright yellow reflective cycling coat with an open pocket in the back. "Maybe it fell out."

Dante stood next to her. "Or she didn't carry any, afraid it would fall out."

"Or the perp stole it," Micah said.

"There was a key in the small bike bag under the seat," Briggs said. "Looked like a house key."

"Who found her?" asked Jade.

"Two runners on their daily run."

"Did you eliminate them?"

He nodded. "A commuter saw the whole thing. Started recording after the stabbing and sent it to us." He pointed south. "The perp took off that way. We're canvassing Crystal City."

Jade waited for the technicians to finish their work.

They finally stood. Recognizing her, one of them nodded.

Snapping on a pair of blue nitrile gloves, Jade crouched next to the body and stared at the victim's face.

"The corpse whisperer," Dante whispered behind her.

"Why do you call her that?" Micah whispered back.

"Because they talk to her. Haven't you noticed?"

"What do they say?"

"I don't know," Dante whispered. "It's like telepathy or something."

"Incredible."

Still crouching, she pivoted to look up at them. "You know I can hear you, right?"

Dante said, "Not saying anything that isn't true." He pointed at the victim. "What's she saying?"

Jade ignored him and turned back to the body. The knife was still rammed in the victim's thigh. Her helmet was removed, and the vivid redness of her medium-length hair splayed across the grass. Her eyes were closed. Other than the stab wound, she appeared to be sleeping. A dark stain covered the ground around her body.

The bike, a few yards away, looked undamaged. Except for the front tire, which was askew.

"Did she fall?" Jade asked.

Briggs nodded toward the techs, who stood off to the side, chatting, waiting for Jade to complete her examination. "They think so."

"Forced off?"

"I would've expected more damage."

Jade scanned the area surrounding the body. "Lots of blood."

"She bled out," Briggs said. "It didn't take long."

Since she'd been wearing a helmet, the victim's face was unblemished. A plethora of freckles dotted her nose and cheeks. Jade thought of Austin.

"Who did this to you?" Jade whispered to her, wishing she knew the victim's name.

"See?" Dante said to Micah.

"When I die," Micah said, "I hope she talks to me like that."

"If you two don't shut up," Jade said, "that might be sooner than you think."

Dante was right. She did talk to her victims, and although they didn't talk back to her, they often led her in the right direction if she stilled herself long enough to listen. She continued to gaze at the dead woman.

Around her, the DC rush hour went on. Bumper-to-bumper commuter traffic crept along GW Parkway. In addition to the normal traffic, drivers squeezed into one lane due to the emergency vehicles blocking the other. The rubbernecking didn't help. Jade tried to ignore the excessive honking and occasional shouting.

She swiveled her head as a plane took off. She grinned despite herself, thinking of her friend Zoe, who would only call the airport by its former name: National. Zoe had a fit when Republicans introduced a bill last year to name this park after the former first lady Nancy Reagan.

Lieutenant Briggs stepped forward. "No ID, but we did find something."

Jade stood as he waved over one of the techs.

"Found this in her jacket pocket," Briggs said.

The female technician—the one who'd recognized Jade earlier—handed her a clear evidence bag with a sheet of beige paper inside. It was handwritten in tight block letters. Black ink. As she started to read, Dante and Micah moved in close—too close—to read over her shoulders.

> *But if thou live, remember'd not to be,*
> *Die single, and thine image dies with thee.*

—Bard of Avon

"What the hell?" Dante said.

Micah shook his head. "The inadequacy of an American education."

"What?" asked Dante.

"The Bard of Avon," said Micah incredulously. "Shakespeare, man."

Jade thought back to a team meeting during the TSK case. After the killer sent an email to a cable news station, the agent who'd brought it to her team's attention said, "Shakespeare strikes again." This homicide couldn't be related to that case. TSK was dead. Jade knew because she had killed him. But somehow he seemed to reach from beyond the grave.

"Was it hers?" she said. "Or did the killer put it there?"

# CHAPTER TWENTY-ONE

## The White House, Washington, DC

*THEY DID IT.*

That morning, the United States Senate had repealed the New New Deal Coalition Act, the final vote along party lines. Soon, the measure would come to Whitney's desk. She would veto it, of course, but the House had secured enough votes to overturn it.

Sitting in the Oval Office, she read a letter from Joseph Babineaux, a worker from Pike County, Missouri. He'd received a call from a construction firm, rescinding an offer of employment on a crew replacing a crumbling bridge that spanned the Mississippi River. Almost a quarter of the bridges in Whitney's home state needed repair.

Placing the letter on her desk, she rubbed her eyes in frustration. It was one of many she'd received. Hundreds of thousands of emails opposing the repeal inundated the White House website, most of them from her base outside of Missouri. Thousands of people signed petitions on MoveOn.org and other political action sites.

Sometimes even *she,* the most powerful person in the world, felt helpless.

Her phone buzzed. It was Sean, her secretary, who sat in the Outer Oval, the office right outside of hers. She didn't want to talk to anyone, but as for any boss, that wasn't always an option. She pressed a button.

"Madam President," he said through the speaker. "Cole Brennan is on the line."

He couldn't be calling to gloat, since he was the one who'd strong-armed Senator Eric Hampton into sponsoring the bill, a major reason it had passed.

She would take the call.

Cole, the most popular conservative radio commentator in the country, was not one of Whitney's biggest fans. He constantly pilloried her legislative positions and accomplishments on his show. Her dress, relationships with her family and celebrities, even her hair—nothing was off-limits to his scrutiny.

Last year, after Cole's son, CJ, was bullied and savagely beaten, Cole's wife, Ashley, had visited her in the White House. As a result of that meeting, Whitney and Cole teamed up to pass the federal Anti-Bullying Act, the first national law protecting children and teachers from bullying.

"Cole," she said. "Is this a condolence call?"

"Madam President, I assure you I had nothing to do with it."

Whitney stayed silent. She believed him.

"I want to wring Hampton's scrawny little neck," he went on, "with one of his little red ties. He's behind this. And Sampson…

Sampson is a two-faced little pri—piece of crap. He's crossed the wrong person."

Whitney said, "You needn't worry about him for long."

"Oh?" he said. "Something I need to know?"

"Perhaps."

"Sexual harassment? Sexting? Embezzlement?"

"You don't think too highly of the senator, do you?"

"I've been in this game for a while."

"How's CJ?" she asked, shifting to Cole's favorite subject.

"He's doing well in school. Even hosting his own show on the radio station at his college. One of those liberal shows, talking about issues that impact LBGT and all those other letters."

Pride in his voice.

"LGBTQIA," she said.

He sighed. "I can never keep up."

"Sounds as if he's following in his dad's footsteps."

"That he is. Well, Madam President, this isn't over. I don't care for your politics much, but I gave you my word, and I'm one of the few people left in this world whose word is his bond."

"I don't care for your politics much either, Cole, but that's kind of you to say."

"Kindness nothing. It's the principle of the thing."

"What are you suggesting?"

"Don't know yet, but I'll think of something." He paused. "In the meantime, is there anything you can do about deregulation? Good God, woman! You're strangling businesses out here!"

Whitney laughed. This was the Cole she knew and had started to respect. "I'll see what I can do."

"I'll be in touch," he said.

## CHAPTER TWENTY-TWO

# Washington, DC

JADE HIT A speed-dial button on her phone. "I need to see you."

A few moments later, Christian's bulky frame filled the doorway.

"Come in," she said, "and close the door."

She signed off on a report and set it aside. Christian sat in one of the chairs across from her. His blond hair, cut military short, stood at attention.

"Missed you this morning," she said.

"I was busy."

Jade mentally reviewed all his cases but didn't come up with anything pressing in his caseload. "Doing what?"

"This."

He handed her a sheet of paper.

A letter addressed to her. His resignation.

She tore it up without reading it in its entirety.

He scrunched up his face. "I could print out another one."

Leaning back in her chair, she said, "I guess the gesture isn't as dramatic as it once was."

This elicited a small smile from him. "No."

"You can't close cases if you don't show up."

Christian stared at a spot on the wall behind her. She followed his gaze to the FBI emblem and looked back at him.

"I no longer want to close cases here," he said.

"We need to talk about this."

"Rather late for that."

"I meant to talk to you beforehand. About my decision. Time got away from me."

He said nothing, his fist clenching and unclenching.

"I stand by my call." She paused. "Give him a chance."

"I. Can't." He stood and turned to leave.

"I wasn't finished," Jade said.

He hesitated before returning to his seat.

"Dante approaches things in a way I've come to appreciate."

Christian winced. "You don't need to explain this to me now."

"I want to."

"He's a hothead and he's lazy."

"He's overcome his anger issues," she said, "and he's not lazy. Rather... unchallenged. This situation won't last forever. Ethan will be back soon. I'll return to my job full time, and you'll report directly to me again. Roll with it for now. This team needs you." She locked eyes with him. "I need you. You're still my rock."

"I'm more experienced. Closed more cases. I'm the better person for the job."

"You're prepared. Smart. One of the best FBI agents I've ever worked with. You'll get your chance. I promise." She stood and extended her hand. "I don't make promises I can't keep."

He sat there, waiting so long she thought he'd leave her hanging. Finally, he grasped her hand.

"Let's go grab a sandwich," she said.

"I need to do something first."

❊

On their way back from lunch, Jade's phone vibrated. She swept it off her hip.

"Talk to me," she said.

"Got an ID back on the victim," Dante said. "Briggs called and said someone from his precinct recognized her photo."

"How?"

"Because she's a bigwig. Her name's Finn Hurley, CEO of Hurley Technologies, a cybersecurity firm headquartered in Crystal City, not too far from the Pentagon. I'm headed over there now to interview her employees."

"Sounds good. Take Micah with you."

"Already asked him."

"What do we know?"

"Divorced. No children. Lived in Old Town."

"Talked to the ex?"

"Still tracking him down. No prints came back on the bike, except for hers. Either the killer didn't touch it or he wore gloves."

"Makes sense, if he was riding a bike."

"And it was cold," he said. "You got jokes?"

"Excuse me?"

"Who hung the poster in my office?"

"What poster?"

"Those dudes from *Miami Vice*. The eighties version. Guys with their shirts open to their belly buttons, lots of chest hair, showing off their bling. Someone wrote 'Dante' and 'Micah' on their chests. You know anything about that?"

Jade stole a glance at Christian, who had found something interesting to admire in the sky.

"No," she said into the phone, "I don't. But you're an FBI agent. Figure it out."

She clicked off and looked at Christian. They both laughed.

Back in her office, Jade grabbed the file on top of a stack. Inside it, she located a phone number with a 312 area code.

"Lieutenant Blanchard."

"Lieutenant, this is Agent Harrington."

"What can I do for you?"

"Learn anything from the head of security at Carr Holdings?"

"He gave us a lot of leads. Too many. Still chasing them down."

"I have a weird question," she said. "Did you find a poem or a sonnet?"

"Not on the victim," he said.

*Wishful thinking.*

"But," he continued, "we found a poem on his computer. Didn't think much of it. It was sent via email. Just the poem. Nothing else. No subject. No greeting. No text. No signature. Thought it was spam. One of a thousand emails he'd received that day."

"Who sent it?"

"Need to double-check. I remember it, though, because I thought it was odd."

"How so?"

"Because it wasn't a modern poem. It was old. Like from Shakespeare's time."

Jade's heart quickened, as it did whenever she uncovered a lead. "Can you send it over?"

"Sure can."

Ten minutes after they hung up, an email arrived in her inbox.

> *So thou, thyself outgoing in thy noon,*
> *Unlook'd on diest, unless thou get a son.*

> —Bard of Avon

Jade was as unfamiliar with this sonnet as the one found on Finn Hurley.

She entered the first line of the poem in the search bar and clicked on the first result. The sonnet sent to Jared Carr was the seventh one. These were its last two lines.

Jade hoped this wasn't the seventh killing.

Next she searched for Sonnet VII. The first link provided an analysis of the seventh sonnet. She read the poem again. It didn't yield any clues as to why Carr was killed.

But it linked the Chicago and Virginia murders. Why did the murderer leave a sonnet on Hurley's person but email one to Carr? Were the sonnets relevant to the victim? Or the killer?

Were there others?

She forwarded the email containing the sonnet to Dante and Pat with the message:

*Dante and Pat,*

*The attached sonnet was found on Jared Carr's computer. Call the detective in New York and ask if they found a sonnet. Also, try to trace the origins of this email.*

*Jade*

A few minutes later she received a reply from Dante.

*I could've done that for you.*

A minute later, a second email arrived from him:

*Isn't this my case?*

# CHAPTER TWENTY-THREE

# Washington, DC

"ACCORDING TO FINN Hurley's coworkers, she rode her bike every morning before work," Dante told Jade later that afternoon in her office. "Sometimes during lunch. Most weekends. She was always training for races, sometimes the distance was over 100 miles."

"They're called centuries," Jade said. "What else did they say?"

"As a boss, she was demanding but fair. Didn't take shit from anyone." Dante grinned. "Sounded like someone else I know."

From him, an unusual compliment.

"She spent most of her time with major clients out of the office," he continued. "Worked late. Competing demands on her time. Quarterly investor calls. Press requests. Information requests." He paused. "Seemed to be under a lot of pressure."

Looking across her desk at him, Jade said, "Customers?"

"Her assistant is sending over a client list with contacts, but the government made up the bulk of their business. Other Fortune 500 companies. Hurley's products and services don't come cheap."

"Could her death be related to her work?"

"Maybe. In the cybersecurity industry, she dealt not only with competitors and suppliers but also hostile agents: Russia, China, Ukraine, et cetera. Or it could have been an employee. They all knew her routine."

Jade frowned. "How does she fit with the other victims?"

"Don't know."

She aligned her basketball paperweight with the edge of the desk. "What happens to the firm now?"

"Although she founded it, it shouldn't die with her. The board will find a replacement."

"And its corporate life will go on. If the perp was a competitor, he bought some time at best. Who are her possible successors?"

"I don't know." He patted his pockets, then looked at her. "Can I borrow a piece of paper?"

Grabbing the legal pad on her desk, she tossed it to him. "You should always keep something to write on with you."

"I thought I was coming in here for a brief chat." He hesitated. "Can I borrow a pen too?"

She handed him one and opened her mouth to share further words of wisdom.

He held up the hand with the pen. "I got it, boss."

As he wrote, she asked, "Was she seeing anyone?"

Dante shook his head. "She didn't discuss her private life. Most of her employees assumed she didn't have one."

"Did you talk to her neighbors?"

"She lived on S. Lee Street, in one of those federal-style townhouses. Micah and I canvassed the neighborhood. It's a quiet one. Neighbors aren't very neighborly. They seldom saw her, except for her comings and goings on her bike. One neighbor resented that sometimes she left her trash and recycling bins out on the street for days after they were emptied."

"Did she entertain much?"

"No."

"Social media?"

"Pat's looking into it."

"Reviewed the autopsy report?"

"Haven't received it yet," he said.

"Anything back on the commuter's recording?"

"I watched it. It's from far away. Looks like a guy riding his bike before work, not like a guy who just stabbed someone. Forensics is going over it frame by frame."

"What about the ex?"

"Talked to him on the phone. He lives in Atlanta and was at the office at the time of the murder. He's an accountant. January is a busy month. Said the two of them barely spoke."

"Bad blood?"

"No. More like indifference."

"Remarried?"

"Live-in boyfriend," Dante said with distaste.

"Oh."

"The ex had no idea who would do this to her. Oh, one more thing: Pat said Hurley was a major contributor to Ellison during the last campaign."

Was that significant? After a moment, she said, "You're going to need a bigger team. A task force. Daily briefings."

"I agree. Is that your approval?"

She nodded. "We can't let the sonnets get out. The media will have a field day."

"Anything else?"

Jade rattled off next steps. "Got it?"

He waggled the legal pad next to his head. "I got it. Thanks."

# CHAPTER TWENTY-FOUR

# The White House, Washington, DC

WHITNEY PUMPED HARD on the elliptical in the Residence gym. The television atop the machine was on, but she wasn't paying much attention to it. She was thinking about how to resurrect her signature legislation.

A breaking news chyron scrolled across the bottom of the screen. The name Sampson snapped her out of her reverie. She pressed the up arrow on the display to increase the volume.

The red-headed male MSNBC commentator said, "This just in. Early this morning, ICE raided the offices of PS Corporation, which owns the farming operations of Republican Senator Paul Sampson and his family. You might remember that Sampson was a vocal proponent of building a wall between the United States and Mexico and a staunch opponent of illegal immigration ever since he switched parties after losing the Democratic nomination for president.

"According to our sources, the government agency searched for evidence that the corporation employs hundreds of illegal immigrants, the majority of whom are Mexican. Senator Sampson was unavailable for comment. After the break, Senator Maureen McAllister will join us to talk about this shocking development."

Whitney wasn't shocked. She wasn't even mildly surprised. She had ordered the raid based on evidence presented to her by the director of the agency. At one time, she would have been surprised by Sampson's hypocrisy. They'd worked together on progressive issues they both cared about. His views flipped 180 degrees when he thought they were his route to the highest office. She wondered how Sampson was handling the negative attention.

He loved his farm.

The screen filled with a headshot of Maureen McAllister. The senior senator from Mississippi stood somewhere in the august halls of the Capitol. She was in her early sixties, her fashionably cut short blond hair interwoven with gray. Her outfit was stylish. It didn't take much of an imagination to understand that she'd been a beautiful woman once. Still was.

"Senator McAllister," the MSNBC commentator said from the studio, "what do you think of all this?"

The senator laughed. "My colleague wasn't thinking. He didn't think he'd get caught? It's like posting a crime that you committed on Facebook. I swear God wasted His time giving some people brains they don't use. I'm from the great state of Mississippi. I know something about farming. Agriculture employs almost thirty percent of our workforce—farmers who farm the right way."

"Should he resign?"

"Not sure if that's for me to say, but I will say that Senator Sampson should be ashamed of himself. Illegal immigration needs to be addressed, but participating in it and then talking out the other side of your mouth isn't the best way to do that. Shame on him."

"He's a rising star in your party, Senator. What happens now?"

"Look up in the sky, young man. You'll see a fallin' star. I hope one day he ends up having to work his farm himself."

When the interview concluded, Whitney muted the sound, pedaling in silence. After several minutes, she pressed a button on the equipment's console.

"Yes, Madam President," Sean said from the Outer Oval.

"Schedule a meeting with Senator Maureen McAllister," she said. "In the Oval."

## CHAPTER TWENTY-FIVE

# Washington, DC

MIDMORNING THE NEXT day, Jade made a trip to the break room for a refill. She could have had a coffee service installed in her office, but she liked how the break room offered chance meetings with her fellow agents. The only way to know how they were doing was to be with them.

On the way back to her office, she stopped in the doorway of Dante's office.

"What did the detective from New York say?"

"You were right," Dante said, looking up. "The perp handed Scofield a piece of paper with a sonnet written on it, tucked into the fundraiser program. NYPD thought it was part of the program, so they didn't think much of it."

"Scofield dropped it?"

"The wife couldn't remember. NYPD is reexamining the sonnet now. Dusting it for prints. I emailed you a copy."

"I don't want to wait. Bring it up."

While Dante searched for the document, she walked behind his desk, holding her recently refilled FBI mug. "Was it the perp's program? Did he attend the event?"

Dante's long, graceful hands typed on the keyboard. "Don't know. Might have slipped the sonnet into Scofield's program."

"But he'd have no guarantee that Scofield would keep it the entire time. Afterward?"

"Not enough time."

She sipped her coffee, avoiding the chip on the rim of the mug. Way past time to get a new one. "Cameras?"

"Front of the library. The detective said a hat obscured the perp's face."

"Unlucky."

"It was more than that. She said his head was tilted away, as if he knew about the camera. She offered to send us a copy of the recording."

"Get it. We need to interview Scofield's tablemates at the event. All the waitstaff."

Dante stared at his computer. "We," he mouthed.

"I saw that," she said.

He opened the email containing the sonnet and swiveled his monitor.

*Pity the world, or else this glutton be,*
*To eat the world's due, by the grave and thee.*

—Bard of Avon

"Which one is this?" she asked.

"Sonnet I."

"New York could have been a warm-up for Chicago."

"Or, since we found Sonnets I, III, and VII, there've been four other murders."

"I hope not," she said. "Any idea what it means? What the other two mean?"

"English was never my best subject."

She thought for a moment. "You should—"

"I put a call in to an English professor at GWU," he said. "My meeting with her is in"—he peeked at his watch—"forty-five minutes."

"Good idea. Mind if I tag along?"

"No."

"We should bring Micah."

"Whatever." Under his breath, he said, "The more the merrier."

"Don't hate," Jade said, draining the dregs of her coffee. "He might surprise you."

## CHAPTER TWENTY-SIX

# Washington, DC

THE PROFESSOR EXAMINED the three sheets of paper on a cleared spot on her cluttered desk. The teetering stacks of papers and files and books reminded Jade of Max's office.

Professor Alaia Bennett stared at the sonnets. She read one, then the second, then the third, then back to the second. She was slender, pretty, and dark skinned, her hair short and natural, shot through with gray. She wore bright red lipstick.

Jade, Dante, and Micah sat in silence, their chairs close together in the professor's cramped office in Rome Hall on the George Washington University campus.

Finally, the professor removed her reading glasses. "The Bard of Avon. Shakespeare. Sonnets I, III, and VII, which you've probably figured out."

"Are those numbers or those sonnets significant?" asked Jade.

"If the numbers are significant, it's not because of the sonnets. Shakespeare didn't number them."

"What do you mean?" asked Dante. "I remember the numbers from high school."

"He wrote the sonnets in the late fifteen hundreds, early sixteen hundreds," the professor said. "They weren't published until 1609, and it was by someone else, without Shakespeare's knowledge. The numbers are arbitrary. No one knows the exact order in which they were written."

"They were circulated among his friends before publication," Micah said.

Bennett appraised Micah. "That accent. And he knows Shakespeare. I think I'm in love."

To Bennett, Micah said, "Shall I compare thee to a summer's day?"

The professor pretended to swoon.

Jade cleared her throat. "You were saying…"

The professor tore her eyes away from Micah. "The sonnets were written at different times in his life, which might've explained the different themes: brevity of life, the transience of beauty, and the trappings of desire. Most were written about obsession and his overwhelming love for a young man, the Fair Youth. Over the centuries, there's been much speculation about whether he was Shakespeare's lover or if their relationship was an intense platonic friendship. Or whether they reflected the writer's personal feelings at all. Most of his work did not. So why would the sonnets?"

A slight head shake from Dante. "Wasn't he married?"

"He was married."

"Then why would he be writing love poems to a guy?"

Micah winked, then blew him a kiss.

Dante shifted uncomfortably in his chair.

It was Alaia Bennett's turn to keep the conversation on track. "Sometimes the men during that age developed strong platonic relationships with other men. For example, artists became attached to the patrons of their work."

Jade pointed at the papers on the desk. "Are these sonnets related?"

"The first seventeen focused on the brevity of life. Shakespeare argued that the way for his young friend's beauty to live forever was for him to beget children."

Dante shook his head. "Why would someone want to read about that?"

The professor stared at him. "Unfortunately, television hadn't been invented yet. Reality TV, a distant art form of the future. Sonnets were one of the few entertainment options at the time."

"What if," Jade said, "Shakespeare was thinking of his own mortality?"

Bennett turned to her. "Excellent."

Jade warmed with unexpected pride as if she were back in school. It had always been about achievement with her, although she refused to explore the issue too deeply. Probably something to do with wanting her father's approval.

"Later," the professor continued, "Shakespeare introduced a Rival Poet, who the Fair Youth ends up preferring."

"Shakespeare was one strange dude," Dante said.

"Didn't the young man reject the procreation argument, starting with sonnet eighteen?" Micah asked the professor.

"He did, but Shakespeare was consoled that the sonnets alone would preserve the young man's beauty forever. And he was right. We're still talking about it, analyzing it, over four hundred years later."

Dante looked at Micah with wonder. "Damn... where did you learn that?"

To Dante, Jade said, "Told you."

Micah grinned at him. "I'm not just a pretty face."

"I remember something about a lady," Jade said.

Bennett nodded. "The remaining sonnets were written about an affair with a woman. Some scholars call her the Dark Lady. Not because she was black, mind you, but because of her hair. I call her his Dark Bae."

Dante sat up. "I want to hear more about *her*. For investigative purposes."

Ignoring him, the professor peered out the window overlooking F Street before turning back. "I would presume your killer is obsessed with the brevity of life." Donning her reading glasses again, she picked up the first sonnet. "*Glutton* means excess." To Jade, "Was the victim rich?"

"Yes."

The professor returned her attention to the sheet of paper. "This sonnet is about selfishness, narcissism, obsession with appearance."

"Sounds like someone I know," Micah said, glancing at Dante.

To Jade, Bennett said, "Is this the best use of my tax dollars?"

"You can request a refund," Jade offered. "Please continue."

"This sonnet is also about usury," Bennett said. "Charging exorbitant interest on money. Commercial profit. Any of that ring true with regard to your victim?"

"He was an attractive hedge fund manager who paid a hundred million dollars to put his name on a building in New York City," Jade said.

"That seems to fit. Did the victim have children?"

"Yes," Dante said.

The professor frowned. "Then I'm not quite seeing the connection."

"Maybe there isn't one," he said.

They sat in silence for a moment. Jade pointed at the sonnet found on the third victim, Finn Hurley. "This one is straightforward. 'But if thou live, remember'd not to be, / Die single, and thine image dies with thee.' You die childless and your beauty dies with you."

"Correct," Bennett said. "The line before this is 'Despite of wrinkles, this thy golden time.' The young man could only experience a 'golden time' in his old age through his children."

"This victim was a divorced woman."

"She won't be having a 'golden time,'" said Dante.

The professor said, "Shakespeare implored his friend not to deny any woman the chance of becoming a mother and a vessel to pass on his beauty."

Dante sat up. "Now you're talking."

"Are you always a pig?" the professor asked him.

"Pretty much," Jade said.

The two women shared a smile.

Picking up the last sonnet, Bennett said, "Number seven. Now, this one is interesting."

Jade leaned forward, hands clasped, arms on her thighs. "How so?"

"In this one, Shakespeare compares the journey of human life to the passage of the sun. Once we reach the apex, like the sun, the only direction is down."

"How depressing," Micah said.

"When you reach 'feeble age,' as he called it," Bennett said, "not only your physical appearance deteriorates, but the people who used to gaze at your beauty with awe will 'look another way.' You will not be remembered."

"That is depressing," Dante said, stroking his chin. "Not much to look forward to."

"That's why," the professor concluded, "he should bear a son. This was the first time the poet specified the gender of the child."

Sitting up, Jade said, "Son. S-O-N. Sun. S-U-N."

"The two of you would receive an A in my class," the professor said to Jade and Micah. To Dante, "*You* need some work."

Jade turned to Dante. "Did Carr have a son?"

He nodded.

Alaia Bennett looked down at the sonnets again. "I wonder why the killer is only providing the last two lines?"

"How many lines are in a sonnet?" Jade asked.

"Fourteen," Micah said.

"Usually," the professor said, "but not always. The last two lines rhyme with each other, unlike the rest of the sonnet, where the rhyme alternates in a pattern. The couplet at the end sums up the previous twelve lines."

"Or provides a surprise ending," Micah added.

"Correct."

"The beginning of the sonnets could have been left with other victims," Jade said.

No one spoke for a moment as they weighed the meaning of that.

"Professor," Jade said, "we've taken up enough of your time. Is there anything else?"

Bennett steepled her fingers. "These sonnets have something in common, which you wouldn't know by looking at the couplet."

"What's that?" asked Dante.

"They all include the word *die*."

Dante said, "I hope he's not planning to kill someone for each sonnet."

"I hope you're right."

"How many sonnets are there?" he asked.

Alaia Bennett said, "A hundred and fifty-four."

## CHAPTER TWENTY-SEVEN

# The White House, Washington, DC

"SENATOR."

The bangles on Maureen McAllister's wrists chimed as she walked toward Whitney, her hand extended. "Madam President, your invitation is an honor and a privilege."

"The honor is mine," Whitney said, taking the other woman's hand in both of hers. She gestured to one of the two matching Queen Anne chairs in the Oval Office. "Please. May I offer you something to drink?"

"Is it too early for a martini?"

Whitney's mouth parted.

Mo rushed on. "I'm just messing with you. How about some sweet tea?"

Picking up the phone on the end table, Whitney placed the order. "The reason I asked you here, Senator—"

"Please call me Mo."

"The reason why I asked you here, Mo—"

Mo held up her hand. "I'm sorry to interrupt again, Madam President, but I do want to ask after your husband and children."

Whitney's smile faltered. One thing she didn't want to discuss with the senator—or anyone, for that matter—was her family. A butler with a gray bob entered carrying a tray with two glasses of iced tea and placed them on the coffee table. Whitney thanked her, and she left without a word.

Whitney handed a glass to Mo. "They're fine. And your family?"

Mo marveled at the glass. "This is how I prefer my tea. Sweatin'. Anyhow, they're fine, thanks for asking. My husband, Jimmy—we call him Nub—can't stand Washington and can't wait for my term to be over." She leaned toward Whitney and said, sotto voce, "He doesn't know I'm running again." She straightened. "Our daughter's fine. She's in Mississippi. Last year, she married one of her classmates from LSU. They just had a baby. He's a Cajun boy—the husband, not the baby—"

"Uh, Mo… unfortunately, I don't have a lot of time. Sean, my secretary, only scheduled us for 15 minutes, so I want to shift the conversation to the purpose of this meeting."

"Well, you asked, Madam President. I can't help myself. There's a difference between how you northern women and us southern women converse."

"Missouri isn't in the north—"

Mo raised and lowered her hand again. "I'm sorry I keep interrupting, Madam President, but this is important. A Yankee woman would say 'She put on her coat and went to the store.' Us *real* Southern women embellish and speak florally. We would say

'Before she went to the store, she put on her mink coat given to her by her third husband three days before he left her.'"

Whitney's laugh was spontaneous and light. While in the Senate, she hadn't worked much with Mo. Now, Whitney wished she had. "I wouldn't want you to go against your grain. Excuse me for a moment."

She picked up the receiver again and pressed a button. "Sean, please clear another fifteen minutes for the Senator."

"But you're meeting with—"

"It will need to be rescheduled." She hung up. "Where were we?"

Mo shifted her gaze from the phone to Whitney. "We were talking about grain, which would be impossible for me to go against, as I'm sure it is for you. Now." She patted her lap with both hands. "Why am I here?"

"I saw your interview about Paul Sampson's troubles."

"One of his troubles. Trying to be someone he isn't. Messing around with Cole Brennan." Mo shook her head. "Senator Sampson also drinks like a fish who hasn't seen water for five days."

Whitney raised her own hand before Mo continued embellishing and speaking florally. "Be that as it may, I think we may be able to help each other."

Mo sipped her tea. "I didn't know I was in need of help."

"This is Washington. We all need help occasionally."

"I'll bite. How can we help each other?"

Setting her glass down on the table, Whitney crossed her legs. "Your party leadership is in a precarious position. With Sampson out, that only leaves Hampton."

Mo made a noise. "Don't get me started about him. I know we're running out of time, but Lord, that man boils my water and chaps my ass."

Whitney leaned forward. "We need someone to lead your party into the next decade. A decade of almost certain turmoil and change."

"I wasn't aware of your concern for my party. I do say that warms my heart."

"Mo, we live in turbulent times. Geopolitical issues. Terrorism. The economy. Income inequality. Gun violence. Climate change. Women's rights. The list goes on. I need to be able to work with someone from across the aisle. To effect real change."

"You and I don't agree on a lot of these issues."

"But we agree on whether they exist. Which is a start. I don't think our positions are all that far apart. Our nation faces significant problems. Unless we work with people we disagree with, our country will be unable to govern itself. 'Alone we can do so little; together we can do so much.'"

"Helen Keller?"

Whitney nodded. "What do you say, Mo?"

"People always say 'Thank God for Mississippi,' but not as a compliment. They're grateful their state doesn't take the lowest ranking in every goddamn survey." Senator Maureen "Mo" McAllister took a final sip of her sweet tea and set her glass down next to Whitney's. "I always knew it would take our state and us women to save this damn country." She stood, holding out her hand. "Where would you like to start?"

# CHAPTER TWENTY-EIGHT

---

# Washington, DC

HER WARNING TO Dante about leaks was for naught.

"This just in. WTOP has learned that the murders of three wealthy and prominent individuals may be connected."

Jade turned up the volume on the car radio.

"Sebastian Scofield, founder and managing director of Scofield Asset Management and a New York philanthropist; Jared Carr Jr., co-CEO of Carr Holdings, Inc. and founder and CEO of conservative Super PAC Freedom of America; and Finn Hurley, CEO of cybersecurity firm Hurley Technologies in Crystal City, Virginia, all died of multiple stab wounds. Three similar murders in three different cities: New York, Chicago, and Arlington."

*So far, so good.*

"But what connects these murders isn't the victims' wealth. Or their method of death. No. What connects them is that the killer left a calling card: sonnets by William Shakespeare. We'll talk more about the Shakespeare Killer after the break."

Jade slammed her hand on the dashboard. "Goddamn it!"

She lowered the radio's volume and pressed a button, drumming her fingers on the steering wheel while she waited for Dante to pick up.

"Yes?" his voice drawled over her car's speakers.

"Who leaked?" she asked. "You or Micah?"

"What do you mean?"

"It's on the news. They're calling him the Shakespeare Killer."

"Damn! It didn't come from me. Micah?" He hesitated. "Or you."

Jade let the accusation slide. Was it Micah? Pat only knew about one sonnet. And Jade trusted Pat. Over the years they'd worked together, she'd proven her discretion.

"The professor?" she asked, doubtful.

"I wouldn't think so, but I'll ask her."

"Set up the task force. We'll need to come up with an action plan quickly before hysteria ensues."

"And before the copycat killers come out of the woodwork."

"That too."

She hung up and pressed another button.

"Yes, boss?" Micah answered.

"You've been hanging around Dante too long."

"Why do you—?"

"Never mind. Did you talk to anyone in the media about the Shakespeare case?"

"Of course not."

"Someone did."

"Wasn't me. But…"

"What?"

"Barringer asked for an update. But he's your boss. He wouldn't say anything to them… would he?"

# CHAPTER TWENTY-NINE

# The White House, Washington, DC

"RAISE A STINK," Sasha said. "That's what I'd do."

On their way to the Cabinet Room, Sasha had stopped Whitney in the hallway outside of the Oval Office.

After three decades of stagnant growth, Japan had come roaring back. One of its major tech houses developed a significant breakthrough in artificial intelligence, resulting in less need for humans in economic production. Given the country's demographic crisis—a population shrinking at an alarming rate—the discovery was auspicious. Recently, Japan had joined the BRICS alliance: Brazil, Russia, India, China, and South America.

It was now JBRICS.

The rising sun had risen again.

Meanwhile, China had solved its debt problems, and its GDP

growth was returning to double digits. And Russia had awakened from its hibernation, the black bear now a political force.

China, Japan, and Russia were increasingly considered the "Big Three."

This morning, the Netherlands, which experienced one of the lowest income inequality rates in the world at 12.4 percent, announced that it would be hosting a summit in three months' time to share the secrets of its success with the invited countries. Japan, China, and Russia were to give keynote addresses. The US was invited, but Whitney hadn't been asked to speak.

Income inequality was *her* issue. The issue she'd campaigned and won on, and the basis for her signature legislation, recently overturned by the US Congress.

How would Americans fare when their country was no longer a superpower? The United States, the world's longest-lasting democracy, was not any more immune to demise than the republics before it.

"Are you listening?" Sasha asked. "You'll be in the room. Speak."

"Don't worry, I will."

"Here's the information you requested." Sasha handed her a folder. "When are we going to start working on New Cubed?"

"New New New?"

"We can do it without Hampton."

Whitney's eyes narrowed. "He thinks I'm Charlie Brown to his Lucy. I will never let him pull the football away from me ever again."

"Hampton isn't the only senator. You should find a different teammate."

This gave Whitney pause. "Like Peppermint Patty?"

"If you want something done."

As they resumed walking, she told Sasha about her conversation with Mo. "Tell Sean to schedule a meeting for me with Senator McAllister and the vice president."

"Will do," Sasha said. "By the way, I have news. About Sampson."

"What did he do now?" Whitney asked.

"He's going to resign," Sasha said.

"How do you know?

"It's my job to know."

Sasha had her sources, and they were usually accurate.

"You're always ten steps ahead of everyone else," Whitney said.

"I know," Sasha said.

Whitney stopped before the Cabinet Room door. "Even me?"

Sasha pressed her lips together but said nothing.

She didn't have to.

Her look, inexplicably, gave Whitney chills.

# CHAPTER THIRTY

## Washington, DC

A PETITE WOMAN WITH funky hair and wearing a rainbow of colors wended her way through the throng of after-work patrons crowding the tables and booths at happy hour.

Taking her foot off the brass rail under the bar, Jade eased off her stool. "Hey, you."

She bent over to give her best friend a hug.

When they pulled apart, Zoe noticed the sleek glass filled with beer waiting for her on the bar top.

"To think people say you're a control freak. What are we drinking?"

"German. Hefe."

"Thank God!" Zoe said, climbing onto her seat. "I couldn't stand to drink a Russian beer today. Or China. They brew the worst beers. Japanese beers aren't bad."

Jade returned to her seat. "What are you talking about? We never drink Russian beer."

"The three superpowers. I refuse to drink their beer now. Germany and the US are on the outside looking in. The only beer I'll drink is our ally's."

"Anything for the cause," Jade said, raising her bottle of beer before taking a sip.

"Pretty soon those three countries will be pushing their beliefs on us—and their beers. As we used to do to other countries. We must take a stand."

"Why is it always about politics for you?"

"The same way it's always about 'winning' for you. What else is there?"

"True."

"I'm glad you called," Zoe said. "It's nice to get out. It's been a rough month."

"Besides what happened to New New... is it work?"

Zoe's nonprofit organization supported progressive issues and female candidates for all levels of political office.

"It's an uphill battle sometimes."

Jade worried the edge of the label on the bottle, wet with condensation. She'd turned down the bartender's offer of a glass. "I wouldn't count the US or Fairchild out."

"I don't." Zoe sipped her beer. "Enough about me. What've you been up to? Any exciting new cases?"

Zoe had been involved in two of Jade's major cases. Too involved. "Not really."

"Hmmm..." Zoe's brow furrowed. "The Shakespeare Killer case seems like something you would take on. I minored in English Literature."

"I remember," Jade said.

Zoe raised her hand to draw the attention of one of the bartenders. The female bartender, wearing a gray vest and a black tie, immediately cut off her conversation with another customer and stood in front of Zoe, who beamed her hundred-watt smile. "Do you have any Belgian beers?"

The bartender leaned in, placing her forearms on the bar. Behind her, a mirrored wall dazzled with strategically placed color-coded liquor bottles. Jade wondered how the bartenders found what they needed. It was comparable to those people who organized their books by color rather than in alphabetical order.

Holding Zoe's gaze, the woman said, "I'm sure I can find something you'd like."

"I'm sure you can too," Zoe said.

Jade imagined a dialogue bubble above her own head. *Puke!*

After the bartender moved away, Jade said, "Seriously?"

"She's cute, isn't she?"

"Do you flirt with every attractive woman you meet?"

Zoe pretended to think about it. "You should try it sometime." Then, slyly, "Maybe you already have."

Jade shot her a warning look.

Zoe's dating habits were legendary and geographically dispersed. If Jade met a lesbian on the other side of the country, there was a distinct possibility that she had dated Zoe. Jade sometimes tired of Zoe babbling about her exploits, although Jade couldn't talk. She ruminated about Blake. And Kyle. She didn't count Micah.

"Here you go," the bartender said, deftly pouring a beer into a Duvel-labeled tulip glass and placing it on the bar before Zoe. She set the other bottle in front of Jade, grabbed her empty, then discreetly laid a folded napkin next to Zoe's glass.

"Thank you," Zoe said, pocketing the napkin with a practiced motion.

The bartender stared at Zoe several seconds longer than necessary before returning to her long-ignored customer.

"Let the woman work," Jade said, taking a drink of her fresh beer.

"Are you jealous?" Zoe asked.

Jade shook her head. "You wish."

She'd never thought of Zoe that way. They were best friends and nothing more. At least from her perspective.

She glanced around the bar. Almost all the patrons were millennials or Generation Z. The few Generation Xers, the "invisible generation," stood out.

A voice rose above the chatter. The guy sitting on the stool next to her, trying to impress his companions.

Jade leaned in to Zoe so she wouldn't be overheard. "What if we were working on that case?"

"The Shakespeare Killer? Is this another hypothetical?"

"Maybe."

"What do you want to know?"

"Tell me about the sonnets."

"They were collected by a Mr. W. H. from private friends of Shakespeare, and published years later, most likely without Shakespeare's permission." Her face brightened. "May I see them? Do you have the evidence on you?"

"Of course not."

"Which sonnets?"

"I can't tell you."

"Ugh! You never let me have any fun."

"There's nothing fun about murder."

"You're right," Zoe said. "I'm sorry."

She proceeded to tell Jade about the sonnets. Much of it Jade had learned from Alaia Bennett, the GWU professor, and Micah.

When Zoe paused to take a breath, Jade asked, "Tell me about the Carr brothers."

Zoe made a face. "Their extremist views changed the direction of this country forever."

Another motive. "Extremist?"

"Some right wingnut philosophies are now considered legitimate schools of thought because of them. Twenty years ago, most Republicans believed that humans caused climate change. Those beliefs were inconvenient for the Carrs' business, so they set about changing them."

"How?"

"Advertising. Forming foundations and deputizing experts to bully and discredit scientists. It worked."

"Tell me more."

"Despite the Carrs claiming ad nauseam that they're for limited government, they have a history of using it to expand their businesses through tax breaks and regulation. Through their company and its subsidiaries, they form nonprofits, which they use to support their beliefs. They hide behind these organizations so they can spend massive amounts of money against their political opponents."

"To the outside world, their philanthropy appears generous."

"Right," Zoe said. "But the money they're giving away is used to manipulate American politics and further their business and private interests."

"And it's all legal," Jade said.

Zoe shrugged. "They're privileged. They can get away with murder."

Jade raised an eyebrow.

"Literally," Zoe said.

The two women drank in silence, and then Zoe leaned in. "Ever check out 'The God of Veritas'?"

"What do you mean?"

"On Twitter. Instagram."

"No."

"Your JadeHarringtonFans account has over two hundred thousand followers."

"Zoe…," Jade said, in a tone that conveyed her impatience. It was one Zoe was familiar with.

"All right, all right. The God of Veritas tweets a lot about the Carr brothers. I follow him on Twitter." She turned to smile at the bartender and held up her glass before turning back to Jade. "You want another one?"

Jade placed her hand over her bottle, still three-quarters full. "I'm fine."

"You should check him out."

After Zoe finished her third drink, the two friends headed to the door. Inclining her head back toward the bar, Jade said, "Aren't you going to say goodbye?"

Zoe didn't look back. "I've got her number."

Leaving the bar, they emerged into the middle of the hustle and bustle of Georgetown's upscale businesses and specialty stores. The northwest neighborhood pulsed with activity, as it usually did this time of night. Diners and partygoers crowded the sidewalk, while drivers honked, protesting the traffic.

"How did you get here?" Jade asked.

Zoe pointed at the curb.

Jade's mouth gaped open. "You bought a motorcycle?" She examined the black and gray Honda sandwiched between two parked cars. "Nice."

"I like it," Zoe said, beaming. "It's a Rebel."

"How appropriate."

Stepping around Jade, she hopped onto the bike. "You wanna go for a ride? I don't have an extra helmet, but I promise to be careful."

Jade surveyed the small bike with its single seat and shook her head. "Nah. I'm good."

In truth, she wouldn't have accepted the offer even if Zoe had lent her an extra helmet and protective clothing, the bike had training wheels, and the streets were empty.

Zoe strapped on her helmet and revved the engine. As she did so, the sleeve of her leather jacket crept up her wrist, exposing a tattoo. Jade recalled the time she'd caught a glimpse of the new tattoo on Zoe's chest, right above her heart, exposed as she covered Jade with a blanket. Jade, in a drunken haze, had asked about it; Zoe claimed it wasn't new.

Now Jade peered closer. "New tat? I haven't seen that one before."

"There are a lot of areas on my body you haven't seen before."

"Stop," Jade said, feigning disgust. She paused. "Is that a tree? What does it represent?"

Zoe shrugged. "Nothing. I just like the way it looks."

Jade squinted at her. "You don't seem happy about it. It didn't come out the way you wanted?"

Glancing at the tattoo for a moment, Zoe readjusted her sleeve to cover it.

"It's what I wanted," Zoe muttered. "It's others who don't care for it."

"When did you start caring about what other people think?"

A faint smile. "You're right. I don't." She revved the engine. "I gotta go. Sure you don't want a ride?"

*I prefer living.*

Frowning, Jade said, "Zoe, what's going on?"

"Thanks for the drinks," Zoe said, brightening, her somber mood over.

Jade placed her hands on her hips. "It's funny how I always get stuck paying the check."

Zoe flashed her characteristic game show–host smile. "Didn't you just earn a promotion?"

As Zoe cut into traffic on M Street, Jade prayed for the other drivers. What was the deal with her friend's melancholy mood? It wasn't like her.

Not like her at all.

# CHAPTER THIRTY-ONE

## Arlington, Virginia

AS JADE LEFT the Chinese restaurant, she thought about what Zoe had said about China, Japan, and Russia taking over the world. Glancing at her takeout bag's greasy bottom, Jade figured she wasn't helping matters.

When she opened the door to her townhouse, her cat, Card, came running from whatever mischief he'd been up to. Scooping him up, she squeezed him and planted several kisses on his head. After ten seconds of bonding, he struggled to free himself and, once liberated, sprinted for the kitchen. After replenishing his water and food bowls on the tile floor, Jade picked up her briefcase and the takeout she'd left in the foyer and plopped cross-legged on the espresso-colored leather couch in her spartan living room. The scuffed hardwood floors needed buffing. Her bookshelves were filled with books and vinyl records, all in alphabetical order. Trophies and medals that she'd collected over the years were packed in cardboard boxes and stored in the basement.

With the case files for the Shakespeare Killer—they were probably stuck with the name now—spread out around her, she fired up her laptop. Using chopsticks, she scooped mouthfuls of the chow mein right out of the carton. She'd forgotten to eat breakfast and lunch. Again.

Jade reflected on her earlier conversation with Micah. Warren Barringer might not be a pleasure to work with, but she didn't want to believe that he'd leak sensitive details about such a high-profile case.

Putting thoughts of Barringer aside, she logged in to her rarely used Twitter account. Jade wasn't on social media much, both because of her job and because she wanted her private life to remain private.

She could've assigned Pat or Cyber to this task, but sometimes she preferred to conduct research herself. She found @TheGodOfVeritas easily. One hundred thousand followers—fewer than her fan account.

*Veritas* meant truth. The God of Truth.

His profile was bereft of description and location. He tweeted. A lot. Specifically about President Whitney Fairchild.

The more Jade read, the more concerned she became. His criticisms of the president were harsh, a recurring theme being that she was too conservative and not a real Democrat. A DINO—Democrat In Name Only.

Reading the replies to his tweets reinforced Jade's decision to avoid the platform. Had the human race always been so hateful, racist, and close-minded? Or did the anonymity of social media foster that behavior?

She kept reading, stopping short when her eyes landed on one particular tweet:

@TheGodOfVeritas: Word on the street is that Finn Hurley is in secret meetings with Senator Hampton. I wonder what Congress will do next to boost her business. #shame

Jade checked the date. About a week before Hurley was killed. Thirty minutes later, she found another tweet of interest.

> @TheGodOfVeritas: It's no secret that the Carr brothers and their Super PAC are behind the push to repeal the #NewNewDeal They should feel #shame

Tweeted a week before Carr was murdered.

The skin on Jade's forearms started to tingle.

Finally, after another hour, she came to:

> @TheGodOfVeritas: While thousands of NYC citizens won't be eating dinner tonight, Sebastian Scofield is attending a $1000-a-plate dinner at the NYPL. #shame

Again, approximately a week before Scofield's death.

When she looked at the clock, it was 1:00 a.m. She'd been reviewing The God of Veritas's timeline for hours. The Chinese food was long gone, as were the two bottles of wheat beer from a microbrewery in California.

Card had fallen asleep next to her, his cocoa-colored head resting against her leg, snoring.

She wondered how long it would have taken the FBI to discover The God of Veritas's tweets if Zoe hadn't pointed her in this direction. The timing of the murders wasn't a coincidence. If his tweets signaled or were associated with the Shakespeare killings, what were the killer's plans for the president?

# CHAPTER THIRTY-TWO

# The White House, Washington, DC

"I APOLOGIZE FOR THE late hour," Whitney said to the senator and the vice president, who shared the cream sofa under the elegant half-moon window in the West Sitting Hall off the Master Bedroom of the Residence. Whitney, sitting in a gray chair perpendicular to them, continued, "but I thought we'd be more comfortable here."

She waited as Senator Maureen McAllister took in the beige walls with landscape prints and white wainscot and chair rail. A bookcase leaned against one wall, filled with coffee table books interspersed with Fairchild family photos. Vice President Josephine Bates didn't need to behold the surroundings; she'd been here before.

"I don't mind," Mo said. "Those drapes! And the flowers are

lovely." Mo's gaze returned to Whitney. "I do declare that I'm starting to enjoy visiting here."

"It can be habit-forming," Jo agreed.

"You're welcome anytime, Senator," said Whitney.

Mo sipped her hot tea before setting her cup on the square wooden coffee table. "I suppose you want to get down to business. Being from the North and West Coast and all."

Whitney asked, "What did you think about our proposal for New Cubed?"

"Why do y'all always go there?" Mo said.

"Pardon me?"

"Income redistribution. I don't believe in it, and it would be political suicide for me. I'd rather give people opportunity. Give them a fair shake."

Jo straightened her back. "Which 'people' are you talking about?"

"All the people who need it. Shoot, Jo, you know I don't care what color you are or whom you pray to."

To Mo, Whitney said, "Opportunity. I've heard that before—more succinctly, by the way—from Senator Hampton."

Mo laughed. "Unlike my esteemed colleague from the Commonwealth of Virginia, I can find my backbone on an anatomical chart."

"Hampton is weak," Jo agreed.

"I believe in creating opportunities for *everyone*," Mo said, glancing at Jo, "especially those who've been left behind by technology or trade. We've been dealing with these issues in Mississippi for a long time."

"Same with California," Jo said.

"If you don't like my proposal," said Whitney, "do you have something better?"

"Instead of free college and all that give-the-store-away foolishness, how about a national apprentice program? There are more jobs than available workers. Jobs that don't require a college degree. Employers want workers with experience. We can give it to them."

Whitney said, "I can support that."

"Me too," said Jo.

"What about providing capital to encourage the creation of small businesses?"

"We tried that with New New," Whitney reminded her.

"But that was the part of your legislation that I *liked*. That most of my party liked, before some of them lost their godforsaken minds. Some of my colleagues aren't *for* anything anymore. They just want to stop progress. Let's keep that part in."

"And increase the federal minimum wage," said Jo.

"To a living wage," Whitney agreed.

"We need to take care of our workers," Jo said. "Notably, workers of color."

Mo shook her head. "No can do. You start fiddling with the market, it gets all messed up."

There was a difference between compromising and, as Mo said, giving away the store. Increasing the minimum wage was important to Whitney's base. She wouldn't forget the people who had voted her into this office.

"What would you suggest?" Whitney asked.

Mo stared at her thoughtfully. "Do you mind if we liven things up in here?"

"In what way?"

The senator reached for her purse, perched next to the lamp on the round end table, and pulled out a flask covered in glitz and sparkle.

She held it up. "I always carry."

"I heard that about you people," Jo kidded.

Mo poured a small amount of the liquid into her tea. She held out the flask to Whitney.

"I'm too old to be drinking out of a flask," Whitney said to the older woman.

"Suit yourself," said fifty-five-year-old Jo, extending her cup. Mo poured a drop. Jo continued to hold out her cup.

"You don't need much," Mo said. "Trust me."

Jo took a sip and swallowed. Beads of sweat dotted her forehead. "She speaks the truth."

Whitney proffered her own cup. "I guess this is our version of breaking bread."

After Mo poured a drop for Whitney, the three women clinked cups.

"Cheers," they said.

Whitney took a sip and coughed from the strong, bitter taste.

"What is this?" asked Whitney, still coughing.

"A little Mississippi moonshine."

"Is it legal?"

Mo winked. "Depends on which state you're in."

"Since we're not in a state," Whitney said, "we should be all right. Now, what were you suggesting before we... livened things up?"

Mo's response was measured. "I could tolerate regional minimum wage increases tied to the standard of living." She waved her hand. "We can let our staffs work out the nitty-gritty details."

"What do you think, Jo?" Whitney said.

"I think we can make that work."

Whitney took another sip of her moonshine-laced tea, this

time without coughing. "Let's also help people save money so they'll be able to retire."

"We can privatize retirement," Mo said. "I could sell that to my colleagues."

"I'm sure you could," said Jo, between sips of tea.

Whitney waved her hand as if shooing a fly. "Now *you've* gone too far, Senator Mo. It won't work. Even if it did, it wouldn't work fast enough. What if we required employers to contribute a mandatory amount to retirement accounts? No matching required. That would go over well with the American people."

"I like the sound of that," Jo said.

Retrieving her flask, Mo poured more moonshine into her own cup. Jo held out hers for a refill. Whitney hesitated but did the same.

"I can't support that," Mo said. "My people want less government intervention, not more."

"Even if it's for their benefit?" Jo asked.

"That's a nonstarter, Madam President. Madam Vice President. Sorry."

Whitney gazed out the window at the West Colonnade, the West Wing, and beyond to the Eisenhower Executive Office Building. The retirement savings of baby boomers and Generation Xers had been depleted or wiped out by the Great Recession. She considered their retirements an impending crisis. It was one of the many worries that kept her up at night.

"I remember that time," Mo said to Whitney, "when you filibustered the Protection of Rights for All Citizens bill. The longer you talked, the more Senator Hampton's face scrunched up, as if he smelled something bad."

"I can top that," Jo said. "I remember when you"—she pointed at Mo—"filibustered a bill by reading *Gone with the Wind*. All one thousand pages of it. Your accent made it seem twice as long."

"You're not disparaging my floral ways, are you?" Mo said.

The three women laughed.

"Hampton was a young pup then," Jo continued, "and he kept interrupting you. And you kept talking over him. I thought you all were on the same side."

"We may be in the same political party," Mo said, wiping the tears of laughter from her eyes, "but that doesn't mean we're always on the same side." She turned to Jo. "Veep, I remember when you were a guest with him on *Meet the Press* while trying to pass the ERA. You told him, 'I'm a strong black woman, and I shall not be intimidated by anyone. Especially by a skinny, spineless little prick like you.' The network didn't beep you fast enough."

"I thought he was going to shit his pants," Jo said.

Mo fell against Jo with the weight of her laughter. Whitney bent over with hers.

Finally, Jo eased Mo off her shoulder, her expression turned serious.

"You'll need to hit the road," Jo said to Whitney. "Sell this thing."

"I can do that," Whitney said.

"I can too," Mo said. "There's only one problem remaining with our proposal."

"What's that?" Whitney said.

"There's no bad guy. If we work together, no one can blame either party. People need someone to blame."

Whitney drained the remainder of her tea. "I'm sure we can find someone for them to hate, Mo and Jo, because... I've got my mojo!"

The three women burst into hysterical laughter.

"Wait! Wait!" Mo said. She held out her cup. "A toast! To the resignation of Senator Paul Sampson!"

"Hear, hear!" said Whitney.

"To one fewer old, out-of-touch white guy making decisions for the rest of us," Jo said. She drank and reached for the flask on the table. "Still almost full. We're going to need some more tea."

Whitney reached for the phone. "I can take care of that."

"Now this," said Mo, spreading out her arms, "is a Tea Party."

# CHAPTER THIRTY-THREE

## Washington, DC

JADE CHECKED HER watch with its slim black band before glancing back at *The Complete Works of William Shakespeare*, perfectly aligned with the right corner of her desk. She lifted the hefty tome and opened it where she'd placed the first blue sticky note.

She checked the time again, then shut the book.

After the third murder, the newly formed Shakespeare Killer task force moved to a major-case room. The team was meeting there now, which was why she remained in her office—to prevent herself from hijacking Dante's meeting.

For a long time, Zoe had been nagging her to meditate, instructing Jade to clear her mind and count her breaths: "one" on the inhale, "two" on the exhale.

Jade closed her eyes and breathed in deeply. *One.* She needed to give Dante the space to do his job. Start over. *One.* She believed he could do it. *One.* She wondered what they were discussing. *One.* Had they thought about—

She popped out of her chair and left her office.

Jade stepped through the doorway into the crowded case room. Christian, Pat, Micah, and Max sat in chairs in the front row. Christian's seat was turned around, his forearms on the top of the chair's backrest. A score of other agents and representatives from other law enforcement jurisdictions were spread out behind them.

Dante, positioned at the front of the room, said, "All the victims were between the ages of thirty-five and fifty-five. Scofield, fifty-four. Carr, fifty-five. Hurley, thirty-five."

"The victims that we're aware of," said Pat. The clicking of her fingers on the keyboard was audible from the back of the room.

"Right," he said. "Pat, check out VICAP"—Violent Criminal Apprehension Program—"for cases with similar characteristics."

"Yes, boss," she said, her fingers tapping furiously.

He squinted at her, as if assessing whether she was making fun of him. After a moment, he seemed to conclude that she wasn't. "No hair, fiber, or other trace evidence was found on any of the victims," he said.

"Were they acquainted with each other?" Micah said.

Pat's eyes stayed glued to her computer. "I'll check that out too."

Glancing back down at his notes, where his index finger kept his place, Dante said, "Both males were married. Hurley, divorced. All three were white." He spotted Jade at the back of the room. "Can I help you, boss?"

Standing just inside the door, Jade shook her head.

"Like I was saying—" he said.

She raised her hand. "How are you doing with Twitter?"

Dante shook his head, smiling, and pointed. "Pat?"

Pat was the team's liaison with the FBI's Cyber Division.

She turned to face Jade. "The company refuses to release the identity of The God of Veritas. Legal is preparing a court order."

"The God of Veritas," Micah said. "Humble that one."

"What about Scofield's, Carr's, and Hurley's social media accounts?" asked Jade.

Pat read off her computer. "Carr and Hurley weren't on social media."

"Carr probably because he was secretive," Dante said. "Hurley, being in cybersecurity, didn't trust it."

"But Scofield lived on social media," Pat said. "He tweeted his every move, making it easy for anyone who wanted to hurt him."

Dante asked Jade. "Anything else?"

She waved her hand. "Carry on."

He turned his attention back to his team.

"As I was saying"—his eyes cut to Jade and then back to his notes—"all the victims came from similar socioeconomic backgrounds."

"They were rich," Christian said.

"More like wealthy," Micah said.

To Max, Dante said, "What are you thinking?"

Jade hadn't seen Max since they'd shared a quiet Christmas dinner at his house. She looked at him now. The faint wisps of blond hair on the top of his head had disappeared after his wife left him.

"Usually, the motive of a serial killer comes down to anger, financial gain, thrill, or attention seeking," Max said. "I can't narrow it down yet. Could be any of them or some combination. There's a lot of rage here. The victims suffered from deep, penetrating wounds through muscles, organs—even to the bone, in Finn Hurley's case. The killer is also organized."

"But an organized killer doesn't usually murder his victim in the same place where the body is found," Jade called out. "Usually, he'll move it and dump it somewhere."

Max pushed up his rimless glasses and then conceded the point. "He might be mixed. I would lean toward organized rather than disorganized. The murders were well planned."

"He seems to enjoy an audience," Dante said. "Scofield and Carr were murdered in front of witnesses, and Hurley's murder was witnessed by the entire GW Parkway's early-morning commuter traffic."

Christian glanced back at Jade. She gave him a look. *This is why I picked him.*

"Signature?" Jade asked, for the benefit of the others in the room.

"The sonnets, of course," Max said. "I'm not sure yet if they relate to the victim, a situation, the perp, or if he wants us to think he's smart. An intellectual."

"What do you make of the absence of defensive wounds on the arms and hands of the victims?" she said.

"You're getting ahead of us here," Dante said, checking his notes.

"Then catch up," she said to him. "Max?"

Max's lips twitched. "That's true. Either the victims knew and trusted the suspect, or the murderer caught all of them unawares."

"The perp possesses some knowledge of anatomy," Micah said thoughtfully. "He stabbed Carr in the aorta and Hurley in the femoral artery. If help didn't come immediately, death was all but certain."

Max looked pleased. "Very good."

Jade did a private eye roll at the teacher praising his favorite pupil.

"Why did he leave the knife in?" Christian asked.

"Good question," Max said. "Extracting the knives would've exacerbated the victims' injuries. Made them suffer."

"Which doesn't fit with the rage or anger motive," Christian pointed out, glancing at Jade as if to say, "You still should have picked me."

"You're right," said Max.

Micah said, "Or he's not totally heartless."

"What else, Max?" asked Dante.

"Serial killers were often abused as children: physically, emotionally, sexually. Usually by a family member."

"Here we go," Dante said sarcastically.

"There's been no evidence of sexual activity with any of the victims," Micah said.

"That doesn't mean he wasn't abused," said Pat.

"Let's move this along, Max," Dante said, "since *everyone's* been abused these days. Let's say he was abused in some way."

"What a twit," Micah whispered to Pat, in a voice that reached Jade in the back of the room.

"I heard that," said Dante.

"Many serial killers were bullied, rejected, and neglected as children," Max said, ignoring them both. "They grow up seeking approval from parents, sexual partners, friends, but they never receive it. Over time, the serial killer develops an inability to attach."

"Psychopathy," said Micah.

Dante said, "Same sad story."

"Unfortunately, it usually is the same sad story," Max said.

"What's unusual in this case is the age of the victims. Your odds of being a victim of a serial killer significantly decrease after thirty."

"Thank God," Pat said as she continued to type.

Dante eyed her. "There are always exceptions."

Pat scratched the side of her head with her middle finger. Some of the other agents laughed. Even Dante cracked a smile.

"New York City, Chicago, and here," Christian said. "The perp has some means."

"He does his homework," Max said. "He studies his victims, learns their habits, where they'll be."

"Not a lot of time between the murders, though," Christian said.

"What if he planned them all beforehand, then struck?" Dante said.

No one had a response.

"Anything else?" Dante asked the group.

"Update them on our meeting with the professor," Jade called out to Dante.

He scowled but did as she said.

"Anything back on the paper the sonnets were written on?" Christian asked.

Pat stopped typing. "The same paper was used in the Scofield and Hurley murders. The analysts believe it was manufactured in England. Same paper used by the royal family."

"Makes sense," Dante said. "Shakespeare and all."

"The perp has fine taste," Micah said.

"What about the kids?" Jade called out.

Brow furrowed, Dante said, "Huh?"

"Shakespeare keeps telling his friend that he should bear children so his beauty can live on for eternity," Jade said. "Maybe this has something to do with the victims' kids."

Dante blinked at her before turning to Christian. "Why don't you take that on?"

Christian smirked. "You sure you're up to this supervising thing, compadre?"

Dante's eyes returned to his notes. "Just check it out, Merritt."

The team discussed next steps and batted ideas back and forth. After a time, no one seemed to remember that Jade was in the room.

As the discussion continued, she slipped out the door without anyone noticing.

Later that afternoon, Dante burst into her office, his eyes alight with excitement.

Jade looked up from the email she was typing.

"We've got a lead," he said. "A solid one."

"What is it?"

"I'll tell you on the way."

"Where are we headed?"

"New York."

# CHAPTER THIRTY-FOUR

# The White House, Washington, DC

"MADAM PRESIDENT, LEI Min is on the line."

Whitney frowned. "Put him through," she told Sean through the speakerphone.

"This is a pleasant surprise," she said to the president of the People's Republic of China.

"You may not think so once I've told you why I've called," he said, his voice clipped. His English was flawless.

"Oh?"

"I want to forewarn you—or, as you Americans say, give you a heads-up."

A pressure in her chest, a foreboding.

"About what?" she said.

"My country signed a deal today," he said. "With Russia. The Sino-Russian Partnership Trade Agreement, or SRPTA."

Whitney almost gasped. This was bad. Why hadn't her team warned her?

Focused on domestic issues during her first year in office, her secretary of state, Charles Staunton, had kept a low profile, making only a few obligatory overseas trips. Except for a brief skirmish with Russia in the Middle East, things had been quiet on the international front. Whitney had encouraged Staunton to resign after the announcement of the income inequality summit.

And she hadn't replaced him yet.

Into the phone, she said, "Is it too late for the United States to come to the table?"

"That ship has sailed," he said. "We will shift some of our exports from the US to our friends in Russia. My staff will send over the details. I thought you should hear it from me. Goodbye."

*As opposed to your new BFF leaking it to the media?*

Pressing the intercom button on the telephone, she said, "Sean, ring Tamirov immediately."

As she waited for the call to go through, she spun her chair around to gaze out the window at the Rose Garden. The foliage was dusted with snow.

The goods trade deficit with China had grown to $500 billion; US companies liked employing cheap labor and materials to manufacture their products, and US consumers liked cheap Chinese imports—"Buy American" notwithstanding.

The US and China shared a strong relationship, an entangled one, based on trade. A trade war could result in their mutual economic destruction.

Russia and China supplied petroleum to the global economy. Perhaps this deal was about staving off the green-energy revolution for a while longer?

Both countries funded antidemocratic and anti-US countries

with arms and currency while playing the peacemaker on the world stage. Whitney—and her foreign policy advisors—had considered them an "axis of convenience." An opportunistic relationship tainted with mistrust. It seemed to be something more now.

Apparently, Tamirov had forgotten his envy of China's sustained economic growth, or he was using Min in some way. Whitney would bet on the latter.

Recently, Russia had stepped up its government-sanctioned cybermeddling in US and European commerce and political elections, weakening the public's perception of institutions and democracy itself on both sides of the Atlantic. The Cold War of the eighties hadn't been resurrected; rather, a new one had been born: a cyberwar. No, this wasn't the same Russia, but this wasn't the same United States either. The US was more polarized. More fractured.

Divided.

Most of Tamirov's moves had heretofore been behind the scenes, but now he'd emerged from behind the Iron Curtain. With one ambition.

To be the only star on the world stage.

"Madam President," the Russian president's smooth, confident voice came over the line, with only a trace of an accent, "what a coincidence. I was just talking about you to our mutual friend, President Lei Min."

"What's going on?" she said, her voice hard.

"Ah," he said, "you heard."

"Tell me about the deal."

"China and Russia have a long history of mutual respect. An alignment of shared interests. Some might call it love."

"Love, Andrei?"

"I love the Chinese people. This Russian-Sino agreement will greatly benefit the citizens of both our great countries."

"I thought it was Sino-Russian."

"Semantics," he said dismissively.

"Oil for consumer products," she said.

"And natural gas and military hardware."

She thought for a moment. "Infrastructure."

He chuckled. "I don't care what your American press says. You are much smarter than your predecessor."

Whitney ignored the compliment, or the dig at former president Richard Ellison. "The United States—"

Tamirov cut her off. "The deal is done. Perhaps next time. Good day, Madam President."

She didn't care for being hung up on twice in the span of thirty minutes. This deal weakened her position. Weakened the United States. The entire premise of international trade was for countries to leverage each other's strengths and support each other's weaknesses, creating greater economic growth for all. Successful trade agreements were essential to the healthy functioning of the US economy. After listening to the dial tone for a few moments, she slowly replaced the receiver.

This would not stand.

She leaned back in her chair, the index finger of her left hand rising to her lips. Her thinking position.

After several minutes, she sat up and called Sean. "Hold my calls for the rest of the day and cancel all my meetings."

"Your afternoon is booked. At noon, you're meeting with the Joint Chiefs—"

"I don't care."

Whitney pressed the End button.

She opened a folio with a pad of paper inside and reached for a pen.

And she started to write.

# CHAPTER THIRTY-FIVE

# New York City, New York

J ADE PACED AS she waited.

Dante stood by the one-way observation window, watching her, a bemused smile on his face. Detective Elaine Katz of the New York Police Department stood next to him.

"Picked him up on 40th, between 7th and 8th," Katz said. "He'd been wearing the coat for a while."

"Anything back on it?" Jade asked.

The detective shook her head. "Still working on it. A lot of fingerprints. Bodily fluids. Probably his." She pointed at the window as a uniformed officer brought the man into the interview room. "It was exposed to the elements for a while. Sorting it all out might take some time. We found blood on the coat."

Jade stopped pacing. "Scofield's?"

"Don't know yet."

"Let's see if he can help us," Jade said. "Shall we?"

She and Dante had taken a shuttle flight to LaGuardia and

come straight to the Manhattan precinct from the airport. Detective Katz—short and solid, with a square face, dark eyes, and dark brown hair—led them into the room.

The pungent smell of body odor hit Jade as soon as she entered. She stilled her face and resisted the urge to cover her nose and mouth with her hand. Behind her, Dante gulped.

The man wore a tattered brown shirt and faded black pants. The toes of his black shoes were scuffed gray.

Jade sat in the chair between Dante and Katz. Thinking the witness might find Jade less threatening, Katz had suggested earlier that Jade conduct the interview.

Dante had leaned in to Jade, whispering, "If she only knew."

Sitting across from them, the man trembled.

Jade relaxed and tried to appear docile and nonthreatening. It was hard. She clasped her hands together on the table.

"You've met Detective Katz. My name is Special Agent in Charge Jade Harrington, and this is Assistant Special Agent in Charge Dante Carlucci. We're from the FBI, and we're here to ask you some questions. That's all, okay?"

He hesitated, then dipped his head.

"What's your name?"

"Ben."

"Ben what?"

"It's just Ben."

"What's your last name?" Dante asked.

"If Oprah's allowed to have only one name, why can't I?"

The two agents and the detective looked at each other. Dante shrugged.

"My mother named me after a damn mouse," Ben said. "Her favorite song."

Jade recognized the song, of course. She fought back

memories of her parents slow dancing in the living room of their California home.

"When the police found you," she said, "you were wearing an attractive coat. Where did you get it?"

Ben fingered the frayed cuff of a shirtsleeve. "May I have some water?"

Katz stood and went to the door. She opened it and said something to someone on the other side. The observers watching through the window had heard Ben's request.

Soon after she was reseated, a police officer entered, placed a cup in front of Ben, and left.

Jade waited for Ben to take a sip. After he'd chugged the contents, she tried again. "Tell us about the coat."

A grin split Ben's gritty, grimy face. Some of his teeth were missing. The remaining ones were a dull brown. He'd been handsome once.

"Did you see it?" he said. "Wasn't it nice?"

"Who gave it to you?"

"Some guy."

"What did he look like?"

Ben shrugged. "Like all those guys, I suppose."

"Those guys?"

"A suit. Slicked hair. White guy. Money."

A faraway look in his eyes.

"What did you do before?" Jade said.

"Before what?"

"Before—" She faltered. "For work."

"I was a head trader at Lehman. Until 2008. Used to be one of them. One of those slick-haired guys in a suit."

"You haven't worked since?"

Ben shook his head and looked at the cup, as if debating

whether to ask for something stronger. "There weren't any jobs after that. Lost the apartment on Park Avenue. Then the Porsche. The house upstate. My wife. Kids. Everything. Now these guys walk around like they're too good for me. Don't even see me."

"Why don't you get back in the game?"

He shook his head, more vigorously this time. "Too old."

"How old are you, Ben?"

Ben thought about it. "What's today?"

Jade told him.

"Thirty-nine."

Jade gasped. She couldn't help it. He looked fifty-nine. Or older. She recovered quickly. "Where were you when the guy gave you the coat?"

"My usual spot. The same place they found me today."

"They?"

"The police."

"Why do you think he gave it to you?"

"I caught him staring at me. Most people look through me, if they notice me at all. He just took it off and gave it to me. The nicest gift I've received in a long time."

"Then where did he go?"

"He kept going down 40th."

She made a mental note to ask Katz about cameras in the area. "Would you do something for me?"

The skin around Ben's eyes tightened, his suspicion returning. "What?"

"If you worked with a sketch artist, do you think you could describe the man?"

Ben considered her, calculating. "As long as you'll do something for me."

Jade was prepared to give him food, drink, and a warm shower, even help him find a place to stay for a short time. It wasn't much or a long-term solution, but it was the least she could do.

"Sure," she said. "What do you want?"

"May I have my coat back?" he asked.

## CHAPTER THIRTY-SIX

# Air Force One

"COME IN, SASHA."

As they soared above the clouds, Sasha crossed the spacious office of the presidential suite and sat in the chair next to the desk.

"Have a seat," Whitney said dryly. "Be with you in a moment."

Sasha waited while Whitney continued to write.

The Boeing 747-200B airplane was en route to the Midwest on a two-day trip to Michigan, Indiana, Ohio, Wisconsin, and Illinois, to sell the slimmed-down version of the New New Deal. Mo was headed to the South, and Jo to the West, to accomplish the same thing. Whitney would be visiting manufacturing plants, colleges, and town halls.

She finally set down her pen. "I've been working on something."

Sasha cocked her head, as she was wont to do. "You sure look proud of yourself."

"I guess I am."

Whitney perused the papers one more time before handing them over to Sasha.

"What's this?" asked Sasha.

Whitney settled back in her chair. "Reagan established the Reagan Doctrine. Truman, the Truman Doctrine. Nixon, the Nixon Doctrine. I can't sit by and watch Min and Tamirov divide up the world like seventeenth-century colonial powers. It's time the United States got back in the game."

"I agree. What are we going to do?"

"In your hands is our approach to foreign policy."

"We don't have a secretary of state," Sasha reminded her.

Waving off this detail as if it were insignificant, Whitney said, "Staunton's departure gives me the opportunity to appoint the best person to carry this out." She pointed at the document. "Someone who supports and shares my beliefs about our place in the world."

"Who?"

Whitney hesitated. "I haven't figured that out yet."

The two women laughed.

"And what is this"? Sasha asked.

"You hold in your hands the Fairchild Doctrine."

Sasha's mouth fell open. "Really!"

Whitney didn't blame Sasha for being surprised. She'd kept her foreign policy views private for the majority of her political career; most people thought Whitney was a pacifist.

For more than a century, the world had been in awe of America's military might. In recent times, public sentiment leaned toward the US focusing on its own problems and letting other countries deal with theirs. The difficulty with that approach was that other countries' problems eventually became America's problems.

Her problems.

While Sasha read through the document, Whitney watched the flat-screen TV on the opposite wall, red and green numbers crawling across the bottom of the screen. The Dow was down one hundred points.

Sasha looked up. "I noticed you didn't mention Russia or China by name."

Whitney returned her gaze to Sasha. "No need. Tamirov and Min will know."

"I love how it's based on *precedent*," Sasha said, "and *presidents*. Everyone's represented." She flipped through the pages. "Truman. Eisenhower. Kennedy. Nixon. Clinton."

"That's the whole idea," Whitney said. "My policy incorporates their legacies, honors tradition, shows continuity, and builds on them for the future."

Sasha handed the document back to her. "I like it."

"Wonderful. I'm going to run it by Jo and Mo."

Sasha cocked her head. "Mo?"

"Yes, Mo."

Affecting a pronounced Southern drawl, the former Texas congresswoman said, "Didn't realize y'all were so close."

Whitney pursed her own lips, imitating Sasha. "As if your accent is any better." She turned her attention to the briefing books on her desk.

Sasha started to rise. "What's next?"

"I need you to find a secretary of state."

## CHAPTER THIRTY-SEVEN

---

# Washington, DC

I N HER OFFICE the next morning, Jade stared at the sketch of the nondescript white man with medium-length brown hair. Pat had sent the image to FACE—Facial Analysis, Comparison, and Evaluation Services—which managed over thirty million mugshots and four hundred million images in its face-recognition database. Many of those images weren't of people who'd committed a crime, but citizens who'd applied for a passport or a driver's license and unwittingly provided law enforcement access to their likeness at any time.

Jade and Dante had reviewed the footage from the camera in front of the New York Public Library. Katz was right. The perp's face was not only obscured by the hat, but it was tilted away from the camera, as if he knew the facial recognition software didn't need much: the width between the eyes, the shape of a nose, the curvature of the lips.

Katz had gotten back to her on the coat. NYPD Forensics found Scofield's blood on it and lots of smudged fingerprints.

Ben had encouraged anyone he encountered to touch his new coat.

After vigorous reassurance, NYPD had obtained Ben's fingerprints. Although he'd already been ruled out as a suspect, his fingerprints would be on file if they showed up later in connection with the case. His name came back as Ben Havenstein. Arrested twice for trespassing. His address of record, a high-end apartment on Park Avenue.

The week of the murder, NYPD had gone door to door within a six-block radius of the library, but no one claimed to have seen the perpetrator/coat-giving Samaritan. After the interview yesterday, Jade and Dante canvassed the Meatpacking District neighborhood. They stopped by a Men's Wearhouse. She selected the item over Dante's protestations.

"I'm choosing it," she said. "I've seen the way you dress."

Later, they found Ben in his regular spot on 40th Street. She handed him his new coat. It wasn't the same one the police had confiscated, but he didn't seem to mind.

After struggling to his feet, Ben modeled it for her and Dante. Stroking the sleeve, he said, "This coat fits even better."

# CHAPTER THIRTY-EIGHT

# Washington, DC

DANTE POPPED HIS head into Jade's office. "We're having a task force meeting. Wanna join us?"

She needed to prepare for afternoon meetings, take care of some bureaucratic details, and go over witness testimonies for other cases. Without answering him, she locked her computer and accompanied him to the major-case room.

It now resembled a war room, with maps, sketches, diagrams, and photographs plastering the walls. Dante had blown up pictures of the victims, in life and in death, and affixed them to the wall. As Jade did for her major cases.

The agents were assembled. Jade stood near the door again. Dante moved to the front of the room.

"What do we got?" he said. "Christian?"

"Why don't you go first?" Christian asked.

Dante's eyes widened, but he said nothing.

Christian gave Dante a look before pulling a small notebook

out of his back pocket. "The first victim, Sebastian Scofield, had two kids. A boy and a girl, ages two and four. Jared Carr, three: two boys, seventeen and nine, and a girl, five. Finn Hurley was childless."

"Did you find out anything that made you think the murders involved the children?"

"Given my limited investigative experience," Christian said, "it's no surprise that I have not."

Dante scowled at him. "Grow up!" He turned to Pat. "Anything on the sketch?"

"No match."

"What about the cameras from 40th Street?" Jade asked.

Dante shook his head, frustrated. He scanned the room. "Does anyone have anything?"

Silence. Then Christian said, "I found the bike." He savored the moment of attention. "In Crystal City. It's one of those bike shares you see all over the city. Although the perp wiped it clean, forensics found blood."

"Whose?" asked Jade.

"Hurley's."

"Did you track down who rented it?"

"Nope. The perp reserved it online. His personal information was fake, the credit card stolen."

"Anything else?" Dante asked, his tone impatient. Jade eyed him. Leading a case could do that to you.

"Got Hurley's client list," Pat said. "Corporations, nonprofits, all levels of government, including the White House, the FBI. Cyber worked with her on the Robin Hood case."

Dante used his pen to scratch behind his ear. "Were the other two victims on the list?"

Pat shook her head. "Although Scofield's firm was private,

we're trying to piece together its client list through SEC and other filings. So far, we've come up with wealthy individuals and pension fund managers. The Carrs' firm is private, too, but a lot more secretive. The surviving brother hasn't been cooperative."

"Let me know if you need help there," Jade said.

Dante held up his hand. "We got it." To Christian, "Anything on the knives?"

"All three were the same brand," Christian. "Maxam hunting knives, which you can buy on Amazon in packs of eight. No prints were found on them. Forensics believes the unsub wore gloves."

"Why did he leave the knives in their bodies?" asked Jade from the back of the room.

Everyone turned to Max.

Max thought for a moment. "I don't think the knives mean anything to him. They're a tool. A means to an end. The weapon of choice might be more important. A knife can be quieter than a gun. It's more personal. If you want to make sure you don't miss, you need to be close."

"But messier," said Dante.

"What if each knife was meant for each victim?" Micah said. "Like the sonnets."

"That's good," Dante said.

Max nodded thoughtfully.

"Or he's trying to make a statement," Christian said.

Dante smirked. "I think we got the point."

Pat, known throughout the bureau for her inappropriate dark humor, said, "That's bad."

# CHAPTER THIRTY-NINE

# The White House, Washington, DC

"EVERYONE," WHITNEY SAID, "please be seated."

Always the last to enter the Cabinet Room, she strode past the fireplace with *The Declaration of Independence, July 4, 1776* hanging above the mantle, the busts of George Washington and Benjamin Franklin, and around the table to the late eighteenth-century replica chair situated in the middle. Affixed to the back of her chair, which was two inches higher than the other chairs, was a brass plate engraved simply with the words The President. The other members' positions were affixed to the backs of their chairs. The elliptical mahogany table was purchased by President Richard Nixon in 1970 with his personal funds. Glancing at the United States flag and the flag of the president behind her, Whitney was awed, not for the first time, by how appropriately the latter represented her position: an eagle clutching white arrows in one talon and an olive branch in the other.

Once everyone was seated, she said, "Shall we begin? Sasha?"

Over the past week, the two of them had refined the document that Whitney had shown Sasha on Air Force One. Sean had typed it up. Whitney had not run it by Mo. Or Jo. The circle—or triangle—of people who knew about its contents had been kept intentionally small.

In front of each member, Sasha placed a folder bearing the presidential seal on the cover.

Whitney looked around the table at the faces of her cabinet members, their deputies and aides sitting behind them in chairs against the walls.

"'Let every nation know,'" she began, "'whether it wishes us well or ill, that we shall pay any price, bear any burden, meet any hardship, support any friend, oppose any foe to assure the survival and the success of liberty.'"

"What?" asked Secretary of Labor Tucker Price, a quizzical expression on his face.

"Kennedy," Secretary of Education Pravir Ratta said out of the side of his mouth. "John," he clarified.

"That's right," Whitney said. "President John F. Kennedy said those words as part of his inaugural address on January 20, 1961. It would later form the basis of the Kennedy Doctrine. To that end, I present to you the Fairchild Doctrine."

The expressions on the members' faces ranged from questioning to shocked.

"The United States will no longer sit on the sidelines of global affairs," Whitney said. "We have a responsibility to be at the center of the international order. Only then will we enjoy global prosperity and international peace and security. At one time, we were the most respected, emulated, and revered country on earth. There is no reason we cannot achieve that again. Starting today, we will strengthen relationships with our key allies and strategic partners and regain their trust."

Price's chair creaked as he shifted. "How are we going to do that?"

She pointed to his folder. "Read."

As they opened their folders, Whitney reached for the delicate cup on the table and took a sip of tea.

Price looked up. "I thought we were focusing on domestic issues this year. Like homelessness."

"Minimum wage," Vice President Josephine Bates said.

"Infrastructure," said Julio Casillas and Ashton Crawford, the secretaries of transportation and commerce.

"What about police brutality?" Jo continued. "African-Americans are more than three times as likely to—"

Whitney held up her hand. "Jo, I'm not abandoning those issues. We will continue to address homelessness, raise the minimum wage, and invest in our crumbling infrastructure—"

"You forgot police brutality," Jo said.

"Things aren't always black and white," Whitney said.

"For some of us, they are."

"Hear, hear," Sasha said.

Whitney flashed Jo a warning. "You didn't let me finish. Those issues are important to me, and my commitment hasn't changed, but I also want to focus on issues that impact everyone, not just Americans."

"Like what?" said Price, doubtful. He scanned his colleagues' faces to ascertain who was with him. Several other cabinet members seemed to share his doubts.

"Create opportunities for women. Reduce income inequality.

Provide an affordable quality education. Eliminate poverty. Combat climate change. Improve health outcomes. Ensure security by cracking down on cyberthreats." She nodded at Malachi Winters, chairman of US Cyber Command. "Private and government-sanctioned groups." A pause. "World peace."

She let the silence linger as they absorbed her words. Whitney gazed at each of their faces. "Franklin Roosevelt won World War I and created the international financial and diplomatic systems that we still use today. Kennedy dreamed about landing the first man on the moon. Johnson expanded civil and voting rights. Reagan helped end the Cold War." She pounded her fist on the table. "Name one watershed accomplishment over the last two decades."

Some of the members flinched. Whitney, typically not one to show emotion—especially anger—had their attention.

"We can no longer go it alone. We will no longer take our allies for granted."

"What about diminished wages and lost jobs in the US?" asked Ashton Crawford. The commerce secretary's hair, makeup, and nails were always flawless. Born in an old money New York family, she'd never had to worry about lost wages or jobs in her life, but Whitney had chosen her because she was smart and got things done.

"You'll be mindful of that in your trade negotiations," Whitney responded. To everyone, she said, "Unless we want to kowtow to authoritarianism or terrorism, we will engage in international diplomacy and continue to be a strong ally with NATO." She raised her hand toward Maricela Salcedo, the secretary of homeland security. "We will support those countries resisting outside agents and protect the territories and independence of such nations. And use military force, if necessary, to defend our economic and national interests."

She scanned the stunned faces of her cabinet.

Jo raised a quizzical eyebrow. "War... and peace?"

Titters from some of the members.

Whitney stood and glanced at the west wall across from her. Each president chose the paintings that hung there. Instead of paintings, she had chosen to hang three black-and-white photographs of suffragettes. Her favorite was one of women picketing in front of the White House.

To Jo, Whitney said, "You must fight for the things that matter."

# CHAPTER FORTY

# Arlington, Virginia

J ADE EXHALED AS she transitioned from the at-rest stance to the first move. Crossing her arms, she extended them to either side, her triceps perpendicular to the floor, her hands in fists, palms facing forward.

She stared into the intensity of her own light-brown eyes in the mirror, pretending she was her opponent. Fists to her hips, she extended her left arm, while her right fist came up in a slow-motion uppercut as she moved to a left front stance. She repeated the movement on the other side. She continued the movements of the *poomsae* against an imaginary opponent, her stances solid. No one could knock her off-balance. Her punches were sharp and swift. Her hands sliced through the air like horizontal guillotines.

When she completed the form, she sat cross-legged on the matted floor in the middle of the room, facing the wall-length mirror, which was split horizontally by a bar, like one found in a ballet studio. But no one performed ballet at Master Won Ho's

Tae Kwon Do school, located at a strip mall within walking distance from her house.

Jade closed her eyes and rested the back of her hands on her knees. "One…"

As she tried to meditate, she thought about her team meeting. Well, Dante's team meeting. Dante had followed up with her later and reported that after she'd left it had continued for another hour without much progress. Despite his frustration with the lack of movement on the case, he seemed motivated since his promotion. He was one of the first agents in the office every morning and one of the last to leave every evening. No one could accuse him of being lazy anymore.

Although she dreamed of being the first black woman FBI director, Jade had never given much thought to how it would feel to attain that goal. She'd always spent the least amount of time behind her desk as possible. It was harder to do while her team pursued the case without her.

Oh… she forgot. She was meditating and wasn't supposed to be thinking about anything at all.

She inhaled. "One."

Her mind drifted to Ethan Lawson, his starched white shirts and suspenders a throwback to bureau agents of days gone by. She wondered if he was ever coming back and why he'd been forced out. She hadn't looked into it.

New cases had gotten in the way.

"One."

"I can tell you're not meditating," said a serene voice.

Jade opened one eye.

In the mirror, she saw a diminutive man with short-cropped silver hair. He was in his blue *dobok*, a white athletic shirt underneath, standing near the entrance behind her. One end of his black belt sported six thin stripes. The other, his name emblazoned in gold cursive writing.

"How?" she asked, opening her other eye.

His soft footsteps padded across the floor until he stood before her. He pointed down.

She looked at her hands. Instead of being relaxed, they were balled into fists. One tapped her knee. "This was never my strong suit," she said. A fourth-degree black belt, she should have mastered meditation by now.

"It's the most important aspect of your training," her longtime instructor said.

"I know," she said, unclenching her fists. "How's the hip?"

He sat next to her, which took a little more effort than normal. Master Ho, in his sixties, was still recovering from hip surgery he'd had this past summer. He was back to work full time but couldn't train. Still, she wouldn't bet against him in a sparring match.

"It feels good."

"Looks as if it still hurts."

"How you feel is a state of mind, grasshopper."

She smiled at his reference to *The Karate Kid*.

Jade envied her teacher's calmness. The peace that radiated within and exuded from him, no matter the situation.

She hadn't mastered that either.

"How have you been?" he said. "You haven't been to class much."

At her rank, Jade could work out by herself, but she needed to attend a certain number of classes before testing for fifth degree. Given her schedule, training was difficult to fit in.

"Been busy."

She never talked about work with him. He knew what she did. Who she was. He focused on helping her achieve her martial arts goals. His only concern was her well-being. Sitting with him helped relieve her stress.

"Care to spar?"

Surprised, she said, "With that hip?"

The corner of his eyes crinkled. "I possess other weapons."

"This I know."

The last time she'd sparred with him, his round kick almost knocked off her head gear—and her head along with it.

The vibration of her phone filled the silence. "Saved by the buzz, I guess."

"Or divine intervention."

They both placed a hand on the floor and stood, Jade in a fluid motion, Master Ho in a more labored one. "I'll leave you to it then." A slight bow. "Good night, Ms. Harrington."

She bowed in return. "Night, sir."

Jogging to her bag resting against the wall, she dug out her phone. A text from Dante.

Pat found The God of Veritas. We're flying out tonight.

Where to?

See for yourself. Meet you at Dulles.

# CHAPTER FORTY-ONE

# The White House, Washington, DC

A SCALED-DOWN VERSION OF the New New Deal Coalition legislation, S.564—Put America Back to Work, sponsored by Senator Maureen McCallister, narrowly passed in the Senate. A similar bill, sponsored by the representative from Jo's state of California, passed in the House. The media—perhaps believing New Cubed would be difficult to understand by the mathematically challenged, a disproportionate segment of the US population—started calling it the New New Redo. With a lot less fanfare than the original, Whitney signed the bill into law at her desk in the Oval Office that afternoon, surrounded by business leaders, union representatives, and labor activists. Afterward, as the cameras of the White House press corps clicked, the three women—the president, the vice president, and the senator—held the document.

As she climbed the stairs, Whitney's mood was light. Mo and Jo had held up their end of the bargain. Arms had been twisted in both chambers of Congress. Cole Brennan had done his part, telling his listeners the bill's benefits and to contact their congressmen, multiple times if necessary.

Employers had started hiring in anticipation of the legislation's passing; unemployment would surely fall when Whitney received the next report. She imagined the discussions being held tonight between Senator Hampton and his lackey, Representative Howard Bell. Senator Sampson was no longer around to commiserate with them. As Sasha had expected, he had resigned last week.

*A win. Finally.*

Secret Service Agent Josh McPherson opened the door to the Residence and said, "Have a good evening, ma'am."

"You too, Josh."

He retreated.

Placing her briefcase on a stand in the foyer, she spotted the suitcase and travel bag.

Her eyes scanned the room until they met her husband's. Sitting on the sofa, he wore slacks, a white shirt, and jacket without a tie. A gin and tonic sat on the glass coffee table in front of him.

"Business trip?" she said, closing the door.

"No."

"Where are you going?"

"Home."

"This is your home."

"I'm needed in Missouri."

She hadn't moved. "Is it the bill?"

Put America Back to Work resurrected the infrastructure program from her defunct legacy legislation, allowing the federal government to administer grants and loans for building and repairing highways, bridges, parks, and low-income housing. Small and midsize businesses would be incentivized to bid on these projects. The increase of the minimum wage, on a regional basis, survived. Whitney still didn't know how Mo had convinced the conservative members of her party to agree to that provision.

Well, she had some idea.

"My brother's going to need some help figuring this out," Grayson said. "Our business—most businesses—won't be able to absorb the increased costs."

"When will you be back?"

"I don't know."

"What about the jobs initiative? Your commitment to the American people?"

"I can't let generations of my family's hard work go to waste," he said, standing. "You can find someone else to help the unemployed. Perhaps your new law will do the trick."

He stepped around the table and walked to the foyer. Hoisting the travel bag over his shoulder, he grabbed the handle of the suitcase.

She waved at the bags. "Grayson, someone can carry those for you."

He grabbed his newest fedora off the coat tree and perched it on his head. "As I said, I can handle my own business."

Whitney caught the double entendre.

He opened the door and turned to her, his expression unreadable. "Even though I don't agree with what you did, I love and support you, Madam President. But I must go."

"Of course. You're becoming an expert."

"At what?"

"Leaving."

## CHAPTER FORTY-TWO

# Seattle, Washington

THE FORD CROWN Victoria climbed a gigantic hill. Jade, sitting shotgun, hoped the traffic light would hold at green, for fear that they might roll backward. She breathed a sigh of relief as they passed under it, only then realizing she'd been rocking forward in her seat to help the car along.

At the top of Queen Anne Hill, a neighborhood north of downtown, the driver, a young agent from the Seattle FBI office named Brian Anderson, made a left on Galer Street, then a right on Fifth Avenue West. Parked cars lined both sides of the street, an inordinate number of them Subarus. Anderson drove slowly, periodically pulling over at an intersection, when a car headed toward them from the opposite direction. The agent finally found a parking spot around the corner from their destination.

Anderson, Jade, Max, Micah, and Dante exited the car and backtracked to a yellow two-story Craftsman house. They had staked out the address for a week, with no sighting of the object of their surveillance. The agents took turns watching the house, the off agents showering and sleeping at a hotel in Lower Queen Anne.

Dante had decided it was time to confront the person of interest.

On the porch, shoes of different sizes and styles—trainers, clogs, sneakers, loafers—were laid in a disorderly fashion just outside the front door. Two rocking chairs, in need of staining, faced the approaching sunset over the agents' shoulders.

A woman of about forty answered the door. "May I help you?"

Dante made the introductions. The woman examined their credentials.

"Does Jacob Collins live here?" Dante asked.

The woman pointed straight up. "He rents out the attic. We converted it into an apartment."

"We're here to ask him a few questions," he said. "Do you mind if we come in?"

He started to push past her to enter the house, but she didn't budge.

The woman gestured to the porch. "You're not very observant for an FBI agent."

"Ma'am, what are you talking about?"

She pointed. "You mind taking off your shoes?"

"I do," Dante said.

The woman looked at Jade, who nodded.

"Regulations," Jade said.

The woman frowned as she stepped back to open the door wider. "He comes in through a separate entrance, but you can come in this way. He's there now. I can hear him. Go up the stairs and turn left at the end of the hall. The last door on the left."

The agents filed past her and down the hallway with its hundred-year-old pine floors.

"What kind of trouble is he in?" the woman said from behind them.

"Don't know yet," Dante said as he started to climb.

"He's a person of interest in a criminal investigation," Jade clarified.

"It was only a matter of time," the homeowner said.

Jade stopped and turned. "Why do you say that?"

"Spends too much time up there alone, if you ask me. I've always wondered what he does up there. Friends never come over. He never goes out. Must be up to something."

"He could be playing video games. Virtual reality. Something like that." Jade thought about the killing sites: New York, Chicago, DC. "Does he travel?"

"Not much that I'm aware of. He works up there. Pays his rent on time and doesn't bother us, so we don't bother him."

"We'll need to talk to you as well."

The woman slipped on a Patagonia vest. "I'll be in my garden out back."

At the end of the hall, they opened the door, not bothering to knock, and climbed the narrow stairs to the attic. Jade's hand moved to the grip of her .40 Glock 23. She paused at the top. It opened to a living room with a green secondhand sofa behind a leaning, low metal coffee table. A thirty-six-inch TV rested on a simple stand. Against one wall, a small table served as a desk, with a desktop computer on it. The table's surface was littered with empty cups, Red Bull cans, and candy wrappers. It seemed The God of Veritas loved Snickers.

The apartment reeked of marijuana.

Above the table was a window you could only peer out of if you were standing. A body of water and snowcapped mountains were visible in the distance. The wind whispered outside.

The low, slanted ceilings, an inverted *V*, prevented Jade from standing at her full height.

A skinny white man in his early to midtwenties, wearing a faded Occupy Seattle T-shirt and jeans, came out of a back room, barefoot, chewing on a candy bar.

"Who the hell are you?"

Dante hunched over, stepped forward, and introduced himself and the other agents.

"Let me see some ID."

They flashed their badges. The man examined each badge, as if the agents were trying to access the San Francisco mint. When he finished, he still seemed unsatisfied.

"How did you get in?" he asked. "Don't you need a warrant or something?"

"Your landlord let us in," Dante said.

"She can do that?" When they didn't respond, he crossed to his computer and locked the screen. Turning his back to it, he said, "Why are you here?"

"We want to ask you some questions," Dante said, moving to the couch. "Take a seat."

"I'll stand, thank you."

"Suit yourself."

Jade and Max joined Dante on the sofa, while Anderson remained in front of the stairs. Micah grabbed a flimsy chair from the small kitchen table.

"What's your full name?" Dante said.

"I don't have to tell you that."

"We're here to talk to you," Jade said. "Or would you rather accompany us downtown to the FBI office and make this official?"

The man stared into Jade's eyes for less than a second before he decided to take the easier path. "Jacob Collins."

"Middle name?" Dante asked.

"Michael."

Pat had already determined his real name. They were testing him.

"Tell us about 'The God of Veritas,'" Dante said.

"How did you find me? My personal information on Twitter is private."

"Nothing is private," Dante said. "I'm waiting."

"I tweet. So what?"

"You tweet a lot."

Dante had obtained a search warrant for all of The God of Veritas's tweets, direct messages, photos, videos, and notifications. Jade had reviewed them on the plane ride west.

The young man shrugged. "Again, so what?"

"Are you the Shakespeare Killer?" asked Jade.

"What?" Collins's eyes bulged. He turned. A tremor was starting to develop in his hand as he pulled out the chair from the table behind him and sat. "Is that why you're here?"

"Answer the question," Dante said.

"Of course not."

"Then why is it," Jade said, "that every time you tweet about someone—especially someone wealthy—they end up dead?"

Sweat popped up on his pale forehead, despite the coolness of the room. "It's… it's a coincidence."

"Three coincidences is a lot, wouldn't you say?"

The curls of his medium-length brown hair began to shake. "That doesn't mean they're not coincidences. Besides, I tweet about a lot of people."

"I hope no one else you tweet about turns up dead," Dante said.

By now, Collins's eyes were ready to burst out of their sockets. "Do I need a lawyer?"

"Do you?" Dante asked.

His mouth opened and closed like a fish. "I don't think so. I didn't do anything. I just tweet, man."

"If you answer our questions truthfully," Jade said in a soothing tone, "you shouldn't need one."

He shot her a grateful look. "Okay."

"Where were you," Dante said, checking his notebook, "on the nights of January 3, January 17, and February 8 of this year?"

"I was here."

"Shouldn't you check a calendar?"

"I don't go anywhere, man. Honest. I'm an *online* activist. I spend most of my life online."

"What do you do," Jade asked, "for work?"

"I write a blog. Sell ads on my site. Generate affiliate income."

Dante took in the small apartment. "That's enough to make a living?"

"I get by."

"Seattle's an expensive place to live," Jade said. She knew this from the time she'd spent in Seattle last year.

Collins said, "This is getting by."

"Your tweets," Max said, "are aggressive. Almost threatening."

"Not to me. I write about stuff. Issues. Injustices. Try to keep our public leaders honest. But I don't *do* anything. I encourage other people to act."

"Like a consultant," Jade said helpfully. Out of the corner of her eye, she saw Max's lips twitch.

"What?" said Collins.

"What about your tweets about President Fairchild?" Jade asked.

The vitriol of his tweets had intensified over the last few months.

"She's a conservative," he said.

"Not a moderate?"

"There's no such thing. Today you must pick a side. It's us versus them. You can't compromise with the enemy."

She leaned forward, interested. "You see this as a war?"

"Of course it's a war. Only one side can win. The winner decides the course of this country for the next forty years. The loser risks oblivion."

"I thought this was the *United* States."

"You haven't been paying attention then," he said, his tone disdainful. "This nation is divided. More so now than at any time since the Civil War." He shook his head. "We use facts that only support our entrenched positions. Watch different news programs. Read different books. Recognize different histories. Live among our own kind. Unofficially, some states have already seceded. There are two Americas. We'll never be united again."

"If that's true," Jade said, "then what's the point?"

"What's the point of what?"

"Your tweets. Being an activist."

He blinked. After a moment, he said in a lame voice, "I still have to try. Even if it's a lost cause."

"How does Fairchild fit into all this?"

"She's a dinosaur. Like the rest of the old guard who've been in office forever. They need to go away and die."

As the other occupants in the room stiffened, Jacob Michael Collins realized he had just threatened the life of the president of the United States and members of other branches of the federal government while in a room full of federal agents.

He held up his hands. "Whoa! Everyone chill! It was a figure of speech." He dropped his hands. "What I meant was, she doesn't represent the progressivism of our party. Our generation."

Jade frowned. "That doesn't sound like the Fairchild I know."

This stopped Collins short. "You know her?"

"Yes, I do."

He seemed stumped.

Dante slid off the sofa. "We need to check out your apartment."

Max moved to the bedroom. Micah covered the kitchen. Dante checked out the bathroom. Jade remained seated on the sofa, studying the books stacked on the floor against the wall.

Collins jumped at the sudden activity.

"We need to take your computer," Jade said.

The God of Veritas backed up until his butt was on the table, his arms wide as if he were a basketball defender, blocking them from taking it. "You can't."

"We'll obtain a court order," Jade said.

Collins's shoulders slumped.

Jade signaled Anderson. With donned gloves, he picked up the computer and headed toward the stairs.

"What am I going to *do* until you return it?"

She thought for a moment. "*Something*?"

Collins looked at her, not understanding.

Jade stood, hitting her head on the ceiling.

That's what she got for being a smart-ass.

# CHAPTER FORTY-THREE

# The White House, Washington, DC

LEANING AGAINST THE back of the loveseat, Whitney puffed on a Cohiba cigar as she stared out the window at the Washington Monument. On the table was a glass of Pavillon Blanc du Château Margaux, the bottle next to it nearly empty.

After Grayson left, she'd gone to the Oval Library and perused her first editions: Louisa May Alcott, Maya Angelou, Jane Austen, Charlotte and Emily Brontë, Toni Morrison, Carson McCullers, Edith Wharton, and Virginia Woolf, among many others. She had kept Alcott's *Little Women,* a gift from Landon Phillips, despite everything he'd done. It wasn't the book's fault. It was one of her favorite stories growing up—Jo March, an early exposure to female independence. Plus, the book was in mint condition.

She had idled in the library, inhaling the calming, musty

aroma. She had brought a few of the books back to the West Sitting Hall, but tonight, no matter which book she picked up, she couldn't concentrate on the words.

Whitney had known Grayson would be upset over the legislation. They'd discussed it beforehand, but he'd seemed nonplussed, perhaps thinking it wouldn't pass.

She'd never thought he would *leave* over it.

His company treated its employees fairly. He'd told her so many times. But not every employer acted like Fairchild Industries. Some required regulation to do the right thing. Didn't he believe every American worker deserved a living wage? He would respond that there was a better way. To let the free market work.

He didn't even need to be present for them to engage in this age-old argument.

The front door of the Residence burst open.

Hurriedly putting out the cigar in the ashtray, Whitney slipped both under the sofa cushion.

"Hey, Mom!"

Whitney rose. "Emma!"

Her daughter ran toward her but pulled up short.

"What's wrong?"

"Nothing."

"Are you crying?"

"No," Whitney said, rubbing imaginary sleep out of her eyes. "Long day."

She hugged Emma but stopped short herself.

Her daughter hadn't come alone.

"Hello," Whitney said to Emma's guest.

Skipping back to her friend, Emma pulled her forward.

"Surprise, Mom! This is Megan. My roommate."

There was trepidation on Emma's face. This young woman

wasn't the same roommate that Whitney had met at the beginning of the school year, when she and Grayson had dropped Emma off. She shook Megan's hand.

"Hello, Megan."

"Madam President."

"I begged Josh to keep Megan's background check a secret," Emma explained, noticing the expression on Whitney's face. "Don't get him in trouble, Mother."

"We can talk about that later. Welcome, Megan. Please," Whitney said, gesturing toward the loveseat. As Whitney settled into one of the matching chairs, the two young women sat on the sofa, close enough that their bodies were almost touching.

Emma's roommate was dressed in a black T-shirt, green army jacket, scruffy jeans, and Birkenstocks, despite the cold weather. Her hair was the same length and style as Emma's. But where Emma's hair was light-brown with a tint of auburn, like Whitney's, Megan's hair was dyed black.

Turning to Emma, Whitney said, "This… is a surprise."

"We should've called," Emma said, missing the point, "but we were here for the Black Lives Still Matter march, and I wasn't sure we'd have time to visit." She gazed around the room. "Where's Dad?"

Whitney shifted her gaze to Megan. "Would you care for something to drink, Megan?"

The young woman's features were strong and feminine, her face unlined and without makeup. She shook her head. "I'm fine, ma'am."

Emma touched Megan's hand. "Are you sure? Don't be shy. She doesn't bite. Except when I bring home bad grades…"

Her hand remained on Megan's.

"Since I presume you're the same age as Emma, and not old enough to drink legally, how about some water? Or juice?"

"Actually," Megan said, "I'm old enough."

Whitney wondered how old she was.

"Do you have any cold-brewed coffee?" Megan asked. "In a can?"

"I'm sure we can scrounge one up." Whitney looked at Emma.

"The same."

"When did you—"

She refrained from completing her inquiry into when Emma had started drinking cold-brewed coffee, or any coffee for that matter, and instead picked up the phone to call the ground-floor kitchen.

"Mom, where's Dad?" Emma asked again.

"He returned to Clayton," Whitney said, tucking her legs beneath her. "Something to do with the business."

"Darn," Emma said. "I wanted him to meet Megan."

*This must be serious.*

"When did you become roommates?" Whitney asked. "I thought you were rooming with—"

Emma shifted on the sofa. "It didn't work out."

"I see."

After a knock on the door, a butler entered, setting a tray with two glasses of ice and two cans on the table in front of the young women.

"Thank you," Whitney said to him. He departed.

Megan poured coffee into a glass and handed it to Emma before pouring a glass for herself. Whitney gazed at her daughter's patrician nose, so much like Grayson's.

To Megan, Whitney asked, "Do you go to Princeton as well?"

"I do. I'm a senior. Majoring in social justice."

Whitney sipped her wine. "That's wonderful. How did you two meet?"

"At the library," Emma said.

"At an event," said Megan, almost at the same time.

Inclining her head, Whitney asked, "Which was it?"

The girls shared a glance.

"It was an event," Emma said. "At the library," they finished together.

"Em and I were working the same event," Megan clarified.

*Em?*

"I see," Whitney said.

Emma said, "Stop 'I seeing' us, Mom."

"What are you talking about?" Whitney asked.

"You 'I see' when you don't want to say how you really feel."

"I was unaware I did that."

"You do."

"I see," Whitney said, smiling, as she rose to retrieve another bottle of white wine from the refrigerator.

The occasion called for it.

Megan whispered to Emma, "Your mother's got jokes."

"She can be humorous in her own way," Emma whispered back.

When Whitney returned, she said to Emma, "How are your classes?"

"Fine. I declared my major."

"And?"

A slight lift of Emma's chin. "Politics."

Whitney sighed. "I failed both my children. Where did I go wrong?"

"I'm not going into politics," Emma said. "I'm going to be a lawyer."

"What kind?"

"Civil rights."

"I see."

"Mom! Stop!"

"Sorry, I forgot."

"We've been going to a lot of events. Talking to the people. Trying to understand their issues. Their concerns."

*The people.*

"What are they telling you?" Whitney asked.

"Things need to change. I want to help them."

"I..."—she almost said "see"—"I'm proud of you." She paused. "Are you staying here tonight?"

"Yeah."

"Your room is always ready," Whitney said.

Even though Chandler and Emma were in college at the time of Whitney's inauguration last year, it was important to her that they have their own rooms when they came "home." Emma's room was the West Bedroom; Chandler slept in the East Bedroom.

"Megan may sleep in the Queens' Bedroom," Whitney added.

She savored another sip of wine, her smile hidden behind the glass, while her daughter and her college roommate shared a disconcerting glance.

# CHAPTER FORTY-FOUR

# Washington, DC

J ADE SPENT THE return trip from Seattle reading Veritas's blog. The topics ranged from free education, the environment, immigration, campaign finance reform, affordable housing, and income inequality.

While the others slept, she had turned to Max in the seat beside her. "You think he's good for it?"

Max shook his head. "He's too disorganized, for one thing. His tweets are reactive. He doesn't present sociopathic or psychopathic tendencies. Plus, he has a moral responsibility and a social conscience. I don't think he's our man."

Over the next week, Pat reported that Veritas hadn't made any trips via plane or train under his own name in the last year, but his alibis weren't airtight either. His landlord couldn't swear he was at home on the nights of the murders. The NSA tracked his phone to the apartment location, which didn't necessarily prove he was there. With no coworkers to interview, and seemingly no offline friends, they were hoping his computer could provide some answers. The activity on it provided an alibi of sorts. He or someone else had tweeted from his computer at the time of the murders. Other than that, the computer offered nothing helpful.

As Jade left the sandwich shop across the street, carrying her lunch, Christian ambled toward her. They stopped in the middle of the sidewalk outside FBI HQ.

"Hey, you," she said.

"Hey, yourself."

She shielded her eyes from the unexpected sunlight. It was supposed to rain today. "Anything new on Hurley?" Dante had left him behind to oversee the Finn Hurley investigation.

Christian shook his head.

"How are you and Dante getting along?"

"He's not you."

They were silent for a moment.

"What are your next steps?" she asked.

His gaze lifted upward as he prepared an answer. "Watch out!"

Christian grabbed her in a bear hug and tackled her to the ground as something crashed into the spot where she'd been standing. He lay on top of her, both of them staring at a chunk of concrete and some scattered pieces.

Shaken but trying not to show it, she said, "You're heavy."

He stood and offered her a hand.

She looked up at the netting installed to prevent an accident like this from occurring. There was a hole in it.

It was no secret that the FBI headquarters was falling apart. If the exterior was bad, the inside was worse. For years, agents had waited for Congress to appropriate funds to replace it with a building better suited for the twenty-first century and equipped for the never-ending war on terrorism. Jade had hoped the money appropriated from the infrastructure legislation would pay for construction of a new building, but those hopes were squashed with the repeal of the New New Deal Coalition Act. Her attitude regarding the president's latest legislative attempt was "wait and see."

After they brushed themselves off, she said, "That was close. Thanks." She told him about hitting her head in Veritas's apartment.

"Two times in one week," he said. "You might want to be more careful."

# CHAPTER FORTY-FIVE

# Washington, DC

DEV SAT ON a stool at the counter by the window, eating a turkey sandwich with cucumbers and sprouts and pretending to read the *Washington Post*. The proprietor was pounding a slab of meat at the back of the establishment. A young man, who resembled him, stood behind the register.

The door chimed as another customer entered.

Dev chanced a glance at Jade Harrington, who waited in line to place her order.

Tall. Striking. Intense. Confident. A formidable opponent.

Something stirred in Dev, a feeling unlike the competitive juices that flowed within her before a game. Before a kill.

The heralded FBI agent took in her surroundings. Dev averted her eyes by gazing out the window at the pedestrian traffic on Ninth Street. Nevertheless, Dev sensed the other woman's eyes lingering on the back of her head for a moment before moving on.

When next Dev stole another glimpse of Harrington, the agent was placing her order.

Dev was in DC on a reconnaissance mission to study this FBI agent who hunted her. She knew of Harrington, of course, but had never met her.

Never worked with her.

Dev had just witnessed the blond agent, who looked like a linebacker, save Harrington from being hit by the concrete debris.

How ironic it would have been if the building in which the agent worked had dispatched Dev's nemesis for her.

Dev waited for the two agents to enter the employees' entrance of the Federal Bureau of Investigation before exiting the shop. She headed in the opposite direction toward Federal Triangle Station.

She had a plane to catch.

# CHAPTER FORTY-SIX

# Washington, DC

"I'M RESPONSIBLE FOR helping you try new things. Otherwise you'd eat the same thing every night."

Jade couldn't disagree with Zoe there. She chewed her spiced grilled chicken, savoring the different flavors. "Good call."

The two friends shared a late dinner at a bistro table for two, enjoying a variety of tapas. In addition to the chicken, they'd ordered the special written in trendy lettering on the sandwich board outside the front door: sautéed shrimp, patatas bravas, and roasted sweet corn. The Spanish restaurant was a new one in Logan Circle, a neighborhood just north of downtown.

"Qué pasa?" Zoe said.

"Not much. You?"

An unusual shadow crossed Zoe's angular face. "'Enough' didn't pass."

"Enough" was the legislation aimed at drastically reducing gun violence in the United States. Last year, a lone white male gunman—it was usually a lone white male gunman—had mowed down over one hundred and fifty elementary school children playing outside at recess. Enclosed in a fenced yard, the kids had offered him a human shooting gallery.

Zoe lowered her head. "I thought we had the votes this time."

"Memories are short," Jade said.

"Mine is long," Zoe said. "I can't forget about those kids. I don't want them to die in vain."

Jade remembered the images from the news: the young man and his vacant countenance, teachers and students scrambling for cover, teachers transforming themselves into human shields to protect their students. Most of the carnage was captured on the school's video surveillance system. A female teacher ended up tackling the gunman, saving an untold number of children's lives. Her heroism was rewarded with the loss of her own.

"It'll pass someday," Jade said. "Mass shootings won't cease on their own."

"Wouldn't it be fabulous to go to a movie theater or a concert or a school and not worry about getting shot?"

"Or a shopping mall."

Zoe cocked her head. "When was the last time you were in a mall?"

"Theoretically," Jade conceded.

"Remember when mass shootings occurred only at post offices?"

"They called it 'going postal,'" Jade said. Impulsively, she grabbed Zoe's hand and stared into her eyes. "You're on the right side of history on this, my friend. Don't give up."

She squeezed and let go. Zoe raised her hand to her heart and bowed her head in thanks. "I can't wait 'to provide new guards for their future security.'"

Not entirely sure what Zoe meant, Jade said, "We will."

The two friends ate in silence for a moment.

"Talked to Kyle lately?" Zoe said, her eyes narrowing, ready to scrutinize every nuance of Jade's response.

"No. The case is over."

"It's over? No one's been charged."

"That's true. Even so, there's no reason for me to talk to Kyle."

Zoe bit her lip to prevent herself from smiling.

*Was that relief?*

"You haven't heard," she said.

Jade sipped her sangria. "Heard what?"

"Kyle is seeing someone."

Swallowing with difficulty, Jade said, "Huh."

"They're engaged," Zoe said, still staring at Jade.

"Huh," Jade said again.

"Aren't you curious who it is?"

Jade popped a shrimp into her mouth. "Not really."

"It's Brittney Summers."

Jade didn't react outwardly, but she forcibly swallowed the shrimp and carefully placed her fork, tines down, on her plate.

Summers played in the WNBA, a point guard with the Seattle Storm, and was a former All-American at the University of Connecticut. Although Jade was a few years older, they had played against each other in AAU, college, and the pros. The rivalry was intense. They didn't hate each other, exactly, but they wouldn't hang out together after a game either.

Zoe searched her face. "Say something."

Jade picked up her glass again. "Good for them."

After dinner, Zoe left on her motorcycle, and Jade sauntered toward her car parked on a side street. She stopped on the sidewalk by a man sitting in front of Le Diplomat on Fourteenth Street. He appeared homeless.

"Do you got any money? I'm hungry."

She glanced at the expensive French restaurant, the scene epitomizing the American divide. Jade handed the man her leftovers. "It doesn't compare to the food in there, but it's pretty good."

He stared into her eyes. "Thank you, Chosen One."

She started at the reminder of what her father used to say to her. A phrase from the Bible. The Gospel of Matthew.

Later, as she drove across the Memorial Bridge, she listened to the eighties station on SiriusXM and softly sang the words to most of the songs, tapping her fingers on the steering wheel to the beat.

As the snow fell, she tried not to think of Kyle with someone else.

Jade didn't enjoy driving in the snow in DC. The transplants from New York and Boston drove too fast, to prove it wasn't a big deal. DC natives couldn't drive in the snow at all. And everyone else was caught in the middle. Fortunately, there weren't many cars on the bridge.

"It's Raining Men" came on.

*Perfect.*

She remembered the barista at the coffee shop singing it at the top of his lungs, oblivious to Kyle and Jade sitting at a table, his only audience.

She hadn't talked to Kyle since her surprise appearance at Jade's team celebration for closing the Robin Hood case. Kyle had been in DC on business. They hadn't talked much that night, and Kyle left the next day to fly home to Seattle.

Jade missed their conversations, a light sparring between two strong women. But Jade couldn't offer Kyle anything more. That was the problem.

Jade's life was here. With the FBI. With her team. With the victims and their families, who depended on her to seek justice for them. To find out the truth. Kyle's life was in Seattle. With her business. Her professional basketball team. Her political influencers. And so Kyle had moved on.

With Summers.

As Jade steered the car carefully over the bridge into Virginia, she changed the radio station to classical music.

# CHAPTER FORTY-SEVEN

# The White House,
# Washington, DC

"DON'T MINCE WORDS."

"It's bad," said Dr. Hayley Copeland, Whitney's chief economic advisor.

"Perhaps mince a little bit," Whitney said.

Copeland's face remained stoic. "Since the Sino-Russian trade agreement went into effect, our exports have fallen one percent, which might not sound like a lot…"

"But…"

"It equates to a hundred and thirty-eight billion dollars in lost revenue for US companies."

Hayley sat in a chair pulled up next to the *Resolute* desk in the Oval Office. Hayley and Whitney had met in college, at Northwestern University. Whitney had gone on to Harvard Law School while Hayley remained in Chicago, attaining a PhD in economics from the University of Chicago and then becoming a tenured professor. Whitney convinced her former classmate to leave academia and join the administration. Smart and attractive, Hayley knew her stuff, but the frustration of dealing with the negative effects of the trade agreement was evident on her middle-aged face.

"Which countries?" Whitney asked.

"Exports are down with all our trading partners, but the major ones have been hit the hardest: UK, Germany, France. Even our buddies to the north."

"Canada," Whitney said, disappointed.

"Canadians aren't any different from the rest. They don't care that their goods are made in China, as long as they're cheap."

"Options?"

"Companies will decrease prices. Promote more heavily. It'll be a downward spiral to the bottom. Not sure there's much we— the government—can do. Maybe talk to China again?"

Whitney shook her head. Min had made it clear that avenue was closed. "What about New Cubed?"

"We won't realize any significant benefits for a few months," Hayley added. "So the situation is bad but hopeful."

"Bad but hopeful. Have you found someone to replace Grayson yet?"

Hayley handed her a sheet of paper. "Here's a list of candidates—"

Sasha knocked and entered without an invitation, looking drained.

Whitney stood, knowing immediately that something was very, very wrong. "Sasha?"

"I need to speak with you," her chief of staff said. "Privately."

Whitney's eyes didn't leave Sasha's. "Hayley?"

Sasha's eyes followed the economic advisor until the door

closed behind her. She stood in front of Whitney's desk. The two women stared at each other.

"What is it?"

"It's CJ Brennan," Sasha said.

"What happened?" Whitney asked. "Was he beaten up again?"

"No," said Sasha, sorrow in her brown eyes. "He committed suicide last night."

# CHAPTER FORTY-EIGHT

# Kensington, Maryland

JADE ATTENDED A lot of funerals, usually for the victims of the serial killers she chased.

CJ Brennan was a victim of a different sort. Bullied most of his short life, first because of his dad and then because he was gay, pretty, and could sing.

And he wasn't afraid to speak his mind.

Depression was a silent, lonely, and relentless killer. No one was immune from its tentacles' reach. No matter how beautiful or rich or famous you were.

Ever since he'd come out last year on a liberal cable news program, despite or because of his conservative father, CJ had become a mini-celebrity. He spoke out about gay and trans rights. His looks and his father's occupation proved a tantalizing combination for social media and the television talk-show circuit.

He'd also become a target for cruelty.

CJ's family sat on chairs set up in a row. The rest of the

gathering stood behind them, Jade off to the side. She smelled the fresh flowers on top of the casket. Cole cried, unashamed, just as he had when Jade entered the church that morning.

The small Presbyterian church near the White House had been packed with a who's who of US politics and media. Cole Brennan, sitting in the front pew, stared at the large portrait of CJ next to the casket, the young man's hair blond and long. Jade touched Cole's arm, and he slowly turned. When he saw her, his face crumpled. Jade tried to take his hand. Instead, he stepped out into the aisle between the pews and wrapped her in a bear hug, which was oddly comforting for her.

And he wouldn't let go.

She peeked over his shoulder. Some of the other guests were looking at them in surprise. Jade guessed they'd never seen the most conservative white guy of them all hugging a black woman before.

After Jade hugged his wife, Ashley, and the children, Cole asked her to sit up front with the family. Jade demurred. During the service, she sat in a pew in the back of the church, flipping through the Bible she grabbed off the back of the pew in front of her, admiring the stained-glass windows high on the wall, studying the intricate sculpture of Jesus nailed to the cross over the altar, and glancing at the back of Cole's head.

Jade wasn't the only one in the church with tears in her eyes when members from CJ's high school glee club came together to sing "Over the Rainbow."

The last one to leave, Cole sat motionless in his pew, staring at the casket long after the funeral director had lowered the lid for the last time.

Now at the memorial park, Ashley sat next to him holding his beefy hand, with their five surviving children sitting next to her in chronological order: Colleen, Madeline, Ryan, Kaitlin, and Ronnie. All of them were crying, except for Kaitlin, who'd had a role in the TSK case.

It was cold but clear. The rain the forecasters predicted never materialized. The park was peaceful, with its manicured lawns, shrubs, and pine trees. The private graveside service included family, select coworkers, and exclusive guests. Mourners sniffled and cried.

Cole wept.

Ashley's face was pale and withered. The former model had aged ten years since Jade last saw her a year ago.

Jade kept her eyes on the family, ignoring the chaplain holding the Bible and tuning out his words of comfort. Looking at him or the casket dredged up memories of her parents' funeral.

After the service, Cole encircled his wife and children in a group hug.

Jade waited her turn and hugged Cole and Ashley again.

"He left a note," Cole said, wiping his nose with a handkerchief.

"Was it the bullying?" Jade asked.

"Partly," he said. "Mostly it was me. He never got over the fact that he let TSK into our home and almost got his sister killed."

"That wasn't your fault. Or his."

"TSK wanted to scare me or kill me. If it weren't for me, that godforsaken liberal killer wouldn't have been there."

Jade said nothing; it was true.

"Thanks for coming, little lady," Cole said, smiling through his pain, knowing she hated the nickname.

Ashley squeezed Jade's arm. "It means a lot."

Before Jade left, she needed to speak to one more person. She walked over.

"Madam President," Jade said.

The two hugged. Although they were separated in age by over twenty years, a kinship had blossomed between them. It was more than their being two alpha women trying to make it in a man's world—it was a strong relationship based on mutual trust and respect. These traits, at a time when they were most needed, were becoming less common between women.

"How's the new job?" President Whitney Fairchild asked her.

"It's been an adjustment," Jade said.

"That's what I like about you; you're always truthful with me."

"Don't know any other way to be." Jade tilted her head toward the grave site. "Like him."

The president nodded, her gaze drifting toward some departing mourners. Jade spotted Senators Hampton and Sampson, and Representative Howard Bell, walking away. Sampson's arm was around a woman's waist, presumably his wife's. "I wish you had taken me up on my offer."

"The FBI is in my blood, ma'am."

"We'll see," Fairchild said. "Well… you're the boss now. 'For unto whomsoever much is given, of him shall be much required.'"

With a faint smile, Jade said, "My father used to say that."

Fairchild cocked her head. "I would like to meet him."

Jade swallowed. "He's gone."

"I should have remembered. I'm sorry."

"No worries," Jade said. "You two would've had a lot to talk about."

A moment of silence.

"He's come around," the president said, waving her hand toward the inscription on the granite headstone.

COLE "CJ" BRENNAN JR.

LOVING SON AND BROTHER
WITH THE VOICE OF AN ANGEL

"What do you mean?"

"Cole never liked the nickname," Fairchild said. "He didn't want anyone to forget who his namesake was named after."

"As if anyone could."

"He also didn't appreciate that his son preferred singing in the glee club to running down a football field."

"Not everyone is destined to be a great athlete."

"No," the president said. "How boring would that be?"

Jade shrugged and smiled. "Well…"

Fairchild smiled. "Ah… right."

"He's come around in more ways than one," Jade said, inclining her head toward Cole, who was shaking hands with friends of CJ's, some prominent activists in the gay community.

Shifting her gaze back to Jade, Fairchild said, "Have you seen Blake?"

"No. How's he doing?"

"He's mending. I was hoping you two would…" She paused. "I must go, but we should get together soon." The president grasped both of Jade's hands in hers. "I miss our talks."

"Me too."

Fairchild started to walk away and then turned. "Agent Harrington?"

"Yes, Madam President?"

"Do you know the secret to success?"

"What?"

"Don't be afraid."

*Afraid of what?* Jade didn't ask.

"Ma'am, we need to go," said Josh McPherson, stepping toward Fairchild and nodding at Jade.

She was acquainted with him but didn't know him well.

He and the rest of the coterie of secret service agents escorted the president to her limousine, idling in the middle of a long line of limousines and black Suburban SUVs on the blocked-off street next to the cemetery. The throng of press waiting there started shouting questions at Fairchild.

Jade walked in the opposite direction.

As she crested the hill on her way to the cemetery's parking lot, from behind her came, "Mrs. Harrington! Wait!"

She turned. Kaitlin Brennan ran toward her. The girl came to an abrupt stop in front of Jade.

Jade crouched, her arms on her thighs, her eyes level with the girl's. She'd be about ten now.

"Yes?"

"I never thanked you for saving my life."

She wasn't sure how Kaitlin remembered, since she was unconscious by the time Jade had reached her on that fateful night. Her parents or siblings could have told her.

Jade smiled. "You don't need to thank me, Kaitlin. I was doing my job."

"When I have nightmares about that night, I think about you, and it makes me happy."

"Why is that?"

"Because you've got girl power. My daddy says you're strong and not afraid of anything."

"Did you tell your parents about these nightmares?"

The girl shook her head.

"Promise me you'll tell them," Jade said.

A solemn nod. "You're my shero."

*She*ro. Not *he*ro.

Kaitlin flung her arms around Jade's neck, almost knocking her off-balance. Jade hesitated, then hugged her back, the child's silky blond hair brushing Jade's cheek. She was surprised by the tears pressing against her own eyelids.

Pulling away, Kaitlin ran off to rejoin her family.

Jade didn't move. Despite all the accomplishments she'd achieved in her life—the trophies, medals, awards, press clippings, accolades—the simple gratitude of this young child might have been the most precious.

You couldn't put that in a box in the basement.

# CHAPTER FORTY-NINE

## Fairfax, Virginia

"YOU AGAIN?" SAID the skinny bartender with the punk-rock black hair. She leaned forward, her hands on the bar. Her rolled-up sleeves revealed a colorful tattoo on her right forearm. "You've got a new partner."

Micah looked from the bartender to Jade, confused. "You've been here with someone else?"

To Jade, the bartender said, "Will there be singing this time?"

Incredulous, Micah said, "You? Singing?" To the bartender, "Tell me more."

Jade said nothing. She gazed at the bartender with a look that said she didn't want to talk about the time she and Christian had gotten drunk in this very bar. By noon on that day, they were sitting on these same wooden stools, heads back, arms slung over each other's shoulders, singing "Bohemian Rhapsody" at the top of their lungs. The bartender gave her an imperceptible nod before turning to Micah. "A Brit?"

He nodded.

"Sweet," she said. "The first one for you is on the house. What can I get for you two? Guinness? Shots?"

She remembered.

"No," said Jade, more sharply than warranted. Softening her voice, she said, "A lager. English. Something on the lighter side."

"We'll take two Golden Glories," Micah said.

"You got it," the young woman said, pushing off the bar and grabbing two pint glasses. She slid one under a draft tap.

Jade eyed him. "Golden Glory?"

"Trust me," he said.

She held his gaze, wondering if she did trust him. Yesterday, after returning to the bureau from CJ's funeral, she'd run into Micah in the hallway. Noticing her subdued manner, he'd asked her what was wrong. When she told him, he invited her here. She protested that she had work to do. He said taking a few hours off from the case wouldn't hurt. She finally agreed.

Pictures of English royalty—including an American princess, political figures and celebrities—pennants of all the English Premier League teams, and English quotes and slogans covered almost every inch of the dark brown wood-paneled walls. An enormous Union Jack flag was displayed prominently on one wall.

The Stratford Arms was crowded because of the soccer game that was showing on every television in the place. Judging by the jerseys they wore, the patrons were evenly split by which team they supported.

"This is the quarterfinal of the FA Cup," Micah explained. "It's a big deal."

"I know," Jade said.

The bartender placed the glasses on cardboard coasters on

the bar. Looking at Jade, she said, "Let me know when you get hungry. The fish and chips are ready this time."

She winked before moving away to help another customer.

"What's up with you two?" Micah asked.

"Nothing," Jade said, picking up her glass and holding it up for a toast. "I guess I'm cheering for Chelsea."

Micah picked up his glass. He looked like a soccer player, the formfitting red Arsenal jersey covering his upper body like a second skin.

"Always the contrarian," he said. "Cheers."

They clinked glasses and drank.

"Up for a bet?" he asked.

"Maybe."

"If my team wins, you have to sing the team fight song. And vice versa."

"I don't know the words."

Waving his arm, taking in the room, he said, "You'll have help."

Noncommittal, Jade changed the subject. "I like Mertens."

Micah nodded a few times at the name of Chelsea's versatile midfielder. "Me too. He just plays for the wrong team."

They sipped their beers as they watched the game on the flat-screen television high on the wall. The crowd in the bar cheered at every scoring chance, exceptional skill, and defensive stop, and groaned at every dispossession, errant pass, and uncalled foul.

At the half, Micah asked, "What do you think?"

"Chelsea is playing too far forward. They're susceptible to an overlap by a defender."

"They have to be. This is all or nothing."

"If they keep playing this way, it'll be nothing," she said. She took a sip of her pint. "Did you play?"

"A little."

Micah was almost as tight-lipped about his past as she was about hers. She didn't tell him she'd also played soccer.

The bartender slammed through the swinging saloon doors and placed two steaming cartons of fish and chips in front of them.

"To soak up the alcohol," she said. "On the house."

Micah followed her with his eyes as she went to help another customer. To Jade, he said, "I need to bring you here more often."

They both dug into their food. Jade hadn't realized she was ravenous. Between bites, she asked, "What are your thoughts on the case?"

"He's not leaving behind a lot of evidence. Almost as if he understands how a law enforcement officer investigates a crime. How are we ever going to find him?"

"Gathering evidence is not about finding him; it's about eliminating everyone else."

"We haven't eliminated anyone." He tilted his glass, staring into it. "I've been racking my brain about the Shakespeare connection. Is it an English bloke? If so, how is he connected to the victims? Why just the last two lines?"

"Go on."

"There's a reason he's leaving the couplet. It connects the victims in some way."

Jade sipped her beer. "I think you're right."

They ordered a few more rounds of beers and, along with the rest of the customers, cheered and groaned and shouted at the TVs. When Chelsea scored its first goal, Jade received a bear hug from the patron next to her, an older man with stale beer breath and a Chelsea jersey stretched tight over his proud beer belly.

During the second half, Micah's seat had moved closer to hers, their elbows occasionally touching.

Jade was feeling good. A little tipsy. She needed this.

"I like seeing you smile," Micah said.

"Don't get used to it."

He laughed and then, almost nonchalantly, said, "Are you still looking into the Robin Hood case?"

Jade shrugged.

"Any new leads?"

She shook her head. "Whoever stole that money was good. Really good."

He took a pull on his beer. "The idea, though, *was* good. Don't you think?"

"What do you mean?"

"The crime."

"Why would you say that?"

"Taking money from people who wouldn't miss it—money they, their children, and their children's children would never need—and giving it to the poor."

She swallowed her beer. "There're better ways to help the poor."

"I'm not saying that committing a crime was the right way to go about it. I think the intention was… noble."

"It was a crime. A lot of good that came out of it had to be undone."

He looked at her thoughtfully. "Do you always do the right thing?"

She stared into those mesmerizing gray eyes, a moment longer than was wise.

Finally, she said, "Nothing can happen between us. You know that, right?"

"Absolutely not," he said, taking a sip of his drink. "Nope. No way. No can do. Not if you were the last woman on earth."

Jade frowned. "Well, you don't have to go *that* far."

"I get it. We're mates."

"I'm not your mate, Micah. I'm your boss."

"Trust me," he mumbled. "I know."

He drained his beer and signaled the bartender, who was close by, for another round. "Don't worry, *boss*. I know my place. I'm a working-class bloke from London, after all."

Micah turned his attention back to the game. She thought about apologizing but decided against it. Better to squash any idea of a romantic future before it bloomed.

The bartender brought them two steaming cups. A tea for Micah and a coffee for Jade. She must have overheard the last part of their conversation. Jade eyed her, grateful. There would be no singing tonight.

At the ninetieth minute, the referee added one minute of stoppage time. The score was tied one to one.

"We're going into extra time," Micah said.

"We'll see," Jade said.

She sipped her coffee as an Arsenal defender dribbled the ball down the sideline. The opposing Chelsea defender, caught too far forward, turned and sprinted to catch up to the speedy Arsenal player. Ten yards from the end line, the Arsenal defender sent a left-footed cross to the team's forward, who left his feet and dove for the ball, heading it past the outstretched hand of Chelsea's six-foot-five goalie and inside the lower part of the goalpost.

As the forward sprinted to the flag in the corner of the field, he dropped to his knees, sliding most of the way. His teammates ran to him and fell on top of him in a heap of masculinity.

The referee blew his whistle to end the game.

Micah placed a hand on Jade's shoulder, his eyes wide with delight, the talk about their relationship forgotten.

"Brilliant!" he shouted. "How did you know?"

Not waiting for an answer, he hugged her, then hurriedly kissed her on the lips before flying out of his seat.

The kiss was an accident. He didn't even notice her reaction as he jumped up and down, fist-pumping, screaming, high-fiving, and bear-hugging his Arsenal compatriots in a bar in Virginia, a former colony far away from his native England.

She stared straight ahead while Micah joined them in the victory song, he forgetting about their bet, she trying to ignore the smell of his cologne.

Jade glanced at the bartender, who stood a few feet away.

To Jade, she mouthed, *He's fiiiiiiiiiine!*

# CHAPTER FIFTY

# The White House, Washington, DC

A KNOCK. SASHA POPPED her head in, her hand remaining on the open door.

"You need to listen to something," she said.

She traversed the Oval Office and entered Whitney's study, not asking for permission nor waiting for Whitney to follow her. Whitney frowned at the unusual lack of protocol but followed her chief of staff just the same.

Sasha turned on the radio.

"It's always been a dream of mine," said a voice through the radio's speakers.

Whitney tensed.

"Why did it take you so long to run?" asked the talk-show host for Patriot News, his tone more subdued than usual. It was one of Cole Brennan's first broadcasts since his son's death.

"Life had other plans for me, I guess."

She envisioned the shrug and the boyish grin of Cole's guest. A grin she knew well.

"My daddy sold cars," the guest continued, "and I was expected to follow in his footsteps."

"I read about that in the *Washington Times*," Cole said. "The only legitimate paper in Washington, by the way. Then what happened?"

"I realized I wanted more out of life."

"You were a state legislator in Missouri," said Cole. "What made you run for Congress?"

"When I learned that Steven Barrett's death wasn't an accident," said the voice, tinged with anger, "and that the FBI covered it up, I had to do something. Congressman Barrett was a Missouri son. Born and raised. He represented our district and state faithfully for many years, and he deserved better than the investigation the federal government conducted for him."

"Those are strong accusations, my friend," Cole said. "Any proof?"

"Not yet, but I'll get it. How the FBI handled his murder was a travesty of justice and an injustice for the congressman's family. I won't rest until they receive the justice they deserve."

"Don't you find it ironic," Cole said, "that you and our president both come from the same district and were elected to the House because of a special election?"

A pause. Whitney held her breath, wondering if the guest would disclose their shared history.

"Her opportunity arose because of the suspicious death of Congressman Barrett," the guest responded. "I was elected after the governor appointed the congressman serving at the time to the president's vacant seat in the Senate. There's a difference."

"Are you implying," Cole said, his voice rising incredulously, "that the president of the United States was involved in Barrett's death?"

Another pause. "I didn't say that."

*Sure you didn't.*

"I know something about insinuation," Cole said, "and that sure sounded like it to me."

"All I'm saying is that it's a curious coincidence."

"If you say so. What are your plans now that you're in Congress?"

"There's plenty we need to do to take the country back, Cole. Decrease regulations, reduce the deficit, and create manufacturing jobs, to name a few."

"Couldn't agree more. Well, that's all the time we have today. Before I go, I want to thank all of you for your phone calls, letters, and emails about my son CJ. They mean a lot to Ashley and me. Now, I'm going to say something else some of you don't want to hear, but you need to. My son wasn't my gay son—he was just my son. Like your children. Depression doesn't happen to only one type of person. Anyone can become depressed: famous actors, celebrities, minorities, teenagers, middle schoolers, men. Anyone. If you or someone you love is depressed, please call the National Suicide Prevention Lifeline. Remember, you're not alone. This is Cole Brennan, protecting your life," he paused, "liberty, and pursuit of happiness. Join us again tomorrow for *The Conservative Voice.*"

During the broadcast, Whitney had glanced at Sasha a few times. The chief of staff had listened intently. The president hadn't told Sasha her entire history, although with Sasha's "sources," Whitney believed she knew.

The guest on Cole's show was Cameron Kelly, the freshman

representative from Missouri and Whitney's former high school boyfriend. She still hadn't told anyone, except for Grayson, that Cameron had once raped her.

"Cole didn't waste any time replacing Sampson as his puppet," Sasha said.

"He does sound smitten," Whitney agreed.

"Sounds as if Kelly has it in for you." Sasha looked at her. "Is there something you want to tell me about your colleague from the great state of Missouri?"

Whitney stared at the woman who had stood by her steadfastly the fourteen months she'd been in office.

"Yes," she said, "it's about time I do."

# CHAPTER FIFTY-ONE

# Washington, DC

I T HAD BEEN over two months since Sebastian Scofield's murder. The Shakespeare task force had interviewed—and sometimes reinterviewed—every witness to the three murders. In addition to driving back and forth across the Potomac River to and from Virginia, Dante and Micah had flown to New York and Chicago multiple times. At one point, Dante grudgingly asked Jade to review the case files again to see if she could spot something he'd missed.

If something was there, she couldn't find it either.

Max had created a psychological profile of the unsub. They knew the type of person they were looking for, but at least a million men fit that description.

Meanwhile, other murders wouldn't wait. Jade had no choice but to assign her team additional cases.

She locked her computer, calling it a day.

Standing, she began to stuff her briefcase with several folders from her desk. She stared at *The Complete Works of William Shakespeare* and grabbed it too.

## CHAPTER FIFTY-TWO

# Arlington, Virginia

THE VIBRATION WOKE her up.

Leaving one arm covering her closed eyes, she swiped her cell phone off the nightstand with the other. Jade didn't think she'd slept long. After leaving work, she'd texted Zoe for a recommendation for Indian food. Zoe was an encyclopedia of DC-area restaurants, her gift all the more remarkable given how often restaurants closed and opened in the city.

Jade had eaten her takeout while watching an episode of an HBO series that held the attention of everyone in the nation except her. Sleep still eluding her, she'd decided to go over the case files again. Sitting at the small desk in her bedroom, she gazed out the window at the unused patio furniture in her postage-stamp-size backyard surrounded by a faded wooden fence.

She fumbled with the phone. "Harrington."

"Coach," the caller said.

Immediately alert, Jade sat up in bed. Her cat, Card, jumped off her chest and onto the bed, circling before settling in next to her in a spot only he occupied.

The clock on the nightstand read 11:30 p.m. "LaKeisha, what is it?"

LaKeisha was the point guard on the high school spring league team that Jade coached every year. Their first practice wasn't until next week, and on top of that, LaKeisha had never called her before.

"I'm in trouble," the girl said simply.

Jade threw off the covers. "Where are you?"

@TheGodOfVeritas: Blayze Tishman may be generous and donate to a lot of causes, but he's also reaping the rewards from exploiting young black men. #shame

## CHAPTER FIFTY-THREE

# Washington, DC

JADE LEANED FORWARD, her arms resting on the steering wheel. She stared through the passenger-side window at the small, well-kept two-story row house on a street in Anacostia. Chain-link fences separated the lawns of the homes. This lower-income Southeast DC neighborhood had so far resisted the gentrification epidemic. Jade wondered what would happen to the residents when that day came.

She had some idea.

A basketball lay in the yard. A streetlight illuminated a solitary chair on the concrete front porch. No lights seemed to be on in the house.

Jade had never been to the house where LaKeisha grew up.

The young woman slouched in the passenger seat next to her. The litheness of last year had transformed into solid muscle. Only a couple of inches shorter than Jade, LaKeisha now outweighed her by twenty pounds.

A sophomore in high school, LaKeisha wore her black hair in long dreadlocks. Her bright smile, made brighter by her dark brown skin, was absent tonight.

Her second-year accomplishments on the hardwood exceeded her first. She was on her way to following in Jade's footsteps: a college scholarship, the WNBA, a professional contract overseas.

Jade wanted to keep it that way.

Although LaKeisha was smart and maintained a 3.0 grade point average, Jade didn't believe that LaKeisha's parents earned enough to pay for college or poor enough to receive sufficient financial aid. Athletics might be her only route to a college education.

When she saw LaKeisha play for the first time at an AAU tournament four years ago, Jade recognized something more than the twelve-year-old girl's talent and natural athletic ability. She had a will to win.

Now, she looked at LaKeisha. "You had one phone call."

The girl nodded.

"And you called me."

"Yeah."

"What happened?" Jade asked.

LaKeisha shifted in her seat. "Some of my friends… on my AAU team… got together to go see a movie. At Gallery Place." She paused. "After the movie, we were all hungry, so we went to a store. Kinda like a 7-Eleven." LaKeisha stopped.

Jade waited, resisting the urge to fill the silence. She wanted to give LaKeisha the time and space to tell the story in her own way.

"They started daring each other," she said. "Stuffing candy bars and snacks into their pockets. Their purses. A security guard came from the back of the store. He looked at all of us and grabbed me. I thought he was going to rip my arm out of the socket."

"And your teammates?"

"They didn't stick around. They ran. I was the only one taken to the station."

"I wonder why."

LaKeisha twisted the thin skin on the back of her hand.

"Ah," Jade said.

The DC Metropolitan PD had transported LaKeisha to the Youth Services Center on H Street NW. Since it was LaKeisha's first offense, CSS—Court Social Services—decided to release her to a guardian. Given their overflowing caseload, and that she was a federal law enforcement officer, Jade qualified. CSS would monitor LaKeisha for six months to make sure she didn't commit additional offenses.

"Did you tell them you didn't take anything?"

"They knew. They'd frisked me. They didn't care." LaKeisha laid her head against the headrest. "My parents are going to kill me."

"If you were my daughter, I would."

A slight smile flickered on the girl's face. After a moment, she said, "Do you know the worst part?"

"What?"

"It's not the getting arrested. Or the racism. Or my parents. It's that my quote-unquote *friends* weren't there for me. They *ran*." She broke eye contact. "They were never my friends."

"My dad used to say that you can count your true friends on one hand," Jade said.

LaKeisha held up her hand, large enough to palm a basketball, and spread her fingers. She retracted her thumb. "I used to count on my four teammates. Not anymore." Her hand dropped. "One reason I didn't take anything was because of you."

"Me?"

"I could never look you in the eye if I did something like that. I have dreams and goals because of you. I'm not going to mess up my future." She opened the passenger-side door. "Thanks for bailing me out, Coach. At least I can count on you. Always."

She slammed the car door shut.

"Always," Jade said into the silence.

## CHAPTER FIFTY-FOUR

# Clayton, Missouri

"TAKE A COOKIE, dear."

Whitney's mother pushed the still-full plate toward her on the coffee table between them.

"Mom, I'm not hungry. Truly," Whitney said.

"I just baked them," her mother said, her tone scolding. "You're getting too thin. That job will be the death of you."

Whitney couldn't disagree on either count.

Hayden and Claire Churchill still lived in the same middle-class ranch in the St. Louis suburb where Whitney had grown up. Earlier, she'd walked through her brothers' and her old rooms. Nothing much had changed since they'd moved out decades ago. A *Grease* movie poster, depicting Olivia Newton-John and John Travolta clutching each other, still hung over her bed. Her cheerleading trophies and academic awards were still on the shelf over the window. Her little desk remained tidy, everything in its place.

Some of her clothes from her teenage years were in her closet. She could probably fit into them again.

Retired now, her father had once been an insurance agent, and her mother was his office manager. Her three brothers lived nearby with families of their own. Whitney didn't see them much and wouldn't have time during this visit. Sitting in a worn yellow chair, she gazed around the living room as she sipped lemonade from a glass. Unless one had been told, it would be hard to fathom that the occupants of this house were the parents of the most powerful person in the world.

"How's Grayson?" her mother asked from the couch across from her.

"He's fine."

"I hear he's back at work," her father said, dressed warmly in a gray-and-blue cardigan over a collared white shirt and dark pants. The house was almost as cold inside as it was outside. Despite her rare visit, he sat in a light-brown suede Barcalounger, reading the newspaper.

"He said the business needed him," Whitney said. "Washington can survive without him for a little while."

"What about you?" her mother said.

"I'm fine."

"I mean, can you survive without him for a little while?"

"Mom, I'm a grown woman. I don't need a man to survive." Whitney forced a laugh. "Besides, we've lived apart for so long over the years, I'm somewhat used to it."

"It can't be healthy for you or your marriage," her mother said.

"Mom, it's temporary. We're fine."

"A lot of 'fines,'" her father said, peering at her over the newspaper. He wore horn-rimmed glasses. "Why are you here? What's going on?"

Whitney said, "Not happy to see me?"

"Of course I am, but we haven't seen much of you since you left home." He paused. "Thirty years ago."

"We have some events in the Midwest, so I thought it would be a good opportunity to visit." Her parents looked unconvinced. "I wanted to see you," she said, simply.

*I wanted to come home,* she didn't say.

"Saw that Kelly boy on the news, yapping his mouth. He's on TV now almost as much as when he hawked cars."

"Hayden," her mother said, "I'm sure Whitney doesn't want to talk about him."

They knew Cameron had raped her. And did nothing. Instead, her liberal, marched-for-civil-rights-in-the-sixties parents had shipped her off to live with her father's sister, Mary, until the baby came. They didn't go to the police. They didn't take her to the hospital. They didn't confront the boy. Whitney dealt with the sexual assault and its aftermath on her own. As she had most situations in her life.

Her parents marched and protested and fought for everyone but her.

Some might say it was a different time then. A he-said, she-said situation. In a small town, where there was an inverse relationship between the maliciousness of the gossip and the size of the population, a girl had her reputation to protect. The boy's reputation would remain intact no matter what happened.

Her parents never explained their actions—or rather, inaction—to her.

"Cameron was an immature kid then," her mom said. "You know how boys are."

The heat rushed to Whitney's face. She placed her glass next to the plate of cookies. "I do."

She hadn't come to fight with her parents. They would never change. That she thought they would be here for her now, when they never were in the past, was the definition of insanity. "I'm going."

"Off to see Grayson?" her mother asked, oblivious to her daughter's feelings.

Whitney rose and went to them, bending over to kiss each of them on their soft, papery cheeks. Her hugs were brief, their bodies frailer than she remembered. She loved them despite their failures.

"I'll call you," she said.

In the Beast, the presidential limousine, Sasha said, "That good?"

Whitney shook her head.

Sasha continued to stare at her. "Are you all right?"

"Please… just head to the airport," Whitney said.

As Sasha picked up the phone to instruct the driver, Whitney donned sunglasses and stared straight ahead, even as the armored car passed the entrance to Fairchild Industries headquarters. The ten-story building and its twenty-acre campus were hard to ignore in this town.

Whitney chastised herself for seeking solace from her troubles at home with her parents. It had been a mistake.

She thought about the time she and Grayson had eaten ice cream in the ground-floor kitchen. It was one of the last romantic moments they had shared.

"Sasha," she said, "let's stop for some ice cream first."

"Ice cream?"

"My treat."

Sasha picked up the phone again.

## CHAPTER FIFTY-FIVE

# Seattle, Washington

S HE DIDN'T UNDERSTAND the last-minute addition. His name wasn't on the original list.

But her job wasn't to question. Or to reason. She was paid to carry out orders. Paid quite handsomely.

She waited.

Fifteen minutes after the appointed hour, a heavyset man tromped through the tall grass.

"Noah? Is that you?" he called out.

"Over here," she said, her voice noncommittal.

"Whew, it's dark! Why did you want to meet out here? You should've come over to the house." The man's loud voice sounded entitled and was already getting on her nerves. He finally reached her. "How was the slammer?" He looked into her eyes. "Wait, you're not—"

Pulling out the knife from behind her back, she stabbed him in the chest. She freed it and stabbed him again.

And again.

And again.

Blood sprayed her black pullover and running tights. She didn't care. She'd rented an Airbnb not far from here and would be ensconced in it soon.

As she continued to stab him, her mind drifted. She wasn't thinking of him as the gurgling sounds stopped.

He was dead.

But Dev was thinking about someone else. The woman who'd ruined her life.

Strike.

The woman who hadn't given her a chance to explain.

Strike.

Or a second chance.

Strike.

The woman who would pay.

# CHAPTER FIFTY-SIX

# Chantilly, Virginia

"WHAT?" JADE ASKED, removing her earplugs.

Max Stover stood ten yards away, sans coat and tie, dressed as if he'd come from the office. He walked past her to tap the smartpad on the wall. "I said you're losing your touch."

As the target drew closer, she scowled. Nine of her shots had gone through the heart. A small hole stood alone, an inch to the left of the others.

Max was right. Between thoughts of Micah's kiss and LaKeisha's troubles and CJ Brennan's suicide, she *had* lost her touch.

She reloaded the mag and clicked it into place.

"Send it back out," she told him, before putting the earplugs back in.

Comparable to the basketball that used to feel like a part of her hand, the heft of the weapon was familiar in Jade's grip. She steadied her breath, held it, and fired.

Jade and her mentor shot for thirty minutes, without speaking, at the range in Fairfax County. The place was crowded because of the unexpected pleasant day. The sounds of birds chirping—and bullets whizzing—filled the air.

She loved spending time on a range, whether here or at FBI HQ. She shot every other week to stay sharp and help take her mind off things. The death of CJ Brennan had hit her hard, although she hadn't known him, except for their brief encounter during the TSK case. Jade had gleaned most of what she knew about the young man from the media. She respected him for standing up for himself and not letting his father push him into being someone he wasn't.

She and Max sat across from each other at a picnic table in an outdoor area where customers took breaks in between rounds. Jade drank a Pepsi, and Max drank an Orange Crush.

"Any leads in the Shakespeare case?" he asked, sipping his drink.

"No leads. No activity. Nothing. At least there's some good news: no new murders."

"What about Veritas?"

"Nothing in the blogs helped. We spoke with all the advertisers; they didn't provide anything useful. He's no longer a person of interest."

"This isn't over," Max said.

She took a long pull of her soft drink. "I don't think so either."

"He's cooling off," he said, "if you call a month a cooling-off period. Perhaps he's gone back to his normal life. Might be years before he strikes again."

Jade raised an eyebrow. "You think?"

"No. He'll start missing the attention, if he doesn't already."

The elusive Shakespeare Killer was the source of rampant

speculation on cable news and social media. MSNBC broadcasted a documentary reenacting the three murders. A sick individual had created a fake Twitter account for the killer. Women from all over the world professed their love to him, offering their bodies or proposals of marriage. These women didn't know or care whether he was married.

Or that he killed people.

What a crazy, crazy world. Or maybe it had always been this way, and the advent of social media only magnified people's basest behaviors and instincts.

"He doesn't want to be caught," she said.

Max nodded. "He likes killing too much. Every murder ups the tension, which can only be satisfied by another murder. Our man will strike again."

"Until he commits the perfect murder," Jade murmured. A perfectionist herself, she should know. "One that can't be topped." After a moment of silence, she said, "Guesses to motive?"

"Robbery has been ruled out," he said. "The murders don't appear to be random. All the victims are not only wealthy, but also major players in their respective fields."

"Don't forget white."

"Right. Did you find a connection?"

"Dante says no. Different industries. Different social circles. None belonged to the same associations or clubs or attended the same conferences."

They both sipped their drinks thoughtfully.

Max said, "How are you adjusting to being a supervisor?"

She didn't respond immediately.

"What is it?" he asked.

His white dress shirt, open at the collar, displayed an off-white undershirt with a wrinkled crew neck. His sleeves were rolled up, exposing his slender arms.

"What if I'm not cut out for this?" she said ruefully. "I want to be where the action is. Not sitting behind a desk full time."

"You're a great agent."

"Maybe so," she said, "but I might suck as a boss."

"It's different," he said. "You're no longer a player. You're the coach."

"Player-coach."

"You've got to accept that it's not only about your success. Your success depends on others." He eyed her. "Is something else holding you back?"

Sheepish, she said, "Being a supervisor is boring."

Max chuckled. "I could see why you would think that." He paused. "How's Micah doing?"

"Not bad."

Max smiled.

"Okay," she conceded. "He's going to be good."

"I know. I taught him." Max wasn't bragging. He was stating a fact.

A man in a blue T-shirt and jeans walked by, his arm around his young son. They carried matching guns. Max followed them with his eyes. His wife had left him last year after thirty years of marriage. Was he thinking about being childless or something else entirely?

Still looking at the pair, he said, "I've watched you two in meetings."

*We have a winner. Something else.*

"Who?"

"You and Micah."

"Why would you do that?"

"That's what I do. Observe." He peered at her over the top of the soda can. "You two have become close."

*Does he know about what happened at the pub?*

She squinted at him. "What are you saying, Max?"

"Be careful, Jade."

Tamping down her temper, she said, "Give me some credit. I don't shit where I eat." She thought briefly of Kyle. *Well, not in the same restaurant.*

"You need to retain the respect of your staff. If they think you and Micah are—"

"I get it," she said tersely.

Jade wasn't sure what angered her about Max's suggestion. His observation? The vibrating phone in the pocket of her black tracksuit pants saved her from continuing the conversation.

Pulling it out, she glanced at the display and smiled, even though the call surely portended bad news. She answered.

"It's been a long time," said the voice.

"My favorite detective. How are you?"

"I fell for that one before," said Detective Kurt McClaine. "What's up?"

"Wish I weren't the bearer of bad news, but unfortunately, that seems to be the basis of our relationship."

"What've you got?"

He sighed. "One with your name written all over it."

"I've been promoted. I no longer work cases. Besides, I've spent way too much time in Seattle."

Two of Jade's most recent major cases had taken her to the Pacific Northwest city, where she'd worked with McClaine. And met Kyle.

*Focus.*

"You're going to want to come out here."

"Tell me why."

"I'm at a scene. The victim's name is Blayze Tishman."

She gasped.

Blayze Tishman retired last year as the CEO of a software company, the number three company in the Fortune 500. He'd recently bought a professional football team with plans to move it to the Bay Area.

"I'm listening," she said.

"It's bad," McClaine said. "The vic's messed up. The perp left a note."

"A sonnet?"

"Let me count the ways."

"That's Elizabeth Barrett Browning."

"Don't you know? I was never *good* in English," he said. "See you in Seattle."

He hung up.

Jade called Dante.

"Call the team together," she said when he answered, looking at Max, "and tell them to pack their bags. I'll meet you at Dulles."

Her next call was to Pat. "Check out Veritas's timeline for a tweet about Blayze Tishman."

# CHAPTER FIFTY-SEVEN

# Casper, Wyoming

"**P**RESIDENT RICHARD ELLISON and First Lady Nancy Ellison, President Timothy Hartman and First Lady Elizabeth Hartman, and President Edward Middleton and First Lady Barbara Middleton, I am honored and delighted to give the opening remarks today.

"I love to read, and libraries are one of my favorite places to spend my time." She paused. "Especially lately."

The one hundred people in attendance laughed. The troubles Whitney had experienced in the infancy of her presidency weren't a secret, nor was her love of reading. Although it was no longer news, the media still accompanied her on monthly trips to independent bookstores.

"Richard and I were involved in a hard-fought presidential campaign, but through it all, he comported himself with integrity and always treated me with respect and dignity. Although we don't agree on many issues—"

"None!" her predecessor joked, standing next to her, his tan, weathered face relaxed.

The crowd laughed again, harder this time.

Whitney joined in. "We weren't as far apart as he led you to believe. Richard was the rare breed of politician who put our country first, who considered issues on their merits rather than toeing the party line. He served as the governor of this great state of Wyoming, as its senator, and finally as our president. He loves his country, loves his family, and loves his ranch."

She remembered fondly her visit there last year. It wasn't far from where she stood now. She took in the scenery through the glass walls: miles of Wyoming dirt and cottonwood trees. A mountain in the distance. She scanned the guests, catching the eye of several familiar faces. Friends and foes alike.

"No matter how much you prepare for the presidency, you aren't truly prepared. A president, as soon as he or she"—she smiled—"sits behind the desk in the Oval Office, has a greater appreciation for all those who served before her. I want to thank Richard for being a resource for me, and now, a friend. This beautiful library represents him. Strong, angular, sturdy, and well crafted."

"You forgot out to pasture," he quipped.

She waited for the laughter to die down.

"The Richard Milhous Ellison Library is a monument to his legacy, for the benefit of his constituents and neighbors, and for posterity. God bless all of you and God bless the United States of America. Ladies and gentlemen, President Richard Ellison."

After the ribbon cutting, Whitney, Richard, and the other former presidents retired to a small room off the main one.

"What've you been up to?" asked former president Timothy Hartman. "Golf?"

Richard shook his head. "I'm not much of a golfer."

"Not sure how you can live out here."

"Casper too dull for you?"

"I've been here for only an afternoon," said Hartman. "It's great to see you again, but I'm ready to leave. I miss the buildings. The action. I want to see cars, not cattle."

Although Hartman had lived in California for most of his life, he'd moved to New York City after his term in office, where he now headed up a foundation named after him. He also jetted around the country, giving six-figure—sometimes seven-figure—speeches. He hadn't been president for over a decade, but the economic prosperity the country enjoyed during his presidency was still a reverent memory for the public.

The three men and Whitney comprised the most exclusive club in the world—the Presidents Club—an unofficial group of the current and former living US presidents. This was the first time during her presidency that all of them had been together.

"Don't talk about our cattle," Richard said. "Besides, the fresh air might do you some good."

"With all this dust? No thanks."

They quieted as a server placed four glasses on the table. He poured a dram into each glass and left the bottle of Macallan.

Whitney and Richard thanked him before he quietly retreated.

"Retirement treating you well?" Hartman asked.

"Can't complain."

The four presidents sat in white-cushioned chairs around a low square table. Despite the modern decor in the rest of the library, this room was bathed in beiges and browns. Built-in bookcases lined the walls with books and artifacts from Ellison's time in office.

They were alone, their secret service details just outside the door.

Hartman raised his glass. "To Richard!"

"To Richard," Whitney and Edward Middleton echoed. Richard nodded in appreciation. The three of them clinked glasses with Richard and each other. Swirling the scotch around in her glass, Whitney lifted it to her lips. She sniffed before taking a small sip, savoring the flavors of dried fruit, wood smoke, and spice.

Middleton looked at Richard. "Milhous, huh? Did your parents hate you?"

Richard Ellison laughed. "Nixon helped push through the Civil Rights Act of 1957 the year before I was born. My mother loved him. My father, not so much."

Middleton shook his head. "Richard Nixon, what a character." He turned to Whitney. "How's it going with you?"

"Slower than I expected," she said.

The three men laughed at the understatement. Her legislative achievements—except for the Equal Rights Amendment, the Anti-Bullying Act, and the slimmed-down New Cubed—were few.

"The job's getting harder," Middleton said. "Harder than in my day. With social media. The pace of the world. Terrorism. Cybercrime."

"Mass shootings," added Hartman.

Richard shook his head. "I disagree. Washington's experience was the toughest. He had no predecessor. Heck, he didn't even have a country—just a bunch of rebellious colonies. He had to make it up as he went along and set the precedent for all who came after him. If he'd messed up, who knows where this nation would've ended up."

"What about Franklin D.?" Hartman said. "He lifted us up out of the Great Depression and steered us through World War II."

"True," Whitney said. "And then there's Lincoln."

His accomplishments—including holding a divided country together—didn't need to be voiced.

"What about me?" Richard asked.

The three other presidents stared at him.

"You?" Middleton said.

Richard said, "Why do you all look surprised?"

"You didn't have it so hard," Hartman said.

"I had Cole Brennan always jabbering in my ear," Richard said, taking a sip of his drink.

"That's true," Middleton held up a hand, conceding.

"Good point," said Hartman.

"You got off easy," Richard continued, looking at Middleton, his Republican colleague. "At least you still had some moderates left in Congress."

After debating for a time who truly had it the toughest, Whitney said, "Perhaps my plight isn't so bad."

Richard leaned forward, reaching for the bottle. He refreshed their drinks, then sat back and crossed his legs, cradling his glass, looking at her. "How can we help?"

*With which problem?*

She thought about Grayson, Chandler, Emma, Min, Tamirov, and Cameron.

"Perhaps there is something you can do," she said.

"Name it," Richard said.

# CHAPTER FIFTY-EIGHT

## Seattle, Washington

J ADE SLOWED HER pace to allow McClaine to catch up to her.

With his long blond hair and small silver star-shaped earring, McClaine didn't look like your typical detective. Over his slight frame, he wore jeans and his customary T-shirt, today's edition light blue with Safer in a Sanctuary City emblazoned in neon-green lettering. A tattoo snaked partway up his neck, reaching higher since the last time Jade saw him.

The footsteps of Dante, Micah, Max, Christian, and Brian Anderson, the local agent, crunched behind her.

McClaine had met Max and Christian during the Robin Hood case. Earlier today, Jade introduced him to Dante and Micah at the Seattle FBI office. He already knew Anderson.

Both cars were parked on the shoulder. Stepping over the guardrail, the detective and the five agents carefully waded their way down through the tall grass toward the water's edge.

"The vic was found there," McClaine said, pointing at a patch of trampled grass the size of a large man.

Jade crouched next to the indentation, the surrounding area littered with cigarette butts and craft beer cans. She didn't see any footprints. "Did it rain last night? Or was it that sprinkle stuff you Seattleites call rain."

McClaine smiled. "The sprinkle stuff."

"Not hard enough to wipe away footprints."

"No."

"Would have been lucky to find impressions in this grass." Jade stood, placing her hands on her hips. "Who found him?"

"UW rowing club," he said. "Women. They row Lake Washington every morning. Saw something on the bank. As they came closer, they realized that it was a body. They almost moved on, thinking it was a homeless person, sleeping."

"But they saw the blood," she said, scanning the drenched ground.

Next to her, Max was taking it all in. He met her eye but said nothing.

"Yep," McClaine said. "They rowed back to the Conibear Shellhouse"—he pointed to the other side of the lake—"and called us."

"Did they check to see if he was alive?"

"No. Claimed they didn't leave the boat."

She gazed out at a lone sailboat braving the cold. Small waves lapped against the shore. "Any witnesses?"

"None have come forward. We went house to house," he said, waving behind him at the houses on the hill overlooking them, "but no one saw anything. Still waiting on one resident to get back to us."

Veritas's house was still under surveillance. Although his real name had been confirmed as Jacob Michael Collins, Jade still thought of him as Veritas. Anderson had reported that he was home all night. NSA tracked his phone to his apartment. This morning, before Jade and the DC contingent arrived in Seattle, Anderson and another local agent paid a visit to Veritas. During the interview, he maintained his innocence. Anderson told her that all the defiance Veritas displayed during their previous trip had dissipated. He was scared. Shaking scared. Though he'd told them he wasn't going to stop tweeting.

Jade didn't think he was responsible for the murders, but the killer could be taking cues from him. She mentally kicked herself. They should have been monitoring his tweets.

She pulled out her phone and sent a text.

Pat's reply came within a minute: Cyber's on it.

Pocketing her phone, Jade inhaled the fresh air. Her eyes returned to the top of the hill. "What neighborhood is that?"

McClaine followed her gaze. "Madison Park."

"Gigantic houses. Great views."

"I should've gone into IT. Or coffee."

McClaine was referencing Seattle's tech hub, home to Amazon and Microsoft, of course, as well as hosting Google, Facebook, and Apple. Costco, Nordstrom, and Starbucks were all headquartered here too.

"You're dressed for it," she said.

"IT? Or coffee?"

"Both. TOD?"

"Coroner said between 10:00 p.m. and 1:00 a.m."

Jade surveyed the ground. "Any trace evidence?"

"Just the knife," McClaine said. "Oh… and a sonnet."

❧

Christian let out a breath. "Jesus."

Standing next to him, Jade said, "Why do you always say that?"

He invoked the Lord's name whenever he saw a naked, dead body.

In the morgue on Jefferson Street, just south of the First Hill neighborhood, the five agents and McClaine stared down at the body of Blayze Tishman on the stainless-steel table.

What remained of the body.

Stab wounds dotted his expansive pale torso, a macabre work of impressionist art.

Tishman's face and legs were unmarred. A tag with his identification information was tied around the big toe of his left foot.

Bright lights illuminated the chilly room, where the smell of antiseptic was overpowering.

Jade scrutinized the wounds. "How many?"

"Twenty-seven," McClaine said. "The victim ended up choking on his own blood."

Dante swallowed slowly. "Jesus is right."

"Such anger," Max murmured, his eyes scanning the body.

To Max, Dante said, "You think the perp knew him?"

"It's possible," came Max's noncommittal response.

"Or Tishman angered him in some way," said Micah.

"He could be abrasive," McClaine said. "It might've been drugs. Seattle has a huge opioid, mental health, and homelessness crisis. A dangerous combination. Or some guy thought the vic encroached on his turf. A quiet place to sleep."

"With a killer view," Dante said.

Jade looked at him. "You're becoming worse than Pat."

McClaine said, "I've seen victims murdered in this city for less."

*DC too.*

"But for the sonnet," she reminded him.

"But for the sonnet," McClaine said. "Let's go to my office."

❀

McClaine passed around copies of the sonnet and the police and autopsy reports to the team, who sat around the rectangular table in a conference room at the downtown precinct. He handed Jade the murder book containing the complete case file: autopsy report, crime scene photos, investigative notes, and witness interview reports.

He waited for the FBI agents to read through the materials.

Jade scanned the autopsy report. Tishman, fifty-eight, weighed two hundred twenty pounds. Manner of death: homicide. Under cause of death, each stab wound was listed. Pasta, tomato sauce, and a brownish liquid were found among the contents of his stomach.

"Tell us about his wife," Jade asked.

"Victoria Tishman. Married twenty-six years. She oversees their family foundation and, from what we've gathered, is very involved in her husband's business interests. She was his partner, personally and professionally. Formidable in her own right."

Jade flipped through the pages. "She give you anything?"

"Nothing helpful."

"We need to talk to her."

"Arranged," he said. "She's expecting us within the next couple of hours."

"Questions?" she asked her team, her eyes landing on Max.

Max looked thoughtful but didn't respond. She didn't press. He would tell her his thoughts when he was ready.

"Tishman was a big bloke," Micah said. "How did the perp overpower him?"

"Maybe he was a slow… bloke," Dante said. "Like Merritt."

Christian cut his eyes at Dante but refused to take the bait.

Jade placed the murder book on the table and picked up a copy of the sonnet.

> *For I am sham'd by that which I bring forth,*
> *And so should you, to love things nothing worth.*
>
> —Bard of Avon

She checked the Shakespeare app on her phone, which she'd downloaded a few weeks ago, having left the tome in DC.

Sonnet LXXII.

Scanning the faces of her team, she said, "Seventy-two. Does this mean anything to anyone?"

Christian, Max, Dante, McClaine, and Anderson gave her blank looks.

"The last line," Micah said. "The perp might have thought Tishman cared about the wrong things. Wealth. Material things."

Jade stood, shaking her head. "Thank God for the Brit. Let's go talk to the wife."

# CHAPTER FIFTY-NINE

# The White House, Washington, DC

"WELL, HELL!" SENATOR Maureen McAllister said. "We're not going to make it."

Vice President Josephine Bates exhaled. "Damn."

"They're right," Sasha said.

A whiteboard set up on an easel had been erected in front of Whitney's desk in the Oval Office. Sasha had written the name of each of the fifty senators and his or her party affiliation—*R* or *D*—in parenthesis. There were no independents in the Senate. In two columns, under the headings "Aye" and "Nay," an *X* was marked next to each senator's name.

The Streamline Regulations Act had been more difficult to push through than Whitney expected, given that the GOP controlled both houses of Congress and deregulation had been a pillar of the party's platform for decades. If she were a Republican president, this legislation would have sailed through last year.

Earlier in the month, question marks accompanied quite a few names, but the Presidents Club had come through. Using their contacts, the weight of their former office, and leverage (read: subtle threats), they helped convert the votes of recalcitrant members of their parties. If successful, it would be the second major legislation passed in as many months.

The four women stood in a row, examining the easel. Although Whitney's high heels were under her desk where she'd kicked them off earlier, she towered over Mo standing next to her.

"Perhaps, if we stare long enough," Whitney said dryly, "the votes will change on their own."

"It'd make my job a lot easier," Sasha said. She'd spent a considerable amount of time on the Hill, persuading senators to change their minds.

Senator Mo looked up at Whitney. "Although I'm a firm believer in positive thinking, I don't think that's going to help us."

Sasha, on the other side of Jo, said, "We need one more."

After a moment, Jo turned to Whitney. "Who owes you a favor?"

"That's cutting to the chase," Mo said.

"I've no time to waste," Jo said. "By the way, where's that moonshine?"

Whitney and Mo giggled. Sasha eyed them, understanding she wasn't privy to the joke, her body language indicating that she didn't want to be.

The laughter died as they all scanned the list again. Whitney went over every name with a "Nay" next to it. Her eyes rested on one halfway down. She pointed to it.

"Scott Harris," she said. "He might not owe me a favor, but he owes me."

# CHAPTER SIXTY

## Medina, Washington

FTER SPEAKING INTO the intercom, McClaine closed the driver's side window and waited for the gate to open. He, Micah, and Dante drove through the entrance, the other agent's car following. The long driveway led to a circle in front of a humongous house of stone and siding and grand windows. The hedges and shrubs were manicured to perfection. Japanese maple trees dotted the lawn.

The Tishmans, like other former and current managers of Blayze's software company, lived in Medina, a city across Lake Washington from Seattle.

Many cars—Mercedes, BMWs, Porsches, a Jaguar, and a Subaru—were parked around the circle. The five-car garage must have been filled.

Max, Christian, Jade, and Anderson—their driver—sat in the car for a moment admiring the house.

"Wow," Christian said.

Max stared at the house but said nothing. Was he thinking about his own empty colonial in Virginia? He had told Jade that his ex-wife had moved in with her new partner.

An abundance of flowers greeted them on either side of the front door.

McClaine knocked. A woman in her midfifties opened the door.

"Detective Kurt McClaine," he said, proffering his badge. "I called earlier."

"Of course," she said. "I'm Victoria's sister, Margaret."

They stepped into a circular entryway with a black-and-white marble floor. A carpeted staircase led to the upper levels.

Margaret escorted them to a room off the foyer. A sitting room. Literally. The long rectangular space was filled with couches, chairs, and coffee and end tables in various groupings. Magnificent paintings hung on the walls. Jade stopped to examine one. A Renoir. It wasn't a reproduction. The soft carpet was identical in color to the carpet on the stairs. French doors led out to a side yard, where a fountain was surrounded by a circular stone path, with two iron benches, a gazebo, a swimming pool, a tennis court, and an outdoor seating area with a bar. The lake began where the lawn ended.

Wealth. This room screamed the word without making a sound. Tishman and Jared Carr could have run in the same circles.

"Please have a seat," Margaret said. "I'll fetch her."

She closed the white sliding door behind her.

Dante surveyed all the seating options. "Where should we sit?"

They selected an arrangement of two couches and two chairs in the center of the room.

The agents and McClaine sat. And waited.

After a while, Jade stood and paced.

Dante stood. "We should remind her that we're here."

"She's in mourning," Micah reminded him. "Tending to her guests. Poor woman."

"Poor my…" Dante started to respond and then saw Jade's expression. He swallowed the rest of his retort.

The door slid open.

Victoria Tishman took in the room with one glance. Also in her fifties, she had dyed blond hair and was dressed in black slacks and a black blouse, the severity of the clothing softened by the string of small pearls around her neck. Jade wondered if this was her mourning outfit or whether she regularly dressed this way. Her bearing was regal, despite her mourning, or, possibly, because of it.

The other agents and McClaine rose.

The woman extended her hand to McClaine. "Detective."

McClaine introduced her to the agents.

"Please sit," she said in a welcoming way. "Would you care for something to drink?"

"We're fine," McClaine said.

She sat in a chair across from one of the couches and leaned forward, her hands clasped. The biggest diamond that Jade had ever seen adorned the ring finger of her left hand.

After offering condolences, Jade asked, "What can you tell us about the night your husband was killed?"

Victoria briefly closed her eyes and exhaled. "I was at a function downtown. A women's group that I belong to. Blayze had called me earlier, telling me he was headed to the club."

"Which club was that?" Dante asked, before turning and widening his eyes at Micah, a request to take notes.

"The WAC," she said. "Washington Athletic Club. We've been

members for decades. Our children practically grew up there with their friends. Whenever he was in town, Blayze played in the basketball league, which has several divisions for all levels of ability. Good thing." A slight smile. "He wasn't as good as he thought he was. He also swam. Worked out. Although, looking at him, you couldn't tell." Her words weren't meant to be hurtful. More of a shared memory with someone who could no longer share it.

"How do you think he ended up on the other side of the lake at that time of night?" Jade asked.

"Blayze loved the lake," the widow said, a tremor in her voice. She paused to compose herself. "One of his favorite things to do was to sit on the terrace off our bedroom upstairs, sipping whiskey and looking at the lake where he'd spent so much time. He used to row. At UW."

"What was he doing there that night?" Jade asked.

"I don't know."

"Thinking about his glory days?" Dante asked.

This made Victoria smile. "Probably. Although he's had a lot of glory days since then. To the world, my husband is a successful businessman and a loud-mouth owner of a professional sports team. To me, he's just Blayze. The same guy I met in college. Studied with. Went to parties and football games with. Fell in love with and married." She waved her hand, taking in the room. "Before we had all this." More quietly. "Before we had anything."

"Tell us about your children," Jade said.

"Our son, Patrick, lives here in Seattle. Our daughter Tara is in New York City, and our other daughter Lindsey lives in Phoenix. They arrived yesterday."

Children weren't mentioned in Sonnet LXXII, but it wouldn't hurt to investigate them. Jade made a mental note to have Pat check them out.

"Did you or your husband know Sebastian Scofield, Jared Carr, or Finn Hurley?" Dante asked.

Victoria Tishman's head jolted in his direction. "You think Blayze was murdered by the Shakespeare Killer?" She scanned the faces of the other agents. "I wondered why the FBI was involved."

"We're exploring every lead, ma'am."

She fingered her pearls. "We didn't socialize with any of them. Neither of us could stand Jared Carr or his politics. But… my husband's former company has dealings with Hurley Technologies."

"How so?"

"You should talk to the current CEO, but I think it had something to do with developing a joint product."

## CHAPTER SIXTY-ONE

# The White House, Washington, DC

"MADAM PRESIDENT."

Whitney's body woman, Sarah, stood just inside the door. Sasha paused handing out the day's agenda.

"I need a private word," Sarah said.

The members glanced at each other. What could be important enough to interrupt this meeting?

Whitney rose.

"Pardon me," she said to her cabinet, hustling out of the room. In the hallway, Josh McPherson closed the door behind her.

"What is it, Sarah?" Whitney said.

"It's about Senator Scott Harris."

*I hope he hasn't died.*

"What about him?"

Sarah looked around. There were only secret service agents

positioned in the hall, staring straight ahead, studiously ignoring them.

"His son's been kidnapped."

❄

"Any news about your son?" Whitney said. She'd called Harris from the Oval Office.

"We haven't received a ransom note. No communication. Nothing." He paused. "I'm a US senator, and I feel helpless."

*I know the feeling.*

"How can I help?"

In a quiet voice, Senator Scott Harris said, "Just find my son."

"Perhaps we can help each other."

"What are you talking about?"

"I missed you last year, during the campaign. At Ohio State. You were supposed to attend and join me on stage before my speech."

"I had a conflict."

"Must have been important." *To stiff your party's nominee for president*, she didn't add.

"Why are you bringing this up?"

"We're one vote short for the SRA."

"Is that what this is all about?"

"What do you mean?"

"Are you holding my son hostage in exchange for my vote?"

Whitney's mouth parted in shock. "Of course not. How dare you?"

"Your timing is impeccable, Madam President." A long silence followed. Then he said, "I can't support the bill. I'm a Democrat. A real one."

He considered her a DINO. "As am I," she said.

It wasn't only through the efforts of the Presidents Club that the legislation was a success. Mo and Jo had worked tirelessly to help Whitney keep this campaign promise.

Cole Brennan had also done his part. Despite his grief, he'd talked to congressional members or called them out on his radio show. Between him and Mo, all the Republicans had fallen in line. They needed one more senator from the Democratic side.

Whitney believed Harris was her best bet. Although she felt badly about the timing, it couldn't be helped.

She crossed her legs. "This is a good bill, Scott. It will help our government work better and save money. This country is on a precipice. Many people believe that this government no longer works. Can no longer function. *Our* government. Let's show them that it still does." She paused. When he didn't respond, she added, "The money we save may be used for more progressive causes."

"Is that all you've got?"

"I'll mobilize the full strength of federal law enforcement to help locate your son."

"All right then," he said.

# CHAPTER SIXTY-TWO

## Seattle, Washington

THEY WERE MEETING at the local FBI office to debrief on the interview with Tishman's wife.

Jade received a call with a 202 area code. She recognized the number. "Excuse me," she said to the team.

"Hold please," she said into the phone as she strode down the hall looking for a vacant office. Finding one, she entered and shut the door. "Hello."

"Please hold for the president," the president's secretary said.

"Agent Harrington," the president said, her voice resonant, powerful.

"Yes, Madam President."

"I need a favor."

She listened, ending the call with, "We'll do our best."

Jade returned to the conference room, signaling Micah to join her in the hallway. She would give him an opportunity to show her how good he was.

"I need you to do something," she said, after he'd closed the conference room door behind him.

"Sure. What is it?"

Jade told him about the senator's son and the president's request.

"My plate's full." She searched his eyes. "Can you handle this?"

"I've got it."

"Make arrangements to return to DC tonight."

"No need," he said. "I just need a private room."

Puzzled, she gestured toward the office she'd just vacated.

"How are you going to take care of this from here?"

"Watch me."

❊

"This is Iyanna Adey. With KIRO7?"

*I need to change my number.*

Holding the cell phone tighter, Jade sat up on the queen-size hotel bed.

"Yes?"

"I heard you were in town investigating the Tishman murder. Anything you can tell me?"

"How did you get my number?"

"Agent Lawson gave it to me, remember?"

"I don't think he did."

"If you're here, this case is connected to the other Shakespeare murders. Did you find a sonnet?"

"No comment."

"Was the knife left in the body?"

She sat forward. "Where are you getting your information?"

No response. Adey had hung up.

Jade held the phone on her lap. Barringer? Who else could it be?

She remembered seeing Adey with Kyle and McClaine at the hearing and made a mental note to ask them about it.

She texted Pat: Check out Iyanna Adey with KIRO7.

A moment later, Pat responded: A reporter now too?

See if she's connected to someone at the FBI.

On it.

Jade stared at the phone for a moment, then placed the call. The professor answered on the first ring.

"How's your case going?" Bennett asked.

"The perpetrator's still at large," she said.

"So not well, I take it."

"No."

"I hoped that I had helped."

"You did. Professor Bennett, I want to email something to you. What's your address?"

"Only if you call me Alaia."

"Alaia."

"Are you always this stiff?"

*Yes.* "I'm working."

"Ah… hence the term 'working stiff.'"

This made Jade smile.

Bennett gave Jade her email address.

"Tell me when you've received it," Jade said.

"Just did. Give me a moment." Then she said, "Where did you find this one?"

"The victim lived in Seattle. Blayze Tishman. Former software CEO. Now the owner of a professional football team. Any thoughts?"

The professor paused. "I don't think the victims were selected at random. Your killer is decompensating."

*Everyone's a profiler these days.*

"I mean about the sonnet," Jade said. "This one doesn't include 'die' in it."

"But there's 'death,'" the professor pointed out. "Same concept. This is seventy-two. Shakespeare moved into a different period with Sonnets LXXI through LXXIV."

"What do you mean by 'a different period'?"

"These sonnets were about anticipated death."

Jade rolled her eyes. Shakespeare—the poet, not the killer—had had too much time on his hands.

While talking to the professor, she stared at the faux impressionist painting on the opposite wall. The elevator dinged out in the hallway. "Of whom? The recipient or the poet?"

"Excellent question. The answer might be both, but I think it's about the poet's impending death."

"Impending?"

"Remember when these sonnets were written. Death was pervasive in England at the time, not too far from a citizen's everyday thoughts. From the plague, which eradicated thousands of people in a short time, to the public execution of criminals and traitors."

Jade absorbed this. "Any other insight you can give me?"

"In the sonnet, 'shame' is mentioned twice and inferred once. The poet is shamed, but so is the recipient. Your killer and the victim might have done something shameful together. I would suggest looking into the victim's background. You might find your killer there."

❋

The four walls of the hotel room were closing in. After her conversation with the professor, Jade needed a walk.

She eschewed an umbrella as well as the hood on her jacket, letting the rain fall on her hair and skin. She remembered Kyle telling her once that precipitation was cleansing.

Her mind was still. Maybe she would eventually get the hang of meditation after all.

She walked alone down Mercer Street. If she were accosted, her attackers would learn immediately that they'd picked the wrong target. At an underpass, she spotted a mural and stopped to admire it. It depicted the reality before her: tents surrounded by garbage bags and litter. A place where homeless people hunkered down for the evening. It was hard for her to grasp the extent of the homelessness crisis in Seattle, one of the wealthiest cities in the country, although DC was one of the most powerful cities in the world and it had the same problem. What was the answer?

She thought about it. And moved on.

Emerging from the underpass, she gazed at the decorative lights strung up on apartments and houses higher up the hill. The holidays were long over. Cranes—she counted at least nineteen—were decorated in bright colors, predominately green and blue, the colors of the Seattle Seahawks.

After talking to the professor, she'd sent Pat an email request to dig further into Blayze Tishman's background, including his current and past associates. Was there a relationship with the other victims that his wife wasn't aware of? Did his company supply software to their firms? Had he partnered with them in a venture? Or were they connected through the football team?

She also asked Pat to check out his children.

The wind picked up. A scrap of newspaper blew across her

path, part of a full-page ad for the software company Tishman used to lead.

What product was Tishman's company working on with Hurley's?

Jade picked up the paper. Next to the ad was an article about Russia meddling in US elections.

A whisper from Tishman?

Balling it up, she tossed the paper into the next trash can and headed back to the hotel.

She had researched the bard's life. She knew more about him now than she ever thought she would. A poet, playwright, and actor, Shakespeare was still considered the greatest English-language writer of all time.

What in the hell did he have in common with modern-day wealthy Americans?

# CHAPTER SIXTY-THREE

## Bellevue, Washington

ON THE DRIVE east to Blayze Tishman's former company, Jade's phone vibrated in her pocket. Eyeing the number, she let it go to voicemail. When they arrived at the software company's campus, Jade said to the others, "I'll be there in a minute."

"Must be important," Christian said.

"Something I need to take care of."

She waited until Brian Anderson, Max, and Christian were out of hearing distance and hit the call back button.

"Hello," Kyle answered. A statement, not a question.

"Ms. Madison."

"Oh, we're back to that again?"

"How are you?" Jade said.

"I heard you were in Seattle. Since you're here, I presume it has to do with the Shakespeare Killer. Blayze?"

Jade might as well have rented a billboard advertising her arrival in Seattle.

"Did you know him?"

"We were involved in a lot of charitable causes together. Attended the same events. Ran in the same political circles."

"Ah… one of Fairchild's army of small donors."

"Something like that."

It used to be a joke between them. Blayze Tishman wasn't a small donor. Neither was Kyle Madison.

"Is it true?" Kyle asked. "He was stabbed to death?"

Through the light fog, Jade admired the fir trees in the distance. Cars blazed by on the nearby freeway. Blaze. Blayze. "I can't discuss an ongoing investigation."

"Oh, right."

"Any idea who could've done this?"

"Always interrogating," she said. "That's the Jade I know."

"Well," Jade said, "since you're on the phone…"

A pause. Then, "Blayze always needed to prove how smart he was. He was loud. Boorish. Offensive. I'm sure anyone that successful developed some enemies along the way."

"Anyone specific?"

"Well…"

"Tell me."

"I hate to do this—he's been through so much—but Blayze never treated Noah very well. He was condescending, belittling to him. I'm sure Noah hated him."

"Enough to kill him?"

Kyle hesitated. "Conceivably."

"Do you know Iyanna Adey?"

"Who?"

"The reporter. Channel seven."

"I've seen her on TV."

"No. I saw you talking to her. At Noah's hearing."

A longer pause. "She interviewed me. For the trial."

"You, Adey, and McClaine seemed familiar with each other."

"We were all involved in Noah's case. Besides, despite its size, Seattle is a small town."

Jade didn't believe she'd misinterpreted what she saw.

❋

The campus was right outside of Bellevue, a city near Medina. Locals called the area east of the lake the Eastside. The agents and McClaine spoke to the current CEO of the global software company, who wouldn't divulge the purpose of the joint project with Hurley Technologies without written authorization from US Cyber Command.

They also spoke to the human resources department. They had received threats targeted at Tishman over the years. The staff provided the names and addresses of all the now former employees involved.

Although described as brash and boorish, Tishman was well respected. The company's financial results spoke for themselves. Everyone agreed on the Tishmans' unparalleled generosity in their efforts to combat numerous social problems plaguing not only Seattle but cities and towns across the United States: homelessness, income disparity, and inequality in education funding.

The agents spent a few hours interviewing staff at all levels of the organization who'd worked with Tishman, but they learned nothing helpful.

Pat sent an email reporting that Tishman's kids were all successful in their own right. Tara was a corporate attorney, Lindsey an investment banker, and Patrick a product manager for Amazon. Victoria divulged that she was the sole heir of her husband's estate. Pat looked into her too, but so far hadn't come up with anything.

On the way back from Bellevue, Jade called AMB International and spoke with Augustus Mathias Blakeley, its CEO and Noah's father. He told her that Noah had moved to Panama shortly after he was exonerated.

To be with "his people."

# CHAPTER SIXTY-FOUR

# Seattle, Washington

LATER, BACK IN a conference room at the local FBI office, Jade, Dante, Max, Micah, Christian, McClaine, and Brian Anderson sat around an oval table discussing the interviews.

Anderson stood. "Anyone want anything? Coffee? Soda? Water?"

There were a few responses for water and coffee.

"Do you have tea, mate?" Micah asked.

"Teammate?" Dante said.

"No, I asked for tea from my mate here."

Shaking his head, Dante said, "A dude who drinks tea. God help me." To Anderson, "Can I have an espresso?"

Micah shook his head.

Once they had their drinks, Dante said to Jade, "We should leave Micah here to coordinate efforts among the locals, our office here, and the bureau."

Sitting across from Micah, she saw his eyes shift to McClaine.

Odd. Was Dante right about him? Was Micah gay? She thought of his kiss.

Definitely not gay.

"I need Micah in DC."

"What about Merritt?"

"I love how you're all talking about us as if we're not here," Micah said, sipping his hot tea out of a cup, his pinkie extended. Dante looked at him with disgust.

Christian rose abruptly and stood by the window, his arms crossed over his chest. She joined him.

As they both stared down on Third Avenue, she said, "I need someone here."

"I'm being forced out."

"That's not what this is."

He looked at her. "What happened to your 'rock'?"

She pushed him. He didn't budge. "See? You're still my rock. Coordinate things here and come back as soon as you can. You're an important member of this team and more valuable to me here."

After a moment, he nodded without looking at her.

They returned to the table.

Dante's head dropped, his expression one of pity. "Robin having trouble leaving Batman?"

Jade opened her mouth to give her usual response, but Christian beat her to it. In her tone of voice, he said, "Shut up, Dante."

The agents' laughter broke the tension.

After deciding on next steps, they stood to leave. McClaine came to stand next to Jade. "Until next time?"

"If you want to work with me so badly," she said, "why don't you move to DC?"

She started to smile, but McClaine's eyes shifted to Micah

and Max, then back to her. It happened swiftly; perhaps she was mistaken.

"Maybe I will," he said.

"How do you know Iyanna Adey?"

An almost imperceptible tug of the eyes. "The reporter? She covers the crime beat, I think."

"I saw you talking to her and Kyle Madison at Noah Blakeley's hearing. The three of you seemed tight."

"Our police department prides itself on knowing the citizens in our community. That's what you saw. Safe travels, Agent Harrington."

He hugged her—he was a hugger—and left.

Retrieving her briefcase and rolling suitcase from against the wall, she said goodbye to Christian and Anderson and headed down the hallway, with Dante, Max, and Micah trailing behind her.

After the elevator doors closed, Jade turned to Micah.

"Do you and McClaine know each other?" Jade asked.

She sensed Max waiting for the answer too.

Micah stared up at the descending numbers. "Why do you ask?"

"A vibe I'm feeling," she said.

"As much as two guys can get to know each other during a car ride," he said. "He's a Sounders fan."

"I think Micah's sweet on him," Dante said.

"Are you jealous?" Micah looked at him. "You want a bromance, bro?"

"I'm serious, Micah," Jade said. "Have you worked with him?"

He turned to her. "Relax, Agent Harrington. We just met and clicked. There's no mystery here. Nothing for you to investigate."

She stared at his face, looking for tells.

There were none.

The car arrived at the lobby.

Micah's phone rang. "Alexander." He listened. "That's great news. Thank you."

He hung up. To Jade, he said, "It's about Senator Harris. We found his son."

"Is he—?"

"He's alive. And he's fine."

"Wow," she said, "good news."

*That was fast.*

# CHAPTER SIXTY-FIVE

# The White House, Washington, DC

"CONGRATULATIONS," SASHA SAID with a broad grin.

The Streamline Regulations Act had passed in the Senate by one vote. Scott Harris, surprising all the media pundits, signed on as a late sponsor of the bill.

In other news, his thirteen-year-old son had returned home unharmed.

No ransom was demanded.

And there was no mention of who had abducted him.

Whitney would partake of a celebratory cigar after Sasha left.

Earlier that evening, they had enjoyed a steak dinner in the Residence dining room, prepared by the White House chef. Now, in the West Sitting Hall, Whitney sat on the sofa with her legs tucked under her; Sasha sat in a matching chair. The television in the corner was muted.

Raising her glass of wine, Whitney acknowledged the compliment. The bottle, three-quarters empty, rested on a side table next to the couch.

"How's the First Gentleman?"

"I wouldn't know," Whitney said as she poured more wine into Sasha's glass.

Sasha hesitated, then said, "'I have been driven many times upon my knees by the overwhelming conviction that I had nowhere else to go.'"

"Lincoln," said Whitney, who had read everything she could about the sixteenth president.

"'Look to the Lord and his strength.' 1 Chronicles. You should try it sometime. It might help."

"I guess if He helped Lincoln, He could help me."

Shaking her head in a tsk-tsk sort of way, Sasha said, "Don't shade scripture. Have you prayed about it?"

"No."

"Is he coming back?"

"I guess I shouldn't joke about whether that's a lowercase or uppercase *h*, but to answer your question… the decision isn't only up to him."

"Is he behaving himself?"

Sasha was referring to Grayson's previous affair.

Whitney shrugged.

Sasha had become more than just an employee during Whitney's first year in office. Whitney considered Sasha a friend, and, in her position, she didn't have many of those. The saying was true: it's lonely at the top. Regardless of how close they were, however, she was uncomfortable talking to Sasha about her relationship with her husband—or lack thereof.

Sasha took in the room. "I could get used to this."

Whitney raised an eyebrow. "Do you have aspirations?"

Sasha's smile was uncharacteristically vulnerable as she gazed into her glass. "Possibly."

Whitney raised her eyebrows. Sasha rubbed some people the wrong way; diplomacy wasn't her strong suit.

"I started out in politics," Sasha continued, "to give a voice to people who didn't have one, but over time, it's become something more."

"This job requires persistence," Whitney said. "A steady hand. Someone who keeps her head and can make decisions when everyone else around her is losing theirs." She paused. "You would make an excellent president."

Her chief of staff's eyes widened. "Thank you, Madam President."

Sasha understood that it was more than a compliment. It would take a strong, resilient, and persistent woman to be the first black woman president of the United States of America.

Something on the television caught Whitney's eye. She exhaled and said, "What is she up to now?"

Judy Porter stood in front of a dark, wooded area, speaking into an ABC microphone.

Reluctantly, Whitney grabbed the remote off the glass table and turned up the volume.

"As previously reported, coincidences and conspiracy theories have swirled around our current president during the campaign and throughout the infancy of her presidency: The death of her aunt. Her mysterious teenage pregnancy. Her meteoric rise in politics. But I believe it all started right here"—the reporter gestured behind her—"with the mysterious, and still unsolved, death of Congressman Steven Barrett."

Whitney stilled her face, not moving her eyes from the television, knowing Sasha's eyes were on her.

"A source within the local police department told me that the FBI's inquiry into the congressman's case was dropped, and all local efforts were to cease. The order came from up high. No reason given. Attempts by state legislator—now Congressman—Cameron Kelly from the 87th district to discover what happened were stonewalled. I wonder by whom?"

Judy scanned the forested area, then looked back into the camera's lens. "I will tell you this. I won't stop digging until I find out what happened here. Our viewers deserve to know. The American people deserve to know. This is Judy Porter reporting from Clayton, Missouri. Back to you, Glenn."

The camera cut to the anchorman in the studio.

Whitney forced a laugh as she picked up the remote and turned off the TV. "Speaking of persistence…"

Sasha shrugged. "She's a woman. She has to be."

As Whitney took another sip of her drink, Sasha swept her phone off the table and sent a quick message.

"Problem?" Whitney asked.

A shake of the head. Sasha set her phone facedown on the table and picked up her glass. Before taking a sip, she peered at Whitney over the rim of her glass. "Why won't she let this go, do you think?"

Biding time, Whitney poured herself some more wine. Sasha, her glass half full, waved away Whitney's offer for a refill.

"Perhaps she doesn't have a personal life," Whitney said, settling back into the sofa, "so she's consumed with mine."

Staring at the blank screen, the chief of staff mumbled something.

"What was that, Sasha?"

Sasha shook her head.

It had sounded like, "Or perhaps where there's smoke, there's fire."

## CHAPTER SIXTY-SIX

# Arlington, Virginia

J ADE ENTERED HER townhouse and stood in the foyer for a moment. Waiting. The house was empty. The quietness enveloped her.

Her cat, Card, was staying with Zoe. It was weird when he wasn't there to greet her. With his unconditional love and complete dependence, he was more than a pet. He was her family.

She set her bag down and started down the hallway toward the kitchen. She'd fallen asleep during takeoff and hadn't eaten on the plane.

As she opened her refrigerator and peered at the slim pickings, her phone buzzed in her pocket.

Dante.

She'd just left him at the airport. Was there a lead in the Tishman case already? Did Pat find something?

"Don't bother unpacking," he said, his breath heavy from running or walking fast.

"I haven't, but I'm hungry."

"Grab something on the way. Shakespeare struck again."

She froze, her hunger pains replaced by a sinking sensation. Closing the refrigerator door, she said, "It hasn't been a week yet." Heading toward the front of the house so she could race upstairs to take a quick shower and pack some fresh clothes, she said, "Where are we going?"

"Missouri."

# CHAPTER SIXTY-SEVEN

## Clayton, Missouri

"WHAT'S HER NAME?" Jade said.

"Judy Porter. Washington driver's license."

"State?" asked Dante.

"DC," said the detective from the Clayton PD.

Jade, Dante, Max, and Micah gathered around the body. Jade had commissioned a private FBI plane, and they were on the ground in St. Louis three hours after she received Dante's call.

The local police had waited for them.

"As soon as we saw that"—the detective pointed to a piece of paper attached with a safety pin to the victim's shirt—"we called you in."

She scanned the area. A well-lit vacancy sign illuminated the front entrance. The body lay beside a dumpster in a parking lot behind the motel, where a putrid combination of trash, grease, and pizza filled the air. The asphalt was littered with needles, chip wrappers, cigarette butts, and dented soda cans. Dried blood formed a circle underneath the upper part of the victim's body.

"Who found her?" she asked.

"Maintenance guy. He was taking out the trash earlier tonight and spotted the body. He dropped the trash," he said, pointing at two large green bags, "and called us. Claimed he didn't touch the body."

"Print him?"

"Yep. He's in the manager's office, if you want to talk to him."

"We do."

She inclined her head toward the victim. "Was she staying here?"

"There's a room registered in her name, yes."

Something was missing. "Where's the murder weapon?"

"No sign of it."

The knife had been left in each of the other victims.

Jade crouched next to the body. Rigor mortis had set in. What appeared to be knife wounds marked the victim's left side. Her breath caught when she saw the auburn hair and pale face, the eyes void of life.

"Judy Porter," she said.

"That's what I said," the detective said roughly.

She looked up at him. "She's a reporter. From ABC News."

He stared at her blankly. "I only watch Fox."

"Why was she here?" Jade asked.

Shaking his head, he excused himself. He walked ten yards away, already on his cell phone.

Jade had never met the reporter and didn't watch her broadcasts often. She remembered the president telling her that ABC News was preparing an investigative report on her political ascendance after the mysterious death of Congressman Steven

Barrett. Fairchild had privately asked Jade to find out what the network knew.

Judy Porter's presence wasn't a coincidence. Neither was her death.

Someone crouched down next to her.

"He's decompensating," Max said. "Organized killers plan their attacks. Planning is part of the fantasy. The other murders appeared to be planned." He pointed at the knife wounds. "This attack was sloppy. Disorganized. Unplanned."

"Judy was a reporter," Jade said, "albeit a national one, but I don't think she would be considered wealthy. At least not in the same class as the other victims. Unless she had money we haven't found out about yet."

"We need to catch him," Max said.

Jade stared at him. She understood. Looking over at the detective, she said, "Where's the manager's office?"

# CHAPTER SIXTY-EIGHT

## Clayton, Missouri

THE MAN IN the maintenance uniform sweated profusely. Although it was warm in the crowded manager's office, Jade suspected his discomfort was primarily due to the presence of law enforcement. In addition to Jade, Dante, Max, and Micah, there was the Clayton police detective, two police officers, and a pretty Hispanic woman in a motel uniform who worked at the front desk. After interviewing her, Jade realized she might be needed. The woman spoke fluent Spanish and English. Although Jade spoke passable Spanish, this interview was too important to allow any room for mistakes. She was grateful for the assistance.

The front desk clerk said Judy and her cameraman—or rather, "the woman and the guy with the bulky camera"—entered and left the motel several times over the past two days. The pair had not eaten in the motel's restaurant or swam in the small pool.

Motel employees said Judy wasn't rude but intense; her mind always seemed focused elsewhere.

The motel's maintenance man was also Hispanic. Jade guessed Mexican. He was stocky, with black hair and a mole dotting his cheek. She pegged him for early forties. From his behavior, he might be working in the country illegally.

Or he was just nervous because he was brown.

"There are a lot of people in here," Jade said to him. "We're here to catch a murderer. That's all. You're not in any trouble. Do you understand?"

The woman translated. He still didn't respond.

Jade stared into his eyes and said to him in Spanish, "We're not ICE."

"I have children," he said.

Jade touched his hand. "I won't let anyone take you away from your children."

*Or take your children away from you.*

Seeing something in her eyes that convinced him to trust her, he gave her a slight nod.

He relayed the same story he'd told the detective. He hadn't seen anyone in the parking lot. After dropping the trash bags, he ran back to this office and told the manager about the dead woman.

"Close your eyes," Jade said, waiting. "Trust me, por favor."

He hesitated, then obeyed her instructions.

"Visualize the scene again," she said. "What do you see?"

He licked his lips.

The agents were quiet as they waited.

"A truck," he said in English, his eyes still closed. "Or an SUV. Black. Idling out on the street near the entrance. When I stopped near the body, it took off." The man opened his eyes in wonder. "I forgot all about that until now."

The front desk clerk started to repeat what he'd said, but Jade raised her hand. His English wasn't perfect, but it was perfectly understandable.

"In which direction?" Jade asked. "Where did it go?"

"Norte. North."

Dante, who'd been leaning against the wall, straightened. "Did you see the license plate? The driver?"

The man shook his head. "Too far away."

Jade thanked the witness and the woman. She tried to be patient as she waited for them to leave the room. A tingle had started in her fingertips and was spreading up her arm.

Their first break.

To the detective she said, "We need to find that vehicle."

❋

Dante used the key card the manager had given him to open the door to a second-floor room. All the motel's rooms faced the parking lot or the street, all the doors and staircases exposed to the elements. He flipped on the light switch.

Scanning the room, Jade wondered if the television network had fallen on hard times.

Why had Judy Porter stayed here?

The carpets were threadbare and stained, the furniture mismatched. Brown stains from past leaks blotched the ceiling tiles. A germaphobe, Jade gladly donned nitrile gloves as they spread out to examine the room. Micah took the closets, Dante checked out the bathroom, Max examined the bed, and Jade headed straight for the desk.

The room had been dusted for fingerprints, but Jade wasn't hopeful that anything useful would come back. A motel room contained hundreds, possibly thousands, of prints. And the killer might not have entered the room.

The desk's surface was spotted with water stains and cigarette burns. A laptop sat open next to a stack of papers. Jade shuffled through it. It appeared to be a transcript. After a cursory scan of the first page, she set it aside for later. A briefcase—one of those old, battered college professor ones—leaned against the desk. Sitting in the chair, Jade sifted through it. Nestled among the pens, Judy's press badge, pads of paper, and folders was a tape recorder. Jade took it out and set it on the desk.

She hit PLAY.

"I live in the neighborhood," said a male voice. "I was out walking my dog."

She turned up the volume to drown out the sounds of the TV in the next room and the traffic outside.

"What did you see?" said a woman's voice. Jade imagined the concerned-reporter expression on Judy's face.

"I was on the other side of the road."

"How far away were you?"

A pause. "Thirty yards. Fifty at the most."

"Tell me what happened."

"A car came toward me."

"Was it speeding?"

"Not really."

"And?"

"All of a sudden, an SUV came out of nowhere and sped up so it was even with the car. At first I thought it would pass, but then it almost seemed like…"

"What?"

"It wanted to race."

Silence from the recorder. While Jade had been listening, the other agents had gathered around her.

"And then?"

"Both of them sped up, as if they *were* racing. Then the SUV bumped the car. The car almost went into the ditch but corrected itself. The SUV bumped it harder. The car swerved again before righting itself. The SUV bumped it a third time. This time the car couldn't right itself. Not sure why the driver didn't use his brakes. The car slammed into a tree. It had been going at a good clip by this point. The car looked like one of those old musical instruments." Finger snaps. "An accordion. That's it."

"You said 'his brakes,'" Judy said. "Did you see the driver?"

"A woman wouldn't drive like that."

Judy paused. "What happened then?"

"The SUV stopped up the road. A man got out and walked back to the wreckage. He squatted and looked inside. I saw the airbag through the shattered window. Smoke came out from under the hood. Like it was going to blow. The man didn't try to help whoever was inside. He stared for a while and then walked back to the SUV and drove away."

"What did he look like?"

"I didn't get a good look. It gets dark out here. He was wearing a coat. It looked like leather. Dark slacks. Short hair. Military or ex-military."

"What did you do then?"

"I picked up my dog and ran back to my house."

"Did you call the police?"

"No."

"Why not?"

"Cell phone service isn't that great out here."

"Is that the reason—"

"I ran... because I was scared. Something about that guy screamed Special Forces. Or an assassin or something." Silence. "I have a family. A new grandson. Thought it best to mind my own business."

Jade let the recording continue, but the rest of the tape was dead air.

She was well aware of what she'd just heard.

Judy Porter was interviewing an eyewitness to the murder of United States Congressman Steven Barrett.

# CHAPTER SIXTY-NINE

## St. Louis, Missouri

*For sweetest things turn sourest by their deeds:*
*Lilies that fester smell far worse than weeds.*

—Bard of Avon

I T WAS EARLY or late, depending on how you looked at it.
Jade leaned against the headboard in a hotel room
downtown. Dante thought it would be bad luck to stay in
the same motel that Judy had stayed in. Jade agreed. Regardless,
she wasn't keen to sleep in a motel one step up from seedy. Jade
understood now why Judy had stayed there. It was the closest
motel to the scene of the congressman's accident.

A pickle on a plate was all that remained from her room-ser-
vice dinner of a double cheeseburger and fries. Sipping a Pepsi, she
checked the Shakespeare app on her phone. The sonnet attached
to Judy Porter was number ninety-four. She read it again.

What did it mean? What did any of them mean? How did the reporter fit in? Had she gotten too close? To what?

This last question made Jade sit up.

Was Judy's investigation connected to the Shakespeare murders? Was the killer acquainted with all his victims? Jade agreed with the professor; she didn't think they were selected at random. What was the glue? Were they looking for an English professor? Teacher? How many serial-killing English teachers could there be in America?

She chuckled. She was tired and being silly.

Earlier, she'd reviewed Veritas's timeline on Twitter, but she couldn't locate a single tweet about Judy Porter during the last month. She made a mental note to tell Pat to check further back and submit another court order to the social media company in case the tweet had been deleted.

Assuming he hadn't tweeted about Judy, why the break in pattern?

She laid each of the partial sonnets in a neat row in front of her on the bedspread and the full texts in a row above them. She wrote the numbers down: 1, 3, 7, 72, 94. After a moment, she wrote their equivalent Roman numerals: I, III, VII, LXXII, and XCIV. She sent Pat a text about the court order and the sonnet numbers, hoping the analysts would find a pattern.

Jade had read every sonnet in its entirety—all hundred and fifty-four of them—along with the online CliffsNotes and SparkNotes analyses of each one. Although she understood the poems better, she hadn't discovered any clues as to their connection with the victims or to the identity of the perpetrator or where he'd strike next.

Her cell phone buzzed. Expecting Dante, she swiped to accept the call without looking at the display.

"What's up?" she asked.

"Pardon me?"

"Oh…"

"It's Blake."

She remembered that he didn't want to see her. "Okay."

"Are you in town?"

"No."

"I want to explain."

She squinted at the generic painting on the opposite wall. It looked like the one in her hotel room in Seattle.

"You're up late," she said.

"I don't sleep much these days."

"Why?"

"It hurts." A pause. "How've you been?"

She glanced down at the sonnets. "Puzzled."

Despite his condition, he'd asked her how she was doing. She imagined the remonstrations of her mother for forgetting her manners.

"How are you feeling?" she asked.

"Been better. I'm home. Finally. I would like to see you sometime, but… not yet."

"I understand." And she did. She wasn't sure she'd want him to visit her under similar circumstances.

"Anything new on who's responsible? For the terrorist attack?"

"No," she said. She'd been too busy with her team's cases to check on his. "Have you found out anything?"

"No."

"I'll check with Counterterrorism."

"No need," he said. "I have my own sources."

The president.

"But that's not why I called," he continued.

"Oh?"

"I heard about Judy Porter."

"I haven't told the president yet."

"Her husband called me."

"How do you—wait!" Jade grabbed the notebook on the nightstand. "You knew her."

"She was in the press corps. We weren't friends and didn't drink together, but we saw each other at events. That's how I met her husband, David."

"What did you think of her?"

"A fine reporter. Did her homework. Practiced journalism the way it's supposed to be. I respected her tremendously. It's a loss for the profession."

"Are you okay?"

"That's not why I called either." He paused. "Did you watch her broadcast the other night?"

"Not yet."

"You should."

"Because…"

"I don't think the Shakespeare Killer killed her. I think it had something to do with Congressman Barrett's murder."

"What makes you say that?"

"Just a feeling," he said. "I'm going to keep digging."

"Blake, you should leave the investigating to the investigators. To me."

"I want to help." Another pause. "I have nothing but time on my hands."

"As a law enforcement officer, I should dissuade you from pursing this matter further."

"Perhaps, but I would pursue it in any event."

---

# CHAPTER SEVENTY

# St. Louis, Missouri

"IT'S LATE. ANOTHER murder?"

"Yes," Jade said into her cell phone.

"Which sonnet?"

"Ninety-four."

"'For sweetest things turn sourest by their deeds," quoted the professor. "Lilies that fester smell far worse than weeds.'"

"That's it."

"At first blush," Alaia Bennett said, "ninety-four is similar to the sonnet preceding it, contrasting virtue with appearance. This one, however, contains no reference to the poet or the young man."

"What's it about then?"

"The difference between outward appearance and inner worth. Or, as my grandma used to say, just because it looks good doesn't mean it's good for you."

How did this sonnet apply to Judy? Was there more to her, or to what she was investigating, than met the eye?

Jade was tired but not sleepy. She stuffed another pillow behind her head. "How did you become a professor?"

"I went to Spelman—the best historically black college in the country, by the way—and loved it. I was an activist before and after graduation, but I realized that no matter how hard I worked or how passionate I was, I wasn't making any progress. *We* weren't making any progress. I decided I could better serve the cause by teaching the next generation about *our* history."

"Through literature?" Jade asked, not bothering to mask her skepticism.

"I don't teach only Shakespeare," Bennett said, "and the other great white writers. I expose my students to the writings of James Baldwin, Zora Neale Hurston, Langston Hughes, Maya Angelou, Richard Wright, Toni Morrison, Ralph Ellison, Octavia Butler, Alex Haley, Alice Walker, and Lorraine Vivian Hansberry."

"Who is Lorraine Vivian Hansberry?"

The professor tsked. "You need to know your history. We are descended from kings and queens. We are their wildest dreams."

Jade thought of her parents. Sounded about right. "Tell me about Hansberry."

"An African-American playwright. She was the first black woman to write a play performed on Broadway. *A Raisin in the Sun.* Heard of it?"

"Sure."

"She was also a civil rights activist in the fifties and sixties. A little militant. Believed that black people should fight back using any means at their disposal, whether legal or illegal, violent or nonviolent, passive or aggressive."

"Do you agree with her?"

"Absolutely. There's no playbook for a revolution."

"Sounds like a formidable woman."

"She was. Married to a Jewish guy. And a closeted lesbian."

Jade wasn't sure what to say to that.

"Have you read any of the other authors?"

"I read *The Color Purple*," Jade said, "and some Toni Morrison in school. *Invisible Man*."

"Pitiful," the professor said. "It's because of people like you that I teach." She paused. "You should take my class."

"Maybe I should."

## CHAPTER SEVENTY-ONE

# The White House, Washington, DC

WHITNEY SPOONED A small wedge of grapefruit into her mouth, her eyes falling on the empty place setting.

She and Grayson had developed a routine of having breakfast and reading major newspapers from around the globe together in the Residence kitchen before heading to their offices in the West Wing.

After he had left, almost two months ago now, whenever they'd called each other, they discussed only the children or their work. They hadn't discussed their relationship.

He hadn't called recently.

She hadn't called him either.

Every day, she ate breakfast alone. In truth, she enjoyed the solitude.

After finishing the grapefruit, she placed her dishes in the sink. The phone rang.

She moved to the counter to answer it.

Only a handful of people in the world could reach her directly. Whitney glanced at the clock: 5:30 a.m. The sun wouldn't rise for another hour. This wasn't good news.

"Madam President, Jade Harrington."

"Agent Harrington. I presume this isn't a social call."

"No, it isn't. I'm in Clayton, Missouri."

Whitney gripped the handset tighter. Grayson lived in Clayton. As did her parents. Her brothers and their families. Were her children visiting? Her mind spun with all the horrendous possibilities.

"I'm listening," she said.

"Judy Porter was murdered here last night."

"My God! I watched her on television the other night. Why was she still in Clayton?" That was the wrong question to ask. "Sorry, this is such a shock. What happened?"

"She was working on a story about Congressman Steven Barrett's accident. She was found dead in the parking lot of the motel where she was staying."

"Why couldn't she let it go?" Whitney murmured.

"Let what go?" the agent asked.

*Did I say that aloud?*

"How did it happen?"

"She was stabbed."

"How awful. Judy was a fine reporter. I truly respected her. She will be missed."

"What couldn't she let go, Madam President?"

Whitney paused, thinking. "A story. Any story."

Silence on the other end. Then, "I wanted you to hear it from me before you heard it on the news." Other voices in the background. Jade said to someone else, "I'll be right there." Into the phone, she said, "Ma'am, I've gotta go."

"Thank you for this call. Please keep me informed."

The agent didn't respond before hanging up.

Whitney slowly replaced the receiver.

She made a mental note to call the reporter's family. Whitney had met her husband once—Daniel? Dylan? David!—and that was the extent of what she knew about Judy's private life.

Judy had kept digging into Whitney's past long after most reporters would have quit.

Despite her sadness for the reporter's family, she would no longer need to worry about Judy Porter.

Whitney's past could finally be buried.

# CHAPTER SEVENTY-TWO

## Washington, DC

JADE FLEW HOME a few hours after talking to Fairchild, leaving Dante and the rest of the team to finish the initial investigation into Judy Porter's murder. They interviewed the motel's guests, Judy's cameraman, and the neighbors that lived along the road where Barrett was killed. Finding the witness to the congressman's death was a top priority.

She thought about the president's question.

*Why couldn't she let it go?*

What was Judy Porter after?

And was she killed for it?

After landing at Reagan, Jade went home for a quick shower and change of clothes.

She dialed the number on the way to work.

"You rang, your highn-ass?"

"Good morning to you too. Why are you still in bed?"

"What time is it?" asked Zoe.

"Eight."

"Damn. I overslept. Where are you?"

"Just flew in from St. Louis. On my way to the office. How's Card?"

"He's fine. Been sleeping with me. Really cramping my style. I put his name on the mailbox, by the way."

"Funny," Jade said, turning right on E Street. "I'm picking up my baby tonight."

"Ooh… am I your baby?"

"My furry one."

"Damn," Zoe said. "We'll be here. Let us know if you'll be joining us for dinner. I'm going back to sleep. Why is the snooze button for only nine minutes?"

"Don't know. I've got my own mysteries to figure out."

She pressed the button near the radio to end the call.

In her office, Jade booted up her computer. An email from Pat, with all of Judy's broadcasts for the past year, awaited her.

She considered Blake's suspicion that Judy's death was a copycat killing, that it wasn't the Shakespeare Killer.

Blake said he had a feeling. Jade made decisions based on evidence, but she, too, placed a great deal of faith in her intuition. She should have dissuaded him from helping her. Despite his investigative reporting skills, he was a civilian. She ignored the small part of her that looked forward to spending more time with him.

Jade clicked on the video that Blake had recommended she watch. Judy Porter stood by the side of the road adjacent to a wooded area, speaking into a microphone, describing the circumstances of the congressman's car accident. She also described the coincidences concerning his death and the special election to replace him. Nothing Jade hadn't heard before. No mention of the witness. Judy might have been trying to locate someone else who could corroborate his story.

She tensed when Judy mentioned that although the death was ruled a homicide, the FBI had dropped its inquiry. Jade paused the recording and leaned back in her chair, closing her eyes. Thinking back to the dinner she'd had with the president in the White House Residence, she remembered that Fairchild asked her to investigate the accident. Jade had delegated the assignment to Pat. Pat discovered that the single-car crash wasn't an accident. The car's brakes were tampered with. The congressman had no chance of navigating the sharp turn or avoiding the oak tree. Since the car was totaled and the family believed it was an accident, they'd sold it to a mechanic, who sold it for parts.

The perpetrator of Jade's first major case, the Talk-Show Killer, happened to be in the area at the time. Judy was right. Many coincidences surrounded this case. Jade didn't believe in coincidences, and she suspected that the reporter hadn't either.

Something wasn't right.

Amid everything else going on, she hadn't kept track of the outcome of the congressman's case.

She called Pat. "How's the court order for Twitter coming?"

"Still waiting."

"Anything back on Adey?"

"No luck so far."

"Whatever happened to your inquiry into Congressman Barrett's death?"

Pat hesitated. "I was told to stop."

Jade had been Pat's direct supervisor at the time.

"I don't recall telling you to stop."

"You didn't."

"Who then?"

Even as she asked, the answer came to Jade.

"Barringer," Pat said.

## CHAPTER SEVENTY-THREE

# The White House, Washington, DC

AFTER ANOTHER DINNER alone, Whitney retreated to the Treaty Room on the second floor of the Residence. Like many of her predecessors, she used the room as a study when she worked late.

The room and the table were named by former first lady Jacqueline Kennedy in honor of the numerous treaties signed there: from the end of the Spanish American War in 1898 to the peace treaty between Egypt and Israel in 1979.

Whitney set the pen down next to the briefing book, still thinking about Judy Porter. Instead of relief, unease weighed on her.

At the knock on her door, she beckoned. "Come in, Sasha."

Sasha had called fifteen minutes ago, asking to see her.

The chief of staff crossed the room and stood looking at the stack of books on the table: biographies (Mikhail Gorbachev, Catherine the Great, and Leo Tolstoy), a book on Russian history, another on Russian politics, and a young adult novel squeezed among them.

"Homework?" Sasha asked.

"'If you know the enemy and know yourself, you need not fear the result of a hundred battles. If you know yourself but not the enemy, for every victory gained you will also suffer a defeat. If you know neither the enemy nor yourself, you will succumb in every battle.'"

"Sun Tzu. *The Art of War*. When do you have time to read all those books?"

Whitney glanced at them. "Reading helped me to get here"— she swept her arm in a gesture that took in the entire White House—"and is sometimes my only salvation. How did it go?"

"Fine. She's at home, resting. Scared more than anything else."

Sasha had flown home to Texas two days ago. Her mother had showed symptoms of a heart attack.

"I'm glad it was just a scare."

"Thank you." Then, her face neutral, Sasha said, "Awful about what happened to Judy."

Whitney sat back in her leather chair and crossed her legs. "Such a tragedy. She was a good reporter."

Sasha held her eyes. "Like a dog with a bone."

"She *was* persistent."

"It was more than that, though."

What was she implying?

Sasha continued, "Well, you won't need to worry about her any longer."

Was her relief that obvious?

"That's an awful thing to say, Sasha!"

"Yes, it is." Sasha handed Whitney a sheaf of papers. "Here are your remarks for tomorrow."

She turned to leave, then turned back. "Since you're always quoting people, I've got one of mine I want to share with you. It's not the dead you need to worry about. It's the living."

Sasha left.

"That's all I ever do," Whitney said to the empty room.

❋

Arriving early to the Oval Office the next day, she finished up her morning briefing with a high-ranking analyst from the Office of the Director of National Intelligence. She was distracted the entire time; her thoughts kept drifting to the conversation with Sasha the night before.

At 8:00 a.m., Sean buzzed her.

"Cole Brennan is on the line."

"Did he say what he wanted?"

"No. He's becoming a regular Chatty Cathy, isn't he?"

She smiled. "Put him through, Sean." Then, "Good morning, Cole."

"I'm getting ready to go on the air, but I have a message for you."

"Oh?"

"I ate breakfast with Congressman Cameron Kelly this morning to discuss the next election."

"Don't you think you're placing your bet too early?" Whitney asked, her tone dry.

"It's never too soon to start. We're up against a formidable opponent."

"Cole, are you complimenting me?"

"I tell it like it is."

"Thank you. What's the message?"

"He wants a meeting with you. Since the two of you are from the same district, I thought it was a good idea and agreed to set it up."

Whitney didn't trust herself to speak. After a moment, she said, "I don't have time."

"I haven't told you when," he said. His media instincts kicked in. "Is there some reason you don't want to meet with him?"

"When?" she managed to say.

"How about tonight?"

# CHAPTER SEVENTY-FOUR

## Washington, DC

FOR THE REMAINDER of the afternoon, Jade viewed the rest of Judy's broadcasts on the computer in her office. The reporter never said it outright, but she insinuated that the president hid her teenage pregnancy from the American people during the presidential campaign because she believed her child had grown up to be the Talk-Show Killer. Judy further implied that then state legislator Whitney Fairchild was involved in Congressman Barrett's death and, as president, had ordered the FBI to cover it up.

Impeachment implications. World-shattering ramifications. Possible criminal charges. Could a sitting president be indicted and sent to jail while in office?

Jade believed so, although it hadn't happened in the United States. Yet.

She stopped herself. What about innocent until proven guilty? This was one reporter's unproven allegations.

Did this jive with the Whitney Fairchild Jade knew?

Judy Porter was the only victim who'd had the knife removed from her body.

It still hadn't been recovered.

The task force hadn't released the detail about the knives being left in the bodies of the first four victims. Not even to local law enforcement agencies. Had Judy Porter's murder been staged to look like the work of the Shakespeare Killer because she possessed incriminating information about the president of the United States?

Jade turned her attention to the file on her desk: a dossier on Judy Porter prepared by Pat.

Judy Porter wasn't wealthy, but she came from money. Her father was the CEO of Adams Appliances, a firm in business for over one hundred years. His great-grandfather started the business in 1905 in a small town in Southern Illinois. The company went from being a small local business to a regional one until the "go-go sixties," when Judy's father took the company public and it became national, and then, in the 1990s, international. As far as Pat could determine, Judy was never involved in the business.

But she ended up investigating the company through her job.

Judy Adams left Illinois after high school to study journalism at Syracuse University. After college, she landed in Chicago and started as an intern at ABC7, the local ABC affiliate. On a Tuesday, the day after the stock market crashed on October 19, 1987—known as Black Monday—she interviewed David Porter, an assistant professor of economics at the University of Chicago and later a full professor at Georgetown University.

Over the next seven years, Judy continued to pay her dues, moving to wherever in the United States the network needed her. She broke the story of accounting shenanigans and possible insider trading at her father's company, forcing the Securities and Exchange Commission to investigate. The SEC had difficulty proving its case against her father's team of high-priced lawyers. No charges were ever filed.

At one of the many interminable DC cocktail parties of political movers and shakers, Judy ran into David Porter. By this time, she was ensconced in the White House press corps and shocked—according to her friends—when the shy economist asked her out for a private drink afterward.

Married almost nine years to the day from when they met on the University of Chicago campus, they now had two grown children. David eventually became the vice chairman of the Board of Governors of the Federal Reserve System in Washington, DC, appointed by President Edward Middleton. The Federal Reserve System was critical to the smooth functioning of the US economy. Although Judy's husband was in a powerful position, and most people would say the same about her, their dual incomes didn't place them in the same strata of wealth as the other Shakespeare victims.

Jade sprang from her chair, left her office, and strode over to Pat's cubicle.

"Adams Appliances," Jade said without preamble. "Find out who took the company public."

"Will do." Pat tapped the reminder on her computer. "Court order came through. I received a listing of all of Veritas's deleted tweets. Nothing about Judy Porter."

"So either his tweets are coincidental or we're dealing with a copycat killer."

"Or he forgot to tweet about it." Pat stopped typing. "I also discovered that a private investigator kept tabs on Jared Carr."

"Who hired him?"

"His brother, Jason."

"Why?"

"Apparently they kept tabs on each other. Sued each other over their inheritance. They signed a decree seven years ago to stop suing each other, but I guess it didn't stop them from spying."

"What else did you find out?"

"The discrimination suits didn't end with their father. Many of the Carr brothers' properties were found to contain hazardous substances. Their tenants got sick. Jared authorized the falsification of documents and intimidation of witnesses, fired whistleblowers, and bribed government officials. Employees hurt on the job were denied workers' comp claims. Some died. He never paid restitution to the families. Not a nice guy, that one."

"Doesn't sound like it."

"Jason's gay."

Jade's eyebrow rose. She knew what their foundation stood for. "How did Jared feel about that?"

"Since Jared's dead, there's only one way to find out."

# CHAPTER SEVENTY-FIVE

## Washington, DC

WHITNEY FOLLOWED JOSH McPherson into the Capital Grille, a restaurant on Pennsylvania Avenue, about nine blocks from the White House. He scanned the interior, confirming again that it was empty of patrons, then led her to a private room in the back. A lone man sat at a table for ten with place settings for two.

He wore a dark suit and purple tie. She hadn't been this close to him in almost thirty-four years. His brown hair was graying at the temples. The lines on his forehead and around his eyes didn't detract from the twinkle in them. He was heavier than he'd been in high school, but not by much. Still handsome, and he knew it.

"Thanks, Josh," she said to the secret service agent. He eyed her before backing away. She had instructed him to leave the door ajar.

"Hello, Whitney," Cameron said, standing. "I'm sorry." He bowed slightly. "Madam President."

She did not want to be here. To face him. Still, it was better to meet him away from all the prying eyes—and cameras—at the White House.

Her house.

*Know thy enemy.*

"What do you want?" she said.

"Please." He moved to pull out a chair for her.

"I'll stand."

Cameron frowned and returned to his seat.

"I met with Cole this morning," he said. A boyish grin. The one that used to melt her insides, make her stomach flip. Now it made her want to throw up. "He's been supportive in my freshman year."

A server joined them, proffering the wine list to Cameron.

To her, Cameron said, "Do you mind if I choose?"

"Not at all, since you'll be the only one drinking."

His nostrils flared. Pointing at the menu, he said, "This one. A glass."

The server retreated.

"Can you please sit down?" Cameron said, looking up at her.

She didn't budge.

He cleared his throat. "We've come a long way since high school." Picking up his fork, he rubbed the handle between his thumb and index finger. "I never knew why you left that year. I thought we had something special. That we were getting serious. Then one day you were gone."

"There's nothing special about rape."

He dropped the fork, his mouth gaping open. "Rape? I didn't rape you. Might've been a little aggressive. But I was young. Didn't know what I was doing. Now"—he grinned—"I do."

If not for the width of the table between them, she would have slapped him. He made her skin crawl.

How could this man make her feel this way? She was the president of the United States.

"I'm leaving." She took a step toward the door.

"Wait a minute." He rose quickly from his chair, trying to block her way.

Josh got there first.

His hand shot to Cameron's chest, pushing him back.

Josh looked at her. "Is there a problem, Madam President?"

To Cameron, she said, "Congressman Kelly?"

Cameron held up both hands. "No problem. I need another minute."

She stared at him. It was better to know what he was thinking than not. She nodded at Josh.

He pressed once on Cameron's chest before backing up to just outside the door.

"Say what you have to say," she said to Cameron, who remained standing.

"I waited for you. I could've had lots of girls, but I stayed single my junior year. When you came back for our senior year, you wouldn't even talk to me. I started seeing someone else, but I wanted to be with you."

Whitney remained silent. She remembered avoiding him their last year of high school. Wouldn't take his calls. This was before cell phones. He wouldn't dare drop by the house and risk running into one of her brothers.

Whitney was relieved when he started dating her eventual neighbor in Missouri. She'd heard they broke up in college.

"I've thought about you over the years," he said. "About

getting back in touch. Trying again. Then I met my future wife, and…"

He shrugged his shoulders.

"A lucky woman," Whitney said, hoping he would pick up on the sarcasm but knowing he wouldn't. "And now I really must be going."

Something in his eyes changed. "Like I said, I've been thinking about that time you were away. And why. About nine months, wasn't it?"

Whitney kept her face composed. Inside she roiled. "I don't recall."

"I think you do," he said. "Whitney, where's my child?"

# CHAPTER SEVENTY-SIX

---

# Chicago, Illinois

J ADE AND MICAH took the first flight out to Chicago the next morning. Dante stayed in DC to oversee the investigation.

The pressure to solve the case had heightened, not only from Barringer but also from the press. Some reporters speculated that Jade had lost her touch.

"Special Agents Harrington and Alexander to see Jason Carr."

"I need to see ID," said the rent-a-cop manning the marble counter in the well-appointed, tasteful lobby of the fifty-five-story office building.

After the security guard examined their IDs and badges with an undue amount of care, they moved away from him to wait.

A few minutes later, a fit, handsome, well-dressed man materialized. Jade pegged him for late twenties and of Filipino ancestry.

"Agent Harrington? I'm Benjie Bautista, Mr. Carr's assistant. Right this way."

Bautista led them to the elevator. The car had one button. The three of them were silent as they ascended. Both men wore cologne; each scent was pleasant, almost complementary. A soft ding greeted them as they reached the top. The doors opened on to another lobby, the entire floor surrounded by glass windows, affording a 360-degree view of the cloudless day. In addition to the waiting room, there were two gigantic offices. Glass walls allowed their occupants to observe everything happening on the floor.

The lobby contained a sofa, a chair, and a glass coffee table, on top of which sat thick glossy magazines. Jade and Micah declined Bautista's offer of refreshments.

On the phone in one of the offices, Jason Carr motioned to his assistant to bring them in.

The furniture was sleek and modern. Jason finished the call and indicated for them to sit in two of the six guest chairs in front of his desk.

"Agent Harrington. This is a surprise. What are you doing in Chicago?"

"We came to ask you a few more questions."

"Shall I ring my mother and my sister-in-law?"

"That won't be necessary."

"Oh. Did you... find my brother's murderer?"

Jade ignored his question. "I want to ask you something."

"What's that?"

"Did Jared know you were gay?"

He stiffened, but after a moment, he said, "I believe so, although I never came out to him."

"Your organization was opposed to homosexuality."

"I kept silent. I didn't grow up in the type of family where you could easily express yourself."

"What changed your brother's mind?"

"I'm not sure. We never discussed it, but I noticed at some point that he became less vocal about his opposition to marriage equality. Then he removed references to it from our marketing materials." He paused. "I assumed it was because of me."

"You hired a private investigator to tail your brother. For years. What were you hoping to find?"

A brief tightening of the eyes, but otherwise no reaction.

"My brother and I were in business together, but that didn't mean we trusted each other. Not many people understand what it's like when there's this much money involved."

"Tell me."

He hesitated before shaking his head. "It would come across as first-world problems." His eyes strayed briefly to his assistant working at a desk adjacent to his office. "Let's just say there was a lot of pressure from our father."

"What about the lawsuits against each other?" Micah asked.

Jason waved this detail away. "We sued each other like other brothers play fantasy football. It was a game to us. To see who could bring the best case against the other one. It didn't mean anything. We bugged each other's offices. I watched him from here, but I wanted to know what he was saying to his visitors and on the phone."

Money never meant much to Jade. Did Jason want them to feel sorry for him? She did, but not in the way he intended. She'd rather be broke than rich and surrounded by people she couldn't trust.

"Do you still have the recordings? From bugging his phone?"

Jason shook his head. "I'd listen to them the same night and delete them."

"There were many lawsuits against the company," Jade said.

"A lot of cases ended unfavorably for the plaintiffs. Do you think any of them would want to kill your brother?"

Jason laughed. "No doubt. Probably all of them. Me too. If you want to investigate all of Jared's enemies, it'll take you twenty years to solve this case." He rose. "Although it's been a pleasure, I have business to attend to. I'm the sole chairman and CEO now. It's difficult to accommodate drop-ins."

A glint in his eye, like a second-born son with a slim chance of becoming king. Jason had surmounted the odds.

A motive.

Did Jason know that Jared would have died from pancreatic cancer?

Jade and Micah remained seated.

"I'm sure it is," Jade said. "If you'd rather, we can finish this conversation in the local FBI office. I'm sure *they* can accommodate us."

Jason sat back down.

Before he got comfortable, Jade asked, "Did you have your brother killed, Jason?"

He didn't bother looking upset. "Truth is, Agent Harrington, I didn't like my brother much. I wished him dead a million times." He smiled. "But I didn't kill him."

# CHAPTER SEVENTY-SEVEN

---

# Washington, DC

THE NEXT MORNING, on the way to her office, Jade stopped by Dante's office to update him on the interview with Jason Carr.

Dante leaned back in his chair. "Even if you peg him for Jared, what's his motive for the other murders?"

"Good question. I need you to take a deeper dive. Bank accounts, associations. We're missing something. And check out Benjie Bautista."

"Who's he?"

"Jason's assistant."

"Right."

"Another motive."

"In what way?"

"I think he's Jason's lover."

"Jesus Christ." He threw up his hands. "Is everyone gay?"

"I don't know," she said. "Do you have something to tell me?"

She left his office before he could respond and stopped by Pat's cubicle next.

"I found out who took Adams Appliances public," Pat said.

Jade raised an eyebrow.

"Goldman Sachs," Pat said. "But what's more important is that Judy Porter's father, Eli Adams, invested his personal funds with Scofield Asset Management."

"You think there's a there there?"

"Maybe. But that's still not the most interesting part."

"You're killing me, Pat."

"Jared Carr."

"Jared Carr what?"

"He invested his personal funds with Scofield too."

Jade took a moment to absorb this. "What about Jason?"

Pat shook her head. "Scofield belonged to a club also. In New York."

"What was it called?"

"The Club."

"Creative. Any affiliation with the Carrs' club in Chicago?"

"No."

"What about the sonnet numbers?" asked Jade. "Did the analysts find anything?"

"If there's a relationship among the numbers, they couldn't find it."

"Roman numerals?"

"Nothing."

"What about Judy Porter's computer?"

Pat's fingers stilled on her keyboard.

"What?" Jade said.

Pat glanced over her shoulder at the other agents working

in their cubicles. Some were in conversation or speaking on the phone. "Let's go to your office."

Locking her computer, she got up and walked away from her desk. Stunned by the request, Jade, for once in her life, followed.

She entered her office and closed the door behind her, gesturing for Pat to take a guest chair, while she took the other.

"What's with the cloak-and-dagger?" Jade said.

"Judy Porter's computer contained a lot of information on Fairchild's stay in Chicago when she was a teenager. Her time with the aunt and at the convent. The adoption records, even a picture of the baby. Also, Landon's work history with the president. That he paged for her in high school. What she didn't have was proof that Fairchild knew—or believed—that he was TSK."

"I still don't understand all the secrecy."

Pat eyed Jade's desk phone, as if it might be bugged. She lowered her voice. "I discovered the identity of the witness."

"What's his name?"

"Joseph Miller."

"Got an address?"

Pat nodded.

"That's great," Jade said. "Why didn't you tell me this earlier?" She sprung from her chair and went behind her desk, grabbing the handset. "I'll call Dante. We can be in St. Louis in a few hours."

Pat walked around the desk, took the phone out of Jade's hand, and returned it to its cradle.

Pat held out her hand. "Where's your cell phone?"

Jade fished her phone out of her pants pocket and handed it to Pat. She took both of their phones and put them in one of Jade's desk drawers.

"You're starting to freak me out," Jade said.

The wrinkles around Pat's eyes seemed to multiply. "Maybe we should be. I'm not sure who's listening."

"What's going on?"

"We don't need Miller's address," Pat said, "because he's not going to be there."

"Did he move?"

"No," she said. "He's dead."

"What happened?"

Pat stared into her eyes. Jade saw fear in them for the first time. Pat motioned for Jade to bend down toward her.

"A car accident," Pat whispered. "Same stretch of road as the congressman, and he hit the same—"

"Tree," Jade finished for her.

❊

After Pat left, Jade paced while she deliberated on next steps. She collapsed in her chair and leaned over the desk, resting her forehead on her arms. She couldn't remember the last time she'd slept through the night.

Jade believed that her current supervisor, Warren Barringer, had halted a federal investigation into the murder of a US congressman, and an eyewitness to that murder who was in a similar accident as Steven Barrett was now dead too. Judy Porter, who'd dogged President Fairchild throughout her candidacy and her time in office, was also dead.

Should she confront Fairchild? Jade didn't have any proof that the president was involved.

Should she confront Barringer?

It would be career suicide.

She picked up the phone. "I need to see him."

Moments later, she marched toward the elevator. Photographs of the many agents who'd served the FBI over the last century hung on the corridor's walls. Some had fallen in the line of duty. Almost all of them were heroes.

Micah jumped up from his cubicle chair and ran to catch up to her. He fell into step. "Where are you going?"

"Headed up to Barringer's office. Why?"

"I wanted to show you something. On the Shakespeare case."

"I can't now."

"It's important."

"I'll be back."

He held her arm, stopping her. "I want to show you now."

Looking into his eyes, she remembered when he'd warned her off reopening the Blakeley case in the bureau's parking garage.

He'd brought up the case at the English bar. What was his interest in it?

Jade looked at his hand, waiting for him to remove it. After he did, she said, "What's this about, Micah? It's almost as if you're trying to stop me from seeing Barringer."

She forced herself not to look away from those damn eyes.

"I can't imagine anyone stopping you from doing anything you want to do," he said. "What I want to show you is more important."

"I'll be the judge of that."

"May I at least walk you to the lift?"

"I can walk myself."

She brushed by him. After she entered the elevator, Jade pressed the button and turned around.

Micah stood in the hallway, staring at her, as the doors closed.

# CHAPTER SEVENTY-EIGHT

## Washington, DC

"WHEN DID YOU last speak to your son?" Sasha asked quietly.

They were ensconced in the back of the Beast. Sarah sat in the adjacent sofa seat, making changes to Whitney's daily schedule. Whitney wanted to spend more time at her next stop, necessitating that they rearrange the entire day.

They were bound for a suburban Maryland elementary school, where Whitney would be giving a speech on the urgent need for girls to pursue STEM careers. The US needed more scientists, technologists, engineers, and mathematicians.

The United States needed women.

Whitney didn't understand the concern on Sasha's face. Perhaps it was because of Whitney's dysfunctional home life. Sasha probably suspected that something was wrong. Grayson resided in Missouri, and neither of her children had visited the White House in a long time.

Immersed in shame, Whitney hadn't spoken to her son since he walked out on them at Camp David.

"I don't recall," Whitney said simply.

"A source tells me that Chandler started a new job."

"Sampson's replacement?" Whitney said. "What of it? I'm glad he no longer works for Sampson. I didn't think he represented his state or the legislative branch well, and I certainly didn't think he was the proper role model for my son."

Sasha pursed her lips. "Lord knows I agree with you. Money doesn't buy class. But you're not going to be happy about his new employer."

"I can live with Hampton, if that's what you're implying. It's not optimal, but at least he possesses some principles and is a master of parliamentary procedure, which could prove helpful if, God forbid, Chandler decides to remain in politics."

"It's not Sampson's replacement, and it's not Senator Eric Hampton."

"Who then?"

"Your son," Sasha said, "is the newest legislative aide for Congressman Cameron Kelly."

# CHAPTER SEVENTY-NINE

---

# Washington, DC

ASSISTANT DIRECTOR, CRIMINAL Investigative Division Warren Barringer's spacious office looked out on Pennsylvania Avenue. Unlike Ethan's office, with the FBI motto displayed behind the desk, photographs of Barringer with the who's who of Washington—President Fairchild, former president Richard Ellison, Senators Eric Hampton and Paul Sampson, Representative Howard Bell—decorated the walls.

After being waved in, Jade walked behind his desk, surveying the photographs.

She pointed at one. "Who's this?"

Barringer strained to turn his bulk in the chair and glance over his shoulder. "That's my latest addition. Congressman Cameron Kelly."

"From what state?"

"Missouri."

Jade thought for a moment. "Which district?"

"Who cares?" he said. "He's a good man. Let's get to it, shall we? I'm meeting with the director in fifteen minutes."

Jade moved to a chair across from him. "Actually, Missouri is what I want to talk to you about."

Barringer shuffled some papers on his desk. "What about it?"

"There was an inquiry. About a congressman from there. Car accident. One of my agents said that you directed her to stop any further inquiries into the case."

"I don't remember that."

"You don't remember the case or calling her off it?"

"Neither."

She pointed at his computer. "Can you check?"

Barringer stopped shuffling. "No, I can't. I'm busy."

"This might be important."

"I decide what's important, and you're working on a major case already, which, I'll remind you, isn't going that well. You don't have time to mess around with an old closed case."

"That's the point. It shouldn't be closed. I think—"

Barringer stood. "I don't care what you think. You've got a job to do, and I expect you to do it."

"I'm doing my job."

"So you say. To be clear, I'm ordering you to drop any further inquiries into Congressman Steven Barrett's death."

The heat flashed in Jade's face. "Ordering?"

"That's what I said, princess."

She stood still.

Motionless.

Stared at him.

"Why did you call me that?"

"It's just a term. I didn't mean anything by it. Don't go charging me with sexual harassment or assault or any of that foolishness."

Jade wasn't angry at the inappropriate endearment. She was stunned. Only her father called her princess.

Striding to the door, she turned back to him. "Given that you don't remember the case, it's funny that you know his name."

She made sure to slam the door on her way out.

On the way back from Barringer's office, Jade stopped by Micah's cubicle, which was decorated with photos of Arsenal football players. A new photo had been added: a beautiful black woman who looked like a model. Jade peered closer. "That's new. Who is it?"

"What do you Yanks say? Noneya?"

"Okay," Jade said, feigning disinterest. She realized for the first time that aside from his love of the English Premier League team, she didn't know much about Special Agent Micah Alexander. "What were you going to tell me?"

Still fuming, she wanted to distract herself from the disturbing conversation with Barringer.

"You said it wasn't important."

"I'll be the judge of that," she said without humor.

He shook his head. "It was about Hurley. She went to the Carr Summit years ago."

She leaned against the edge of his cubicle wall. "What's that?"

"It's where a bunch of conservative blokes and ladies congregate, donate a lot of money, and carve up the world."

"Any of the other victims there?"

He shrugged. "I only know Hurley was there, because she told her ex-husband."

"We need the list of attendees," Jade said.

"That'll be hard to do. Not only is the invitation list a secret, but so is the event itself. If you tell anyone that you've been invited or discuss anything that takes place there, you'll never be invited back."

"You learned all this from her ex?"

"Hurley sometimes got drunk and would call him late at night. I guess being a CEO, she didn't have a lot of people to speak freely with. He said he's never told anyone."

"And now it doesn't matter that she won't be invited back," she said. "Solid, Micah."

"Told you."

She turned to go.

"That wasn't all," he said. "I found a link between Scofield and Carr."

"Pat told me Scofield handled Carr's money."

"Did she also tell you that they went to prep school together?" He checked his notes. "The Phillips Academy in Andover, Massachusetts."

CHAPTER EIGHTY

---

# The White House, Washington, DC

WHITNEY OCCUPIED A lounge chair on the Truman Balcony just off the Yellow Oval Room, which afforded a view of the South Lawn, the National Mall, the Washington Monument, and the Lincoln Memorial. A few small trees and fresh flowers were interspersed with chairs, couches, and tables grouped in various arrangements. The balcony was used for entertaining foreign heads of state, diplomats, members of the other branches of government, and celebrities.

It was becoming Whitney's favorite spot in the White House. She enjoyed breakfast out here on the weekends, and, on warm nights, she worked or read.

The phone rang. She picked up the extension on a side table.

"Madam President," Sasha said, her voice tight, "you're needed in the Situation Room. Now."

"Sasha, what's happened?"

"Reports are coming in that a number of power plants and electrical grids are down along the West Coast."

"What's the cause?"

"We don't know yet."

"You don't think it's a coincidence?"

"No."

"Tamirov."

"Or Min. Or both."

China and Russia had reportedly infiltrated the electrical grid of the US back in 2009, leaving behind software that could disrupt several regions of the country.

"We've received word that at least three large corporations were breached. Social security numbers, email addresses, personal information. Cyber Command thinks there will be more."

"My God," Whitney said. "I'll be right there."

She hung up.

Whitney looked longingly at her glass before picking it and the bottle up and heading inside. She poured the remaining wine in the glass down the sink and capped the bottle, returning it to the wine refrigerator.

She called the ground-floor kitchen for a pot of coffee to be delivered to the Situation Room.

Time to go to work.

Whitney scanned the intense faces around the table.

"Dani?" she said.

"Electric power grids, water systems, and energy were impacted on the West Coast," said Danielle Oliver, the secretary of energy.

"Ditto for telecommunications and transportation," said Julio Casillas from transportation.

"Automatic cars crashed. Interstate trucking has been impacted. Grocery stores won't receive deliveries on time, if at all. If this goes on a lot longer, they'll run out of food. Same with gas stations."

Oliver said, "Blackouts in LA, San Francisco, Seattle, Las Vegas, and Portland."

"I'm worried about the inner cities," Vice President Josephine Bates said.

"What time did this happen?" Whitney asked no one in particular.

"Midnight," responded several of them.

Energy Secretary Oliver caught her eye. "Exactly midnight."

"Personal computers and cell phones aren't working at all," Transportation Secretary Casillas said. "Some are displaying gibberish."

"Manufacturing facilities have been infiltrated," said Tucker Price, secretary of labor. The sweat from his underarms formed gray semicircles on his white shirt.

Smaller than most citizens imagined, the Situation Room now smelled of a mix of sweat, cologne, perfume, and coffee.

Secretary of Homeland Security Maricela Salcedo said, "Several banks and credit card companies were hit with denial-of-service attacks. Corporate servers, ISPs are down. Folks will panic when they can't email, Skype, text, or conduct online transactions. Even the RainForest, which provides cloud-based solutions that support many businesses around the world, including eighty percent of the Fortune 500, was hit. When the public starts realizing what's happening… we need to be prepared. For possible violence."

"This will disproportionately hit poor people," Jo said. "Minorities. They'll freak the fuck out."

"Everyone's going to freak out," wailed Price. "It's a fuckin' mess."

"Calm down, Tucker," Whitney said.

Jo said to him, "Why are you always so emotional?"

Whitney cut her a look. "Jo. Please."

"Asian markets are plummeting," said London James, secretary of the treasury. "I expect US markets to plunge. Thousands of points." She paused. "Should we stop the market from opening?"

"No," Whitney said. "The world needs to know that the United States of America is open for business."

"How can we be open for business when a quarter of the country is in the dark?" said Oliver.

*Good question.*

She turned to James. "What's the impact?"

London James was the first female CEO in Goldman Sachs's history and another in a long succession of former Goldman Sachs CEOs to join presidential cabinets. Whitney liked the tenaciousness it took for James to claw her way to the top spot at the top investment bank in the world.

"Daily?"

Whitney nodded.

James shrugged. "Trillions."

"Go on," Whitney said.

"Banks will shut down. Customers won't be able to access cash or credit. People will panic. Demand for food, gas, and other necessities will outstrip supply. A US panic will cause a global panic. Demand for the dollar will plummet. Inflation will rise. If it goes on for long, hyperinflation will ensue. Interest rates will increase. Investors will invest in other currencies. Shall I continue?"

Whitney held up her hand. "Who benefits?"

"China most likely. They can fill the void. No one else."

Whitney turned to Edison Banks, secretary of health and human services. "Hospitals?"

"It's a crisis. Medical care facilities rely on power. We'll need to move people soon."

Whitney eyed Pravir Ratta, her secretary of education.

"Nothing's come in so far," he said.

"Media?"

"No reports that they've been hit," Energy Secretary Oliver said.

"But what do we tell them?" asked Lena, the acting press secretary.

"Nothing for now," Whitney said. "Until we know our plan."

Lena leaned forward. "With all due respect, Madam President, the East Coast is asleep now, but they won't be for much longer. Some people might still be up—

"As we are," murmured Secretary of Commerce Ashton Crawford.

"—trying to contact loved ones on the West Coast. We won't be able to keep this under wraps for long."

Whitney turned to Secretary of Defense Leyton Quinn. "Military systems?"

She shook her head.

Breathing a sigh of relief, Whitney shuddered to think of the consequences of the infiltration of their nuclear or missile systems.

"Winters, what's your assessment? Did you see this coming?"

General Malachi Winters was the chairman of the US Cyber Command and head of the NSA. Now, in addition to land, sea, air, and space, his responsibilities included a new battlefield: cyberspace. Cyber Command's mission was to neutralize cyberattacks and defend military computer network systems.

"We had an inkling," Winters said, shaking his head. Deep lines furrowed his dark forehead. "But nothing like this. I would've told you. Do you want my resignation?"

Whitney waved this thought away. "Options?"

"At first," said Defense Secretary Quinn, "we thought it was a massive outage, but now I think…"

"What?" Whitney asked.

"It was a military attack," Quinn said.

Her words silenced the room.

After a moment, she added, "This was an act of war."

"By whom?" said Winters. "A sovereign state? A nonstate? A bunch of teenagers playing a game?"

"Or a fat guy lying on his bed," said Commerce Secretary Crawford.

The nervous giggles died quickly.

Whitney eyed a woman dressed in a military uniform decorated with five stars on her shoulder straps. "General?"

Chairwoman of the Joint Chiefs of Staff, General Frances Wilkerson was the first woman to hold the title. Possessing a high standard of integrity, she guided the military with restraint. She despised partisan politics, especially when they got in the way of doing the right thing. Whitney trusted her completely.

The general gazed at her, calm and unflappable. "At your command, we are ready."

Whitney broke the stare and scanned the cabinet members' faces again. "Is there any good news?"

No one met her eyes. Some of them doodled on the notepads in front of them. Some stared off into the distance.

"I think it was Tamirov," said Defense Secretary Quinn.

Russia had done something like this before. A decade ago, to Ukraine. Ukraine, however, was not the most powerful country in the world.

"Could be Min," said Maricela Salcedo from Homeland Security.

"He possesses a hacker army of hundreds of thousands of private citizens," Winters said, "while we employ a few thousand civil servants to protect us. It's not a fair fight." He hesitated, then looked at Salcedo. "Could it be both?"

Whitney thought it was plausible.

"Let's talk to Min," she said, nodding at Secretary of State Park Chui. "Instead of mutually assured destruction, we want mutually assured restraint. Otherwise, this will not end well. For anyone."

"What about Tamirov?" asked Leyton Quinn, the defense secretary.

"I'll talk to him," Whitney said. She looked at her team again. "Come up with a plan for bringing our citizens back online." She stood. "I want it on my desk within the hour."

"An hour?" said Oliver, voicing—if their expressions were any indication—the concern shared by most of the other members.

"One hour," said Whitney. "We're at war."

"With all due respect, Madam President," Winters said, "we've been in a cyberwar for a long time, and we're losing. Most Americans just don't know it."

## CHAPTER EIGHTY-ONE

# Washington, DC

S HE WASN'T SURE how she'd ended up here.

Well, she knew how, but not why.

Jade had spent that afternoon discussing next steps on the Shakespeare case with Dante and dealing with other matters. The conversation with Barringer continued to bother her.

When she called it a night, Jade didn't feel like going home, and she wasn't up for Zoe's upbeat company. Zoe lit up a room, but the energy she needed to fuel herself could drain those around her.

Instead, Jade stopped by a small dive bar in Capitol Hill, a place where she hoped no one would recognize her. A jazz trio played near the entrance. Photographs of jazz and blues artists— recent and seasoned, young and old—dotted the walls. When she arrived, there were no vacant seats at the bar, but there was an empty semicircle booth for two in the back.

She removed her suit jacket, laid it next to her, and ordered a Heineken.

Taking a pull on the beer, she closed her eyes, allowing her head to bob to the music.

"Is this seat taken?"

Jade opened her eyes. A woman stood across the table. She was about five eight, with light-brown hair, attractive in an androgynous sort of way.

"No."

"This place is always crowded. Do you mind?"

Jade moved her jacket closer to her. The woman slid into the booth.

"You look familiar," Jade said.

"I live nearby, so you might've seen me here." To the server, "I'll have what she's having."

"Glass?" the server asked.

The woman glanced at Jade's bottle. "No."

The server left.

The woman smiled, embarrassed. "Forgive me. My name's Brooklyn. My friends call me Brook."

"Jade."

They shook hands.

After receiving her beer, Brooklyn raised her glass. "To jazz?"

"To jazz."

They clinked bottles and drank.

"Thanks for letting me share your table."

The two women listened to the music and sipped their drinks.

"What do you do?" Brooklyn asked.

If this woman didn't recognize her, Jade wasn't going to be the one to inform her.

"Security," Jade said. "You?"

A pause. "Customer service."

Brook turned to face the band. Her neck was taut, her forearms sinewy.

Jade sipped her beer. "Athlete?"

The woman turned back to her. "Volleyball. Setter."

"Do you still play?"

Brooklyn shook her head as she signaled for two more beers. "I'm more of a triathlete now."

"Impressive."

The two women talked as they listened to the first set. Brooklyn was also a fan of all the DC sports teams, including soccer, and they discussed the prospects for DC United this season. Jade was enjoying herself immensely. She hadn't talked sports with another woman in a long time. For the moment, she forgot about Barringer, Shakespeare, Judy Porter, and Whitney Fairchild.

They ordered a bucket of Heinekens and stayed for the second set.

That was several hours ago.

The bedroom was dark.

"Brook, I gotta go," Jade said. "Thanks for tonight."

Brooklyn turned to face her, her head still on the pillow. "It was nice."

Jade rolled out of the bed, gathered her clothes, which were scattered all over the floor, and dressed hurriedly.

She quietly let herself out of the Capitol Hill townhouse.

Driving home, Jade realized she didn't know Brook's last name.

# CHAPTER EIGHTY-TWO

# Washington, DC

"CRAZY WHAT HAPPENED on the West Coast last night," Pat said, looking up from her computer.

"What happened?" Jade asked.

"Where were you? Sleeping under a rock?"

*Sort of.*

Early the next morning, head pounding, she'd stopped by Pat's cubicle on the way to her office. Jade still hadn't processed her feelings about sleeping with Brooklyn.

"Tell me," she said.

Pat told her about the blackouts.

"Sounds like a test," Jade said.

Pat ceased her typing and squinted up at her. "You okay?"

Jade yawned. "Late night."

Pat looked hopeful.

"Noneya," Jade said.

Pat raised both of her arms, as if Jade had hit a three-pointer. "Yes!"

Christian looked over from his cubicle. Since he'd returned from Seattle the night before, Jade had told him to take the day off. He'd come in anyway.

"What's up, Pat?" he called over.

"Jade got some last night!"

He lumbered over. "Really? Who!?"

Jade's face flushed. "Noneya. Chill."

Dante came out of his office. "What's going on?"

"Shit," Jade said under her breath.

"Boss got some," Pat and Christian answered, almost simultaneously.

"It's about time. Maybe now you can get off my back," Dante said. He raised his hand to give her a high five. "Male, female, or both?"

Jade ignored him. "Can you all get back to work? I'm talking to Pat."

"We're happy for you, that's all," Christian said, grinning.

A parting, suggestive smile from Dante. "Can't wait to hear more."

As she watched Christian return to his cubicle, her gaze landed on Micah. Still seated at his desk chair, he glared at her, his jaw clenched, his face a mask. He averted his eyes and turned to face his computer.

Jade couldn't help him.

To Pat, she said sarcastically, "Thanks."

"Sorry." Pat suppressed a smile. "Couple of things for you. After running into a dead end with the Barrett witness—"

"Pat," Jade warned.

"—I found out that the SUV used in the Porter killing was

out of range of the motel's camera, which pointed toward the parking lot."

"But…"

"A traffic light camera caught it. The license plate turned out to be fake. Indiana. Unregistered. They still haven't been able to locate the vehicle."

"I wonder if it's the same SUV as the one used to kill Barrett."

"I doubt it. That was a long time ago. Plus, there aren't any cameras on that country road, and our only witness is dead."

"Unless we lifted something off the congressman's car."

"Which is in pieces and part of other vehicles now."

"True. What else?"

"Sebastian Scofield also attended the Carr Summit. He and Hurley belonged to the Carrs' billion-dollar donor club."

"Someone might be targeting the attendees. These people are at risk. Micah tried to obtain a list. Can you check it out?"

Pat rolled her chair a few paces to the other end of the desk. She returned, handing Jade a file.

Jade opened it to find a list of attendees. "All righty then. Tishman and Porter on the list?"

"No. Tishman was a progressive. Still unsure how he fits in. Or Porter. She had no connection to the other victims. She wasn't a conservative. Quite the opposite. Her husband said she voted for Fairchild. She was a strong supporter and respected the president tremendously, but she hid it behind journalistic impartiality. He said she felt sick breaking the news about the first man's affair."

Jade closed the file; she'd review it later. It was a long list. "Come with me."

Once they were both seated in her office, Jade said, "I need a favor."

Pat's arms were on the guest chair's armrest, her hands clasped. "Sure."

"I need you to explore Barrett's death again." Jade straightened the already-straightened items on her desk. Without looking at Pat, she said, "Also, find out why Barringer would want us to stop the investigation."

"Are you sure?" Pat said. "You're treading on dangerous territory, Jade. We could lose our jobs."

*We.*

Pat just called her Jade. She didn't remember the last time that Pat called her by her given name. If she ever had.

"I've thought a lot about this," Jade said. "Some things are more important than a job. We swore to obey the Constitution with uncompromising integrity. That case stinks. Something's not right."

"We're not only talking about losing our jobs here," Pat said in a quiet voice.

"I know."

The older woman gazed down at the floor, then raised her head. "I'm in."

"This stays between us."

"I got it, boss."

*Shit. Now Dante has everyone saying it.*

Jade had secretly started to like it.

"I need you to do something else for me," she said. She spun around in her chair and grabbed a sheet of blank paper from the stack next to the printer.

Placing the paper on her desk, she sketched two objects from memory.

When she finished, Pat gave her a puzzled look. "A tree?"

Jade nodded. "Find out what kind it is."

Pat pointed. "What about this symbol? It looks Japanese."

進捗

"I believe it's 'progress,'" Jade said, "but find out for sure. My Japanese is a little rusty."

Jade's mother was Japanese, and at one time, Jade spoke it fluently. With her mother gone, she no longer spoke it every day. Another piece of her parents that she'd allowed to slip away.

While Jade ruminated about them, Pat grabbed the sketches and left her office.

## CHAPTER EIGHTY-THREE

# Washington, DC

"WHAT'S THE LATEST?"

Sasha stood in front of Whitney's desk in the Oval Office, looking no worse for wear. "Power grids, water systems, and energy are back online. Transportation is up and running, although with significant delays."

"Roads?"

"Cleanup has commenced on the highways." Sasha paused. "Although the cars were driverless, it doesn't mean they were without passengers. At least five hundred deaths and counting. We were blessed that the event happened at midnight, or there would have been more. Many more."

"There were enough."

Sasha gave her a solemn nod. "Thank God there weren't many planes in the sky."

"I wonder if that was why that particular time was selected. To minimize casualties."

"Several planes made emergency landings. Reports of injuries—some severe—but no deaths. Factories are up and running. A lot of wasted product, but otherwise no long-term damage."

"What else?"

"Internet's back up. Most personal computers and cell phones are working, but…"

"What?"

"We're encouraging the public to download antivirus software on their computers, servers, and smart TVs to combat any malware installed during this event. There's no guarantee that people will do it."

"Likely adding identities to the list of casualties," Whitney said, leaning back in her chair.

Sasha waited.

"It was a test," Whitney said.

She was more convinced that Russia was the culprit.

The former Soviet Union hadn't forgotten that the CIA had planted the computer malware that blew up part of the Trans-Siberian pipeline back in 1982, causing the biggest non-nuclear explosion the world had ever seen. The country didn't publicly blame the US at the time.

"I think you're right." Sasha cocked her head. "Did you sleep?"

"No. I took a cold shower. You?"

"I tried to sleep on the couch in my office, but it was clearly made for a skinny girl, not a voluptuous woman like me."

Whitney held up her hand. "Don't start shimmying. Care to watch the opening bell with me? Instead of Breakfast at Wimbledon, let's enjoy Breakfast at Wall Street." She punched the speakerphone, not waiting for Sasha's answer. "Sean, please bring breakfast into my study. Something hearty. For two."

"Has the First Gentleman returned?" he said, hopeful.

"Thank you, Sean," Whitney said, hanging up.

Twenty minutes later, a butler wheeled in a cart with several covered trays. He lifted each cover and described the tray's contents before departing.

The two women sat a table in front of the television eating eggs and bacon and toast—Sasha asked Whitney to call back and add pancakes to the order—as they watched the negative red numbers light up the screen.

"We should do this every day," said Sasha. "Not that,"—she pointed her forkful of eggs at the television—"this." She slipped the fork into her mouth.

The Dow dropped two thousand points by 9:31 a.m.

By 9:35, the New York Stock Exchange halted trading.

Whitney dabbed her mouth with a white linen napkin. "I guess you should call Lena in here."

"She can wait a few minutes." Sasha lifted a tray cover, heaping another helping of eggs onto her plate. "We need to fortify ourselves. It's going to be a long day."

Whitney looked at the second helping on Sasha's plate, suddenly not hungry. "By all means. Any word from Chui?"

"He said that Min categorically denies any involvement and is open to further discussions of mutually assured restraint." Sasha chewed and swallowed. "Tamirov?"

"Still waiting for him to call me back."

"Normally he's available to take your calls or responds immediately." Sasha eyed her. "I always thought he was sweet on you."

Whitney was saved from responding—and analyzing why this comment pleased her—by Sean's voice coming over the speakerphone. "Madam President, President Tamirov is on the line."

She gave Sasha a "this is it" look before moving behind her desk and picking up the handset.

"Andrei."

"Whitney, good morning. I hear you are having difficulty keeping the lights on."

"With your help?"

"Why would you think I was involved in your recent troubles?"

She sat in her chair. "I could think of a thousand reasons. Were you?"

"Your recovery has been swift. Impressive. It seems the rumors of the decline of the alleged greatest nation on earth are vastly exaggerated."

"You shouldn't listen to rumors."

"Maybe so," he said, "but unlike you Americans, Russians have suffered throughout history. The unforgiving cold weather. The wars and endless conflicts. The revolutions. The scarcity. Nevertheless, we always come through every challenge better off because of it."

"Why are you telling me this?"

"We are a proud people, and we don't forget even the smallest of slights. We are also patient."

"Andrei, if I have slighted you in some way—"

"That," he said, "was for the pipeline."

# PART III

# CHAPTER EIGHTY-FOUR

# Washington, DC

JADE STRODE DOWN a path near the reflecting pool. She spotted Pat sitting on a bench underneath a shade tree, eating a hot dog.

"Late lunch?" Jade said.

"You work me too hard."

Jade smiled before glancing around the crowded National Mall. On one of the first days of spring, people were out eating, walking, and running. Workers pecked away on their laptops. Students relaxed on the grass, studying, their backpacks lying next to them. Groups of color-coordinated tourists trekked up the Lincoln Memorial stairs.

"Here," Pat said, handing a hot dog to Jade. "You work yourself too hard too."

"Thanks. I forgot to eat."

"You usually do."

Jade took a bite of the dog, which was still warm and loaded with melted cheese and chili. "That's good. Thank you."

Pat waved behind her. "Food truck. One of my go-to places."

The two ate in silence.

Finally, Jade said, "Why did you call me out here, Pat? It wasn't to eat lunch together."

"You're right," she said, lifting a file from her lap and handing it to Jade. "I found your tree."

Jade scanned the document inside the folder. She looked at Pat. "The Liberty Tree?"

"It was an elm tree planted in Boston in 1646, on the only road into or out of the city. After the British Parliament passed the Stamp Act in 1765, a band of merchants and artisans formed a radical secret society called the Sons of Liberty, or the Loyal Nine. They hung items on the tree, including an image in effigy of the tax collector. A mob gathered and started breaking into houses, destroying furniture, raiding liquor cabinets, that sort of thing. For the next decade, Boston's angriest demonstrations took place there, symbolizing the violent aspect of the Revolutionary War—a side that the colonists we're still too sensitive to see."

Jade said, "What happened to the tree?"

"The British Army chopped it down in 1775, which is why most Americans haven't heard of it. Towns throughout the colonies planted Liberty Trees in protest. One of the founding fathers, Thomas Paine, wrote a song about the tree and its importance to all Americans." She glanced down at the folder that now lay on the bench between them. "The lyrics are in there."

"Anything else?"

"Thomas Jefferson tried to make the Liberty Tree a lasting metaphor." Pat quoted from memory, "'The tree of liberty must be refreshed from time to time with the blood of patriots and tyrants.'"

"Sounds dangerous," Jade said.

Pat searched her face. "What's this about?"

*Why would Zoe tattoo the Liberty Tree on her wrist?*

"What about the symbol?" Jade asked, ignoring Pat's question.

"You were right. It's the Japanese word for 'progress.'"

"What else?"

"I've also looked into Barrett's death, as you asked. You're right about that too—it stinks."

"How so?"

"I obtained a copy of the original airplane manifest and compared it to the one we had on file. It'd been altered."

Jade stopped chewing. "What?"

"Rick Cheney, the alias that Caleb Hewitt used on that flight, appeared on the second manifest, but not the first."

"Meaning…"

"Rick Cheney didn't replace another passenger. He was an addition."

"So we would deduce that it was an alias for Hewitt."

"Correct. I don't think Hewitt was in St. Louis at the time of the murder."

"Then where was he?"

"I don't know," Pat said. "There's more."

"Go on."

"Since the manifest for the flight from Philadelphia to St. Louis was altered, I decided to check out the flight from Newark to Chicago."

Caleb Hewitt had used the alias Walker G. Bush on that flight, putting him in the vicinity around the time the president's aunt, Mary Churchill, was killed.

A sense of foreboding settled over Jade. "And?"

"That manifest was altered too."

No longer hungry, Jade balled up the uneaten remainder of the hot dog in its wrapper and lobbed it into the trash can a few feet away. Swish. Nothing but net.

"Hewitt hated the Bush administration," Jade recalled. "Rick Cheney represented Dick Cheney. Walker G. Bush was obviously George W. Bush. We copped Hewitt for both murders, tying them in with the TSK murders. Someone handed us a gift wrapped with a bow."

"And we opened it," Pat said.

Jade paused. "It's more than that. Evidence tampering of this magnitude would need to come from the highest of levels."

Pat nodded. "That's why we're eating lunch out here."

"And Barringer asked us to stop looking into the Barrett case."

The two women looked at each other for a moment.

Pat stood. "Be careful, Jade."

She walked away.

Jade glanced down at the folder.

A feeling of dread came to life in the pit of her stomach. And, if she were being honest, not a small amount of fear.

## CHAPTER EIGHTY-FIVE

# Arlington, Virginia

"HEY," BLAKE SAID.

Jade had been shooting around on the court at the park by her house. It was dusk, the basket swathed in shadows. During her routine, she thought about her conversation with Pat earlier that afternoon. Holding the basketball in one hand and her phone in the other, she sat cross-legged underneath the basket. No need to worry about being hit by a stray ball. She was the only one on the court.

She was disappointed that none of the usual crowd had showed up. She loved playing ball with the fellas. Well-earned respect reflected in their eyes when they realized—or knew—that she could (still) hold her own. It gave her a sense of pride. And she could use a vigorous game about now.

Blake's call surprised her.

"Hey, yourself," she said.

"How's your investigation going?"

Instead of the Shakespeare case, she contemplated the Barrett and Churchill cases. Which weren't officially her cases. Or open ones, for that matter.

"It's going. Still at home?"

"Yes," Blake said, "in bed, where I've been spending a lot of time."

"Are you up for visitors yet?"

"No," he said in a quiet voice. "I'm still not ready."

"When are you returning to work?"

He sighed. "Not sure I'm ready for the pressures of the White House yet either."

"I hear you."

She enjoyed the quiet of the park. The crickets chirped. Through the trees, she saw lights coming on in some of the townhouses. A squirrel darted onto the court and stopped to look at her. Finding nothing of interest, he moved on.

"I've been doing a little digging into what Judy was working on."

"Blake…"

"She *was* onto something."

"Such as?"

"I'm not sure I should tell you."

"You did call."

"Right." He hesitated. "I don't think Congressman Barrett's death was an accident."

Of course it wasn't. "Why do you say that?"

"At first I believed the news reports. An unfortunate accident for him, and serendipity for the future president. I checked in with the police in Clayton, Missouri. They're now saying that it wasn't an accident, but they are tight-lipped about the details.

After the congressman died, Fairchild ran and won the special election to replace him."

"Everyone knows about the special election. Are you saying there's a connection?"

"I think there is. Yes."

"There was no assurance she would win," Jade pointed out.

"Maybe not," he said, "but a significant amount of money for her poured in from outside the state. I'm still trying to track down the sources of the contributions, but it was a disproportionate amount for a special election House race, especially back then for an unknown, unproven candidate."

"You're talking about the president." She paused. "Your boss."

"I don't like corruption. Something about this stinks. My boss and mo—" He hesitated. "Notwithstanding."

"And what?"

"Nothing."

"You think someone was behind her getting elected?"

"Someone," he said, "or something."

Jade picked up Card from the sheet of paper on the couch next to her. The cat possessed an uncanny ability to sit on whatever she was about to read. Kissing him on the top of his head, she placed him in her lap.

She reread Thomas Paine's song about the Liberty Tree, which ended:

BUT HEAR, O YE SWAINS ('TIS A TALE MOST PROFANE),
HOW ALL THE TYRANNICAL POWERS,
KINGS, COMMONS, AND LORDS, ARE UNITING AMAIN

TO CUT DOWN THIS GUARDIAN OF OURS.
FROM THE EAST TO THE WEST BLOW THE TRUMPET TO ARMS,
THRO' THE LAND LET THE SOUND OF IT FLEE:
LET THE FAR AND THE NEAR ALL UNITE WITH A CHEER,
IN DEFENSE OF OUR LIBERTY TREE.

She'd heard of Thomas Paine, of course, and read *Common Sense* in high school. That didn't mean she remembered any of it. Tapping a key to bring her laptop to life, she googled his name and clicked on his Wikipedia page.

*Common Sense* was originally titled *Plain Truth*.

Was this connected to Veritas?

After a few hours of reading about the man and his work, she understood why Zoe identified with him. A lot of his views were progressive: human rights, progressive taxation to combat poverty, egalitarian society, world peace, social security for the elderly and the poor, the evils of arbitrary government, combating illiteracy, the need for insurances against unemployment. Paine was staunchly antislavery and believed in religious tolerance.

"'Every religion is good that teaches man to be good,'" Jade read aloud.

She liked that.

Paine sounded like Zoe's kind of founding father. Was that why she'd tatted the Liberty Tree on her wrist? Zoe didn't need a reason to do anything, but a tattoo was a permanent declaration. At least, until it was removed.

The tattoo must represent something political. Politics was Zoe's life. Why was she seeking liberty?

And progress.

Jade's eyes drifted to the wooden triangle frame perched on

a shelf of her bookcase. Jonathan Harrington's sacrifice. A soldier had handed the flag to her at her parents' funeral.

What did Zoe say that time? Something about a new guard for future security? She googled this phrase and got a hit on the first link:

... IT IS THEIR RIGHT, IT IS THEIR DUTY, TO THROW OFF SUCH GOVERNMENT, AND TO PROVIDE NEW GUARDS FOR THEIR FUTURE SECURITY.

Part of a sentence from the Declaration of Independence.

Jade leaned back, frowning.

Her doorbell rang.

Visitors to her home, unannounced or otherwise, were rare. She set Card and the paper aside. Looking through the peephole, she saw Pat Turner glancing over both shoulders.

Jade opened the door. "How do you know where I live?"

Pat gave her a look that said *I know everything.* "I need to talk to you," she said.

Jade opened the door wider. "Come in."

Pat shook her head. "No. Let's go to that park you're always talking about." She mouthed, *Leave your phone.*

Grabbing her keys, Jade pulled a light jacket over her Stanford Women's Basketball T-shirt and Adidas track pants. The night was cool but pleasant. The two women didn't speak as they walked along the sidewalk, then cut between a break in the townhouses to travel the short distance to the park.

Pat didn't stop walking until she'd arrived at the center of the court. The lights surrounding the court were off. Jade could barely make out Pat's face.

"I found an encrypted file hidden on Judy Porter's computer," Pat whispered.

"What was in it?" Jade whispered back.

"I haven't been able to open it yet."

Jade put her hands on her hips. "Then why are we here?"

"Because of the name of the file."

"Which is?"

"Paine," Pat said.

# CHAPTER EIGHTY-SIX

# Washington, DC

"DO YOU THINK that's a good idea?" Dante asked the next morning.

Jade stood in Dante's doorway, as he used to when she occupied this office.

Christian slid in next to her. "Morning. What were you talking about when I got here?"

"What we can do to flush out Shakespeare," she said.

"That rhymed," said Micah, standing with them in the now crowded hallway. "Almost sounds like a couplet." He rapped: "What were you talking about when I got here? What we can do to flush out Shakespeare."

"She's a poet and doesn't know it," said Dante.

Christian moved his head to an imaginary beat. "Don't mess with Jade if you can't abade."

Micah looked puzzled. "Is 'abade' a word?"

"I might have just made it up," Christian replied.

Jade rolled her eyes. "I'm leaving."

She turned, hiding her smile, and headed down the hallway, while her team continued to make up rhymes behind her.

She'd been thinking about this plan for some time. She was desperate. There hadn't been any movement on the Shakespeare Killer case. Barrington was still griping about her solve rate. The drumbeat of his impatience—and the public's—rumbled louder.

Picking up the handset in her office, she checked the Seattle number and dialed.

Three rings. She was about to hang up when he answered.

"Yeah."

"This is Agent Jade Harrington."

"What do you want?"

"Now that's not very nice. Not even 'Seattle nice.'"

He didn't laugh.

"I need you to do something for me," she said.

"What?"

She told him.

There was silence for several moments.

"If I do it, will you get off my case?"

"Yes," she said.

"I can do that," said The God of Veritas.

❋

"Tell me about the Liberty Tree," Jade said.

Zoe, puzzled, said, "What are you talking about?"

Jade pointed at Zoe's wrist. "That."

Zoe scoffed. "It's a tree. I like trees."

"Since when?"

"I'm an environmentalist. Always have been. What of it? Why

are you questioning my tattoo? I can tat whatever I want on *my* body. A naked woman or a—"

Jade held up her hand. "Stop."

Zoe closed her mouth.

"The tree is significant," Jade said. "It's a symbol of the American Revolution. Rebellion. Of a dark side of US history. Why is it tatted on your wrist?"

Zoe examined her wrist, pouting, a look Jade had seen many times before. "I wanted a tree. It's no big deal."

"I think it's a big deal and means a lot to you." Jade leaned forward and placed her hands on the counter that separated Zoe's kitchen from the rest of her Adams Morgan apartment. "Who's the artist?"

Zoe swept her arm toward the living room. "Can we at least sit down?"

She went to sprawl on her favorite circular wicker chair with beige cushions, perching her feet on the coffee table. Jade sat on the couch. For once, she didn't grab the round orange pillow and start shooting it like a basketball. Zoe looked at the pillow and back at Jade.

"This *must* be serious," Zoe said.

In contrast to the minimalist decor in Jade's townhouse, Zoe's apartment was eclectic: walls of indigo, eggplant, and lime. Bookshelves crowded with African knickknacks obtained during her time in the Peace Corps.

The aroma of patchouli incense did not put Jade at ease today.

She gazed at the new posters on the wall. One had a 1950s-looking woman flexing her bicep above the words "ERA Amendment Now," the legislation that passed during Fairchild's first year in office. The other showed an arcade gallery from the point of view of someone holding an assault rifle. People were the rotating targets. Underneath was the word "Enough," the name of the gun reform bill that didn't pass after the elementary school shooting.

Zoe pointed up. "Do you hear what's playing?"

"Sade," Jade said.

"Thought you would like that, being from your era and all. Do you want to order takeout? There's a great new Japanese restaurant in Dupont Circle that delivers."

"You know I don't eat Japanese food."

"Why not? You're half Japanese. Your mother—"

"Zoe," Jade said, "this isn't a social visit."

She placed a blown-up drawing of Zoe's tree tattoo on the coffee table between them.

"What is this?" asked Zoe, sitting up.

Jade placed another drawing on the table and tapped it. "The Japanese symbol for 'progress.'"

Zoe's eyes became huge. "How do you know about that?"

"I saw it. Last year. When you covered me with a blanket."

"I need to wear tighter clothes," Zoe muttered to herself.

"These tats are related to some cases I'm working on. Who's the artist?"

Zoe stood. "This is crazy. Are you investigating *me*? Again? What for? I thought we were friends. Best friends. If this is the way you treat me, I feel sorry for your enemies. Isn't this abuse of power or something? Doesn't a crime have to be committed?"

"We are friends," Jade said, standing as well. "That's why I'm here. Alone. This is your chance to tell me the truth." Jade picked up the photographs and returned them to her briefcase. "Crimes have been committed, and I think you're involved. Do you have something to tell me? I can get you immunity."

"I still have no idea what you're talking about."

"Were you involved with the death of Congressman Barrett or setting up Noah Blakeley? You were a hacker in college. A good one. All along, we've thought foreign agents were responsible, but now I think you were involved in one or both cases."

Jade's eyes never left Zoe's face.

She looked for a sign that Zoe was lying: A shifting of the eyes. Swallowing. Clearing of the throat. Grooming gestures. A pause before responding.

Zoe paused, swallowed, cleared her throat, and ran her hand through her short hair. Her eyes blinked rapidly.

The FBI believed that only a sophisticated hacker—or hackers—had the ability to pull off the Robin Hood heist of millions of dollars from corporate and individual bank accounts. All the ill-gotten funds had been used to help people by providing low-income housing, jobs, and education. All good causes. All causes that Zoe believed in.

Cyber didn't believe the perp kept any money for himself.

Or herself.

In college, Stanford had suspended Zoe for two weeks for changing everyone's grades in her poli-sci class to As. The reason: she wanted everyone to be a winner. She was reinstated only when she agreed to join the university's information security department, assist with counter-cyberthreat efforts, and promise never to use her skills improperly at the university again. As far as Jade knew, Zoe had kept her promise.

And Jade should know; she'd been Zoe's roommate.

Although Zoe was capable of committing the Robin Hood heist and altering the manifests in the Barrett case, she didn't possess the resources to pull off these crimes alone.

Jade hadn't told anyone of her suspicions. Her friend deserved a chance to come clean first.

Zoe's silence spoke volumes.

"Who are you working for?" Jade asked.

"My organization helps pro—"

Jade stepped closer, looking down at her friend. "Zoe, who do you really work for?"

"Get out!"

The two women stared at each other for what felt to Jade like minutes.

Placing a hand on Zoe's shoulder, she said, "I'm worried about you. Are you in over your head? If so, I can get you out. But if you don't tell me, I might not be able to protect you."

Anger flitted across Zoe's face before compassion took its place. She placed her hand over Jade's. "You're my best friend, and I love you. I can't tell you *anything*, but I will tell you that you need to stop investigating me or anything else to do with the Robin Hood and Barrett cases."

Something in Zoe's words reminded Jade of what Micah had said at the conclusion of the Robin Hood case: "Move on."

It wasn't a suggestion. It was a command.

"Do you know Micah Alexander?"

Zoe blinked. "No."

Jade yelled, "Why are you lying to me?"

Zoe put her hands over her ears. "Stop! Stop with the questions. Or else!"

"Or else what? Is that a threat?"

Sighing, Zoe pulled her hands away and shook her head. Her eyes beseeched Jade's.

"It's not a threat, Jade. It's a warning."

@TheGodOfVeritas: President Fairchild invited some important people to a Kennedy Center Gala next week. Why doesn't she ever invite the common people? #shame

# CHAPTER EIGHTY-SEVEN

## Washington, DC

JADE READ THE paragraph again, still disturbed by her conversation with Zoe the night before. A chasm had erupted between them, and Jade wasn't sure it could be crossed.

Movement at her office door made Jade shift her gaze from the email she'd been reading.

A man poked his head in. "I love what you've done with the place."

Jade laughed—she hadn't done anything. It still looked the same as when he'd occupied it. "Ethan!"

Hopping out of her chair—*his* chair—she ran to him, giving him an uncharacteristic hug.

He hesitated, then hugged her back.

She pulled away from him. "What are you doing here?"

He was dressed impeccably, as always, in a black suit, pressed white shirt, and—she knew without looking—suspenders underneath his jacket. She could see her reflection in his polished shoes.

Looking rested and fit, he smiled. "Running, as a pastime, is overrated. I'm ready to get to work. And I want my office back."

※

Jade sipped champagne in the small red-and-gold room adjacent to the presidential box at the Kennedy Center. She had come alone and was unacquainted with the other invitees. She watched them mingle with each other.

She wasn't one for mingling.

She was still thinking of Zoe. Had she been too hard on her? But Zoe was involved somehow in whatever was going on with the president as well as the Robin Hood case.

She and Zoe hadn't spoken today.

The door opened, and she started to rise, expecting President Whitney Fairchild. Instead, Kyle Madison entered, wearing her customary tailored black pantsuit and crisp white shirt, an outfit that cost more than Jade's monthly rent. Kyle's medium-length shampoo-commercial hair shimmered as her green eyes found Jade's. Jade froze momentarily midrise and then stood to greet Kyle, who smiled. Jade started to respond in kind until she realized Kyle wasn't alone.

Following close behind Kyle was Brittney Summers, with her sandy complexion and long blond braids. She sort of looked like Prince in her purple women's tux.

"I'm surprised you're here, Agent Harrington." Kyle held out her hand, squeezing Jade's hand firmly before letting go.

There was a diamond on the ring finger of her other hand.

"Same here, Ms. Madison," Jade said.

"Being one of her minor donors has its privileges," she said, smiling. "I believe you've met Brittney."

Jade locked eyes with Summers, the tension between the baller and former baller on display like a scene from a bad teen movie.

Jade shook Summers's hand. "How's it going?" she said.

Summers raised her chin. "What's up?"

This had been the extent of their conversations when they played against each other.

As the mature adult, Jade broke eye contact first.

"I love the symphony," Kyle said, seeming to enjoy the tension. "Don't you?"

Jade wouldn't know. This was her first time. Before she could respond, an older woman made an entrance. And it was an entrance. Jade recognized her from television. She wore a black fitted dress, her neck wrapped in gold. Her bracelets tinkled as she made a beeline for Jade.

"Hello, I'm Senator Maureen McAllister, but you may call me Mo." The tiny woman hugged Jade, and Jade awkwardly hugged her back. The senator pulled away. "I don't believe in highfalutin titles. Do you? You're that famous agent I've read so much about. What a pleasure to meet you. You're prettier in person. Where's your family from?"

Slightly off-balance in the wake of the senator's staccato delivery, Jade responded, "Uh… I'm an army brat, so… everywhere."

"Well, thank you and your family for your service. This here is my husband, Jimmy." Mo patted his chest. "We call him Nub. He doesn't want to be here, but he knows who wears the dresses in the family." She winked at Jade.

Jimmy's eyes sparkled—he was a man who liked a good time. The way he looked at his wife reminded Jade of how her father used to look at her mother.

"How're you doing, darlin'?"

Jade pointed at the small Mississippi State pin on his collar. "Basketball or football?"

He grinned. "All sports. But women's basketball is my favorite."

"Good man," she said.

Mo and her husband moved on to introduce themselves to Kyle and her fiancée and the others in the box.

Next to enter was an attractive middle-aged black woman also wearing a black dress. She, too, came straight over to Jade.

Jade was anxious to meet her as well.

"Vice President Bates," Jade said. "Truly an honor."

"Oh, put your hand down and give me a hug. I'm a fan of yours. Please call me Jo. All my friends do."

Jade glanced over at Mo and back at her. "The three of you are the real deal. You, the senator, and the president are as close as it appears on TV."

"If we were younger, the press would call us Charlie's Angels, but at our age, they'll probably call us the Golden Girls. And we're just getting started. You haven't seen anything yet."

"I bet," Jade said.

A man stepped into the box. "Ladies and gentlemen, the President of the United States of America."

Everyone turned to face the door. Entering alone, Fairchild wore a gorgeous blue evening gown with a diamond necklace and earrings. She was followed closely by Secret Service Agent Josh McPherson.

Fairchild shook hands with the other guests in the box before approaching Jade. After exchanging pleasantries, she asked quietly, "Any progress on the Shakespeare Killer?"

"Not yet. I hope to have something to report soon."

*Hopefully tomorrow.*

As the president asked to be kept informed, Jade gazed over Fairchild's shoulder; there was movement by the door.

Another secret service agent had entered.

Jade stared open-mouthed at the agent.

The president followed Jade's gaze.

"Remember me?"

The agent wasn't speaking to Jade, but to Fairchild, who appeared confused.

The agent whipped a gun from behind her back and pointed it at the president.

For Jade, everything slowed down.

"What are you doing here?" someone yelled. It sounded like Kyle.

Jade wondered the same thing. She had a brief vision of a woman coming up to her table at the jazz club on Capitol Hill, and another of eyes meeting hers across the pillows.

Jade pushed the president to the floor. Josh dove to cover Fairchild as Jade lunged for the gun.

*Don't be afraid*, the president had said at CJ's funeral.

A loud boom filled the enclosed space.

Something pinged into Jade's chest.

A grunt, sounding as if it came from her, preceded a burning sensation that radiated to other parts of her body. She slammed into the floor where the agent had stood.

Why would Brook be dressed up like a secret service agent?

Why would she try to kill the president?

Kill me?

Screaming. Footsteps. Someone shouting Jade's name. Sounded like Kyle again.

Suddenly she felt tired. So tired.

Touching her chest, she gazed at the dark liquid on her fingers.

She needed to stay awake.
The pain was unbearable.
*I need to close my eyes. Just for a little while.*
She saw her parents' faces.
*I can't wait to see you.*
Then she felt nothing.

# CHAPTER EIGHTY-EIGHT

## The White House, Washington, DC

"HOW'S OUR FRIEND?"

"The same."

"I hope she makes it," he said.

"Me too." Whitney spun in her chair to look out the window at the Rose Garden. "What's on your mind, Cole?"

He never called to chat.

"Wanted to tell you something before you heard it from one of those busybodies in Washington."

Whitney's heart dropped. Was it about Cameron?

Keeping her voice light, she said, "Present company excluded?"

"Ashley's pregnant."

"Oh… that's wonderful news."

"Speak for yourself. I'm too old to have another kid."

"You have some control over that, you know."

He laughed. "That I do. By the time this kid graduates from college, I'll be seventy-eight years old. They'll be wheeling me in on a gurney to his graduation ceremony. If I make it that long."

"Age gives us perspective," she said.

"Tell that to my body."

"You're a good dad."

His breathing heavy, he said, "I miss my boy. CJ. I should've been more understanding, but I didn't understand him. He was different from the boys I hung out with growing up. From me. I won't make the same mistakes this time."

"All parents make mistakes, Cole. No one provided us with a manual. You can only do your best."

"I don't feel like I did my best with CJ."

He sniffed. She gave him a moment.

"But that's not the only reason I called."

She braced herself. "Oh?"

"We've selected a name, regardless of sex."

Whitney was perplexed. Perhaps he *did* just want to chat. "Okay…"

"Reagan Fairchild Brennan, after our two favorite presidents. You're Ashley's, by the way, so don't get the wrong idea. I'm not sure what you said to her when she came to visit you at the White House. Girl power stuff, I bet."

Caught off guard, Whitney teared up. This time, she needed a moment. "I'm speechless. Honored. And it's women power, Cole."

"Oh brother," he said. "We're not going to let the kid tell anyone his middle name. It'll be one of those old embarrassing family names that no one ever talks about."

She smiled. "Even so."

"And that's not all. You know how every time there's a mass

shooting, and we conservatives say we need to put money toward mental health, but we never do it?"

She didn't bother to answer.

"Let's do something about it. For real this time. In honor of my son. What do you say?"

"I say yes."

He clapped. "Hot dog! I'll start twisting some arms on my side of the aisle. Have a good evening, Madam President."

"You too. And thank you, Cole. Give Ashley my best."

❋

Whitney packed her briefcase. Grayson, Chandler, and Emma were upstairs in the Residence. After the assassination attempt, the Secret Service had located each of them and brought them back to the White House as a precaution.

Josh McPherson waited for her just outside the door to the Oval Office. He opened it for her as she approached.

He held an envelope.

She stepped outside. "Is that what I think it is?"

He tried to hand it to her.

She gripped her briefcase handle in front of her with both hands, not taking it.

"It's my fault. She was one of ours."

"Any news on her whereabouts?"

"Not yet."

"As I've told you every day since the… attempt, I won't accept your resignation. So put that away."

He held it out for a second longer, then slid the letter into a pocket inside his suit jacket.

"And I don't want to see it again," she said, holding his gaze, "until the next time you allow one of my children to bring home a date I haven't met."

He grinned. "Your daughter can be persuasive."

"So can I," she said. "Walk with me."

Whitney and Josh strolled along the West Wing Colonnade. The evening was balmy. Summer was coming.

"How are your children, Josh?"

His brown eyes lit up. "They're fine, ma'am. Ava and Mia are almost two."

"Ah... the terrible twos."

"I'm ready."

She shook her head at the muscular agent. "No, you're not."

They shared a smile.

She stopped walking. "Jade Harrington risked her life for me. For all of us. Without hesitation. Without a thought to her own well-being. She... reacted."

"It was her duty."

She looked at him. "Would you do the same for me?"

"Without a thought."

## CHAPTER EIGHTY-NINE

# Washington, DC

KURT MCCLAINE, IYANNA Adey, and Kyle Madison stood in the hallway of the Seattle courthouse. Jade couldn't hear their conversation from the other end of the hall. She crept closer, as she used to do as a kid when she spied on her parents.

Kyle did nearly all the talking. She was giving instructions, not being interviewed as Adey had told her. McClaine and Adey eventually left.

After a time, Zoe joined Kyle.

*What is she doing here?*

By now, Jade hovered next to them, but for some reason, they couldn't see her.

"She's getting close," Zoe said. "I'm not sure how long I can hold out."

"You'd better find a way."

"I hate lying to her."

*Why would you lie to me?*

"It can't be helped."

A sob. "What if she never comes out of the coma? What if she dies?"

"She won't."

"If she does, Paine won't be happy."

"Don't ever say that name in public again."

Jade was falling away from them. She could no longer hear their voices.

*Paine?*

Darkness enveloped her again.

❧

She was treading water. It felt warm and embracing. Above her she saw a glimmer of light. She knew she must swim toward it.

If she didn't, she would die.

She'd never backed away from a challenge. A fight. Her dad used to say, "For many are called, but few are chosen." A passage from the Bible. Although he wasn't a religious man, it was the code he lived by. The way he wanted her to live.

He would want her to fight.

Did they fight when they were trapped in a car at the bottom of a ravine off the Pacific Coast Highway? Did they try to come back to her? For her?

When Jade was a child, her mom would sometimes take her to the convenience store and allow her to buy a bag of M&M's. But she would let Jade eat only one M&M a day, no matter how much she begged for more. Her mother wanted Jade to learn self-control.

When her mom wasn't looking, her dad would sneak the rest of the bag to her.

Jade wanted to be with them. But she wasn't ready. Yet.

She started to swim.

Fifty yards. Twenty yards. Ten. Five. Three. Two. One. She broke through the water's surface.

And opened her eyes.

"Blimey!" a voice with a British accent said. "She's awake!"

Hazy. Everything hazy. Thankfully it wasn't too bright. She tried to say something, but her mouth wasn't working. It felt as if it were stuffed with cotton balls.

The person who'd spoken dashed out of the room. A moment later, a woman in a white coat stood in his place.

"Welcome back," said the woman. She had a friendly voice, and her English was precise with a slight Indian accent. "I am Dr. Sati Sangha, the president's personal physician. And now, it seems, yours as well. You're in the George Washington University Hospital."

"Wa—"

The doctor reached toward the bedside table and produced a clear plastic cup. She bent the straw to Jade's lips. The water burned her throat on the way down.

Jade swallowed. "The president?"

"She's fine. Thanks to you. She's been by to see you. She's quite worried."

"How long?" Jade croaked.

"You've been out for a few days."

"Damage?"

"Nothing permanent. You won't be working for a while. Or playing basketball." The doctor patted her arm. "I want you to rest now. You've had a lot of visitors."

"Who?"

Jade couldn't wait for the answer. She fell back asleep.

# CHAPTER NINETY

# Washington, DC

"I THOUGHT YOU WERE angry at me."

"I was," Zoe said. "I am. But you almost died, so I forgive you. Besides, you're a hero. Again. It's hard sometimes, being best friends with all this greatness. May I have some of that?"

Jade was sitting up in bed. Bandages were wrapped around her chest and left arm. She shifted the bowl of Jell-O away from Zoe. "No."

The room resembled a living room from a TV sitcom. There was a recliner near the bed, a couch, and a small round table with four chairs. The beeping and hissing noises from the medical equipment were muted.

"You were lucky. The bullet barely missed your heart."

Jade spooned some Jell-O into her mouth.

"Kyle was there," Zoe continued. "How was that?"

Jade stared at her snack as if it were a work of art, while Zoe examined her face for any sign of interest in Kyle.

"I don't really remember."

Zoe frowned. "That's too bad. I wanted to hear how it went with Brittney."

She regaled Jade of the press coverage from her exploits, how Jade had trended on Twitter for almost an entire day, with people of all ages posting videos of themselves diving into the air and landing on the floor or the ground ("Jading"), and that she had been named one of *People* magazine's Most Beautiful People.

"Must be a down year," Jade said.

"You're really famous now!"

Jade eventually tuned her friend out. Something tugged at her. Something about Kyle. And Zoe.

What was it?

A few minutes after Zoe left, there was a knock at her hospital room door.

Kyle Madison popped her head in. "Up for another visitor?"

"Of course."

At least Zoe had left. What a disaster that would've been.

Kyle entered with a dozen roses.

The clack of Kyle's high heels stopped as she looked around the room. "Oh my."

Most of the horizontal surfaces were covered with get-well cards and flower arrangements from friends, coworkers, former teammates, other students from the tae kwon do school, and the president of the United States of America.

Shifting some vases from other well-wishers, Kyle placed hers in a prominent position on the table.

She sat in the chair next to the bed and leaned forward, hands clasped, arms resting on her legs. She wore a gray shirt with black pants. Her makeup and hair were impeccable.

"I finally saw you in action," Kyle said. "You saved her life. All our lives." She touched Jade's hand. The skin on Kyle's finger was lighter where the engagement ring had been. "I, for one, will be forever grateful. Thank you."

"I was only doing my job," Jade said.

Kyle tilted her head. "I thought that was the Secret Service's job."

"Yeah... well," Jade said.

"When in Rome?"

"Something like that." Jade paused. "Did you know her?"

"Who?"

"Brooklyn."

"Who?"

"The secret service agent."

Kyle pulled her hand away. "No."

"You yelled at her."

"Everyone was yelling."

They were silent for a moment.

"In town on business?" Jade said.

Kyle didn't answer at first, turning instead to gaze out the window. She turned back to Jade. "I haven't gone home. I've been here since... the assassination attempt."

"Why?" Jade said. "What about your businesses?"

"That's what technology is for."

"I still don't understand why you're here."

"Because of you, silly."

Jade wasn't sure what to say, so she did what she did best: deflected. "Is Summers here too?"

Kyle crossed her legs, resting her elbow on her thigh, chin in hand. "I wouldn't know."

Silence again.

Jade said, "I enjoyed the time we spent together in Seattle, but—"

"When I saw you lying there," Kyle said, "I didn't know whether you were alive or dead. Whether you would live or die. Things suddenly became clear to me. My feelings became clear." She gazed at Jade, her eyes as blue as a perfect sea. "I told Brittney about my feelings for you."

Jade was speechless.

"Don't say a word. We'll talk about this later. I've realized tomorrow isn't promised."

Jade looked at Kyle. She felt… nothing.

"I—"

They both turned at the knock on the door. Kyle was agitated at the interruption. Jade was relieved.

At the threshold stood Professor Alaia Bennett, carrying a stack of books.

Jade smiled. "Hi."

Mouth parted, Kyle looked from Alaia to Jade. "Did I realize it too late?"

# CHAPTER NINETY-ONE

# The White House, Washington, DC

WHITNEY KNOCKED ON Emma's bedroom door. "Hello?" said a female voice that was not her daughter's.

She frowned. "Emma?"

Talking to Cole the night before had made her think of mistakes she'd made with her own children. Chandler had been avoiding her, staying in his room and leaving it only for work. They still hadn't spoken. She should have made more of an effort. How could she bring a divided country together if she couldn't do the same for her family? She was a mother first. Other mothers found the time.

The door cracked open, revealing half of Megan's face. Emma had insisted that Megan come with her to the White House. "Are you looking for Em?"

"Well, yes."

"Hold on a minute, Madam President. She's just getting out of the shower."

Whitney debated whether to leave but remained where she was.

Megan called out to Emma. "It's your mom!"

A moment later, Emma emerged from her room, closing the door behind her. Her hair was dry. "Mom."

"I wanted to make sure you're all right."

"I'm fine. We were studying."

Did college students typically study in the shower these days?

"I'll let you... study."

"That reminds me, Mom, I have something to tell you."

Whitney looked at her, questioning.

Her daughter hesitated. "Megan and I are sort of a couple."

"Sort of."

"Well, we are a couple."

Emma's secret service detail must know. Who else? Obviously the press hadn't caught on yet.

"I see."

Emma exhaled. "There you go again."

"Forgive me, but my daughter just came out to me." She glanced around the hall. There was no one there. "Perhaps we should talk about this some other time."

"Will there ever be a good time?"

The news wasn't a total surprise. The noise that Whitney heard last night—the same noise she'd heard last time Emma and Megan had spent the night in the White House—was Emma sneaking off to the Queens' Bedroom.

A mother knew.

After a moment, Emma said, "I didn't think so. I thought you would be cool with it, given your politics. Or is tolerance reserved for your base?"

"I don't care that you're gay. I'm upset that you didn't tell me." She paused. "We used to be close."

"We're still close, Mom. Just because we don't talk every day doesn't mean I don't love you."

"Emma," Whitney said, placing her hands on both of her daughter's shoulders, "I love you, and I respect who you are. I'm proud to be your mother, and I can't wait to become better acquainted with Megan."

"That's great, Mom," Emma said, "because I have something else to tell you."

"Oh?"

"Megan and I... we're going to live together, after the semester is over."

❄

"When you weren't in your library, I thought I might find you here."

Whitney remained in the plank position. "I wanted to be alone."

Her husband took a step into the White House Residence gym. "Where's Nicki?"

Nicki was her private yoga instructor.

"As I said, I wanted to be alone."

"Even from me?"

"I will not repeat myself again."

Grayson crossed the room and stopped a few feet away from her. He sat cross-legged on the floor.

Whitney clenched her butt cheeks and sucked in her stomach.

Her palms pressed into the yoga mat, a small tremor shooting up her forearms. She had been holding the pose for a while.

She lowered herself, not wanting him to see her shake. Matching his cross-legged position, she faced him.

Classical spa music played through the in-wall speakers, the relaxing sounds juxtaposed by the tension between them.

"While I've been here," he said, "I've had time to think. About what's important."

She waited.

"You. Us. I'm back."

"What about… ?"

"It's nothing."

"Another mistake?" she said.

He opened his mouth, then closed it.

The first time he engaged in an affair with their next-door neighbor in Missouri, he claimed it was a one-night stand. It was a mistake, the result of consuming too much wine.

Now Grayson's eyes beseeched hers. "It's over. For good this time. I've learned that I need to keep the politics and our relationship separate. I won't make the same mistake again."

That word. Again.

She stared at the face of the man she had loved for most of her life. The father of two of her children. Her best friend.

"No," she said, "you won't."

He exhaled with relief. "Thank you. I promise to be the husband I should've been."

"I hope she appreciates that, since you weren't for me. Every time it got hard, you left, and I had to get through it alone. And now I've realized that I don't need you." Rising, she walked by him without looking down. "Now get the fuck out of my house."

# CHAPTER NINETY-TWO

# Washington, DC

"HI."

Jade looked up from the novel she was reading, *Their Eyes Were Watching God* by Zora Neale Hurston.

She hadn't seen him in almost six months. His face still showed the aftermath of the Rockefeller Center bombing, although the scars were healing.

"Hi," she said, setting the open book facedown beside her on the bed.

Entering the room, he sat in the chair that Alaia Bennett had vacated an hour ago.

He took in the books on the nightstand: *The Bluest Eye* by Toni Morrison. *Native Son* by Richard Wright. *Kindred* by Octavia Butler.

"Light reading," he said. "I detect a theme."

"A friend brought them over," she said. "You look great."

"Liar. I'm supposed to be saying that to you. Thanks for seeing me."

"At least I put you on the list," she said, teasing. Then, "I can't wait to get out of here."

"I know the feeling. I can't imagine that lying here all day suits you."

She smiled. "No. How's it going?"

"My doctor said I should make a complete recovery. Additional surgery will take care of the rest." He surveyed her bandages. "We make quite a pair, don't we?"

"I'm glad you came."

He shrugged. "I missed you."

She should respond in kind, but instead she allowed the silence to drag on too long.

Finally she asked, "Back at work?"

"Not yet. But it won't be long. President Fairchild thinks it's important to show the public that terrorism didn't win." He pointed to his face. "I'm going to need lots of makeup."

As the White House press secretary, Blake gave on-camera daily briefings to the American people.

She decided to trust him. She needed to.

"I've been thinking a lot about our discussions," she said. "About the coincidences. Your conspiracy theories. I think it's a good thing you're back at work."

"Why?" he said.

She told him about Zoe's tattoos, her reaction when Jade confronted her, and her warning. Blake had worked with Zoe on political campaigns.

Jade stared at him, gauging his reaction to what she was going to say next.

"I think Fairchild had something to do with Judy Porter's murder."

He looked into her eyes, his tone flat. "I do too."

❁

"Hey, Coach."

Taking a hesitant step into the room, LaKeisha smiled, but it wasn't as bright as it once was.

She glanced around as she sat in the chair next to the hospital bed. "Nicer than my house."

"Mine too."

"How can you afford this?"

"I can't," Jade said, looking around the room herself. "Let's just say our president is grateful."

"You're the best FBI agent ever. You're friends with the president. You were a great basketball player. And you're not a bad coach either."

"Thanks. I think."

"Some of my AAU teammates can't believe you're my coach. You're the truth. It means you're the shit." LaKeisha grinned. "Oops. Sorry, Coach."

Jade smiled. "I know what it means."

Jade thought about her plan with Veritas to flush out the killer. It almost worked. Too well.

"Are you in pain?"

Jade shook her head. "The nurses are taking care of me." She felt groggy from the medication; the nurses had administered the drugs before the next round of pain could commence. "Sorry I couldn't coach the spring league team this year."

"No worries. We knew you were busy."

"How's AAU going?"

"We're going to nationals next month. New Orleans."

"Next time you find yourself in a potentially compromising situation, leave."

"Don't worry about me, Coach." Subdued, she said, "I learned my lesson."

Jade studied her face.

"What lesson is that?"

"I need to pick better friends," LaKeisha said, forcing a laugh.

"No, really," Jade said. Although this girl looked tough, she held a lot of things inside. Jade needed to draw her out.

LaKeisha looked down at her red long-sleeve Adidas T-shirt and black track pants. "That it's different for me. Because of what I look like. How I dress." She pulled at a braid. "My hair."

"It can be. Yes."

LaKeisha's eyes met hers. "Is it that way for you, Coach?"

Jade wondered if LaKeisha would ever trust the system again. Jade had been fortunate that she hadn't suffered much racism during her life, but she wasn't immune.

She believed Barringer was a racist, for example.

"Sometimes. As a black person, your standards must be higher."

The girl's expression was anguished behind her cool facade. "How do you deal with it?"

Jade thought for a moment, not wanting to give LaKeisha a pat answer. "I try to focus on me. What I'm trying to do. Being the best me I can be." Jade held her eyes. "Racism isn't about you. There isn't anything wrong with you. Or the color of your skin. It's about them. Something is wrong with *them*. Their insecurity. Their fear of uncertainty. You need to keep doing you." She thought about what Alaia had said to her. "You're descended from kings and queens. You are their wildest dreams."

LaKeisha's eyes shone. "I'm focusing on my game. Scholarship offers are coming in."

"Let me know if you ever want to talk about that. I've been through the process."

"I'll take you up on that."

"You should focus on your studies."

"I will."

"And don't worry about the charges," Jade said. "They've been dropped. Your record was expunged."

Jade had called in a favor at CSS before the assassination attempt. She hadn't had a chance to tell LaKeisha until now.

The girl swallowed hard, about to cry. She didn't. Instead, she stood and extended her hand. Jade slapped LaKeisha's hand and held it.

"No matter if you coach me or not," the girl said, "you'll always be my coach."

# CHAPTER NINETY-THREE

# The White House, Washington, DC

I N THE ROSE Garden the next morning, Whitney stood at the podium set up for the occasion. She was flanked on either side by Senator Maureen McAllister and Vice President Josephine Bates. Next to Jo stood radio talk-show host Cole Brennan. The two women wore smart suits with skirts. Cole's tan suit fit. He had lost weight.

The weather was perfect, the arrival of the suffocating DC humidity still a month away.

She gazed out over the assembled audience.

Whitney concluded her speech, "Suicides are at an all-time high in this country. This legislation will not prevent a mass murderer from easily obtaining a gun, but it will decrease the number of suicides. Especially among our teens." She turned to Cole. "It won't bring CJ back, but I believe he would have liked this bill.

He fought for the causes he believed in, like his daddy… although he chose the right side."

Cole laughed. "Not going to debate you here, Madam President, but you're right. CJ would have liked this bill." He gave her a slight bow. "Thank you."

The CJ Brennan Mental Health Act would create a department within the executive branch to coordinate mental health programs across federal, state, and local agencies in order to help Americans in need find care, housing, job assistance, and other services.

She moved to the small mahogany table with the presidential seal affixed to its front and waited for Mo, Jo, Cole, Sasha, and several other supportive members of Congress to gather behind her. Selecting one of the many Cross Townsend pens, Whitney signed the act using one pen for every two to three letters of her name. When she finished, she stood and gave one pen to Jo, one to Mo, and one to Sasha. The last three pens she handed to Cole.

"One for you. One for Ashley. And one for CJ."

Tears fell from Cole's eyes, and he pulled her toward him in a bear hug. Josh McPherson took a step toward her, but she held out a hand to stop him.

After a moment, she disengaged and slipped her arms around the waists of Mo and Jo. The four of them posed as the press pool cameras clicked away.

"Cole, I want one with just the women."

He made a face, pretending to be offended. "Aren't you always complaining about sexism and discrimination?"

"It's *our* turn," she said simply.

Raising his arms in surrender, Cole walked away.

As she posed for the cameras, Cole went to stand by Cameron Kelly.

And her son, Chandler.

*What is Cameron doing here?*

After the last photo was taken, she said to Mo and Jo, "Thank you both. I could not have done this without you."

"We should do it again," said Jo. "We're on a roll."

"It was a hoot!" said Mo. "I love working with you two."

"We *should* get together again," Whitney said, "but for fun. Dinner. Once a month. Just us. What do you say?"

"I'm in," said Jo.

"I'll bring the moonshine!" said Mo.

"I would certainly hope so," Whitney said, smiling.

*I don't need him.*

A weight she had borne for as long as she could remember had lifted. There was life—a good life—after Grayson.

"Madam President, a few questions!" said one of the White House press corps.

Whitney returned to the podium. She spotted Judy's replacement at ABC and pointed at the reporter.

"What's your question, Mike?"

"You said this mental health act would've helped CJ Brennan. Can you think of a time in your life when it would've helped you?"

The conversational noise ceased. Everyone looked at her, waiting for her answer.

*It was time.*

"Yes, Mike, I can. When I was a junior in high school, I went to live with my aunt, Mary Churchill, and transferred to a school in a suburb outside of Chicago. Winters there can be frigid. I wore bulky coats and sweaters every day. For the last three months of my stay, I lived at a convent where my aunt volunteered."

She paused.

A few reporters raised their hands, some shouting "Madam President!" or "President Fairchild!"

Holding up a hand, she said, "Let me finish. There's been a lot of speculation out there. You've waited a long time for this story. It's my story; let me tell it. If you're patient, I'll answer most of your questions."

"I doubt it!" shouted one reporter.

The others laughed.

She waited for the laughter to subside.

"The entire experience was a painful one. Living away from my family and friends. Attending a new school where I knew no one, with only my aunt for company. I was all alone. It would have been helpful to have someone to talk to. A professional.

"Being there wasn't a choice. At least, not my choice. It was my parents' decision. They believed they needed to protect me and my reputation from the inevitable small-town gossip.

"I had a secret, you see. I was pregnant." The reporters started to murmur. "After the baby was born, I held him once before I signed the papers giving him up for adoption. Before he was taken away from me forever. I was promised he would be brought up in a good home. With parents who would love him. And I returned home to Missouri.

"My story is far from unique. There are women across this country and around the world with similar stories. Similar situations that happened *to* them. Not because of anything they did or the clothes they wore, but because they are women. I applaud the brave women speaking out. Remember, what happened to you is not your fault.

"Over a decade ago, an African-American civil rights activist named Tarana Burke started a movement called Me Too." She stared at Cameron Kelly. "I stand here today to tell you that I was raped. I am your president, and I am a survivor. Yes. Me too."

The press corps and other guests were silent. Stunned. A bird chirped.

Chandler looked from Whitney to Cameron and then backed to Whitney. He roared: "You!"

An ugly look consumed her son's face, now inches from Cameron's. Chandler's hands encircled Cameron's neck and squeezed. Cameron's face turned red as the two men fell to the ground. Whitney took a step toward them before Josh grasped her wrist and held her in place. Two secret service agents sprinted past him, each of them grabbing one of Chandler's arms.

They pulled him off Cameron.

"You fucking asshole!" Chandler tried to shake off the agents, his face also a deep shade of red. Spittle leaked out of the corner of his mouth. "You raped my mother! And you hired me anyway? You goddamn—"

"Josh," Whitney said to her lead agent. "I have to do something. I need to protect my baby."

Josh stared at her. He looked around and called two agents over. "Watch her."

Sasha yelled at the press corps, "Stop taking pictures!"

Sprinting toward Chandler, Josh encircled her son in his powerful arms. Chandler struggled all the way as Josh carried him into the White House.

Cameron staggered to his feet, holding his neck and coughing. "Did you see what that little fucker did?" he gasped to Cole.

Cole looked at him. "Is it true? Did you rape the president?"

Cameron was caught off guard by the question. And then he grinned. "She begged for it."

"Did she now?" Cole was agile for a big man. His right arm

shot out, making contact with Cameron's jaw. Whitney's ex-boy-friend fell backward with the impact of the knock-out punch.

Sasha continued to yell at the camera people and everyone who had pulled out their smartphones.

To no avail.

# CHAPTER NINETY-FOUR

# Washington, DC

"AREN'T YOU TIRED of lazing around?" Dante said. "You need to get back to work, boss."

He was followed into the hospital room by Micah, Pat, Christian, Max, and Ethan. Micah moved the metal IV stand and LED heart monitor out of the way so the six of them could gather around the bed.

Jade lifted her chin toward the equipment. "I hope I won't need that." She scanned their faces. "Can you help bust me out of here?"

"Don't tempt them," Max said.

Christian surveyed the room and spotted the refrigerator.

"How are you feeling?" Ethan asked.

"Bored. Any sign of the perp?"

He shook his head.

Jade finally asked the question that had consumed her for the last several days. "Who is she?"

"Her name's Devon Mattix," said Dante, "a former secret service agent."

"Secret Service?" she said.

Christian returned, popping open a Pepsi. "She was fired from the first daughter's detail last year when Emma Fairchild sneaked out of her dorm."

"I remember that. And she blamed Fairchild?"

"She wanted revenge," Dante said.

With a proud smile, Micah said, "Told you she was in law enforcement."

"You also thought she was a he," she reminded him. He frowned. "Nine millimeter?"

"Ruger LC9s," Dante said.

"You should've worn a vest," Max said, his voice soft.

"Didn't think I'd need one at the symphony," she said. "How did she get the gun in?"

Dante plopped himself in the recliner. "She had help. One of the president's secret service detail disappeared the night of the assassination attempt."

That was too scary to contemplate. She sat up higher in the bed. "We should inform the—"

"We're on it," Dante said. "Every law enforcement agency in the country is looking for both of them."

"McPherson wasn't in on it, right?"

"No."

She exhaled. She thought of Josh as one of the good guys. If he were dirty, it would've shaken her worldview. "What's new with the Shakespeare case?"

"Not much," Dante said.

"Did you find anything tying Brook—Mattix to the murders?" she asked.

Her talkative team became silent. Christian looked up at the ceiling. Micah studied the books on her nightstand. Max gazed out the window. Pat studied her cell phone. Dante and Ethan stared down at the floor.

Dante looked at her. "What if she was hired to kill them?"

Doubtful, Christian said, "Contract killings?"

Jade remembered what Brooklyn had said she did for a living. *Customer service.*

"Thought of something?" Max asked.

"I might—"

She should tell them she'd already "caught" Mattix. Or rather, Mattix had caught her. Seduced her.

Why?

She could tell them where Mattix lived, but she wasn't sure of the address. Only the neighborhood.

Jade closed her mouth, averting her gaze. "I thought I did, but it's gone."

"A contract killing does seem farfetched," Micah said.

"Does it?" Dante said. "She was a well-trained agent out for revenge."

"And fit," Jade said.

"How do you know that?" Micah asked.

"Uh… I got a glimpse of her before she shot me."

"That still doesn't answer why," Ethan said. "Or who took out the contracts."

"We've examined Mattix's bank accounts," Pat said, "and haven't come up with any unusual or significant deposits."

"Doesn't prove anything," Dante said. "She could have off-shore accounts."

"We're working on that," Pat said.

As Micah opened his mouth to say something, his hand

accidentally knocked into the rolling table that Jade used to eat her meals. A stainless-steel tray clattered to the floor.

Jade yelled, "Everybody down!"

Her heart pounded as she glanced around wildly at her colleagues.

"It was just a tray, Jade," Micah said, bending to pick it up.

Concern was etched on the faces of her fellow agents.

Laughing it off, she said, "It was so loud."

Silence descended.

"We should go," Ethan said.

"Pat and Max," Jade said, "can you stay for a moment?"

Micah frowned.

Christian, Ethan, and Dante hugged her and shuffled out.

Micah stared down at her, concern still evident in those gray eyes. "You sure you're going to be all right?"

"I'll be beating your butt up the Lincoln steps in no time."

Micah looked unconvinced. "Can't wait." Glancing at Max, he hugged her. "See ya, Jade."

He sauntered out of the room.

Jade watched him leave.

Her heart pounded again, as if it would bust out of her gown.

But not in a lovelorn way.

She had never seen Micah shirtless. But when he leaned over, she happened to peek under his open-collared shirt. A chill went through her as she caught a glimpse of the tattoo on his chest.

The same as Zoe's.

In the exact same place.

進捗

# CHAPTER NINETY-FIVE

# The White House, Washington, DC

"HOW BAD IS it?"

"Actually," Sasha said, sitting in the chair alongside Whitney's desk in the study, "it's quite the opposite. Your approval ratings are up."

Whitney shook her head. "Of course they are."

That morning, the headline of the *Washington Post* was "The Melee in the Rose Garden." The entire front page comprised stories about Whitney and her family: Whitney's confession, Chandler fighting with Cameron, Cole punching Cameron, and speculation—once again—about the identity of Whitney's baby. The passing of the mental health act warranted two small paragraphs in the lower right corner.

Cameron declared he wouldn't press charges against either Chandler or Cole, probably figuring it wasn't a wise career move.

Women took to social and traditional media to tell their stories of sexual assault using the hashtag #MeTooWhitney.

"You just have to look outside," Sasha said.

Earlier, from the Residence, Whitney had looked out the window at the many women standing just outside the White House fence, most of them holding signs. In addition to #MeTooWhitney, there was #MeToo, #IBelieveYou, and #ItsNeverTooLateToBeFree.

Whitney wasn't sure why it had taken her so long to speak out about what had happened to her. None of her reasons seemed to matter now.

She *was* free.

"Cole's on."

"Turn it up," Whitney said.

"It's been quite a week," Cole said. "Who knew White House press conferences could be so lively? Thank you all for the cards and emails. Yes, my hand is fine, and no, I shouldn't have hit him harder. I apologize to you folks that I was such a bad judge of character. I thought Kelly was a better man. I want to tell the fellas something. Are you listening? Come closer to the radio or the computer. Are you ready?

"No means no. It's not code for yes. Guys like Cameron Kelly have no place in the Republican Party or in Congress.

"If he should run again when he's up for reelection, I promise to God I will do everything in my power to defeat him. Are you with me?

"We need to pay the bills now, but after the break, my guest will be a former legislative aide to Cameron Kelly, Chandler Fairchild. Yes, that Chandler Fairchild. Stay tuned."

Whitney looked at Sasha. "You knew?"

Sasha cocked her head and pursed her lips.

After the intermission, Cole introduced Chandler.

"What are you going to do now, champ?" Cole asked.

"I'm not sure yet, Mr. Brennan. I might take a break from politics."

"Why?"

"My last two bosses weren't very good."

Cole's high-pitched laugh squealed over the airwaves. "That's true. How did you feel when you realized the truth about Kelly?"

"Blindsided. This guy hired me, showed an interest in my career, in me. Now I know it was to spite her."

"Not very nice of him."

"I was just as bad. A real sh—jerk to my mom."

"Who knows, son? She might be listening. You do listen to my show, President Fairchild, don't you?"

Whitney smiled.

"What would you say to her," Cole said, "if she were listening?"

"Mom, I love you, and I'm so proud of you and all your accomplishments. I'm sorry I ever went to work for that douchebag."

"What do you think about your mom? After what she went through."

"She's a badass. I should've been there for her like she's always been there for me. Chosen her over politics. Sons are supposed to protect their mothers."

"Are you going to switch parties?"

"I'm still a Republican, but I respect my mom's views, as she's always respected mine."

"She has?"

"Well… most of the time."

"We need a loyal guy like you at the network."

Chandler paused. "Have your people call my people."

Cole laughed. "We'll leave it right there for today. Thank you, Chandler Fairchild. Good luck to you, young man."

"Thank you, Mr. Brennan."

Cole signed off.

Sasha turned off the radio. Whitney wiped her eyes.

"Sounds as if you've got your son back," Sasha said.

Chopin's Nocturne in E-flat major, op. 55, no. 2 trilled from Whitney's cell phone. A ringtone she hadn't heard in a while.

"I need to take this, Sasha," Whitney said.

Her younger son was calling.

After she hung up with Chandler, she returned to the paperwork on her desk. She caught herself humming. She was happy.

She glanced at the credenza. Sasha had left her purse.

Whitney picked up the handset to ask Sean to retrieve it, then set it back down. She needed to stretch her legs. She could return the purse to her chief of staff's office herself.

As she got closer, she noticed that the black patent leather purse was open.

She peered inside. A sheet of parchment paper.

A familiar color.

The texture was familiar to her touch.

Pulling it out, she unfolded it, already knowing its contents.

A letter addressed to her. From Landon Phillips.

Worn from the many times she had read it.

The same letter stolen from Whitney's purse several months ago.

Sasha had known all along that Landon believed he was Whitney's son.

Why did Sasha take the letter?

Why hadn't she returned it?

What else was she keeping from Whitney?

A heaviness overcame her. She slipped the letter back inside Sasha's purse and picked up the phone to call Sean.

# CHAPTER NINETY-SIX

## Washington, DC

"MAY I SPEAK to Pat first?" Jade said to Max.

"Of course," he said.

She waited for the wide hospital room door to close behind him. "Anything new on Barrett?"

The other woman shook her head.

Jade looked at Pat for a long time, then said, "'For sweetest things turn sourest by their deeds.'"

"Ninety-four," Pat said. "The sonnet left with Judy Porter. What of it?"

"I think it's a message."

"Meaning?"

"I need you to run a check on someone."

"Sure. Who?"

Jade put a finger to her lips. She scribbled a name and an address on a sheet of paper from a notepad on her nightstand and held it up.

"Memorize it."

Pat's eyes narrowed. "Isn't that your friend?"

Jade nodded.

Pat stared at the paper and then nodded.

Jade ripped off the piece of paper with Zoe's name and address and handed it to Pat. "Flush it."

Pat did as she was asked.

Jade thought about seeing Kyle, McClaine, and Iyanna Adey at the Seattle courthouse. There was something between them. Something involving Zoe.

But what?

"Look into Kyle Madison."

"We ran a check on her for the Robin Hood case."

"Do it again," Jade said. "We missed something. And one more thing."

Pat looked at her, questioning.

"There's another person I need information on."

"Who?"

"Micah."

# CHAPTER NINETY-SEVEN

## Washington, DC

"THIS IS UNEXPECTED," Blake said.

He stood in the doorway, his normally styled hair tousled. He was barefoot and dressed in a plain black T-shirt and jeans.

"I was just visiting Jade," Whitney said.

"How's she doing?"

"You haven't seen her?"

"I have."

This pleased her. "Aren't you going to invite me in?"

"Uh… sure."

She entered Blake's condo, which opened to a living and dining room area. The furniture was modern, the walls gray and white. Crossing the cherry floors, she gazed out the window at the George Washington University Hospital across the street and listened to the rhythm of the city outside.

"How convenient," she said.

"I could've walked home."

Behind her, he picked up papers and files from the sofa and rectangular wooden coffee table. She turned, watching him. "What are you working on?"

"Nothing," he said, cradling all the material in his arms. "Trying to catch up on what I missed while I was out. Please sit down. I'll be right back."

He walked past her to where there were two other rooms: his bedroom and the guest room he used as an office.

Sitting on the sofa, she admired the white marble flecked with gray that surrounded the fireplace.

He wasn't gone long.

"Your fireplace is beautiful," she said.

"I lucked out, finding a place like this close to the White House. Would you like something to drink?"

"I'm fine."

Opting to sit on a chair across from her, he crossed his legs at the ankles.

"I can imagine the traffic jam you're causing outside," he said.

"I won't be long. I suppose you're wondering why I'm here."

"You've never visited me at home before."

"It's about what happened in the Rose Garden."

"Sorry to miss all the excitement. Do you want me to write up a statement?"

"This has nothing to do with your job," she said. "It's about you."

"What about me?"

"It's time."

He sat up straighter. "Time?"

"For us to tell everyone who you are."

"Why?"

"It will come out eventually. We need to craft the story the way we want it to be told."

"Okay." He dragged the word out, unconvinced.

"Your life is about to change," she said, noticing his discomfort. "Everything you do will be scrutinized and commented on, worse than in your role as press secretary. You'll receive protection from the Secret Service."

He looked sharply at her, as if he hadn't considered this.

"I don't want their protection."

"It's a hassle sometimes," she said, "but you'll get used to it."

"I'm of age. I can decline it."

"Given what happened to me, I wouldn't recommend that. Everyone will come after you."

Standing, he moved to the window behind him, gazing down at the traffic jam around Washington Circle.

"I like my life the way it is," he said.

She came and stood by him, following his gaze.

"You are my son. This is your life now."

## CHAPTER NINETY-EIGHT

# Washington, DC

"HOW LONG?" MAX said upon reentering the room after Pat had departed. He sat down in the chair next to the bed.

"How long what?"

"Have you been jumpy like this."

She started to blow him off, then looked at him. "Ever since it happened."

"Is there anything else that's different?" Max asked.

She thought about it for a moment. She was exhausted from all the visitors. "My chest hurts before it rains."

"Nightmares?"

"Every night. But not about that night."

"About what then?"

"My parents."

His brow furrowed. "What about them?"

"I'm trying to find them."

The last word hung in the air. After a while, Max said, "I looked into their deaths. At the time. I met with the local chief of police and the detective in charge of the case." He stared into her eyes. "It was officially ruled an accident, Jade. They're gone."

She was never satisfied with that conclusion. They died in a one-car accident on the Pacific Coast Highway. There were other tread marks at the scene. The police thought that it might have been a hit-and-run. The other car was never found.

Fire had consumed her parents' car. There were no remains. Their caskets, laid to rest in Arlington National Cemetery, were empty.

Glancing down, she said, "I blamed myself. Believed that the accident was somehow my fault. That I could've prevented it."

"You've never told me that," Max said. Then, quieter, "I miss your parents too. I'm your godfather for a reason." A pause. "Did you know your dad was a spiritual man?"

"We never went to church."

"But he read the Bible. Every day. 'For unto whomsoever much is given, of him shall be much required.' He believed privilege bestowed responsibility."

"I know," she said. "He told me that many times." She paused. "I want to get back to it, Max."

"It's going to take some time before they'll allow it," he said. "Even a desk job."

"Can't you pull some strings?"

"You need to rest."

"Being here has given me a lot of time to think," she said.

"About?"

"I'm not ready to sit behind a desk."

"I could've told you that."

"I miss my previous job. Being an ASAC. I miss the hunt."

"It's what you were born to do."

"Did my father say that too?"

Max hesitated. "Possibly."

"I'm glad Ethan's back," she said, fiddling with her hospital wristband.

His expression changed. "So am I."

She wondered what that was about. "Did you have something to do with that?"

"I don't possess that type of pull. I should go, let you rest. When will they discharge you?"

"Tomorrow?"

"Need a ride?"

"Zoe's coming." She hesitated. She wanted to tell him her suspicions about the president. About Zoe. Something made her hold back. She wasn't sure what. Max was one of the few people in her life whom she'd always trusted.

He'd always been there.

"What about you?" she asked.

"What about me?"

"How are you doing?"

"I'm fine," he said. "I started writing."

This made Jade sit up. "Writing what?"

"Fiction."

"Crime fiction?"

"No," he said. "A historical thriller. Set during the Shakespearean era."

"Can't let all that research go to waste."

"That," he said, "and it fills the hours." Max was never one to rush to fill silences, even awkward ones. He surprised her. "We need to talk about Micah."

She looked at him. "What about him?"

"The way he looks at you." Max pushed his glasses farther up on his nose. "You shouldn't let him be so attached."

Jade didn't like anyone telling her what to do. "He works for me."

"All the more reason to keep it professional."

"We *are* professional," she said. "Is there more to this? What's going on, Max?"

"Just take my word for it."

"What've you got against Micah?" Jade said, eyeing him with suspicion. "Isn't he your platinum child? I thought you'd want us to be close. Your two protégés. You know something about him that I don't?"

He stared at her for a long while, an inner debate taking place. "I do."

"What? Tell me."

Max swallowed. "He's your brother."

## CHAPTER NINETY-NINE

# The White House, Washington, DC

**W**HITNEY STEPPED TO the podium.

Gathered before her in the James S. Brady Press Briefing Room, the press corps sensed a major announcement forthcoming.

"Good afternoon, ladies and gentlemen," she said into the microphone. "I want to share something with you. Please hold your questions until the end.

"After the Rockefeller Center terrorist attack, Blake Haynes, who stands here before you every day speaking on my behalf, needed a blood transfusion. Without it, he would have died. Blake has a rare blood type, shared by few people. My chief of staff, Sasha Scott, led the effort to find someone with a match. It turned out I was one of those people."

The press started to murmur.

She plowed on. "I donated my blood to him." She turned to the wings and motioned to him. "Come out here, Blake."

He came and stood next to her, smiling bashfully at his colleagues.

"When are you coming back to work, Blake?" shouted a male reporter. "We miss you!"

"I bet," Blake said.

Whitney held up a hand. "Please. During this process, our DNA was tested." The murmurs were getting louder. She glanced at the empty chair where Judy used to sit, her colleagues still leaving it vacant in her honor. "It was confirmed that Blake Haynes is not only a valuable member of the White House staff, but he is also my biological son.

"And now," she said, "I'd like to bring out his brother and sister."

Chandler and Emma joined them on stage. She placed her arms around Blake's and Emma's waists. Chandler stood on the other side of Blake, his arm around his brother's shoulders.

They'd met their new brother at dinner the night before. They'd listened as Blake told them about his upbringing. He listened as Chandler and Emma told him how much it sucked to be the president's children.

"Where's your husband?" shouted Mike from ABC News.

Whitney gave a wry smile. "I'll leave that for another press conference. Thank you, everyone. I hope I've answered all your questions."

Every reporter's hand was raised, all of them shouting questions at her.

Whitney looked at her three children.

And laughed.

❋

Sasha crossed the Oval Office and handed Whitney some papers. "It's good to see you happy."

Whitney hadn't forgotten Sasha's betrayal, but she believed that it was best to keep her friends close and her enemies closer. Her frenemies, even more so.

"I *am* happy," Whitney said.

Sasha cocked her head. "It's not awkward?"

"A little. For all of us. Chandler and Blake are attending a Nationals game tonight." Whitney held up the papers. "Anything important? I want to spend some time with Emma before she heads back to school."

Sasha shook her hand. "It can wait. Have a good night, Madam President."

"You too, Sasha."

Sasha left.

Whitney retrieved her purse from her desk, leaving her brief-case on the credenza.

No work tonight.

Her phone rang. "Yes, Sean."

"Secretary Salcedo is here."

Whitney frowned. The secretary of homeland security didn't usually drop by unannounced.

"Send her in. And get Sasha back here, will you?"

"Will do."

The secretary entered a few moments later, followed by Sasha.

Salcedo stopped a few paces from her. Glancing at the purse in Whitney's hand, she said, "Madam President, sorry to disturb you. It's about the Rockefeller Center bombing."

"Someone claimed responsibility?"

"There's been an arrest."

Whitney laid her purse on her desk and returned to her seat. "That's excellent."

"I hadn't heard," Sasha said. "Who?"

"Isaiah and Jeremiah Johnson, ages twenty-four and twenty, respectively. They're brothers."

Whitney's mouth parted in surprise. "American?"

Salcedo nodded. "Members of a white nationalist organization with a grudge against the cable network."

"My God!" Whitney said.

"Terrorism knows no color," said Sasha.

"The FBI director is on his way."

"What do we know?" asked Whitney.

"FBI Counterterrorism traced significant payments to their personal bank accounts."

"Any idea who was behind it?"

Salcedo hesitated. "We believe that it was the Carr brothers. The FBI office in Chicago is en route to pick up Jason Carr."

Whitney's mind raced as she tried to absorb what she had just learned. "Any connection with the Shakespeare Killer?"

"We're not sure," Salcedo said, "but there's more. The brothers received financial backing from another party. We don't know for sure if the Carrs were cognizant of the other funding source."

"Who was it?"

Salcedo's stare didn't waver. "Russia."

*The bear never forgets.*

Whitney picked up the phone to say goodbye to her daughter.

# Washington, DC

"NICE DIGS," HE said as she let him into the Ritz-Carlton suite in Georgetown.

"My home away from home for the moment. Charming earring. What is it, a star?"

"It's a tree. How is she?"

"She's going to be fine. She knows you're here?"

"No. I was asked to check on the situation. Jade would think it was odd if I visited her."

"Are you hungry?" She waved a hand toward the dining room. "We can have something brought in. Or eat downstairs."

"I'm not sure if being seen together here is a good idea," he said.

"You're right. I believe that Jade's already suspicious. We can order in."

"I'm not that hungry."

She gestured to the living room. "Well, then, have a seat."

"I'll stand, thanks. I've been sitting for five hours."

"It is a long flight." She moved to a beige chair by the unlit fireplace. "I'll sit, if you don't mind."

"Suit yourself," he said. "I see that Collins stopped tweeting."

"The silly little activist served his purpose."

"You paid him to tweet to throw off the feds. And then what? Were you going to set him up as the fall guy?"

"He was paid handsomely for his insignificant efforts."

"Were the sonnets supposed to throw them off too?"

She nodded. "I tried to select the most appropriate sonnet for each victim, but I knew the media and the FBI wouldn't be able to resist murders with a literary connection. Zoe, of all people, gave me the idea. Before she came up with the name Astrea, she was going to name the program Dark Lady."

"She knows what you've been up to?"

"She didn't. She might've figured it out by now, though."

He seemed to consider this.

"It was a means to accomplish our goals while throwing law enforcement off the scent," she continued. "They were looking for a serial killer with a passion for Shakespeare. While we were eliminating the enemies of the republic one by one."

"'Our goals.'"

"The end justified the means."

"Why Hurley? You did the Russians a favor."

"She's the CEO of a public company. She can be replaced."

"And Tishman? He brokered the deal with Hurley to create a product to protect our election system. Didn't you think he was of some utility?"

She shrugged. "I never liked him."

"Seems rash."

"Good riddance. But Judy Porter wasn't me."

"I know," he said. "What about Fairchild? Was assassinating her a means to an end?"

"God, no," she said, horrified. "That wasn't part of the plan. How was I to know she'd go rogue?"

"How did you connect with her?"

"Dev? We knew each other from another life."

"You dated?"

"We went to school together."

"Paine isn't happy," he said, stepping forward to admire the painting over the fireplace, his hands behind his back. "*You* shouldn't have gone rogue."

"It had to be done." She shook her head, her hair cascading over her shoulders and down her back. "Besides, it was a one-time thing. It won't happen again."

"You're right about that." Detective Kurt McClaine touched the silencer to the middle of Kyle Madison's forehead. "Hurley isn't the only one who can be replaced."

He fired.

THE END

# ACKNOWLEDGEMENTS

MANY THANKS TO:

My editor: Leah Wohl-Pollack.

My proofreader: Michael Manahan.

Jim and Mo Herring. It was a privilege to meet you and share that magical Final Four weekend. Go Dawgs!

My writing companion and king of our household: Fitzgerald, my cat.

My children Jasmine, Travis, and Brandon for being a part of the jlbrownauthor crew.

My amazing wife, manager, and editor, Audi, who is with me on every page. Your love and support are invaluable. Always.

My readers who read, reviewed, followed me on social media, subscribed to my newsletter, and spread the word about *Don't Speak*, *Rule of Law*, and *Few Are Chosen*. Thank you for allowing Jade, Whitney, Cole, and the rest of the Jade Harrington family into your lives. You have no idea how much it means to me.

# ABOUT THE AUTHOR

Julie L. Brown is the author of the historical fiction, *Bend, Don't Break*, the alternative-history novel, *No One Will Save Us*, and the creator, under the pen name J. L. Brown, of the Jade Harrington series, political thrillers which include the novels, *Don't Speak, Rule of Law*, and *The Divide*, and the short story, "Few Are Chosen."

Julie earned an MFA in Creative Writing from the Stonecoast program at the University of Southern Maine. She resides with her family in the Pacific Northwest, where she is working on her next novel.

You can find her on:
Website: julielbrown.com
Instagram: @julielbrownwrites

If you would like to receive an email when I release my next book and other exclusive offers and updates, you may sign up for my newsletter at bit.ly/JLBNews. Your privacy is important. Your address will never be shared, and you can unsubscribe at any time.

Thank you for reading *The Divide* and don't forget to leave a short review on Goodreads and your favorite bookstore's website.